CASTING BONES

CASTING BONES

Don Bruns

This first world edition published 2016
in Great Britain and the USA by
SEVERN HOUSE PUBLISHERS LTD of
19 Cedar Road, Sutton, Surrey, England, SM2 5DA.
Trade paperback edition first published
in Great Britain and the USA 2016 by
SEVERN HOUSE PUBLISHERS LTD

British Library Cataloguing in Publication Data
A CIP catalogue record for this title is available from the British Library.

ISBN-13: 978-0-7278-8636-1 (cased)
ISBN-13: 978-1-84751-732-6 (trade paper)
ISBN-13: 978-1-78010-796-7 (e-book)

All Severn House titles are printed on acid-free paper.

Severn House Publishers support the Forest Stewardship Council™ [FSC™],
the leading international forest certification organisation.
All our titles that are printed on FSC certified paper carry the FSC logo.

Typeset by Palimpsest Book Production Ltd.,
Falkirk, Stirlingshire, Scotland.
Printed and bound in Great Britain by
TJ International, Padstow, Cornwall.

Do snakes and spiders cast spells? Are they integral in the design of a man's life? I think not. While spirits do influence people's lives, the people themselves control their own destiny.
The Spider Lady

Voodoo doll, work your magic. All ends well or all ends tragic.
Mason Doyle, historian

The houngan danced, the snake wrapped tight. The lady's eyes were wide with fright.
A voodoo journal, author unknown

Author's Note

Casting Bones is a work of fiction. Most of it. I talked to a number of law enforcement officers during my research for this book and have the utmost respect for the New Orleans Police Department and the people who work there. They are true professionals, still trying to overcome the negative impact on their organization from the aftermath of hurricane Katrina. I have taken some liberties with the police procedures and departmental policies. New Orleans remains today as it appears in this book. Louisiana is peppered with private prisons and towns where the main industry is criminal rehabilitation. Still, this story is largely fiction. Some of it is spot on. I'll leave it to the reader to decide what is factual and what isn't.

I asked a detective if the department ever consulted with voodoo practitioners when investigating a crime. The answer was quite simple. "If they approach us with information, we definitely listen."

Acknowledgements

Thank you Victoria Alman and Steven Stegall for your invaluable help in geographic, cultural and atmospheric realities. Thank you to the members of the NOPD for your time and information. Thanks for the tours my friend taxi driver Yerga Beraki. You helped me understand your city. And thank you to the number of other residents who live in this exciting town. Thank you authors Heather Graham, Laura Morrigan, Cara Brookins and Sandra Balzo and my good friends Connie Perry and Nancy Merwin. Thank you Linda Bruns for your editing. I've had some amazing moments and conversations at the Hotel Monteleone. Thank you to the help and guests for those interesting times, and I highly recommend their Carrousel Bar on Royal Street. Thanks to my agent, Jill Marr, and to all at Severn House.

I

'He's going to be killed.'

'What?' She turned and studied him.

'He's going to be killed. Murdered. You need to know that.'

'Who is going to be killed?' The statement had startled her. His mouth never moved but his statement was crystal clear.

The young black woman stared at her charge, the pale old man slumped over in a motorized wheelchair on the levee above the dirty Mississippi River rushing by. She was simply a volunteer caregiver, and had no idea how to deal with this information.

'The judge, of course. Shot in the head.' Very matter-of-fact as if everyone knew.

The wizened, white-haired octogenarian gazed at the brackish water, never saying a thing.

The girl with the soft skin spoke in a hushed tone, afraid those nearby would hear her and think she was crazy, having conversation with a silent man. In a sense, she knew she was. Crazy. Like her mother before her. Her mother, who once upon a time cast spells and prayed for interventions, and now spent her days in a wheelchair, staring vacantly at whatever was in front of her. Dementia had robbed her mother of all her abilities and now she was the one casting spells, praying for the souls of others. She was a voodoo lady who could suddenly hear a voice and read the mind of someone who could not speak for himself. This hearing of voices was something brand new. It scared her. Scared the hell out of her.

'Please, tell me. What judge? Can someone stop this killing?'

There was silence. Just as there had been silence before. It was all in her head, the words of the decrepit old man. She heard him, clear and precise, yet his voice never uttered a sound. His mind lost in the fog of dementia.

'Speak to me,' she said firmly.

'There is nothing you can do. The Krewe has made its decision.' His mouth never moved. Eerie.

The young voodoo practitioner approached him from behind, brushing a helix of black hair back from her face. She placed her hands on his shoulders and stared at the water as well. Looking down she saw the wrinkled hands, thick with gnarled veins. There on his right wrist was the faded tattoo of a green coiled snake. She squeezed his arms, venting some of her hurt and anger.

'You have caused a lot of people a lot of problems.' Whispering the words, knowing, as a volunteer at the center, that she was out of line. Her job was to care for her patients, not abuse them. Still she continued. 'You are the scum of the earth. You have caused a lot of people a lot of pain and I believe with all my heart, old man, that you will have to answer for your sins. You polluted this river with your chemicals, you raped the land and you stole the souls of people who worked for you.'

He showed no sign that he heard or understood a word she spoke.

'And now you have the audacity to communicate with me, telling me that a judge will be murdered by one of the Krewes and yet you give me no other information? Damn you.' Closing her eyes she took a deep, cleansing breath, relieving some of the tension. 'I feel if you help stop this killing, you will start to amend your evil ways. Not completely, but some. Help yourself, I implore you. Tell me who will be murdered and let me stop this assassination.'

Nothing.

Releasing the grip on the man's shoulders, the young lady once again closed her eyes. Silently she prayed to Damballa. 'Deliver me from this burden. I have one purpose here, my creator. To help make my Ma whole. With your help we can bring her back. I ask that you take away other obligations. She alone needs me to make her well again. Give this murder, this killing to someone else. Another mambo, a houngan. I need time to help my mother heal, and I do not want the burden of someone's death on my conscience.'

Again, there was only silence.

The girl shivered in the warm, humid air. She was now the bearer of important information, an impending death that was known to only a few. She had the power to inform authorities and even stop the killing. But her source, this man, was incapable of communicating with anyone through traditional means. An advanced case of dementia had terminated that possibility. And he apparently was very selective in the information he was giving her.

'So you won't talk?'

A slight move of his head, almost as if he'd heard her. But his mouth never moved. There was no sound from his formerly raspy vocal chords. No sound, yet she heard him loud and clear.

'The judge, the judge who will be killed, he belongs to Krewe Charbonerrie. Someone must be told.'

2

Five months later

T he judge had known at four a.m. that it was going to be a really bad day. Struggling, trying to breathe, he woke up sputtering, choking, deep under swirling dirty water and desperate for a breath of air. Five seconds later he caught that breath, realizing it had all been a dream. He woke up drenched in sweat. The rest of the morning hadn't gotten much better.

He was going out on a limb today, turning over evidence that could put him away for life. If he didn't, they would nail him anyway. They knew enough to destroy him, but at least he had a bargaining chip – or multiple chips, as the case may be. His meeting with Paul Trueblood was in less than half an hour. Trueblood, who said he could make a deal with the government. He just wanted it all to be over.

'Judge Lerner?'

The judge jerked his head upright and looked over the boxes he had been positioning in the trunk of the cream-colored Jaguar XK-E.

'Yes?' Where had this punk come from?

'Nice car.'

The young man stood out in the driveway, smiling in at him in the garage. A goofy, lopsided kind of smile, as if he'd had too much to drink. Dressed in a tight white T-shirt and skin-tight jeans, he turned his head furtively to the right, then to the left, then finally looking once more over his right shoulder.

'I want to make certain that no one is watching.' He giggled.

Lerner glanced in the same directions.

'Watching what?' He was confused.

'Our conversation, of course. I want it to be private. Very private.'

Lerner studied the man for a moment, then turned back to the trunk of his car.

'You got nosy neighbors? Behind the curtains over there?' The intruder motioned to one of the houses across the street.

'Go away. I don't have time to stand around talking.'

The judge closed the steel-gray lid on a file box and straightened up.

'No one appears to be watching.' The man's high-pitched voice was sibilant, and Lerner reckoned the guy might be gay. Maybe a friend of Rodger's. Although he knew most of Rodger's friends.

'What do you want?' Now there was a hint of irritation in his voice. 'Do I know you?'

The young man shrugged his shoulders. 'I'm about to be an important part of your life.' He paused. 'Or . . .' his voice trailed off.

'Oh, shit.' Disbelief in the judge's voice. A touch of fear. 'Did I sentence you? You did time? You were in my court, right? Is that it?'

A nightmare for every criminal judge. Someone you convicted comes back to seek revenge. *Deliver me from that scenario*, he thought.

'No. This is nothing personal.' A reassuring tone. 'Just a message I was asked to deliver.'

'Thank God.' Lerner let out a sigh of relief. Then what was the line about 'your life. Or . . .?' Lerner studied him. The kid bore a trace of an effete James Dean, in *Rebel Without A Cause*. Or a young, camp Brando, in *On The Waterfront*.

'Give me the message and then I've really got to go.' The judge slammed the trunk lid shut and walked round the car. 'Be quick about it – I've got an appointment in about ten minutes.' All he needed was to be late and have this Trueblood walk out. He was about to make a deal that might save his life. The day was new and already there appeared to be a problem. He didn't need more problems.

Lerner stared at the man. The high whiney voice, the air of affected boredom. God, the guy really was going for James Dean, although in New Orleans anything went. Tight jeans, a tight white T-shirt that showed off his flat abs and biceps, and too much product in his carefully coifed hair, the judge thought.

'Did Rodger put you up to this? Is this his way of getting back at me?' Rodger had been furious. He told Lerner he wasn't about to be dumped by someone like him. It would be like Rodger to put a young punk up to this.

'No. I don't know a Rodger.' He shook his head.

'No? Then what's the message?'

The young man wore the same crooked smile.

Lerner motioned him back with a sweep of his hand, as he started toward the driver's side.

'Please, get out of my way. Now. Either tell me what you want or get off of my property.'

A black Escalade pulled off the side street, and backed onto his concrete driveway. It happened a lot at the dead end. Drivers didn't realize there was no exit. They pulled into his drive to turn around.

The judge raised his left hand to the driver, barely outlined behind the dark tinted glass. At the same time he reached into his pocket for his iPhone and surreptitiously activated the recording app with his right hand. He wanted a copy of this conversation.

'Driver, please, be a witness.' He shouted it out, hoping the motorist could hear him.

'This guy is threatening me.' It couldn't be about what was in that gray file box, the one in his trunk. He'd only told one other person that it existed, and even they didn't know exactly what the box contained. He was supposed to meet that person at the Cochon in just about ten minutes. Paul Trueblood. The contents of that box contained evidence to bring down some very high figures in New Orleans, and he was ready to make a case for his own immunity. This couldn't be about that. Could it? Dear God. Of course it could.

'Are you here because of the Krewe? Is that it? Tell me. We can work this out. Seriously.'

The young man smiled, still standing in the middle of the concrete driveway, now shielded from the neighbors' view by the vehicle. Reaching behind his back with his right hand, he pulled out a pistol and pointed it directly at Lerner's face. The end of the barrel was huge, like an open drainpipe.

'Jesus.'

'Do you pray often?' The gun never wavered.

'No.' He was shaking now, trembling. 'Not often enough apparently,' he muttered, and closed his eyes. 'Are you going to shoot me? Right now? In front of this witness? Please, tell me before you pull the trigger.' Shuddering, he felt the blood drain from his face.

'Get in.' The man spoke in a singsong voice.

'Get in . . .?' It was then he realized the Escalade was for him. This was no lost driver who wanted a quick turnaround.

'Look,' perspiration covered his body and he felt a slight chill on his skin, 'if it's Rodger, tell him I'm sorry. It wasn't going to work from the beginning. Seriously. I offered him cash, a lot of cash. Enough to go away and start over. Please don't do something you'll regret. Something he'll regret.'

'Get in.' The voice a little deeper now, more demanding. None of the feminine tones from earlier on.

'What are you going to do?'

'Get the fuck in.' The man stepped forward and with a hard thrust he rammed the barrel of the gun into Lerner's soft stomach. The judge doubled over in crippling pain, tears welling in his pale blue eyes. It felt like the metal rod might come out the other side. Lerner fought for a breath, gasping, sucking in air. This guy wasn't fooling around.

The man in the cotton tee opened the rear door and motioned to the judge.

Still hunched over, Lerner staggered to the door. Where were his neighbors? The loud, brassy soccer mom next door, or the retired couple with the yapping Labrador retriever across the street? Where the hell was the dog? He was out every night Lerner got home, barking in a frenzy. So the canine takes a break on the one afternoon the judge needs him?

'In.' The kid grabbed Lerner's arm and pushed the shirt cuff from his right wrist. Peeling back the sleeve he unveiled the green coiled snake tattooed just above the judge's gold chain bracelet. He smiled, nodding to the driver. 'It's him. No doubt.'

The sting of the pistol barrel smashing into the bone over Lerner's right ear took him by surprise. He found himself thinking, as his brain processed the pain, that the blow had been strong enough to cause a large bruise. Maybe even concussion. His entire skull throbbed. The judge shook his head, trying valiantly to keep his consciousness.

He felt hands pushing him as he tried his best to climb into the rear seat of the black Cadillac.

'It's the right guy, James. Let's go.'

The voice faded in and out as he tried to suppress the nausea. Concentrating on his immediate condition he feared only that he would vomit on the soft leather seats. He did not want to embarrass himself.

It had to be Rodger. The guy just couldn't let it go. As a public figure of some repute, Lerner had decided that he needed a more appropriate lifestyle. He had decided that he didn't like Rodger Claim so much anymore. You fell in and out of love with people for a variety of reasons, didn't you? There were lots of reasons to fall out of love with Claim.

'The warehouse next to the Napoleon Avenue Wharf, James. You know where that is?'

'I know, Skeeter.'

They didn't care if he knew where they were taking him. They didn't care if he knew their names. So obviously he was expendable. Expendable. They were going to kill him.

'I've got money. God knows, lots of money. Hidden money.'

A wave of dizziness came over him.

'Please, whatever he's paying, I can pay more.'

No response.

'Oh, God, please.'

The man named Skeeter turned to him and this time he wore a tight, thin-lipped smile.

'You seem to pray a lot, Judge Lerner. But I don't think that God or Jesus is going to do much to save your soul.'

Lerner thrust his hand into his pocket. The punk hadn't bothered to check to see if Lerner had a phone. He could still call 911. A wave of nausea overcame him and he collapsed on the seat, his last attempt at freedom lost forever.

3

The pale bloated body bobbed in the muddy Mississippi, bumping the seawall just down from the *Creole Queen* steamboat and across from the Crazy Lobster riverfront restaurant. Detective Quentin Archer peered down as the two divers maneuvered the floating corpse to a submerged rubber sling, which hung from the small crane anchored on the brick walkway.

Detective Adam Strand joined him, nodding at the unfolding scene.

'You swallow any of that water, you're poisoned. That's some nasty shit, Q.'

Brushing back his thick brown hair with his fingers, Archer nodded. 'You should see the Detroit River. Can't be any worse than that.'

The grinding of the winch's gears echoed off the concrete as the limp body slowly rose from its watery grave. A curious seagull swooped low as two officers in wetsuits grabbed the sling when it reached the plaza, gently lowered the body and pulled the rubber contraption from around the corpse.

'Detectives?' A uniformed officer motioned to Archer and Strand, inviting them to view the body.

A crowd had gathered on the steamboat, tourists straining to see the grizzly scene just yards from where they stood. Yellow crime scene tape wrapped the area and uniformed officers faced the growing throng, waiting for a reporter to attempt an end run.

Archer bent down, rubber gloves on, and gently rolled the body, running his hands over the man's rear pockets. He pulled out a wallet. Opening it, he glanced at the driver's license. Then he pulled open the soaked wallet pocket where the deceased kept his money.

'Wasn't a robbery.'

'No?'

Separating the wet bills, Archer said, 'Must be a couple hundred bucks.'

Strand glanced at the bills.

'Not that anyone would miss the money much now. You know what I'm saying?' Strand studied Quentin Archer for a moment.

Archer frowned. He still didn't know Strand that well.

'Hey, it's a joke, OK? Money stays where it is. Well, someone must have gotten something out of it. Look at this. Shot right through his eye.'

They studied the wound, a round hole bored through the right socket.

'Wasn't the water after all.'

Archer shook his head. 'Do you know a David Lerner?'

'Judge David Lerner?' Strand rose from his kneeling position and brushed at his trousers.

'I'm new in town. You tell me.'

'Yeah, I know of him. Works in the juvie section. Tough guy. Kids don't want to go before him. They usually get a long sentence.'

'Kids won't have to worry anymore.'

He palmed the driver's license, handing it to Strand.

'Jesus. Somebody's kid didn't like his sentence.'

'It would appear.'

Archer reached into the man's inside jacket pocket and pulled out a cell phone. Studying it for a moment, he handed it to Davis, another detective, who was standing nearby.

'Davis, have lab pull the SIM card and use discovery software on the computer. See if we can retrieve contacts, calls . . . you know the drill.'

'A judge.' Strand looked out at the water, shaking his head. 'That's gonna stink up the place. And we had to draw lead on this one. There's gonna be some serious pressure on this case.'

A department photographer snapped pictures, walking around the body taking close-ups and long shots from every angle possible. A young lady from NOPD with a video camera was filming the entire event. Photos and video often helped when you stumbled on the scene of a crime. In this case Archer knew that this wasn't the scene of the crime. Could have happened anywhere.

'Detective,' the photographer called to Archer, 'check this out.' He pointed to the right arm, a gold bracelet dangling from the wrist.

'A judge with a tattoo?'

'We see the tattoos every day, just not on people like a judge. And a snake? I would bet a lot of people consider a judge as low as a snake.'

Archer nodded. He filed it away for future consideration.

An ambulance drove up slowly, giving the crowd a blast of its siren to move them along. No rush. The damage had already been done.

'Welcome to the Big Easy, Q.' Strand and Archer watched the attendants hoist the gray body bag onto a stretcher. 'Let's see what a Michigan cop can teach us Louisiana boys.'

And just for a moment, Quentin Archer shuddered, staring at the bag covering the swollen body of a high-ranking judge. Fighting back the nausea he felt, his eyes clouded over. The pallid corpse seemed to have an aura, a faint shimmering light that emanated from within, shining through the vinyl. Just for a brief moment. He closed his eyes to block the vision. Like he'd tried to block the vision of his wife, after a Detroit driver hit her on a sidewalk then sped off.

That was a sensation he had hoped would never happen again. Archer put his palm to his forehead, searching for a fever. He was light-headed, a little warm and his stomach was queasy. He'd seen some pretty gruesome deaths before, and they'd never affected him like this. There was something different about this, but nothing he could put his finger on.

'Q, you OK?'

Adam Strand raised his eyebrows, noticing the look on Archer's face, flush, with perspiration dotting his brow.

'Sure. Fine. It must be . . .' he trailed off, not sure what it must be.

The two detectives stripped off their gloves.

'You want to sit down, partner?'

'No.' He shook his head. 'Really, I'm good.'

'Look, the crack about the judge's money—'

Archer shook his head. Regaining his composure, he walked over to the four other detectives on the scene, two in sport coats, the others in long-sleeved shirts and ties.

'Two of you pick up anything you see and someone talk to the deckhands on the *Queen*. We'll cover the restaurant up there, and you' – pointing to the other two detectives – 'see if any of these tourists saw anything.' His breathing had returned to normal and he felt his heart rate slowing down.

Strand stood back and nodded.

'You know it didn't happen here.'

'And you know we've got to cover every base,' Archer responded.

They walked away from the river, heading toward the Crazy Lobster.

'How many cases you worked?'

Archer put his hand to his head, a slight feeling of uneasiness still lingering. 'Never counted them.'

'As of now, we've got the highest per capita murder rate in the country.' Strand pointed beyond the restaurant where New Orleans spread out into the downtown area. 'About one hundred eighty murders a year. Mostly young kids who've got nothing to lose.'

'Three hundred plus in Detroit.'

'Jesus.'

'Still, you've got the highest per capita. Pretty impressive.'

'We duke it out with Baltimore or Flint, Michigan for bragging rights every year.'

They reached the brown pavers strewn with green tables and chairs that sat in the brilliant sun outside the Crazy Lobster. Patrons of the trendy restaurant drank Abita beers, sucked meat from red, boiled crawfish and warily watched the two detectives as they approached.

'Can you get the manager?' Archer touched a waitress on the shoulder and she nodded, walking quickly into the restaurant. In a moment, a young black man walked out, an apron tied around his waist.

'You dealing with the dead guy?'

'We are. I'm Quentin Archer, and this is my partner, Adam Strand.'

The two offered their badges and the manager nodded.

'I'm Marcus Walker. We sort of talked about it while you were down there,' he motioned to the muddy river. 'Nobody noticed anything. My guess is the guy washed up or somebody dumped him recent.'

'You don't mind if we talk to your staff?'

'Not at all. You'd do it anyway.'

'We would,' Strand said. 'You get any judges, court people who come down here for a meal? A drink?'

'Detective, we get everybody. We're on the water and if I do say so we put out a really good product. Listen, if people don't come here, we've probably catered something for them. We go to their place, you know what I'm sayin'? Sure, we do some parties at City Hall.'

'Know a guy named David Lerner? Judge?'

'Is it the *late* David Lerner? Was that his body they found?'

Q shook his head. 'No positive identification yet. We just wondered if you recognized the name.'

'Sure. I've seen his name on the news. Hard guy. He gets a lot of press because of his stiff sentences. We've got a couple young guys in the kitchen who received some of his tough love.' The manager offered a weak smile. 'That's who we're talking about, right? Lerner?'

'Has he been here?'

'I can ask around. I wouldn't recognize him.'

'Let's find out. Can you get your wait staff one at a time? Then the kitchen crew?'

Walker nodded and walked back toward the bar.

'Maybe the judge complained about some bad service?' Strand watched the manager as he brought a waitress to them.

'Or somebody didn't like *his* service.'

'Maybe one of the boys in the kitchen?'

Q motioned the lady to a seat at an empty table and took a deep breath. He'd done this too many times. At thirty-six, young by most standards, he was already burned out. Detroit, New Orleans, a body in the river . . . same story, different city.

'Hey, Q, how many murders do you solve in Detroit? What's your percentage?' Strand straddled a chair as Archer sat down.

'Fifty percent, maybe less.' There was only one that haunted him every day. One unsolved murder. Denise, his wife. The love of his life. One of the reasons he'd left Detroit.

'We've got an impressive record here,' Strand said. Highest murder rate per capita, and last year we solved about twenty-two percent. Maybe with you on board our percentage goes up.'

Archer frowned, drumming his fingers on the table. He hadn't solved Denise's murder, so his track record wasn't that good. But to be fair, he hadn't given up trying.

4

His father had bitched about filing reports. Banging away on a manual Underwood, going through a bottle of Wite-Out every week to correct all the mistakes. He'd told Quentin how cops today had it easy, with computers and everything. It didn't feel that easy.

One day, when Q was maybe ten years old, the old man had taken him to the precinct house. Must have been summer because otherwise he'd have been at school, and when they entered the old brick building he smelled the pungent odor of sweat, smoke and burned coffee. The smell stuck with him almost as strong in memory. Even with air conditioning in all the offices and a no smoking policy, he expected to breathe in the aroma of sour body odor and cigarette smoke every time he walked into a police station.

'Damn,' Sergeant Dan Sullivan hovered over his shoulder. 'Had to be a judge.'

Archer nodded and continued to peck away on the keyboard. Fastest two-finger typist in the building.

'I'd expect this to happen in One,' the balding man said. 'Across Rampart Street. But I can't picture Lerner hanging out over there. Bad neighborhood.'

'Could have happened anywhere,' Archer replied, hitting the keys with his index fingers.

'Any reports back from the interviews?' Sullivan continued to press. 'We can put some more manpower down there, if need be.'

'Nothing yet. Strand may have heard something. He was finishing up with the kitchen crew.'

'The minute you know anything I want to know. Anything at all, Q.' He drifted down the row, talking to another detective.

'Got it, Sarge.'

The manager of the Crazy Lobster, Marcus Walker had said point-blank that some of his help had been sentenced by the dead judge. He continued to hunt and peck while detectives drifted in and out of the room.

Thirty-two homicide detectives, all of them in a pressure cooker situation, working third floor of headquarters in a bullpen setup. An open room, devoid of personality, with gunmetal gray desks crowding each other. Sixteen on one side of the hall, sixteen on the other.

Archer knew there was manpower if needed, and he also knew the department was down three detectives. Recruiting was apparently not going well. And the guys who had been brought in for relief were all working their own cases. With eighty-some murders already committed for the year, they were busy. Very busy.

'I knew him,' Sullivan was back. 'Played some charity golf with him a couple of years ago.'

'Raising money for what charity?' Archer didn't look up.

'No, no. I mean, nobody would ever play with the guy. That was the problem. Judge David Lerner was a duffer with an ugly attitude and a really bad hook. Spent half the time looking for lost balls and bitching his head off. This one time he needed a partner, so I drew the short straw.'

'Uh-huh. *Charity* golf.' Archer got it.

'Cocky guy.'

'Not anymore, Sarge.'

'No, I suppose not.'

Archer finally looked up. 'You got any thoughts on why someone would want him dead?'

'He was a judge. A heavy-handed judge. There are probably hundreds of reasons why people would want him dead. This one may not be easy.'

Archer turned back to the flat screen. When he had exited the force up north, even Detroit had sprung for the big flat-screen monitors. Technology was changing so fast, and he was still a two-finger wonder at typing. Get with the program, Archer.

What had Strand told him? Only twenty-two percent of all murders were solved?

'My father was a cop.'

'Yeah?' Sullivan sounded half interested.

'He taught me one thing. The most important thing to look for in any case.'

'What was that?'

'Keep asking why.'

'"Why"?'

'You start every case by asking why. Why did someone kill this person? You follow up with a why, and a why, and a why. When you run out of whys, when you run out of questions and answers, you've solved the murder.'

'Well, you know it's not that simple,' Sullivan said.

'No, Sergeant, I don't know that. It pretty much works every time. And if the crime is still unsolved, it's because you haven't answered every *why*.'

Sullivan cocked his head, staring at Archer.

'We all have our methods, Archer.'

'We do. Mine makes the most sense.'

The officer turned to walk away.

'Oh, Sergeant, you think of anything, *you* let me know. You know this town a whole lot better than I do.'

The other equation was who. He knew why they killed Denise.

To send him the sternest of warnings, that if he didn't quit pushing the case against a certain drug ring, they would make his life miserable. But he didn't know exactly who had committed the crime. He didn't know yet. He kept it low-key, but there were friends in Detroit. People who were in his corner, working the edges.

Archer finished the report along with his third cup of green tea. The caffeine in coffee drove him crazy so he settled for this thin bitter liquid. It was healthier, too, so he'd been told.

Throwing on his dark blue sport coat, he stood up and took the elevator to the lobby. Nodding to the young black woman who doubled as dispatcher and information officer he said, 'Gonna grab a bite to eat, Cheryl. Call me on the cell if anything comes in from the coroner's office, OK?'

One o'clock and he was hungry. And thirsty.

He rented a little cottage in the French Quarter, ten minutes by car. A car that NOPD provided. Probably some drug dealer's ride or a repo. No restrictions. Archer used it for work, and to drive to lunch. But when he went home in the evening and to work the next morning, he took the streetcar. It beat getting towed every week or so when they hosed down the streets in the Quarter and he'd forget if it was odd or even streets. Paying for impounded cars applied to everyone, even detectives.

Driving to Decatur he turned left. There was a parking spot on the street and he pulled in.

The nice thing about the French Quarter was that you didn't really need a car. It was made for walking. He could pass dozens of restaurants, bars and coffee shops on foot. He'd stand outside, study the menu on the wall or window, look inside and see what kind of clientele frequented the place, breathe in the unique aromas from the kitchen and then move on to the next establishment. A quick course on the French Quarter cuisine. You couldn't do that on the east side of Detroit. Where he'd been stationed, around Warren and Conner, you very seldom ventured out on foot. If someone didn't steal your wallet or cell phone, they'd slice your throat for your Nike LeBron X Cork shoes. Not that the French Quarter here in New Orleans was safe. Far from it. Still . . .

The French Market on San Felipe was one of his favorites. So far. Spicy shrimp, crawfish, oysters, done just about anyway you could imagine. And he loved talking with Mike, with his wild wiry hair and jovial manner.

'Hey, Q! You're a little early. The good lookin' *femmes infidèles* show up a little later in the evening.'

'Coke, Mike. And what else do I want?'

'Goin' light?'

'I am.'

'Half a dozen of the char-grilled oysters. You're gonna love 'em, man.'

Archer smiled. 'Haven't had a bad meal here yet.'

Mike nodded. 'You've been here what? Couple months now?'

'A couple.'

'Just breakin' you in and you draw the dead judge.'

Archer looked at him inquisitively. It had only been a couple of hours. 'And where did you hear this?'

Mike walked back toward the kitchen shouting over his shoulder. 'This is the Quarter, Q. I know everything that happens down here, man.'

'Mike. Wait.'

The frizzy-haired man turned, his big eyes boring into Archer's. 'What, *mon ami*?'

'You know everything that happens down here?'

'Most things. *Most.*'

'Then answer the obvious question. My life would be a lot easier.'

'Who killed the judge? Is that your question?'

'Go ahead.'

'I know most things that happen in the *Quarter*, Q.'

'And?'

'Didn't happen in the Quarter. That's a sure thing.'

'We figured as much.'

'So I don't have the answer. Not yet. What's your next question?' Archer gave him a grim smile.

'The next logical question, Mike. What do you think it is?'

'I know what it should be, *inspecteur*.'

'What should it be?'

'The question should be why? Why was the judge murdered?'

'Exactly.'

'Don't have that answer either. Not yet. But check back soon. Eventually I'll have the answer. I always do.'

5

The char-grilled oysters were anything but light. The butter and Romano cheese lay heavy in his stomach. Or was it the quarter loaf of French bread he'd used to sop up every last drop of flavor in the shells? He walked toward his car, wondering if Strand had any new information. Unless they received a fabulous stroke of luck, it was going to be a late, late night.

And then he saw her, a brief glimpse, walking across the street with a lanky young man wearing a sleeveless tee. The familiar sharp pain gripped his chest. She turned, and of course it wasn't her. He saw Denise daily. And he didn't see her at all.

A short black man wearing a shaved head and a worn burgundy sport coat walked toward him staggering slightly, too many drinks too early in the day. He appeared to step out of Archer's way, then stumbled as he bumped the cop.

'So sorry,' he mumbled, continuing down the cobblestone sidewalk.

Archer brushed his hand over his rear pocket, spun around and in that single motion pulled his pistol from the shoulder holster under his jacket.

'Freeze.' His voice chilling, no-nonsense. 'NOPD. Turn around.'

The little guy hesitated, as if he might run or he might comply.

Slowly turning around, he put his hands out, palms up. At five three, even his hands only came up as high as Archer's shoulders.

'A gun? Isn't that a little severe, Jack? I done nothing to warrant a gun. What you want me for?'

'I thought about public intoxication, but if I arrested everyone down here for drinking, the jails would be overflowing right now.'

'I didn't know you was a police officer. Plain clothes and all,' a grim smile on his face. 'So sorry, man. Please, let's just forget about it.'

He stood firm as Archer approached, the pistol leveled at him.

'You probably make more at your little business than I do at mine,' Q said. 'I need every cent I've got, police pay being what it is.'

'Listen, Mr . . .'

'Not Mister. Detective. Detective Archer. Detective Quentin Archer.'

He stepped closer, and the dark man with the shaved head cringed.

'What? You gonna shoot me? Arrest me?'

'I'm going to get my wallet back.' He stuck out his hand and the man reached into his waistband and handed Archer the wallet.

With one hand he thumbed it open.

'What's your name? Your real name.'

'Samuel.'

'Samuel. I want the cash.'

'Damn, man. Wasn't but twenty-seven dollars.'

Archer nodded, somewhat surprised. It had only been in his possession a few seconds yet the man had already counted the money. He reached out and grabbed the little guy by his shirt collar.

'I don't care if it was one dollar. Do you know what happens if I take you in? Do you?'

The short man reared back, a sly smile on his face as if he'd been waiting for the question.

'Yeah. I know what happens. I'm out in two hours.'

'The money.'

He reached into his pants pocket and handed the detective the twenty-seven dollars folded in half.

'Another twenty,' Archer said.

'Now you crazy. Weren't but twenty-seven. You know it, I know it. You can go fuck yourself.'

'Another twenty, Samuel.'

The man pursed his lips, squinted and looked up at Archer. 'So you just like all the rest of 'em. On the take.'

Same shit, no matter where you were.

Pulling him closer, his hand still clenching the shirt collar, Archer looked him in the eyes. 'I'll give it to the poor children's fund. Maybe it's a donation for injured cops. I haven't decided yet, but yeah, I want twenty for not turning you in.'

'Damn, man.'

Shorty was right, of course. The conman would be out in two hours. The jails would be overflowing if they arrested every pickpocket, every public drunk in town. This was a drinking town with a murder problem. That's where the effort should be directed. With his best hard-assed cop attitude, he repeated.

'Twenty.'

Samuel reached back into his pocket and pulled out the Andrew Jackson.

'What's your last name?'

Samuel smiled, handing him the bill. 'Jackson.'

'Right.'

'No, 'tis. Jackson. No relation.'

'Samuel, if I catch you again—'

'You won't, brother, because I've learned my lesson. Believe me, Detective, I'll recognize you.'

'If I do catch you again, I'll run you in. And I won't let you out in two hours. I promise.'

'Just tryin' to make a livin', dude.'

Archer nodded, putting his pistol back in the holster. Samuel Jackson shook his head, sighed, and continued staggering down the sidewalk. Probably already plotting his next sleight of hand.

Archer's cell phone jangled and he glanced at the caller ID. Strand.

'Partner, I'm in the Quarter. Where are you?'

Archer gave him the address and two minutes later Strand pulled up in a blue Buick LeSabre, turn of the century vintage.

'Q, I figured I'd find you down here somewhere. We might have this thing wrapped.' Strand motioned him to the passenger side. 'Get in.'

'Only twenty-two percent of your cases are solved, and you're telling me we might already have the killer?'

Strand stepped on the gas and the Buick shot forward.

'Those interviews you and I did at the lobster place?'

'Yeah?' Archer detected a slight odor of alcohol on his partner's breath.

'One of the line cooks got a year from the good judge. For some petty theft when he was a minor.'

'Priors?'

'Looks like it was his first.'

'A year? Sounds a little harsh.'

Strand wrapped his hands around the hard plastic steering wheel, staring intently at the narrow street as shops and small houses rolled by.

'He thought so too. Complained about it to some of his coworkers. Anyway, five minutes after I talked to him, he walked off the job. He was two hours into an eight-hour shift.'

'Maybe he got sick?'

'Maybe. But that manager, Marcus Walker, says the kid was one of his best workers. Today, he never said anything to anyone. Just took a powder. I got the call five minutes ago. We're going to the guy's house. I got a feeling about this, Q. We've got a disgruntled ex-con who found a way to get his payback. What do you think?'

'I hope you're right.'

'Even if we solve it, I can't begin to tell you how much pressure there's going to be. The victim was a white judge. And this guy, this cook, he was a black thief. You were in Detroit. You know how these things play out.'

Archer nodded.

'We've always been a town with a race relations problem.'

Among many other problems, Q thought.

Strand only slowed slightly at the stop sign, glancing both ways, then stepping on the gas.

'You didn't hear so much about it before Katrina. I mean, on a major playing field, it didn't get that much attention.' Strand took a deep breath, delving into a theme he was passionate about. 'You knew it was there, but it was an undercurrent. Then Katrina hits and boom, the national press, they played it up really big. White cops shooting black looters. People saying Bush delayed national aid to run the blacks out of New Orleans. Oh, it got nasty. Q, you know you've always had the R problem in Detroit, but here it wasn't so in your face. You know what I'm sayin'? Now the world pays a whole lot more attention to us. Black versus white, my friend. Detroit's got nothing on the Crescent City.'

A white judge oversteps his bounds and a black ex-con extracts his vengeance. There could be riots in the street.

'Are you rooting for the kid to be the killer?'

Strand took his eyes off the road for a brief moment to look at Archer. 'I'm rooting for us, Q. I became a cop because,' he paused, 'well, because I wanted to be on top. I like being in control. You either lead, or you follow, you know what I mean? I want to be the guy who calls the shots.'

'You want to be on top?'

He nodded. 'I grew up as a scrawny kid in a neighborhood where you got shoved around a lot. By adults, by other kids. I always ended up on the wrong side of a fist, an open hand, a knife and a gun. I swore that when I grew up, if there was shoving going on, I was going to be the one doing it.'

'I get it. You need to be in charge.'

'You and I both know a lot of cops with answers weaker than that. So it's a power thing. So what? There are benefits, dude, so don't be critical.'

There were dozens of reasons. Q had become a cop because of his family. Not so much the history of the Archer family, but because of Archer family problems. His dad had been a cop, but when Archer chose law enforcement, it was his way of righting the ship. His two brothers had tilted it just short of going under. Quentin Archer wanted to prove that not all of his father's offspring were as bad as Jason and Brian Archer. Both had been part of the drug ring he'd tried to expose. He'd busted his ass to prove there was at least one member of the clan who turned out all right. And look where it got him.

'So you do want this kid to be guilty.'

'Sure. Anything to make this job easier. Anything to make us a hero. That's what it's about, Q. We come off like heroes and the world is good. Let's make this guy the killer. All of our problems go away.'

'Where does he live?'

'The Lower Ninth.'

Q nodded. 'How do we play it?'

'Probably two doors. I'll knock on the front, you cover the back.'

The Buick cruised by Mango Mango on Conti and Bourbon, the original absinthe house where such notables as Andrew Jackson and Mark Twain had hoisted a drink. The garish neon sign advertising daiquiris was a more recent addition.

Out of the Quarter the route took a stranger twist, Strand pointing out the old Intracoastal, showing Archer where the water had overflowed the banks when Katrina hit.

'Hell of a mess, Q. I saw it with my own eyes. Some of it in my old neighborhood.'

Payback for some of the pushers, Archer thought as two young men walked toward them on the brown worn lawn. One of the boys raised his middle finger, sneering at the detectives.

'Cover's already blown, Q. Two guys wearing ties in this neigh-borhood got to be cops.'

Further into the Lower Ninth, Archer saw the crudely drawn tattoos on the houses.

Archer had researched the drawings. They appeared on specific homes. The search-and-rescue teams had marked those that had already been searched so that people would know not to re-search. The signals also marked which houses had dead bodies so that workers could come for them. Very sad.

'Badges of courage, man. Some of these homes, no one's there. But some of them remodeled and they leave that information on the front. The Katrina tattoo. It's an honor.'

He pointed to the left.

'Down here, Fats Domino's studio. And the Ellis Marsalis School of Music in Musician Village. Man, Harry Connick Jr and Wynton Marsalis, they helped a lot. But look at those homes there.'

The detective pointed to an odd-looking shotgun house, narrow and two stories high.

'This is what's happening, man. The actor Brad Pitt and some other guys have invested some serious jack in building new homes. These people who live here, they buy the place, they pay an agreed-upon monthly and they get a really inexpensive house. On stilts, see?'

Archer saw the new construction, complete with solar panels that heated the homes. Wouldn't happen in Detroit. Detroit registered a little colder in the winter months. A lot colder. And the sun didn't shine like it did here.

'Kid lives up about two streets.' Strand stared straight ahead now, focused like a laser beam.

Turning left, he passed four houses, before pulling up to the curb. 1323 Barataria. The number was poorly scrawled on the mailbox.

'This is it?'

''Tis.' He reached across Archer and opened the glove box. Pulling out a silver pint-sized flask he twisted off the cap and, tilting it back, took a slug. 'You want some, Archer?'

'No. I'm on duty.'

'Duty gets a little easier, my man. Jack Daniel's has been my partner for several years.'

'I'll cover the back,' Archer hesitated, 'and the side. Sometimes there's a—'

'Side door. I know. Chances aren't likely. These older homes were built on the cheap. Front door, back door . . .'

Strand wiped his lips, put the flask back into the compartment and they both stepped from the car.

'Give me a second to hit the rear and—'

Archer was interrupted by a tall figure who appeared from behind the house, running full pelt. In seven seconds the runner was behind the ramshackle building to the south. Q bolted after him, Detroit Crockett High School linebacker style, his feet beating the pavement, then the grass. He agreed with Strand. Archer wanted this guy, this petty thief with an axe to grind. Archer, Strand, Sullivan and the entire department needed to make this case go away.

6

Feeling the holster tight against his chest, he took short, powerful strides, covering ground as if there was a goalpost just ahead. Sparse grass turned to bare earth as he caught a glimpse of the tall black man running a straight path two houses up. Kid had done some time and maybe he was gym tough from the prison. Maybe, but prison was strength training. Pull-ups on upper-level bunk beds, lifting heavy pots of water in the kitchen, and working on push-ups and sit-ups. Not much attention was given to endurance. There was no track, no long-distance course. Nowhere to run.

Archer was gaining, his breathing coming a little harder now. He had no idea where Strand was. Probably calling for backup. The gangly kid threw a quick glance over his shoulder and Archer could tell he was gasping for air. The detective started stretching his stride. Back in the groove. The rasping sound of the runner's breath told Archer it wouldn't be long. Gliding over the ground, Q closed in as the black runner veered right, heading for the street. *Cut the angle, take twenty feet off the chase and hit him just as he reaches the sidewalk.*

He closed the gap, ten feet, five feet, and leaped in the air, tackling the kid mid-thigh as their bodies crashed to the ground.

Pulling his weapon from the holster, he jumped to his feet, staring down at the suspect crumpled on the dirt, his chest heaving.

'You work too hard at it, Q.'

He spun around and there was a smiling Strand, standing by the car door, gun drawn.

'Got your back, partner,' he said smugly.

Archer was taking deep breaths, as his eyes looked back to the man sprawled on the ground.

'Next time,' he said breathlessly, 'you do the running. Then I get to cover your back.'

Strand shrugged his shoulders. 'Deal.'

'I ain't no killer, man.' Antoine Duvay glared across the bare table. A bandage covered the two-inch gash on his forehead above the right eye from where he'd hit a stone as he landed.

'But you are a thief. You got into some fights while you were doing time. Your record doesn't exactly sparkle, Antoine.' Strand stood and walked behind the young man. 'We talked to some of your coworkers, and they say you're a bitter guy. Pissed at the system, pissed at the judge that put you away. We don't expect you to be happy, but when you get bitter and—'

'Yeah? You gonna haul in every nigger that's bitter? They got white boys up there, bitter too. I don't see them down here.'

'They didn't take off running when the cops showed up.'

Duvay took a deep breath, his eyes narrowing. Archer thought he saw some fear showing through the tough exterior.

'Why did you run, Antoine?'

'That's what you've got, man? I run so I must be the killer? I been here before, motherfucker. Shit. You can manufacture whatever you want, but you got nothing. Cracker makin' shit up about me.' He folded his hands defiantly on the gray metal tabletop and looked at the wall in silence.

The door opened and a uniform walked in with a Styrofoam cup of coffee. He handed Archer a piece of paper and exited.

'Here's that coffee, Antoine. Station-house brand. The best we can do.'

The suspect ignored it, staring straight ahead.

Archer examined the blank piece of paper, holding it in his right hand. He glanced at Strand and nodded.

'We've got a witness, Antoine.'

The young man squinted, turning and now looking puzzled. 'You got shit. You know it and I know it.'

'We've got someone.'

He was quiet for a moment.

'Who you got?'

'Someone who is willing to testify. Testify that you made serious threats on the judge's life. Said you were going to get him someday. According to this person, a couple of times you described in detail how you were going to kill him. Put a bullet in his head.'

The tall man let out a breath. 'I don't remember ever sayin' I was gonna kill that fucker.'

'It's enough to hold you, man. You want to confess now, we can make a plea. My suggestion.'

Strand sat down across from Duvay, pursed his lips and put his hands on the tabletop palms up.

'We build up frustrations, Antoine. Then, one day, things just break loose. You tell us what happened now and we're open to a lot of options. You don't tell us, those options go away. We've got the arrest. We need to know how and why you did it.'

'Let me see that paper.'

'No. I told you what we've got.'

Duvay shook his head. 'Detective. My momma told me every night that she was gonna kill me for what I did every day. She was gonna skin me alive. She was gonna beat my sorry ass till there was nothin' left of me. Every day she told me this. You understand?'

His eyes opened wide and he focused on Strand's face.

'You find me dead some morning, you gonna arrest my momma?' He smiled, a grim grin. 'I don't think so. And you ain't gonna get more than you got. A couple of loudmouths talkin' shit about me. Because I didn't kill no judge, and unless you go back out there and do a better job of lookin', there be a killer on the loose. And I ain't lyin'.'

'Antoine—' Strand turned his hands over.

'Get me a lawyer, Mr Policeman. I know my rights.'

7

'We can hold him overnight.' His breath smelled faintly like Jack and Coke. The on-duty cop, with a little bit of fortification.

'We can hold him on what?' Archer looked at the clock in the lobby. Time to check out. 'What do you have?'

'Suspicion.'

'Come on, Strand. There was no accusation. Nobody ratted him out at the restaurant. We made it up. It was a desperation move. He called our bluff and didn't fold. We've got nothing and you know it.'

'We'll find something. It's the way we do it in Nola. I say we hold him. If we just cut him loose we'll never see him again. He'll disappear into thin air, Q. I say we get him his attorney in the morning. Until then, we'll let him think about it and I'll do a little background work. I'll get a warrant to search the house tomorrow. I'll find something, I promise you.'

Archer stepped outside, holding the door open. Turning to Strand, he was quiet for a second.

'You do that, but the kid did a year, for God's sake. I mean, one night in the city jail isn't going to rattle him, Strand.'

'You don't know the Orleans Parish jail, Q. It's not your everyday prison. Honest to God, he's going to go through a lot of shit in twenty-four hours, Q. And besides, I think he's our guy.'

Archer had an idea of what their suspect was going to go through. The jail had a national reputation as one of the worst in the country. Squalid conditions, abusive situations, drugs, weapons and whatever else you could find.

'We don't have enough to hold him, Strand.'

Bullheaded. His partner was an ego-driven, bullheaded son of a bitch, but he was saddled with him so he had to at least pretend to be nice. It wasn't going to be easy. It never was.

'Let's do it my way, Q. I'm trying to make it easier on us. You're new to the system, so let me lead, OK?'

'We've got absolutely nothing. No motivation. Why did he do it?'

'Revenge.'

'I don't believe it. Look, tomorrow I'm going to go downtown and talk with everyone in Lerner's office. I think you should come down, too. Two of us would lighten the workload.'

'Christ, Archer, let's work this guy. We should stick around and revisit our runner. Where he lives, where he worked, you know.'

Archer nodded. 'OK. You follow that lead and you know where I'll be. You've got my cell. Call me if you get a conviction.'

'At least maybe I'll have a confession by the time you get back. Don't forget where you heard it.'

'I've got a feeling about this, Adam.'

'And I've got a feeling too, Quentin.' He stared at Archer. 'This can be an easy case, open and shut. You got a problem with open-and-shut cases?'

'It's not him.'

'Kid ran. He's hiding something and it has to do with the judge, I'm telling you.'

Archer shook his head and let the door go as Strand said, 'See you tomorrow morning. Tonight I'm going to be with my girl.'

'You've got a girl?'

'A real sweetheart.' Strand turned abruptly and walked back into the bullpen.

Archer was certain it wasn't the kid, Antoine Duvay. Maybe Duvay was scared they'd single him out. That may have been the reason to run, but he wasn't the killer. Archer was sure of it. His partner was looking for the easy way out. Quentin Archer took the elevator to the ground and walked to the street. He headed left, hoofing it to Canal. Three minutes later he was on a streetcar to the Quarter. No vehicle tonight. He'd have a couple of beers and hole up in his rented cottage. He had vowed to keep it simple this time. Start fresh, no baggage.

And it did seem much simpler. Until now. He'd drawn a high-profile murder, and the entire investigative team would be subjected to scrutiny. As co-lead on the case, he knew what to expect. The press would be on him every minute, making judgment calls, criticizing every move the team made. Making his job all that more difficult, just like in Detroit.

But Detroit had been more than just pressure and criticism. It had been accusations directed at his family. Accusations *from* his family. The finger pointing that came from his relatives regarding *his* charges against *his* brothers. That had been all over the *Detroit Free Press*. All over the Detroit media. Scrutiny at the highest level. And in Detroit, he'd alienated the one group he couldn't afford to antagonize. The department he worked for and its employees. No matter who was right, he'd found it didn't pay to piss off the cops. There had been blood spilled, largely because he'd taken on the establishment, and a life lost. His wife, murdered in cold blood on the streets of Motor City and no one had yet paid for that crime. Tears formed in the corners of his eyes. OK, lesson learned. The blue brotherhood was strong, loyal – *Serpico*, the story of a New York cop who ratted on his fellow police officers, that story did not resonate anymore. Archer had to regroup. And there wasn't a day that went by, not an hour that passed, that he didn't try to figure out his next plan of attack. There wasn't an hour that passed that he didn't think about revenge for the murder of his young, innocent wife. He never gave up. And there was a handful of faithfuls who hadn't given up either.

Archer's attention went back to Antoine Duvay. The young man may have had serious issues with the dead judge, but in the brief conversation Archer had had with the kid there hadn't been a lot of emotion. The man had denied ever threatening to kill the judge, and Archer believed him. He was usually right about things like this.

His cell rang, an actual telephone ring instead of some popular song. The phone showed a blocked call, and he immediately knew how it would play out. It always did. He always answered it anyway. Connection with the bad guys. Someday one of these calls would lead to the killer. Someone on the other end would say something that would give him a lead. He prayed that it would. 'Archer.'

'Quentin Archer? Is that you?'

'You know it is.'

'Just checking.'

The line went dead. He could swear it was his brother's voice, thinly disguised. Jason Archer, playing mind games. Brief and to the point. It was his job to torture his brother, remind him that he and the Detroit force were still there should Quentin ever decide to push further with his allegations. Jason had walked away from his charges and was now officially on the run. Jason, who would give himself away with his stutter if he spoke more than two sentences.

Archer placed the phone back in his pocket. The calls didn't bother him so much, but in the two months since he moved in weird things had happened. He'd found misplaced items in his small place. The chair and table moved. A nightstand overturned.

A week ago, he'd walked into his bedroom, bone tired from a long day working four new cases. Across the room he saw the iron bed, spread thrown on the floor. The sheets were streaked blood red and wet, liquid still dripping to the floor. He flashed briefly on the scene from *The Godfather*, where the film producer woke up with a bloody horse head in his bed. Archer had seen a lot of grisly murder scenes, and prepared for the worst he pulled his gun and braced himself, holding his breath as he walked softly to the scene. The killer could still be in the small room. The body could be in several places. Taking a deep breath he bent and looked under the bed then stepped to the closet. He paused for several seconds then yanked on the door handle, bracing himself as he aimed directly at the entrance. No body. No killer. He let out his breath and prayed a silent thanks. His next thought was of Jason.

He'd taken a sample to the lab and they identified it as animal blood, probably a rabbit. And there was the evening when he arrived to find a dead black cat in front of his door, its head twisted in a grotesque tableau. The body was still warm. No notes, no warnings, just a reminder that there were people from Detroit who knew where he was and were likely to kill him if they felt like it. Archer was a target and he knew it. Secretly it frightened him, but outwardly he had a life to live. He looked over his shoulder more than usual and at his own expense added a security alarm to the small cottage, but there was only so much you could do. He'd warned his wife to be vigilant as well. That hadn't worked out at all. It was all a warning. If he pushed any harder, they wanted him to know, they'd take him out too.

Archer jumped off the trolley and walked north to Bourbon, ducking into an alley behind the Cat's Meow, a balconied drinking establishment. His six hundred square foot cottage was nestled into the corner of a small courtyard, a well-worn brick walk leading to the door of this former slave quarters. A quick stroll through showed him nothing disturbed this time.

The wailing of an off-key karaoke singer in the bar bled into his cramped one room abode, and Archer switched on the TV, partly to drown out the caterwauling and partly to see how the murder

was being played out by the local media. He didn't have to wait
long for either.

The NBC affiliate broke into programming, news anchor Alicia
Manor announcing that the police department had a suspect in the
murder of Judge David Lerner. The suspect, name withheld, was
in custody at the moment, and was rumored to be someone Lerner
had sentenced to prison three or four years ago. Archer knew that
Strand had leaked the arrest. Some people couldn't leave well
enough alone.

She finished the two-minute bulletin by saying lead investigator
Adam Strand said there would be more information released in the
next twenty-four hours.

Lead investigator. Adam Strand? He shook his head. It was a
shared title, but just as well. In the short time he'd known him, he
already realized Strand was a showboater, someone who would
always be proving to himself that he wouldn't be bullied again. He
was now in charge. That was fine by Quentin; he was happy to just
try to fly low, staying off the radar screen.

Detective Adam Strand might have to eat his words tomorrow
because he wasn't going to be able to make the charge stick. Archer
was sure of it.

Walking to his compact refrigerator, he pulled out a Dixie beer
and popped the top. A New Orleans beer, now made in Wisconsin.
The plant had been looted after Katrina and the owners had moved
the operation to a more friendly location.

He sipped the beer and decided he was going to have a talk with
the landlord about getting a new fridge. It was nothing close to
cold.

Closing his eyes, Archer ran the day's events through his mind
like a newsreel, starting with the call from a dispatcher this morning.
Duvay's attempt at evasion was cause for concern, yes; but young
black men in Detroit, especially ex-cons, distanced themselves from
cops with regularity. They didn't trust law enforcement officers.
How many times had he shouted out 'Police' and watched people
race from a scene. Almost *every* time. It didn't always equate to
specific guilt. They may have been guilty of *something,* but not
necessarily of the crime he was investigating. Why should it be any
different in New Orleans?

The oysters still heavy in his stomach, he drank part of another beer and fell asleep in the worn pea-green lounge chair, NBC still broadcasting in the background and Bourbon Street music still ringing in his ears.

The young, light-skinned black girl stood on the carriageway that led to his courtyard unit, breathing in the pungent odor of a ripe gardenia bush. Her dark eyes darted right, then left and settled on the brick building as she brushed coal-black curls from her face. Blocking the music from her mind, she concentrated on Archer and wondered if the time was right. She needed to tell him, to warn him about the death of the judge. She studied the small home, drumming fingers against her jean-covered thigh. Then, with a frown, she walked back out onto Bourbon Street. Tomorrow would be preferable. The detective would be fresh, rested and better able to deal with her. Then she wondered if he would be receptive to dealing with her at all.

'Damballa,' she whispered, 'you who makes valleys with your passing, bring me an inquiring mind. Bring me a sponge that I may let it soak up the knowledge.'

A breeze kicked up a cloud of dust from the sidewalks, blowing fine particles of dust into the eyes of the Bourbon Street crowd, and drunken revelers on the street looked skyward, wondering where this puff of wind had come from.

Archer sat bolt up in his chair, an icy chill racing through his body. The man's heart skipped a beat and he quickly surveyed the small living space. Instinctively he reached for his Glock 22, feeling some comfort in the grip of the handle. Nothing seemed to be disturbed. Nothing out of place. It wasn't a dream, but something had invaded his space. Music still blared from Bourbon Street, the sound of a noisy throng only slightly muffled in his courtyard. Everything was as it had been, but he knew something had happened. Wiping a sheen of perspiration from his forehead and rising from the chair, he grabbed his beer bottle and dumped the remainder in the white porcelain sink. He needed a clear head.

With one more sweep of the tiny room, then the bath, he re-holstered his pistol and checked the deadbolt and cheap lock on the front door. He had been getting used to someone playing mind games with him, but this felt different. Stripping off his clothes he lay back on the bed staring at the cracked ceiling. The Glock rested on the cheap vinyl end table, within easy reach. If he was threatened, he was ready. Never afraid to pull the pistol and use it.

Archer had drawn parallels between Motor City and New Orleans. Some of them were crystal clear. With roiling racial biases, drug trafficking, a corrupt police force and a murder rate that seemed to increase every year, the two cities resembled each other in many ways. But there were differences. He'd felt it the moment they'd seen the body. The bloated, dead body of Judge David Lerner. He'd never encountered anything like that in Detroit. Something about this case continued to haunt him. He hadn't been able to put his finger on it, but something floated in front of him, nagged at his inner core and clouded his brain. He'd always been a man who crystallized his thoughts, his methods, his purpose. Not anymore. Not after the body in the Mississippi River had surfaced. The murder of David Lerner, the case itself confused him. It was as if a ghostly presence surrounded the situation.

Through the turmoil in his life, the cases, the family crisis, his romantic disasters, his wife's murder, Archer's grounded sense of reason and justice had been the rock. He could always sort out the good and the bad and arrive at a logical conclusion.

Not here. Not now. There was interference, and the intrusion was disturbing his ability to think things clearly through.

On Bourbon Street the tipsy crowd on the Cat's Meow's second floor balcony was at capacity. The roar of the crowd and the blaring music filled the air as she glanced up at the spring breakers, the Mardi Gras faithful, and the drunken locals who patronized the Quarter. Plastic cups in hand, they swilled their drinks and at least a dozen young men shouted down to the assembled in boisterous voices, 'Show us your tits.'

Three young women on the street pulled up their tops and bras, shaking their breasts as plastic beads cascaded from above. Two girls on the balcony shouted, 'Show us your cocks,' and ten feet away from her a drunken twenty-year-old pulled down his pants.

The young black woman walked away, head down. Her town never seemed to change.

8

Even in Detroit, the badge garnered respect. A flash of the brass and doors opened. Important people ushered you into their inner sanctums and told you stories that no one else would ever hear.

Not so in New Orleans. There was a hierarchy that ruled. Some of it from organized crime. Some from crooked politicians who controlled the city. And often the snub was the result of a distrust of any law enforcement agency. Four police officers had recently been convicted of shooting unarmed residents in the aftermath of Katrina. In the last five days one cop had been arrested for rape, another for domestic violence and two had been charged for excessive use of force. Then there was the female detective from the Fourth who had stolen money from a charity for the homeless. A lot of money. There was only so much tolerance from the populace regarding the police abusing their power.

Sergeant Dan Sullivan met him in the lobby.

'Archer. A brief meeting in my office.'

Quentin Archer followed him into the small room. The desk was piled with paper, and his laptop was pushed to the side. Several commendations were framed on the wall behind him, and someone had made a stained-glass NOPD logo that he'd propped up on the remaining space of the crowded surface. The man needed a bigger desk.

'Strand thinks he might sweat this Duvay kid. What's your take on it?'

'It's the first lead, Sergeant.' Still too new to know how far to go. Going on record as criticizing his partner might not play so well. 'You know. Sometimes that pans out. He's got a warrant to search the house this morning, so there's that.'

'I've been here awhile, Archer. This isn't my first Mardi Gras. I think it's a little presumptuous. There's no evidence to back it up. Do you agree?'

'The kid took a hard hit from Judge Lerner. Most minors do community service for shoplifting. Duvay got a year. He may have a reason to be angry. As soon as we questioned him, he bolted from work, and when he realized we'd located him he took off running again.'

'I rest my case.' Sullivan folded his hands. 'No evidence. None. Am I right?'

'To be fair, Sergeant, Strand can use today to find evidence.'

The sergeant glanced at his cheap Timex with its large black face. 'Whoever the attorney turns out to be, he'll have him out in an hour.'

'But that's an hour that lets Strand investigate without the kid interfering.'

Every minute you could buy meant you might be that much closer to solid evidence. And he had to back his partner.

'This morning, where are you?'

'Courthouse. I've made a list of people who worked with the judge, liked him, hated him, including an ex-secretary who filed a sexual harassment case against him four years ago. She's agreed to talk.'

'The judge? A sexual harassment charge? Really? I never heard about that.'

'She dropped the charges, and they moved her to traffic court. She's still there, so I figured . . .'

'Interesting.'

'Oh, there's more.' He'd searched the Internet late in the night, called up police records and found quite a bit of information. Missing a lot of sleep, he'd turned up one important fact. The dead Judge Lerner was no saint.

'There's also a retired judge, name of Raft, who went public with a claim that Judge Lerner was possibly taking money to throw out cases. The backup on this charge comes through an anonymous source, and I'm not sure this Judge Raft will agree to talk anymore. He claimed his family had been threatened.'

'What?' Sullivan was obviously shocked. 'I've played golf with Judge Lerner. Not to speak ill of the dead, but I will agree he was pretty much an asshole. However, throwing cases? Sexual harassment? I would think charges like that would have gone public. I mean, I know he was maybe a little overly aggressive, but that's not in the same league.'

'Judge Raft was reassigned. Then he took an early retirement.'

Sullivan shook his head. 'Let me guess. Assigned to traffic court. It's a pattern. Am I right?'

Archer nodded. 'I made the calls yesterday, Sergeant. It sounds to me like this guy had a lot of power, and it didn't pay to fuck with him. If any of this pans out, there would be several people who had it out for him.'

Sullivan nodded. 'You tell me everything, Archer. Anything at all that you uncover, you get to me immediately.'

'Of course.'

'You're on top of his house?'

'Detective Levy has a crew. They're looking at it later today.'

'How many cases are you two covering right now?'

'Seven. And with the murder rate in this town, that's bound to go up.'

'I don't have to tell you, Archer, this is priority one. They're gonna come up my butt if we don't have something real soon. And I'm pretty sure this kid in lockup isn't what we're looking for.'

'Time will tell, Sergeant.' Archer remained circumspect.

'That's the point. We don't have time.'

Archer turned to leave the office.

'Good luck, Archer. Make your visit, interview everyone you can, and please, bring back something substantial, because I don't believe your partner has squat.'

Archer clenched his teeth. He wanted to agree. Couldn't. Shouldn't. But he knew deep in his soul that Antoine Duvay was not guilty. It probably went a lot higher than some ex-con kitchen worker.

On his way out, he stopped in the lobby, glancing at Cheryl, who was, just like yesterday, working behind the counter, talking on the phone, keying information into her computer and apparently reading a memo propped up in front of her.

'Hold on,' she said into the phone. She pushed her long dreadlocks behind her ears and looked up at Archer.

'Detective, what can I do for you?'

Archer gave her his best smile. He appreciated her dedication.

'Do we have a fund for cops who are down and out?'

'Relief and pension fund.'

He reached into his pocket and pulled out forty-seven bucks.

'Can you see this gets in the right hands?'

She nodded, smiling. 'Sure. Thank you.'

'It's not all from me. A guy on the street donated some of that.'

'Oh, wow. I don't think that happens very often,' she said. 'I guess there are some good guys out there, huh?'

'Yeah.' He walked out of the station house, muttering under his breath. 'Or not.'

9

Archer answered the phone on the second ring. A Detroit area code and he knew the number. Detective Tom Lyons, putting his job and maybe his life on the line.

'Quentin, we've got a partial on the plates.'

'Enough to get a name?'

'No, but we're working on it. The guys think we'll be able to get it.'

'How many cameras?'

'The corner where Denise was killed, we've been able to isolate three. Service station, a drug store and a camera at the stoplight where they ticket drivers who run the light.'

'Look, I'll find a way to pay you. Just keep the pressure on. It wasn't a hit-and-run. You know it, I know it.'

'You don't owe us shit, Q. We're going to get to the bottom of this, OK? Everything OK in Nawlins?'

'It's Nawlins. What do you think?'

'Detroit only ten times worse?'

'I would agree,' Archer said. 'Except that Denise was killed in Motor City.'

'Quentin, you've got friends. We're doing everything we can, no matter what you hear.'

'And I hear you. Thanks, man. Let me know the minute you have any information.'

He held the phone tight in his hand, staring into space. There were those who believed, and now a glimmer of hope.

10

'**M**a?'

Solange Cordray studied the old black woman's wispy white hair. She sat on a straight-back couch, a blanket thrown over her slender frame. The frail woman stared out the window, never acknowledging the girl.

'Ma?'

'Ah, the silent treatment again.' Kathy Bavely looked over Cordray's shoulder. 'You know, Solange, most of what you say to her she doesn't even hear. Maybe none of it.'

'She hears,' Cordray said, never turning. And looking at the ancient one, she said, 'They all hear.'

'You sound so confident.'

Solange said nothing, but turned from her mother and gently guided Bavely out the door.

'I know what the past has been and what the present brings. You don't have to believe me, but I swear to you, they hear us.'

Bavely shook her head.

'Sometimes you make no sense.'

Solange smiled. 'I know more than you give me credit for.' Changing the subject quickly she said, 'So, how was your date last night?'

The petite blond gave her a broad grin. 'Not good enough for me. You know, the older most people get the more desperate they become. They settle. I'm not a settler. This Craig Landis, he's a pretender. He barely got a kiss goodnight. And believe this, it's the last one from me.'

'You're too hard on these boys,' Cordray smiled at her.

'*You* need a man to be hard on, Solange. Or, the other way around.'

Laughing they walked down the hall, footsteps echoing off the walls.

'I'm taking Mr Essex and Mrs Abrahms out to the banks in,' Kathy Bavely checked her watch, 'fifteen minutes. Do you have time for a coffee?'

They continued the walk to the small break room. Pushing a five-dollar bill into the machine, Bavely programmed two lattes, and passed one to Solange.

'Ma and the two ladies in the lobby, my job today.' She motioned to two women down the hall, a vacant stare in their eyes as they sat in rocking chairs, looking at nothing.

'Do you ever wonder if they really do hear, what are they thinking? To be locked up with their thoughts, not being able to talk, to express themselves and never—'

'And you, Kathy, with no filter, if you weren't crazy already, it would drive *you* crazy. Am I right?'

'You are,' she chuckled.

'So, what was wrong with Craig Landis?'

'Talked all night about himself.'

'Which stopped you from talking about yourself?'

They both laughed.

Picking up their coffees, they saluted each other then sat back and watched the Mississippi River as it flowed outside the window. More at home in the quietness of their relationship than with a constant stream of conversation.

Twenty minutes later, Solange Cordray and her three charges were perched on vinyl lawn chairs on the grass, enjoying the seventy-five-degree weather and a gentle breeze off the river. In front of them the brackish water swirled by, pieces of wood and debris riding on the surface.

'Thelma, are you enjoying the day?'

The woman to her right didn't respond. The second woman nodded.

'The day. The sun. And fried chicken tonight.'

'You're having chicken, Ruthy?' Cordray asked.

'I'd better hurry home. Harold will be coming in the door just any minute. Loves my fried chicken, he does.'

Harold had been dead for ten years, killed by a drunk driver in the Garden District. Records confirmed that the lady's mental condition deteriorated from that point.

'Ma, are you comfortable?'

Her mother looked up, staring into her eyes.

'Yes, dear.'

Then she looked away, gazing at the dirty river.

It was the first time in three days she had spoken to her daughter, and Solange's heart actually skipped a beat.

'Ma,' she touched her arm but there was no response. It was as if her comment had never happened. 'I almost talked to the detective. I almost told him last night what Mr Foster knows.'

She heard. She heard everything. But her lack of response was the issue.

'I'll find him today, and I'll make my case. I know, I know, you're thinking I don't know him. He may not take me seriously. Or, he may not care what I have to say. And you and I both know that trying to explain *how* I got the information won't be easy. It may be impossible.'

The Big Muddy stretched out wide, bank to bank. She never tired of the river. She was glad to be a part of it, every day. The water gave her energy, strength, and renewed her courage. And God knew she needed that. The courage to face these people each day, and to deal with their problems, their quirks, idiosyncrasies and their secrets.

'I'm going to confront him, Ma. You would. You *did*. But I will be careful. It won't be like in your time. I know you used what you had for good. Not like some. But *they* didn't understand. And that only seemed to make you stronger. You know that. Still, you told me, always use the gift for something good. To make something better. I'm doing that, Ma. You taught me well.'

The hour went by slowly and a uniformed orderly with his name tag prominently displayed arrived at the appointed time and gathered up the lawn chairs, helping the older women to their feet.

'Thank you, Clarence.'

'My pleasure, Mrs Cordray. You're looking good today. Very good.' He wore a thin smile, his eyes looking into hers with an interest that was not reciprocal. Then his eyes lowered as he took in her person. The man stared at her upper body, that smile still plastered on his face. The way he studied her and spoke made her uneasy. The guy was creepy.

'Ma, I'm seeing Matebo soon. I'll tell him you asked about him.'

The old woman turned her head and Solange thought she caught a small smile on her lips. Matebo. Maybe her mother's best friend. Someone Solange had grown up with, a partner in the voodoo practice, a true medicine man who worked in the bayou, cultivating herbs and flowers and all kinds of wild things. Just one name, Matebo. It's all she'd ever heard him called.

Kissing her mother on the cheek, she walked to the desk and logged out, the day of volunteering at an end. Solange walked past the sign, *Water's Edge Care Center*, and continued up Barracks Street, turning left on Dauphine.

There was a sense of danger in the air. She was receiving far more information than she was comfortable with. And she didn't know what to do with most of it. The detective from Michigan somehow had the background to put it all together. She was convinced that Archer could make sense of it all.

Clarence the orderly was a minor disturbance. Still, the man was a problem. He worked the center for his own amusement. Seeing how many women he could score with. Workers, patients, it probably didn't matter to him. She'd heard the rumors. Solange shuddered, thinking about all the problems at the center. And the most important problem? Ma.

Ma had spoken to her today. Actually seemed engaged. For about two seconds. She'd actually said two words. Two whole words. And the world was a brighter place.

11

He'd taken a long swallow from the flask of Jack Daniel's, a little courage, a little fortitude. It made the job a little easier.

Strand stood in the small living room of Duvay's shotgun house. A threadbare green sofa and chair, a couple of cheap store-bought prints on the wall and an old black man in a threadbare undershirt, his back plastered against the far wall. The narrow house had a living room, hallway, a kitchen at the end, two very small bedrooms and a bath. Long, narrow, you could fire a shotgun from the open front door and through the rear exit without hitting anything else.

'You flash your badge and a piece of paper and espect me to let you in here?' The man pointed his thumb and index finger at the detective.

Gun drawn, Strand nodded.

'Look, Dad, I expect you to back off and allow these two detectives and myself to do our job. We will search this home, and we will look at everything we possibly can. If you get in the way, we can and will arrest you. Do you understand?'

'I have a question, officer.'

'What?'

'Would I be in trouble if I said "go fuck yourself"?'

'I'm trying to make it easy on you, Dad. Just hold it inside. We'll be in here for twenty minutes.' Less than twenty. Much less. 'If you want to jeopardize your situation, keep on talking. We've already got your son downtown, and if you want to smart off, we'll be happy to bring you in as well.'

Adam Strand nodded to a detective named Rooney, who promptly drew his Glock 22, keeping it by his side as he eyed Antoine Duvay's father.

Moving back down the hall, Strand reached into his jacket pocket and pulled out a fist-sized package wrapped in a white cloth. Two small bedrooms opened off the short hallway and he chose the first one. It had to be Antoine Duvay's room. A few posters of obscure rappers tacked on the wall and some T-shirts thrown on the unmade bed confirmed it. A shirt flung on the rumpled sheets boasted the slogan *Don't Be a Sexist. Bitches Hate That*. Pulling open the top drawer of a chipped and faded white dresser he dropped a cloth-covered package inside on the pile of underwear and closed the drawer.

'Cassidy?'

'I've got nothing so far, Strand.' The paunchy, balding detective walked out of the kitchen. 'Kitchen, bath, standard fare.'

Strand nodded.

'You?'

'I'm going to check the old man's room. You give a thorough to Antoine's room here.'

'Got it.'

Fifteen seconds later, Strand heard Cassidy shout it out.

'Detective. We've got a gun.'

Strand allowed himself a brief moment. In this city, in this department, a man had to do what a man had to do.

They met in the boy's room.

'Sig Sauer P290.' He held the small pistol in his gloved hand. 'Wrapped up in this handkerchief. I'm gonna bet it's wiped clean.'

Strand smiled. 'This should hold him for a while. See what else there is.'

An ex-con with a gun. That wouldn't play well at all. He'd bought himself some time. But tying the gun to the murder of Judge David Lerner, *that* might be harder to do.

Archer left the precinct and drove his Chevy downtown, the faulty air conditioner cranked to the max to combat the humidity. Not much relief. The car was a perk, but the department never guaranteed the quality of the vehicles. He was sweating profusely by the time he arrived. There was a story about the cops, after Katrina, looting citizens' Cadillacs and patrolling in the 'borrowed' vehicles. Totally unacceptable, but anything was better than this beat-up Chevy.

He found the four-story courthouse at 421 Loyola.

Clearing the metal detector, he introduced himself at the front desk and told the receptionist his business. The older woman waved him to the elevators.

'Judge Lerner's office is second floor,' she said, 'to the left, and it's clearly marked. Very sad about the judge.'

Her flat voice belied any sincerity.

He found the office five doors down. Turning the handle, Archer walked in and glanced around the reception area. The actual office was in the back, the door wide open.

The attractive woman sitting behind the judge's desk looked up. The pile of papers in front of her must have been eight inches high.

'Yes? Can I help you?'

Her voice was a little brusque, and she seemed somewhat perturbed that he'd interrupted.

Palming his badge, he introduced himself.

'I'm obviously here to get as much information on Judge Lerner as possible.'

'Well of course,' she said. 'I'm Sue Waronker. I worked with the judge for twelve years. He was a tough judge, but a fair man, Detective. Most of the time.' She paused, then glanced down at her desk. 'Some of the time.'

She sounded less than sincere.

'I'm sure he was, ma'am.' The lady sounded like she had memorized the line. Tough but fair. As if she was used to defending him.

'I've been working with Traci next door.' She brushed back her dark hair; she looked haggard.

'Traci?'

'Yes, Traci Hall. She's a judge as well. We've been sorting out some of the immediate things that have to be done.'

'Everything is documented?'

'Not as well as I'd hoped. Or assumed. David was a very organized man, but there are some things that don't seem to be where they should.'

The dark-haired woman waved her hand at the computer monitor in front of her and the stack of papers and files.

'We're only dealing with immediate issues. Court dates in the next week, obligations that he had to meet tomorrow and the next day. Even that is a bit overwhelming.'

'I'm going to need to talk with you. Is now a good time?'

Shrugging her shoulders, she motioned for him to sit down. Archer took a seat across the desk, a seat that over a fifteen-year career had probably seen its share of attorneys, offenders and a whole cast of characters who influenced the justice meted out to young people.

'Twelve years? That's a long time.'

'Twelve. This August.'

'Tough man to work for?'

She frowned. 'Is everything you say going to lead to a negative response from me? Is that your intent?'

'I don't follow.'

'You start out with "a tough man to work for"? And if I say yes, then do you keep probing? Trying to get me to tell you all of his negatives? And does that lead to you measuring my responses and weighing whether I might be a suspect in his death? Because, I am not going to be a person of interest, Mr Archer. I don't like the tone of your voice.'

A lady who had seen twelve years of lawyers, probing for the defense, for the prosecution.

'Whoa.' Archer motioned for a timeout. 'Miss Waronker . . .'

'Mrs.' Her voice very firm.

'*Mrs* Waronker, I'm not playing games here. I'm not a trial attorney. Just a cop trying to solve a murder. I want to know this man inside and out. I want to know who his friends were, who his enemies were, who his contacts were. The question was somewhat of an icebreaker. I'd heard he was a little harsh in his opinions, in his judgment. Let's start over, OK. It is not my intention to back you into the corner.'

Her eyes boring into his, she studied him for a moment, and he straightened his posture, shifting his shoulders.

'OK. Yes, he was tough to work for.' She spit out the words. 'He could be a real son of a bitch at times. Demanding as hell, but I put up with that for twelve years. There was another lady who didn't last twelve years. There's a story there. I suppose,' she hesitated, 'I suppose I should point out that there were some good things about him too.'

Archer nodded, folding his hands in his lap. He had the distinct impression there really weren't too many positive qualities about the deceased.

'All right, let's start there.'

Sue Waronker leaned forward, her elbows on the dark wooden desk. Letting out a slow breath she said, 'I've lived the last twelve years making excuses for Judge David Lerner. That was my job. And, Detective, I'm paid to do my job. You give me a check and I'll do almost anything you want done. Almost. Understand? And, I've been led to believe that part of my job is to support the judges in this division. Not just Lerner, but the others as well.'

Archer nodded, hoping to encourage her narrative.

'Well, one of those judges is no longer among us. While he was alive, I lived with his arrogance, I put up with his superior attitude and the harsh sentences that he passed on young men and women in this city. It was a job that I sometimes couldn't stomach, Detective. Judge Lerner destroyed a lot of young lives – especially the men's – and their families because of harsh penalties that very few of those people actually deserved. He wasn't the only one on this floor. But I worked for him and I apologize to anyone if I turned a blind eye to some of his corrections.'

'You say this without a background in the justice system? Without any education in criminal law?'

The lady gripped the edge of her desk, her knuckles white.

'I say this, Detective Archer, with a compassion for people. Judge

Lerner and Judge Warren,' she hesitated, 'and there are others, believe me, I'm sorry, but there are, were, several judges who seemed to revel in harsh sentencing on young people who I believe deserved a second chance. It's my thought, but as you point out, I haven't one good reason or qualification to make that statement.'

'Mrs Waronker, I was simply pointing out that there may be legal reasons beyond your, or my understanding. No offense.'

'I'm going to be totally honest with you, Detective Archer. You seem to have been honest with me.'

His innocent face on, Archer smiled.

'I worked for him almost twelve years. The pay was decent, the hours sometimes long, but I fit in well, and I'm really good at what I do.' She hesitated. 'One of the girls who worked with him is now tending traffic court. Abruptly dismissed. So obviously, the man had issues with employees.'

'OK.' He nodded, feeling like the other shoe was about to drop. Which was the reason for his visit.

'That said, I go back to my statement.' She wore a weak smile. 'Or my outburst about the judge.'

Q nodded again, trying to encourage the lady.

'I've known him a long time, and Judge David Lerner didn't really have a lot of redeeming qualities. Pressed, I'm not sure I could name one. I'm not sorry he's gone, Detective. Part of his job seemed to be making people's lives a living hell. My honest answer to your question is this: there could be all kinds of reasons and all kinds of people who would want him dead. All kinds.'

She'd given him a copy of the judge's calendar, his Rolodex, plus the names of the other six juvenile judges who worked in the building. He checked at the front desk to see if any of them were available.

'Richard Warren. He's the only one who isn't busy at the moment. He's in his office. Do you want me to see if he can work you in? Would you like to see him?' the plump honey-blond receptionist asked.

Archer walked down the hall and into a cramped office. After introducing himself, he said, 'You worked with David Lerner? Judge David Lerner?'

The judge looked up, peering skeptically at Archer through large black-framed glasses. A small wiry man, about forty and quite pale. Someone who spent a lot of time inside.

'I did.'

'Did you have much interaction?'

'Interaction?'

'Did you work together? I'm sorry, Judge Warren, I'm not exactly sure how your system works. Maybe you could help me out. Tell me how things progress in this court.'

'We handle our own caseloads, Detective. I may have a day, or a moment when I deal with one of the other judges' cases, but for the most part we are independent of each other.'

'Judge Lerner had a reputation for being a little harsh in his sentencing. Did you have any feelings about that?'

'Judge Lerner,' he leaned on the man's last name, 'called his own shots. He didn't ask my opinion on how to adjudicate.' Warren crossed his arms over his chest and dared the detective to keep up the interrogation.

'Judge, we're trying to find out who murdered your colleague. I'm asking you if you have any idea who might have had a reason to—'

'Detective, New Orleans has a lot of bad characters who are underage. And when those kids get out, I'm well aware some of them are not happy with our part in their incarceration.'

'So you think that offenders may—'

'Offenders. Their family. Their friends. We get threats from all of them. You want to go back twelve years and look into every kid Judge Lerner convicted? Or every threat he received in his tenure? Do you want to put your staff through that process? Good luck with that, Detective.'

'How about you, Judge? Do you give harsh sentences? A little over the top? A little severe for the offense?'

Warren stood. His gaze went beyond Archer, to the entrance to his office, the wall in the hallway. His stare had a distant look.

'Detective, Judge Lerner was a zero-tolerance judge. If you break the law, you pay for that transgression. Some of us feel that's following the letter of the law. Some of us agree with that philosophy. Some of us.' Standing up he walked to one of the three windows in his office. 'We all have a sense of responsibility, Mr Archer. We need to rid our streets of these punks. Teach them a lesson, OK?'

Archer remembered the song from Gilbert and Sullivan's *The Mikado*. 'Let the Punishment Fit the Crime'.

'Some of us? You must be someone who believes in harsh penalties. You must be one of the good guys.'

Warren wet his lips with his tongue.

'I am a fair judge, Detective. That is what I believe.'

'Judge Warren, I sincerely hope that whoever committed this crime isn't thinking about killing more judges.'

'What?' Rearing back, Warren stared at Archer's face. 'Is that a threat?' He threw his arms out, an expression of bewilderment on his face. 'What are you saying? Are you suggesting—?'

'A threat? No, I—' Archer had said it as a thought, a warning. The man's life could be in danger. Didn't he get that? Maybe even the judges in New Orleans were suspicious of the police and questioned their motives. 'Definitely not. I'm not in a position to threaten you. It's a sincere warning. As of this moment, we don't know who killed Judge Lerner, or why, but if I were you, I'd be watching my back.'

Warren walked from behind the desk and forced Archer into the hall. 'Detective Archer, if you want to file a grievance about the way I handle *my* business, you can take it up with the state board. Judge Lerner isn't around to explain the way *he* did things.'

Archer nodded. The guy was very touchy. As if Archer had touched a nerve.

'I don't understand your business, Judge. But, you need to understand it may be possible someone doesn't like the way you do things. Be careful, Mr Warren. I'm serious.'

'Fuck you, Detective. I'm serious as well.'

12

I t was mid-afternoon when he left the building. Three judges, the Waronker lady, and he wasn't much further ahead than he had been. The judges were closed-mouthed, a brotherhood and all that. Judge Traci Hall, who worked in the next office, admitted that the punishment David Lerner handed down often seemed excessive, but that was the most she would say. She was guarded in her comments and Q quickly understood that brotherhood, sisterhood, was paramount. No one wanted to be the snitch. Much like the Detroit Police Department, and he assumed with the NOPD as well.

Archer guessed none of Lerner's fellow judges would venture a reason why someone would gun down the man. Richard Warren had been sullen and defensive and would probably rate another interview.

Sue Waronker, on the other hand, gave him several reasons. None that he took too seriously, although a lead was a lead. She seemed to have some issues with a couple of offenders the judge had sentenced, and she had suggested he talk with the secretary who had claimed sexual harassment. Archer intended to follow up on her immediately as he walked to traffic court on Broad Street.

The detective was starting to have a better understanding of the murdered judge. Twice divorced, twenty years on the bench, drove a Jaguar convertible and seemed well off, supposedly because of good investments. Then there were the rumors that he'd thrown cases for money. It was going to be hard to prove those stories.

He had a daughter named Alison, who, by Lerner's own admission to his colleagues, never talked to him. The judge apparently hadn't seen her in over ten years. No inquiries from either of the wives or the daughter. Nobody cared about this guy.

Walking over to the traffic court, Archer found the maligned secretary in a small office buried in the back of the building. One metal desk, a laptop Dell computer, a couple of file cabinets and two chairs. The name on the desk plate said Brandy Lane. To him, it sounded like a stripper's name.

When he made his introduction she said, 'I thought you'd be visiting.' Brandy had a soft face, expressive eyes and short brown hair. Not a raving beauty, but not totally unattractive.

'I'd like to ask you some questions.'

'Sure.' She motioned for him to sit across from her. 'I'm not sure I can tell you that much. It happened several years ago. It happened, it's over, and I'm here now.' She sounded resigned.

'I looked it up and apparently you dropped the charges.'

'I only filed to get him to stop. It started with rude comments. He'd comment on the clothes I wore, then he'd talk to me about my body. He accused me of coming on to him, and believe me, Detective, if you've seen pictures of him, he wasn't the most attractive man in the world. There was no way I ever would have made advances on that man. No way.'

Archer had seen the real body. Water logged, and not a pretty sight.

'And then he kept commenting on my name. Said it sounded like a stripper's name or a porn star.'

He swallowed and glanced again at the name on her desk. Brandy Lane. Were all guys on the same wavelength?

She studied Archer for a moment, then said, 'The strange thing about all of that, was, I was certain he was gay. I think he used sexual harassment with women to cover that fact.'

'Gay?'

'Please, don't take that in a wrong way. My thoughts, no proof. He was an asshole. Not because I thought he was on the other side.'

'So you filed charges?'

'I did. And I learned something, Detective Archer. You don't file charges on a judge when you're surrounded by other judges. Great lesson, but I wish I'd never been in a position to be schooled. I never should have made any waves. I know that now. A very bad decision. Judges in New Orleans are very powerful. I worked for one and had no idea. Honest to God, they will kick your ass.'

He nodded, understanding only too well. Judges, officers on the force, they stood up for each other, right or wrong. No question about it. In Detroit, it involved the cop who was in business with Archer's brothers. He fronted a drug running business, but as bad as the drug business was, the police fraternity did not approve of Quentin Archer's crusade against Officer Bobby Mercer. The force as one stood up for Mercer. They made it very clear. And six months and twelve hundred miles later, here he was. Not guilty, but he was the one who exited. He'd been certain Mercer had committed murder, to cover his drug running, but that same police officer still walked the streets of Motown. Don't go after a judge when you're surrounded by other judges? The same philosophy seemed to apply to cops.

'Ever have any thoughts about getting revenge?'

She smiled softly. 'Sure. All the time.'

'Ever act on any of those thoughts?'

'No. Sometimes I wish I had. Guy was a son of a bitch. Actually, I probably would have, at one time. I might have killed him, Detective.'

'Why didn't you?'

'Someone else beat me to it.'

* * *

The parking ticket was wedged between the windshield wiper and the glass. Archer ripped it out and thought about tearing it into a thousand pieces. Some meter maid had already gone out of her way to incite his wrath.

The Chevy was sticky hot inside as he drove back to the office, both windows down. Parking the car, he took the elevator to the third floor. At his desk he sorted through handwritten notes and keyed them into his computer. Scrawled notes. The department had recently bought new recording devices but Archer worked better off his paper trail. Half of his life was trying to organize things. Lost in his own world of reconstructing his morning, Archer jerked when he felt a hand on his shoulder.

'Found a gun, partner.'

Archer turned and stared at Strand. A sick little grin was on his partner's face and Archer knew immediately.

'Recently fired?'

'How did you know?'

'How long can you hold him?'

'Don't give me any shit, Q.'

'How long, Strand?'

'We'll see. Ex-con with a gun? Dead judge? I think we've got some time to work him.'

'You're still pretty sure, aren't you?'

'I want it to be him, Q. Makes our world a lot simpler.'

'And justice?'

'It will be served.'

Archer just shook his head.

'Look, Q, I'm not looking for a bad collar. Last thing I want is six months down the road we find we nailed the wrong guy. But right now, I like this kid for the murder. He ran. He walked out of that restaurant right after we questioned him. We need to hold him till we can work the case.' Shrugging his shoulders he said, 'Besides, I wasn't the one who found the gun.'

'Sergeant Sullivan talked to me this morning. He said he doesn't believe the kid is guilty.'

'He's singing a different tune now.' Strand walked into the hall, then turned and looked at Archer. 'You know the old saying? When you want someone's attention, you pull a gun. I think we've got this kid, Q.'

'And I think it goes further than the kid.'

'All right, what have *you* got, hotshot? Interviews today, talking to his colleagues. What did you learn?'

'The guy was a bit of a jerk.'

'We knew that, man. Come on, you want me to believe, give me something, Quentin. What do you have?'

'He was rough on offenders.'

'Yeah, yeah. What's new?'

Archer shrugged his shoulders.

'I'll send you the report.'

Turning away from his partner he continued keying in his notes. He was angry and he was hungry and it was going to take an hour or more to put this report together. Time was slipping away, the killer getting further from the crime, and all they had was a planted gun, and an ex-con who never killed anyone.

Detective Adam Strand was pushing just a little too hard. And if someone did plant the weapon, it was just like the killings on the bridge after Katrina. The cops had planted guns then too. Hadn't they learned anything? It was just Archer's luck to have drawn Strand on this case.

13

He checked his watch, knowing he only had a small window of time to make the call. They had offered him a nice bonus if he gave them something solid.

'Hello.' The voice on the other end was quiet and the 'hello' almost a soft question.

The caller didn't recognize the voice. 'You wanted to know about the murder investigation. Where it stood. You're going to make it worth my while if I give you good information?'

'What have you got?'

'We've got an ex-con with a gun. This ex-con, he was sentenced by Lerner.'

'Anything else?'

'A detective is interviewing other judges. He's not convinced yet.'

'What's your take?'

He hesitated with his answer. 'The ex-con with a gun. I don't think we can prove it's the murder weapon but it's a pretty good lead. We're hoping to wrap it up soon.'

'Call me with any updates.'

'I will.'

'Oh, and find out who he's talking to, this detective. I need to know what judges he's contacting.'

The informant hesitated. 'Should I stop by the restaurant? Compensation and all that?'

'I think something a little more solid would justify payment. We'll try to accommodate on your next phone call.'

The line went dead. They weren't going to pay him for this information. Damn. Maybe when he had a little more juice. He'd tried to trace the number he was calling, but to no avail. With all the technology in the world today, there were still ways to hide.

14

Yo Mama's Bar and Grill was headquartered on St Peter's between Bourbon and Royal. It was close to his home and the burgers were good, the beer cold. And they served a New Orleans draft.

Driving from the office, he'd circled the block several times, finally finding a spot about thirty yards from the restaurant. The early revelers had already replaced the more sedate tourist trade as Archer walked the walk, dodging several drunks, an Uncle Sam on stilts trolling for money and a one-man band playing drums, guitar and a kazoo. The crowd was avoiding him. Inside the small bar he sat in one of the booths, immediately ordered a Tin Roof and drained it while waiting for the barmaid to bring the food. An open-faced chili cheeseburger. The perfect meal.

He was checking his cell phone when he glanced up and there she was, sitting across the booth from him. He'd missed it altogether, and that didn't happen very often. Almost never. A chill went down his spine and he actually shivered. She was beautiful. Simple, unadorned and naturally beautiful. Archer tried to catch his breath as the young lady gave him a wry smile.

'Ma'am, if you're selling something, roses, or something else . . .' and immediately he knew she wasn't.

'Detective Archer.' A smile played on her lips, inviting and friendly. There was no question she knew him.

He continued to be struck by her presence, struck by an emptiness where his heart should have been. Dark skin, but not black. Eyelashes longer than those of anyone he'd ever met. Cute? No, it wasn't just cute. She was striking to look at, the kind of girl you dreamed about but never had a chance with. And she was probably ten years his junior. High cheekbones, that flirtatious smile on her face, perfect teeth and, from the waist up at least, a perfect figure. He couldn't see any more than that. He struggled to regain his composure.

'I believe I may have some information you might be interested in.' Now a more somber tone.

He found his tongue not responding. Attractive women like this one did not normally seek him out.

'You have no questions?' Now more of a quizzical smile and she ducked her head just a little. 'About what this information is? How I knew where to find you? Detective, you must be skeptical, am I right?'

Archer took a quick swallow of his beer to give him time to think. It almost felt like the girl was toying with him, but it was more than that.

'Mr Archer, please, I've searched you out. It's not easy for me to approach someone like yourself. In your position. There are people like *you* who don't understand people like *me*. I speak from experience. Please, let me try to explain that.'

Archer studied her face and nodded. He had yet to say a meaningful word to the young, mysterious woman.

'OK, let me start the conversation. I'm here because I believe I have some information on the death of Judge David Lerner. Information that could help in your investigation.'

Finally he found his voice. 'I don't know what people like *you* are like,' he wrapped his hand around his beer bottle, squeezing it, 'but I'm always accessible when it comes to information on one of my cases.'

He saw his reflection in her brown eyes, her look almost inviting. Almost, but not quite.

'No matter how the information came about?'

'You stole it? Bought it? You're divulging some sort of secret you promised to keep?'

'Here's your chili cheeseburger, hon.'

The waitress with a dragon tattoo from wrist to shoulder set it on the vinyl tabletop. The sandwich was a picture of excess. Half a pound of meat covered in chili and gooey melted cheese, presented as an open-faced sandwich.

'You having anything, sweetie?' She looked at the girl, did a second take, backing away.

Archer noticed, wondering what kind of aura this young woman was radiating.

'Please,' Archer asked, 'can I order you a drink?' He couldn't enjoy this dinner or even partake of it if she just sat there with nothing. 'Have you had dinner because I'm not going to finish this thing by myself.'

The young lady shook her head, the soft black hair moving like a gentle wave.

'Please?'

'Coffee, black,' she said.

The waitress nodded, her frozen gaze focused on the young lady. Finally, she turned and hurried back to the bar.

Archer gained his composure, and tried a smile.

'I'd like to tell you that good police work solves most crimes, but the truth is,' he paused, still taken aback that she'd come to him, this strange, beautiful woman, 'most crimes are solved because people like you come forward. You fill in some blanks. Is that what you're going to do? Fill in some of the blanks?'

'I'll tell you my story.'

He couldn't wait.

'You haven't told me who you are.'

'You are not from New Orleans.' She made the statement matter-of-fact, not a question.

'No.' He put his hands on the table, not even thinking about the large patty of meat, chili and cheese in front of him.

'So the name Clotille Trouville doesn't mean anything to you, am I right? You've never heard the name?'

He would have remembered a name like that.

'You are Clotille Trouville?'

'No. I'm her daughter. My name is Solange Cordray.'

Strange names. Clotille. Solange.

'And why should I know your mother?'

'My mother practiced,' she cleared her throat and just for a second he thought he saw her eyes cloud over, 'she practiced voodoo. She was somewhat famous in this area. Her name and her story made national news a number of years ago.'

The waitress with the twisted dragon on her arm set the coffee cup in front of the young lady. Staring at her for a moment, she said, 'Here you go, hon.'

'I don't know her.' Archer admitted. 'Obviously I'm not from here; and I know very little about voodoo.'

'And I could spend a week and not explain everything the religion of voodoo has to offer. Briefly, Detective Archer, in the early 1700s, when African slaves from Benin were shipped to the French colony of Louisiana, they introduced voodoo to the community. Haitians brought their version to Louisiana. We are an active faith, one that is much like the Catholic religion. Followers often practice in the Catholic faith as well. Voodoo believes in one deity, Damballa, the snake god. Then, just as the Catholic religion has their saints, we have our spirits. For money, for love, for faithfulness, happiness . . .'

'There's a famous voodoo lady who's buried not too far from here, isn't there?' One of the few cultural stories he'd heard since moving to the city.

'Marie Laveau, the Voodoo Queen. She is buried in Saint Louis Cemetery Number One, off Basin Street. A very mystical woman. People who don't believe at all visit her gravesite and make wishes. They draw three Xs on her tombstone.' She paused and shook her head. 'Religion in all forms is very strange, don't you agree?'

Archer stabbed a piece of burger with his fork, feeling glutinous while the young lady across from him demurely sipped her freshly poured coffee. No cream or sugar.

'So your mother cast spells and made people's lives better? Or worse?'

'This is why it's not easy to talk to someone like you. You make light of what is often very serious.'

Taking a deep breath, he resolved to concentrate on the story at hand.

'Your mother has something to do with the case I'm working on? Is that what you are telling me?'

'My mother has Alzheimer's disease. Her memory is fading, and she rarely communicates with me or anyone.'

'I'm sorry to hear that.' His mother didn't communicate with him anymore, but it had nothing to do with dementia. 'So what's the connection? To her and the murder of David Lerner?'

The young girl put both arms on the table, presenting a diminutive but formidable presence.

'Records will show, Detective, that my mother came to the police fifteen years ago. I was ten years old. She had a premonition that one of her clients was going to be killed. She could see the killer's face and warned her client and your police department. She gave them all the time of the killing, the place it would happen and the identity of the killer. She saw it very clearly. The lady who was to be the victim, her very own client, told her she was wrong. Called her an insane bitch. This was a woman who had paid for my mother's advice.'

Archer nodded, hearing the pain in the young lady's voice. Obviously it was hard to tell this story.

'The police told my mother she was a crazy woman. They laughed in her face and called her *anraje*. A lunatic. I was there when it happened. At the police station in the Quarter. The most humiliating moment of my mother's life. Of my life.' She paused, and breathed a ragged breath.

Finally, regaining her composure, she said, 'I was by her side when they threw her out. She was trying to save a life, Detective.'

And Archer could see the young girl, holding tight to her mother's hand while a cynical policeman escorted her from the building. He could see it as if it was happening at this very moment. As if he were there in the precinct house.

'And this murder took place, am I right?'

'It did. Mrs Robert James, the wife of a prominent businessman in New Orleans. The killing happened at the place my mother said it would. It happened at the same time she said it would.'

'And the cops and Mrs James ignored it.' He cut off another bite of the burger, wondering where the story was going.

The young lady paused. She struggled for the words and Archer struggled with her, a strange feeling.

'My mother paid dearly for sharing that information.'

'What price?'

Deeply engrossed in the dialogue, he wanted answers, even though he had no idea where the conversation was going.

'The police arrested her, Detective. They accused Ma of the murder.'

Ma. The story had turned very personal.

Her voice broke, and she blinked her eyes. 'They put her in jail and she sat there for six weeks, Detective Archer. Six weeks before Mrs James's *infidèle* husband finally confessed.'

A tear trickled down her cheek and Archer wanted to console her, touch her hand or say something. Instead he looked away.

'Now do you understand why I hesitate bringing this story to you?'

'Yeah. I do.' His uneasiness at listening to her most intimate feelings was apparent. 'Whatever you tell me, I'll never divulge where I heard it.'

'You can't. Ever.'

'You have my word.'

'I'm a good judge of character, Quentin Archer. But I'm also wary of the police. I do have one thing in my favor, if you should ever divulge your source.'

'What's that?' She intrigued him. He was under her spell, hanging on her next thought, her next utterance.

'I *also* practice voodoo.'

There was no smile on her face.

Archer felt the familiar chill running down his back. Silly. This voodoo was a witch doctor thing. A religion designed to keep the slaves in line. He should be amused, but for some reason he wasn't. She was very serious, and so was he. She was threatening him and he could do nothing.

'And I do cast spells, Detective. I do cast spells. You mentioned Marie Laveau? She was my great, great aunt.'

Her somber stare scared him. And he didn't scare easily.

15

Strand sat across from the young black man, trying to be Mister Nice Guy. Soft tone of voice, a gentle smile on his face. If Antoine Duvay did not respond, Strand would turn bad cop. It was easier to do this with two men, but he'd have to do the best he could. Archer had phoned in and was busy talking to a lead.

'We visited your house, man.'

'You promised me an attorney.'

Duvay watched him through squinted eyes.

'Met your dad. What a charming man.' Strand's own dad had been a disaster. Constantly berating his son for being a wimp, a cowering idiot, or the word he used most: a pussy.

'You mess with my pop?'

Both hands on the table, Strand shook his head.

'We didn't mess with anybody. We had a warrant and—'

'How the hell did you get a warrant? Man, you got no reason to hold me. Who is gonna give you a fuckin' search warrant?'

'Antoine, Antoine, *judges* issue search warrants. We've got a dead judge, my friend. That's the reason you're here. Almost any judge I call is going to bend over backwards to help me.'

The ex-con grunted in disgust. 'Where's my lawyer, man?'

'Why did you run, Antoine?'

There was a flash of fear in the young man's eyes, and just for a moment Strand saw through him. Here was a kid who had been pushed around and bullied by the system. Just like Strand. Strand understood. And the kid was scared, just like he'd been scared his entire life. But Strand needed a confession and now was not the time to be sympathetic. Get the confession, solve the case. Not the moment to go soft.

'You going to tell me?'

He shook his head. 'I was in prison for a crime I shouldn't have committed. I was on the warden's honor role, Detective. I had house duty where I took care of Warden Jakes's grounds. I swept his walk, I washed his cars. I greeted visitors to his home.' Duvay swallowed hard as if he shouldn't have divulged his position. 'Anyway, dude, I was a model prisoner, and that's the end of it. There was never any idea of getting even with that cracker judge. OK?'

'We went through the house, and you'll never guess what we found.'

'If you found the pot, it was pop's.'

'Ex-cons aren't allowed to have illegal substances, you know that, right?' Strand folded his hands, calm, methodical.

'Hell, man, you gonna bust me on a chickenshit weed charge? That's all you got? You better get somethin' bigger than that. Bring me my lawyer, cop.' His eyes were bright and wide open. Strand could see veins on his forehead. The suspect was working up a head of steam.

'Didn't even see the pot. Maybe your old man smoked it while you were here. He does seem a little out of touch.'

'Then let me go, muthafucker.'

'Well, we considered that. Letting you go. But then Detective Cassidy, he was helping me search the house, he found a gun, Antoine.'

The boy's jaw dropped, and his eyes almost popped out of his dark head.

'A Sig Sauer P290. Little thing, but we found it.'

Duvay started to get up, shackled to the table. He jerked at the chain and leaned toward the detective.

'You lyin' sack of shit. There be no gun. You makin' it up, you dirty no good cop.'

'Got it, Antoine. I didn't find it. Cassidy did.'

'Fuck this Cassidy. Prove it's mine.'

'We're working on it, but in the meantime, young man, we've got reason to hold you for a little while.'

'You gonna prove that this gun was the murder weapon? Are you?'

'Hard to do. By the time a bullet goes in and out, through flesh and bone, it does so much damage you can't usually tell what gun it came from.'

'So you can't prove shit.'

'The fact that you have a gun—'

'I never owned a gun. In my life.'

'The fact that we found a gun, that might be good enough. Ex-con, kid who had a vendetta against a judge, and a gun that could have been the murder weapon. You do the math, hotshot.'

'Oh, Lord Almighty. You can't be serious.'

'We're building a pretty good case here, Antoine.'

'Fuck your case.'

Now the hands had become fists and Strand raised his voice.

'Look, you little turd, I've *got* a case. You confess, right now, and we can make some good things happen. We can take away some of the bad things that *are* going to happen to you. But if you don't confess, then everything is off the table. Do you understand me?'

'You, you mouth, you told me this the last time we talked. "Plea," you said. Well fuck you, motherfucker. Where is my lawyer, dude? I'll tell him what I know.'

Strand stood back, not sure what the young man was saying. So he did know something? The detective shook his head, not certain where to take the next line of questioning. In an instant it was forgotten.

'Damn. I want an attorney. Don't fuck with me any longer, you piece of shit. Give me my attorney now.'

'You're positive there isn't anything you want to say?'

Strand felt the pressure. He was losing the battle and he didn't want it to be over. Not yet.

Duvay looked like he might explode. His eyes were wide open, his voice gravelly and he appeared to be shaking.

'Bring me my attorney.' He screamed at the top of his voice, straining at the chain. 'You better damned well have me an attorney. No more stallin' cause I got nothin' else to say!'

Strand stood slowly, knocked on the door and an officer opened it.

'Send in Witter.' Bitterness dripped from his words. 'Antoine Duvay wants to lawyer up.'

16

'**M**a spends her time at Water's Edge Care Center. End of the French Market. I'm sure you've seen it.' Leaning over the table, her hands clasped in front of her.

Archer sat back in the booth and nodded, not exactly sure where the facility was located.

'It's a home for dementia patients.'

'Your mother. The practitioner?'

'Let me tell the story, Detective. Then you can decide if you want to take it seriously. OK?'

Archer quelled his desire to ask more questions and settled back to listen. If this was going to help solve the crime, then so be it.

'I volunteer at Water's Edge three days a week. I talk to the patients, take them on walks, and basically spend as much quality time as possible with them. I have no training in this field, but with Ma being a patient there . . .'

She sipped her coffee and he tipped his beer, quenching his thirst.

'Possibly six months ago, one of the patients spoke to me. Out of the blue. We were on an outing.' She paused for a moment. 'We take the patients up on the levee and spend an hour with them. I try to engage them in conversation.'

'I understand.' Archer, ever supportive.

'I'm out with Ma, another woman and a man. And they are just sitting there, non-communicative. I bring up different topics, like how nice the river is, or how warm the temperature is, and this day no one was responding. Some days they do, some days they don't.'

'This has to do with your information regarding David Lerner, right?'

Cordray frowned. 'Let me tell my story, Detective Archer. Be patient. This isn't easy.'

Archer signaled the waitress for another beer. Technically he was off the clock and right now he needed a drink.

'The man, Rayland Foster, was staring at the river water, zoned out, and I heard his voice. Not from his mouth. His mouth had nothing to say.'

'I'm afraid I'm not sure what *you're* saying.'

'His voice was inside my head.'

'So you were channeling—'

'Mr Archer, I heard him. As clearly as I can hear you.'

The detective scrutinized the young beauty. She was struggling with the story, trying to make a spiritual connection sound credible.

'And he said to me, 'the judge, the judge who will be killed, he belongs to Krewe Charbonerrie. Someone must be told.'

His sandwich long since forgotten, Archer leaned across the booth, looking into the young girl's face.

'Solange, that's it, right? Solange, help me out here. I want to hear your story, but I have no idea what you're talking about. Six months ago someone communicated with you about the death of the judge? But the murder just happened.'

'I'm well aware of the timeline.'

There was a moment of silence at the booth.

'All right, go on.' He was used to getting right to the heart of the matter. Just the facts, ma'am, just the facts. *Dragnet*. Joe Friday.

'Krewes are the backbone of Mardi Gras. Since 1857, Krewes, the families of wealthy locals, have sponsored our holiday. Some of the Krewes are social. They build the floats that you see during our celebration, they make the costumes and purchase the throws – doubloons and beads – that are tossed to the crowds. You may have heard of Rex? Or Mistic Krewe of Comus? Krewe of Proteus, and the Zulu Social Aid and Pleasure Club?'

She leaned into the booth, her face a little closer to his and he could detect a delicate scent, like frangipani.

'And some of these Krewes are made up of rich, highly influential members of society who have the power and influence to control whatever they want. And,' she paused, 'they often want everything.' Solange sat back in the booth and closed her eyes, saying nothing else.

After fifteen seconds Archer figured it was OK to talk.

'Solange, so what? What does membership in a society have to do with a murder? And, let's assume you are right. The judge was a member of this Krewe Whatever-you-said. Does belonging to this Krewe make a person a target for murder?'

'Krewe Charbonerrie. Named after a young group of radicals in the early 1800s who tried to overthrow the French government.'

She stared into his eyes, making a strong connection. He shrank back into his booth as she continued.

'Membership, as I understand it, is very restrictive and very pricey. The Krewe is open only to the rich and powerful.'

'And?'

'It struck me that a judge in the juvenile system, while powerful in certain circles, is probably not a rich person.'

'So he was a member. Someone sponsored him. Gave him the money to join the organization,' Archer said. 'Isn't that possible? Or maybe he inherited a lot of money. A lot of folks are not what they appear, Miss Cordray.'

'It was a voice of desperation, Detective. This Rayland Foster wanted to be heard. He was telling me, six months out, that this killing had been planned. I had no idea where to go with the information. There was no dead judge when he spoke to me, and I was confused. You, Detective Archer, were not even on the force at that time. You were still dealing with your problems in Detroit.'

Archer blinked. What could she possibly know about his problems?

'You see, I had no idea who to contact, or whether I even should. I had no name, no time frame, nothing.'

Archer understood. The girl didn't want a repeat of her mother's mistake.

'But knowing now what I know, I believe very strongly that this information is correct. Mr Foster knows.'

'About what?'

'He believes that the death of David Lerner is related to the judge's membership in this Krewe.'

'David Lerner, belonging to a Krewe—'

'As I said, a very expensive Krewe. You must put up one hundred thousand dollars just to apply. Then, if you are accepted into Krewe Charbonerrie, another one hundred thousand dollars is required. Detective, the cost to join this organization is two hundred thousand dollars. Not an insignificant sum.'

'Jesus.'

'I think, if you look into it, you will see that a judge in this city makes about one hundred fifty thousand dollars a year. Maybe one ten after taxes. So where does he come up with the membership money?'

'So, he spent almost two years' salary to belong to this club.'

'Krewe. It's called a Krewe. On the surface, the judge did not show a large inheritance and his investment strategies were suspect.'

'How do you know this?'

'I know, Detective. I know.'

Archer nodded in frustration. 'We're working on his background.' This wisp of a girl seemed to have all the knowledge at her fingertips and his department had just started. It pissed him off.

'I have a very strong feeling, Detective, that if you look into his membership to Krewe Charbonerrie, you will find your killer. At the very least you will find the reason he was killed.'

The why factor.

'It's that simple?'

'It may be. Mr Foster feels it's very important.'

'But he never vocalized that feeling. You just told me that. You never heard him tell you that.'

'He put his information in my head.'

'Who is this Mr Foster?'

'He is at this time a pathetic, failing man. He's sick, old, and his family doesn't see him anymore. And besides his dementia, he has mobility issues. He's confined to a wheelchair.' She paused. 'And he is insanely rich, and he has made everyone in his immediate circle rich.'

Archer missed any empathy in her description of the patient.

'Who was he? What's his past?'

'He was an industrialist. Rayland Foster made a fortune in the chemical manufacturing business, and in the process poisoned as much of the Mississippi River as he possibly could. According to everything I've learned, he dumped tons of waste into our river. He used people and natural resources like they were his personal property. From what I have heard, he was not a nice man.'

The beer gone warm, he pushed it aside.

'And was he in this Krewe?'

'Detective Archer, he was the grand leader of this Krewe. A powerful, cruel man who won his place by domination.'

'Apparently that power has ended.'

She smiled faintly, shrugging her shoulders.

'Maybe. But as long as he lives, he poses a threat. You may find this hard to believe, Detective, but when someone is impotent, they often find other ways to impregnate. As long as this man is alive, he is a concern.'

'That's it? Rayland Foster, in a nursing home with no way to communicate to the outside world, is still a danger?'

'Detective, this reprobate wears the tattoo of a coiled snake on his right wrist.'

The coiled serpent. He'd seen it on Judge Lerner's pale, bloated hand. Maybe she was on to something.

'The snake is a voodoo symbol, but apparently it is the symbol of Krewe Charbonerrie as well. Rest assured, his tattoo and the symbol of Krewe Charbonerrie has nothing to do with the spirit of voodoo. I can guarantee that. I feel very strongly that his tattoo physically ties him to the Krewe.'

Reaching into her bag, the petite lady pulled out a small brown pouch. 'This, Detective, is for you.'

Archer picked it up and studied the brown cloth. It fit in the palm of his hand. Whatever was inside was lumpy, uneven, like tiny twigs and stones.

'It's *gris gris*,' she said. 'Powerful stuff, made from a swamp man's ingredients.'

'Swamp man?'

'Matebo, a man my mother holds dear. That's not important.'

'And this *gris gris*?'

'I made it for you. Keep it with you at all times.'

'And why would I do that?'

'It will keep you safe.'

'Am I currently in danger?'

The young girl took a deep breath, held it for a second, then let it out.

'I know you are skeptical right now. But you are walking into some serious situations. I feel it. Life and death.'

'Really.'

'You've been in that situation before, Detective Archer. In Detroit. You survived. This time, without some intervention' – she pointed to the bag – 'you may not be so fortunate.'

Archer looked over his shoulder, searching for his waitress. Finally spotting her, he signaled for the check. When he turned back, Solange Cordray was gone.

His eyes searched the small area, but she had disappeared and there was a sensation in his ears as if all the oxygen had been sucked from the room.

17

The streets were crowded with tourists, even at this early hour. Archer walked to his car, kicking cheap plastic beaded neck-laces, to-go drink cups and beer cans into the gutter. Street cleaning was a full time job in this city. He saw the bobbing blond head in the crowd and blocked the view and the idea from his head. Just blend in, ignore the pain, the visions of her. Archer drove back to the station, deciding to check on the Krewe and on Solange Cordray's background before he returned to his tiny cottage. The girl had grabbed his attention and as far-fetched as it seemed, he hoped she could bring some serious information to the case.

'Hey, Q.' Detective Josh Levy called out as Archer entered the bullpen. 'We tore up the judge's house today.'

He turned and nodded. 'Anything interesting?' Another piece of the puzzle.

'Not much to look at from the outside. A little place down in the Garden District. Dead end street. Guy lived alone, but lived well.'

'Yeah?'

'I'm no connoisseur of art but this guy had some classy stuff. Some pretty fancy pieces. Take a look.'

Levy held out his iPhone as he scrolled through photographs of some of the paintings in Lerner's home. A couple drawings of nudes, men and women, and some nicely framed city scenes, possibly Paris or London.

'Nice furniture, sixty-eight-inch flat screen, and a cream-colored Jag convertible in the garage. I could learn to live like that. We've got the Jag and we're going through it.'

'He was a judge. You know they tend to make a little more than detectives.' He smiled at Levy.

'Strange coincidence happened while we were checking the place out.'

'Yeah?'

'Welker is outside, taking a smoke break, and down the road comes a car. Now this guy, Judge Lerner, lives on a dead end street, so according to the neighbors there's always somebody driving down this street, and turning around in Lerner's driveway. They finally realize it's not a through street. But this was a bit unusual.'

'And you're going to tell me why.'

'The car, according to Welker, was a cream-colored Jag. Identical to the one in the garage.'

'There are people who have the money to buy those kinds of cars. It can't be that unique.'

'Driver pulls into the drive, sees Welker and our unmarked car, backs up and peels out. Maybe you're right. It could be a strange coincidence. I don't know if we'll ever know.'

'Did you run it?'

'Of course. Nothing yet.'

'We're grasping for anything,' Archer said.

'You know, someday I'll go to law school and get me a promotion so I can afford some high-end car. But here's the kicker. Check it out.'

He held the phone up and Archer stared at the screen.

'What am I looking at?'

'A bunch of small photos that sit on his white Young Chang baby grand piano. About forty mug shots of kids that we think he sentenced. That's Lerner' – he scrolled to another photograph on the screen of two men standing in front of the same Young Chang, the same collection of framed mug shots in the background – 'and the guy next to him, smiling, is the warden at the juvie prison up the river. Russell Jakes. And there are maybe a couple hundred more of these framed mug shots scattered around the house.'

'He's proud of his record.' Archer studied the picture, wondering what kind of man would glorify his conquests.

'Look, he's got some kind of number on each photo.' Levy pointed. 'You can see the ones closer to the front. This smacks of spiking the ball, Detective.' Levy gave him a frown.

Archer paused for a moment.

'You're a cop. You should applaud the arrests, and the convictions. That's what we're here for.' He knew the detective was right, but here he was, standing up for the judge.

'Not necessarily.' Levy turned from the phone photograph. 'These are kids, Q. Young, screwed-up kids. You were one, I was one, and I venture to say that ninety percent of the people functioning today as adults were screwed-up kids.'

'What's your point, Levy?'

'Not necessarily a point. More like an observation.'

'That would be?'

'Here's a guy who put some serious effort into exalting in his convictions. He wanted the world to realize that he'd put these juveniles behind bars. When I was a patrolman, I was judged by my collars, Q, but sometimes I wasn't proud of them. Oftentimes they were folks who were flat-busted broke and just looking for their next meal. So I understand that not every kid who is busted is a hard-core criminal who should be displayed on some judge's piano. Do you understand what I'm saying?'

He did. 'Maybe he was proud of the fact that the kids would come out and go straight?'

Levy squared his jaw. 'That doesn't happen. You know it and I know it. They call these prisons correctional facilities but there's no correction going on. Hell, more than fifty percent of the juveniles in jail right now are repeat offenders. They don't go straight. It's more like half of them go straight back to jail. The phrase "correctional facilities" is a joke.'

He was right. Short sentences, long sentences, it made no difference. The young people went back to the streets, to the drugs and to the same conditions that put them in prison in the first place.

'Address books?'

Levy nodded. 'We're going through them.'

'Other photos? Girlfriends? Anything else jump out at you?'

'House was pretty much sterile. Except for those photographs. Mug shots, each one. Like a trophy shelf.'

'The neighborhood?'

'Yeah, we found a lady who pretty much stares out her window most of the day. Doesn't watch TV, just watches the comings and goings of the neighbors. This house, as I said, it's on a dead end street, and unsuspecting drivers sometimes wander down there and have to turn around and go back. Lerner was at the end, so his driveway was a turnaround spot for a lot of these people.'

'And?'

'She's watching,' he paused, 'what she *thinks* is about six hours before we found the body, and she sees a black Cadillac Escalade pull into Lerner's driveway.'

'License?'

'No.'

'Description of the driver? Passenger?'

'Maybe some guy talking to Lerner by his garage but she lost interest. Figured it was another driver who wants to turn around and leave.'

'Still' – Archer was searching for anything – 'bring her in. Maybe she'll remember something if we coax?'

'All right, but I think she's a bit of a flake.'

'Invite her.'

'I'll do it, Archer.'

The officer walked away.

Archer pulled the calendar. He concentrated on the day before they'd found the body, the day of and the day after. Trace the steps that the man took the last forty-eight hours of his life. And keep asking why. Why did Lerner venerate his sentences with photos in his home? Why did a cream-colored Jag high-tail it out of the neighborhood when the driver saw detectives working the scene? Why did Solange Cordray receive a mystic message from the former head of Krewe Charbonerrie?

Too many whys, and until he answered them all, he was afraid this case was not going to be solved.

His cell phone buzzed and Archer answered.

'Archer, there's a press conference happening tomorrow morning.'

'And?'

The sergeant continued. 'The lieutenant, chief and mayor are all going to be there.'

'And just what the hell are they going to say?' Archer was bristling. The sarge was probably just down the hall, but he couldn't be bothered to check and see if Archer was in the building.

'They're going to say they are very close to charging someone with the murder.'

'We need a little more time. They can't make this shit up.'

'Don't have much time, Q. This was a judge. It's like a cop. Everything else pales in comparison, you know what I mean?'

He did.

'If you've got something, Quentin, bring it now, because the mayor is telling the public that charges will be filed by week's end. Got that?'

He got it. Loud and clear.

'You're going with the runner? Duvay?'

'End of the week.'

'And the real killer will just laugh and walk.'

'We're giving 'em something, Archer. It may be political, but it tells the people we're on the ball.'

And the truth was, they were far from the ball. Some ex-con was going to be charged for something the poor guy knew nothing about. It was time to get very serious about finding the real killer.

'Check out the headlines for tomorrow's *Advocate* online. That paper is forcing our hand.'

Archer ran it on his computer.

COPS STYMIED BY JUDGE'S MURDER.

'You can read on if you want to, Archer, because the story is worse than the headline. The words *inept* and *incompetent* are repeated. We've got to show some progress. You have a prostitute murdered, a drug dealer, some poor black in the projects – they don't ride us about that. You kill a cop or a judge . . .' He let it hang.

The detective was very much aware of the power of the press.

'Archer, you know we probably have the guy. Strand found a gun. It's a big step. The mayor's going to comment, possibly the governor, and who knows, maybe the president next. He tends to mouth off on local issues.'

'Well . . .'

'No *well*. We've got a guy who took off running when there was a confrontation. I'm starting to think that if he isn't our man, at least he's a link. He was scared, Archer. He ran. We want to tie him to this murder. This *Advocate* story, it just doubles the pressure. You honest to God can't imagine. We're going with Duvay week's end, and that's that.'

'Sergeant, do we want a conviction or do we want to find the person who actually killed the judge?'

'Jesus, Archer. If the kid looks good for the hit, please, get on board, OK?'

'I'd rather bring in the murderer, Sergeant. Not someone we've framed.'

18

Solange Cordray showed up in a Google search. Five mentions, one relating to her involvement in a renovation project on Dauphine Street and two mentioning her in certain social situations.

'*Solange Cordray and husband, financier Joseph Cordray, attended the festive event at Woldenberg Park . . .*'

The two that especially interested him were dated a year later. The first mention was factual.

'*Solange Cordray was granted a divorce from Joseph Cordray.*'

The date, place and time were listed. The second mention dealt with some of the terms of the settlement.

'*New Orleans financier Joseph Cordray tried to hide several million dollars in assets from his ex-wife, Solange Cordray, to avoid paying out in his divorce settlement, according to charges filed by the woman's attorney. Cordray, a venture capitalist has major holdings in a company called Secure Force which owns twenty-five private prisons in a three state area.*'

Judge Lerner was putting juveniles in a private prison just outside of the city. Detective Levy had just shown him a picture of the prison warden standing by the piano with Lerner. They were friends or at least acquaintances. What did he say the warden's name was? Jakes. Russell Jakes. Archer keyed in another search.

Jakes, Russell. Warden.

The hits appeared immediately. Hundreds of postings, all mentioning one Russell Jakes, Warden, at River Bend Prison. River Bend Prison, a part of Secure Force, a holding company for twenty-five private prisons. Duvay had been an inmate there.

And he suddenly remembered. Archer had recently seen an article regarding public versus private prisons. The private groups, cutting expenses to the bone, made a fortune compared to state and federal facilities which drain government coffers.

Scrolling through the information he found what he was looking for. Mixed in with prison history and statistics were new stories of charges that had been filed against River Bend and Warden Jakes. Charges of harassment, physical abuse, favoritism – the list went on.

Many of the juvenile offenders who saw Judge David Lerner were sent to River Bend. Now, Solange Cordray was coming to Archer with information about the death of Lerner, and her ex-husband had been a major stock holder in Secure Force and River Bend. He closed his eyes and rubbed the lids with his fingertips. It might mean nothing. Still, it was an interesting coincidence.

Sergeant Sullivan approached his desk.

'Hey, you're here. Thought you'd be out gathering evidence or . . .'

'I'm here. Are we going to visit the *Advocate* headline again?'

'Don't be flippant with me. It's a big deal, Detective. A huge deal. Like it or not, we live in the media and if they say we're even more inept than before, there are repercussions. The state, Feds, everyone steps in and they take even more control. But here's another big deal. Got a complaint on you about half an hour ago.'

'Me?' Maybe the pickpocket? Doubtful.

'Intimidation.'

'I've been asking questions, Sergeant. You want me to solve this murder, I've got to get under some people's skin. It's part of my job. But I don't think I intimidated anyone.' Hell, it's what he did, he and every other homicide detective. When they chained a suspect in the interview room and kept them up for hours, trying to break them? That would qualify as intimidation.

'Judge Richard Warren, juvenile—'

'I know who he is. Didn't like my line of questions.'

'Says you almost threatened him.'

Archer shook his head. 'I'll try to improve my bedside manner.'

Sullivan frowned.

'Sergeant, I didn't threaten him, I warned him. We've actually sent out warnings to all the judges. A precaution to watch where they walk, drive, who they talk to, whatever.'

'Jesus, Archer. We're going to get crucified tomorrow in the paper. Please, just find this guy, or sign on that Duvay is the killer. OK?'

'I may have some inside information.'

'Inside? What? Who?'

'Can't say. But it involves Lerner's association with a Krewe.'

'A crew? What kind of a—? Oh, a Krewe.'

'Have you ever heard of Krewe Charbonerrie?'

Sullivan studied him for a moment, a dark look on his face.

'What about them?'

'Apparently Lerner was a member.'

The sergeant nodded. 'Someone told you this?'

'Yes.'

'And you think, or this person thinks, that membership in this Krewe may have something to do with the murder?'

'Yeah. But they're not sure how it links.'

The man let out a long sigh.

'Detective Archer, I hope that's not the case. This organization lists some pretty powerful people on its roster.'

'Politically powerful?'

'Powerful. They don't go public with their membership roster. However, speculation runs rampant and they are probably powerful enough to stop this investigation if they wanted to.'

'Really?' A group of Detroit cops had brought the drug ring investigation to a screeching halt. He knew how that worked.

'Let's hope this is just a wild goose chase. You don't want to fuck around with these guys, Archer.'

'So you're telling me to pull up short if it looks like this group was involved?'

Sullivan clenched his teeth and paused.

'Look, we are always under pressure. But I've never felt it like this before. How many cases are you working right now?'

Without hesitating Archer answered, 'Seven.'

'Drop every one. I don't care what it is. I'll assign someone else. Let's get this one solved, because I just got definite word that the governor will probably be on the phone for this press conference tomorrow. The goddamned governor, Archer. He's going to want to say that we are very close to a charge.'

'Can we just do our job?'

The sergeant looked down at him, circles under his eyes, his face haggard and pale.

'How do I play this, Sergeant Sullivan? I'm new in town. If there are rules—'

'I've watched you, Archer, and I've heard stories about your Detroit experience. You're the kind of guy that if there are rules, you'd probably break them. You tried to take down the Detroit force, right or wrong, and created quite a problem. You had to leave. Well, I can't have you doing that here. We've got enough of a problem without you piling on.'

'Someday I'll give you the facts, Sergeant; and by the way, rules are highly overrated. Sometimes you get in more trouble if you enforce the rules.' Archer looked into his superior's eyes. 'How do you want it?'

'You be damned careful, and report to me on any progress. Report to me on any problems. When you intimidate someone, when you decide it's time to break a rule. This is some uncharted territory you're dealing with. Let's just hope that this lead goes nowhere.' He glanced at his watch. 'Week's end . . .'

'You've made your case, Sergeant. You're charging Duvay.'

The sergeant straightened up, put his hands in his pockets and started to walk away. He turned back to Archer when he entered the hallway.

'You're positive that Lerner was a member of Charbonerrie?'

'Pretty sure.' Based on the word of a mind-reading Voodoo Queen. Maybe he was stretching it. Maybe he was crazy. Maybe this was getting way too serious to be trusting some female witch doctor. But Solange was compelling.

'That's the thing about that Krewe. You never know who is a member. You could say something to their face and you'd never know it.'

Sullivan sounded like it may have happened to him.

'I thought these organizations were social. They helped sponsor Mardi Gras, children's programs, stuff like that.'

'Yeah. That's what you'd think. And some of them are. Some of them go beyond that and work hard to raise funds for charitable organizations. Women's shelters, the Make-A-Wish Foundation, inner-city kids' clubs.'

'These guys?'

'I've never heard of them sponsoring any type of non-profit.' Pausing, he stared at Archer. 'It's made up of a lot of influential people. Very connected. They've got connections to the very top.'

'Mayor's office?'

Pursing his lips, Sullivan stared off into space for a moment, alone with his thoughts.

Finally, 'I'd guess a lot higher than the mayor,' he said. 'If this group wanted to shut down a business, big, small, they could do it. State wide.' He rolled his eyes. 'Hell, they *have* done it. I don't pretend to understand it all, but it's a lot of rich guys who will do whatever it takes to get richer and keep that wealth; and if you're not with them, you're against them. It's a very powerful society and very secretive and again, I've said way too much all ready.'

Archer saw the frown lines on the man's face, etched into his pale skin.

'I don't get the impression that Lerner was a rich man.'

Sullivan nodded. 'I agree. But you never know. There are million-aires working here. On our own force. Had a detective a couple of years ago. Turns out he was worth a couple million. He probably could have quit, but he liked the job.'

'What happened to him?'

'Got killed in a car accident while he was on duty.'

'If it's any consolation, this Krewe thing is just one of the leads I'm working. I need to talk to Strand about the warden at River Bend, Russell Jakes.'

'What about Jakes?'

'Lerner was sending him a lot of prisoners. There was a collection of mug shots of juvenile offenders displayed on the piano in Lerner's home, and a photo of him with Jakes was in the middle of them.'

'You're stepping into a lot of shit, Archer.'

'It's what's out there.'

'Jakes is a tough guy. He's been brought up on charges numerous times for his treatment of prisoners, treatment of staff—'

'And what I saw online says he's skated on all of them.'

'Largely because the prison is owned by a private company. If it had been State or Fed, chances are he would have been forced out. As it is, every time he walks on another charge, he gets that much stronger. Stock in that company is pretty healthy and the shareholders tend to keep someone who's making them money.'

'You know,' Archer stretched and took a deep breath, 'I feel right at home. We had the same bad characters in Detroit.'

'And you got out of town.'

'No one is going to push me out of this town.'

'You've seen the murder statistics, Archer. They don't push you out of New Orleans. They carry you out of town in a coffin. Buy into Antoine Duvay, Archer. The kid had a gun and a reason. This could be a lot easier for everyone.'

He stood there in the doorway for a moment, then walked out of the room.

Archer glanced through his handwritten notes once more, making sure he'd left out of his report any mention of Solange Cordray. Getting up to use the restroom he returned to his desk and saw someone had riffled through his papers. They were just slightly shuffled. He glanced around but there was no one in the room.

Couldn't trust anyone.

19

The photos were on Archer's computer. Fuzzy, long shots and close-ups of the car and license plates.

The accompanying note was short.

Q, this is what we have so far. Late-model Chevy sedan, looks like an Impala. We've got three cameras, three angles, but as you can see, only a partial on the plate. Running it, but trying to be careful. You understand. We've got families, Archer. TL

Tom Lyons, one of the handful of cops who believed in him. One of the cops who was putting his career – hell, his life – on the line to find Denise's killer.

Archer printed off the pictures. He wanted to study them, memorize them, hang them on his wall at the cottage. Along with the phone calls and the intrusions at his cottage, it was all part of the puzzle. He knew why they killed her. Now he needed to know who had run her down.

20

The stories were told by candlelight, by firelight, by moonlight, by starlight. Voodoo Queen Marie Laveau had danced topless, breasts exposed in their splendid glory, with a snake named Zombi wrapped around her supple frame, taunting the men in her audience, mocking the young women who stared wide-eyed as the voluptuous voodoo priestess worked her way through the throng. People of both sexes, all colors, would reach out to touch her, feel her firm flesh, caress her breasts and buttocks. Some of them felt her loins and encouraged her to touch theirs. The act of healing, affirmation and lust. Some of them, men and women, stripped naked and danced on the bare earth, where sometimes a massive orgy occurred. Hundreds of locals and dozens of visitors, who needed to see it for themselves, convened on the grounds deep in the bayous and later on Rampart Street, whipped into a frenzy, believing that the vision they saw would fulfil their dreams. Wealth, security, love, prosperity: dreams that were fueled also by the fermented drink served from large oak barrels.

The high priestess, Queen Marie, would solicit white married men of wealth, finding them fine mistresses of color to bed, house, feed and clothe. The voodoo madam. She accepted up to one hundred dollars from white businessmen who wanted to eliminate rivals and she accepted up to one thousand dollars from local judges who were determined to be re-elected.

This is what she heard, read, and this is what disturbed her. So many people believed that the spirit of voodoo was sexual in nature. The queen had turned the serpent into a sexual organ. Sex, salacious moments, baptism by sperm, retributions, whatever they wanted would be granted by the voodoo witch.

Solange Cordray lit the thin blue candle, silently praying to a special spirit.

'The void, the voodoo emptiness, let it be filled with the power to heal my mother. This I pray and send the scent of my candle to the goddess of health. Loa, hear me. Make my mother whole again.'

The gods were tired of hearing from her, she was certain of it. Yet it gave her comfort and a feeling of being needed. She would go to her grave seeking a way to bring her mother back to full mental stability.

Twenty minutes later the candle was a puddle of wax, and then it extinguished itself. She heard it, the slight whoosh of air that rustled the papers on the counter. The spell had been cast. No naked dancing, no snakes slithering over her oiled body. If it took all of that to save her Ma, she would do it. But in her heart she knew this was all in the hands of the spirits, and all she could do was continue to pray.

21

Archer decided to check in with Strand as he walked to the streetcar. He figured he might as well make good use of his time. Past the jail with its stainless steel concertina wire boundaries, the bail bond stores, and the carry-outs with garish window signs advertising po-boys, check-cashing, fried chicken and lotto tickets. Across the cracked, pitted pavement to the next block where everyone on the sidewalk seemed to be on their phone. Not a soul looked up or acknowledged him. As he pulled out his phone to call Strand, it rang.

'I heard they did Lerner's house today.' Strand was already home and Archer could hear the drone of a TV in the background.

'Yeah. Lots of framed mug shots on his piano. Guy used them like decorations or trophies.'

'You've got the day-planner from his office?'

'Got it with me. I'll look at it tonight and see if anything jumps out.'

'Q, we've got an ex-con and we've got a gun. Tomorrow the press is going to tear us a new asshole. Why not get on board? Back me on this and let's get this guy convicted. We'll be heroes, Archer, instead of idiots.'

'Strand, there are a lot of other things going on. I want to wrap it, too, but I've got some leads.'

'If we don't get this solved by week's end, they'll involve the FBI. They'll have state officials on our ass. The governor is going to nail us to the wall. Come on, Q.' There was a pleading in his voice.

He'd reached Canal Street and the streetcar was just pulling up to the stop.

'Look, I've got to catch the trolley and . . .'

'Streetcar, Q. This is New Orleans.'

'Whatever. I'll call you later tonight.'

There was a slight hesitation. Archer heard a young girl's voice in the background.

'No, wouldn't be a good idea tonight. I've got someone here. We'll touch base tomorrow morning and you can tell me about these other things.'

Archer stepped up on the streetcar, and pushed his ticket into the machine. A heavyset black woman in a red-and-yellow bandana brushed by him, pushing her ample breasts into his arm. An old man with a foot-long white beard and creased face grinned at him, relishing in Archer's discomfort, the man's lack of teeth giving his face a death-mask appearance.

The walk from Canal to his small cottage was five minutes and he paused at the door. The odd things that had been happening at his new home caused him to be a little hesitant before entering. Archer reached under his jacket and touched the handle of his Glock. Booming karaoke tracks echoed down the walkway to his courtyard as he unlocked and slowly opened the door. Apparently the newly passed sound ordinance wasn't in force just yet.

The door squealed like a cat whose tail had been stepped on. He mentally noted he needed some WD-40. The lubricant would immediately take care of *one* of the loud noises in his courtyard.

Flipping on the light switch, Archer's gaze swept the room. Nothing out of place, nothing out of the ordinary.

His phone rang. Glancing at the screen he saw the sender was blocked. It rang again and Archer considered not answering. He hated these people, but he needed to stay connected. To keep the line open to the people who had alienated him from his family. To the people who had probably killed his wife. Eventually he would use it all to nail the bastards. He clicked in on the fourth ring.

'Archer.'

'Hey, Quentin.'

Silence. He knew the voice. Very well. It was Mercer. While one of his brothers was doing time in Detroit for dealing drugs, Bobby Mercer still worked for the DPD. The slimeball still drew a paycheck. Detroit taxpayers still paid for his benefits. No one had ever been able to prove that the crooked cop was behind hundreds of thousands of dollars' worth of drug deals. No one.

But damn. Archer had tried.

'Bobby.'

'Just wanted to say hi, Quentin.'

'How's my brother?'

'The one in prison? Or the one who's on the run?'

'Never mind.'

'Wondered how the job was going, Quentin. Wondered if you'd pissed off any of the NOPD yet.'

'Is my brother down here? The one who's on the run?'

'Down where?' Sarcasm dripping from his voice.

'You know where. New Orleans.'

'Now why would you ask me something like that?'

'Little things, Mercer. Like a dead cat on my doorstep.'

He laughed. 'Really, a dead cat? Somebody putting a hex on you,

my man? Watch yourself. It's voodoo country. Next thing you know
you'll have zombies for neighbors.'

Archer stood still, tight-lipped. He shouldn't have said anything.
Just adding fuel to the fire.

'Hey, Q, I'd think Jason would get as far away from you as
possible. After you tried to have him put away and all. Besides,
he's a wanted felon. If I knew where he was, I'd have him arrested
and returned. You know me. Following the letter of the law, Archer.'

The detective squeezed the handset.

'Just want to make sure you know we haven't forgotten what
you tried to do up here, Detective. Keep your distance, because
you've got a lot of people who don't like you in Detroit. Do you
understand? We just think you need a reminder from time to time.'

'Tell me, Bobby,' Archer said, 'because I don't think you ever
answered the question. Who killed my wife? Who ran her over?
Was that you? Did you kill Denise? Because eventually, you fucking
piece of scum, I will come after you, and—'

'Keep your distance, Archer. Stay away. This is not a game.'

The phone went dead. Mercer had terminated the call. There was
so much he wanted to say to the man, but it was better to stop
before he started something he couldn't finish. Maybe he'd already
said too much. He'd tried to finish it, and had his ass handed to
him. Not only that, he'd lost the love of his life in the process. It
left an empty hole that he was finding impossible to fill.

There was one Archer doing time. One was on the run. And
Mercer was biding his time in Detroit, still working the streets and
probably still organizing drug rings. Quentin Archer wondered where
his brother Jason had decided to hide out. If he was smart, and he
was, Jason would be out of the country by now. Maybe hiding on
some Caribbean island. He probably had enough money to stay
hidden a long time.

Placing his gun on the small kitchen table, he sat down on the
bed, taking deep breaths. Relaxation methods usually calmed him
down. His wife's murder, the Detroit threat and now the New Orleans
press calling for an answer. It was a lot to shoulder. He unfolded
the printouts of the vehicle and license plate responsible for Denise's
death and placed them on his nightstand.

Picking up Lerner's day-planner, he moved to the table to work.
He studied the page filled with appointments, notations, sidebars

and scrawled initials. Some of the information would take a code-breaker. But looking at the pages, he could loosely put together what the judge had on his agenda the day before and the day that they found the body. Archer placed a yellow legal pad next to the judge's schedule and started making notes. Trying to put together the hour to hour life of the magistrate just before his death.

An hour later he rubbed his eyes and glanced at the clock. 11 p.m. The muffled sound of Bourbon Street wafted through the doors and windows and he stood, stretching his aching back. He needed a break.

Locking the pistol in the cottage's only closet, he put on his sport coat and walked outside, heading toward the fabled street named after a French ruling family, the House of Bourbon. Archer preferred to think of its hard drinking heritage and the bourbon that was consumed on this famous stretch of pavement. The street was steeped in the lore of musicians, actors, writers and characters that prowled its rowdy bars and strip clubs. Strand had told him that Bourbon Street was where they quarantined the tourists so they didn't fuck up the rest of the city.

Throngs of revelers roamed the street in various states of inebriation, and the smell of stale beer and sweet incense filled the air. Avoiding the slop that filled the gutters, Archer dodged small groups of tourists as he avoided colliding with a tall woman in tight black slacks and long hair, who was screaming at a short, scruffily bearded man who was walking away.

Ten young women crossed the street in front of him, identically dressed in skin-hugging black leggings and tees that said *Goodbye, Julianne.* One of the girls sported a crown and veil. Weaving out of the line she approached Archer.

'Want to join us?' she asked.

'No, not right now.'

'I'm getting married,' she informed him in a slurred voice. 'This is my last night on the town.'

'Good luck,' Archer said. She was going to need it.

The short man with the scruffy beard turned back to yell at the tall, angular woman.

'You are a fucking bitch. Do you know that?'

She yelled down at him, shaking her fist. 'I'm your wife, damn it. You can't say things like that to me. I love you.'

A quartet of old black men sang some tight harmony doo-wop on the street corner as a small crowd gathered and from a block up strains of a brass section floated on the air. Following the music, he walked into a bar. A hot young band was playing Motown on the stage to his right. Four brass players and a rhythm section with a guy and girl singing outrageous vocals. He downed his first American Blonde, then ordered another and sat halfway back, enjoying the music and the euphoric feeling. The bar was crowded and the musicians ripped through songs from the Temptations, Ben E. King, Wilson Pickett and more. With shrill brass, bottom-thumping bass and a soaring, brilliant guitarist who shredded a solo on Pickett's 'Fire and Water', the band was spot on, almost making him homesick for Detroit. Almost.

Forty minutes later, after one more beer, he walked back to his cramped residence, threading his way through the packs of people that were milling in the busy street. An aimless crowd that wandered up and down Bourbon without any purpose other than to party and drink themselves into oblivion.

Reaching the cottage, he automatically checked for any distur-bance. Everything seemed to be the way he'd left it. He sat back down at the table and reviewed his notes. Alcohol and work never seemed to mix, but he kept looking, trying to find the magical solu-tion, hoping something from the judge's calendar would give him a clue to the murderer. Week's end, they were going to charge Duvay. And then throw everything they could at the boy to get the conviction. He had to get some answers.

There were notations of things Lerner had to do, almost like an odd jobs list. Archer was sorting through the judge's style of short-hand, trying to decipher exactly what the man was thinking. The appointments were easier. The day of the murder, he'd had five of them. Three in his office, one at a restaurant called Cochon in the warehouse district, and one where he'd written to be decided. Possibly by phone. Archer made a note to check with Detective Davis on progress recovering the phone record and any data off the SIM card from the victim's phone. Initials were listed for four of the appointments. He'd ask Sue Waronker who the people were. The to be decided meeting had no identifying initials. He'd check with the Waronker lady about that too, and if Davis had the restored phone records he could start poring through those. And, suspect and gun be damned, Strand could help. He didn't seem to be around most of the time. If the cocky detective was taking credit as lead on this case, he could do some of the tedious work. Archer considered the handwritten notes that someone had perused on his desk and wondered if Strand had riffled through them, catching up on what Archer had learned.

With an idea of where tomorrow was going, he stood up and walked the seven steps to the tiny bathroom.

Three minutes later he lay down on his bed and placed the Glock pistol on the nightstand. He closed his eyes, drifting into a dream state. There was the dark girl, whispering in his ear, and the dead bloated body of Judge Lerner, lying on the floor. Sergeant Sullivan was leaning over him, urging him to do what was right, and he kept wondering what was right, and then he heard a rustling sound.

Scratching, scraping, grating, a sound from outside. He'd had drinks. It could be his imagination, or just the wind. Sometimes curious tourists or drunks made their way back behind the Cat's Meow into the tiny courtyard. It could be one of them.

Then there was a bump at the window, like a bird flying into its own reflection. The pane of glass not five feet from his bed. The creaking sound surprised him, like someone trying to pry it open.

Grabbing his gun he sat upright, all senses suddenly on high alert. Was the window locked? He couldn't remember. Clutching the grip he tried to recall. If someone was trying to break in, if they were successful, would he shoot them? There was a huge difference in being a regular citizen home owner or renter, and being an off-duty cop. Archer felt perspiration on his brow.

And then it came to him. Of course there was a lock. Archer had checked it when he first noticed strange things at the ramshackle little cottage. But had he opened the window since then? Possibly he wasn't as vigilant as he should have been. The detective slowly swung his legs over the edge of the bed. He never should have had the beers, but someone was trying to break in, there was no question. In the dark he pulled on his pants and quietly stepped to the window, praying for a moment of total sobriety.

The sound suddenly ceased and pressing against the wall to minimize his exposure, he reached out and slowly parted the curtains. That's when he saw the small wrapped package sitting on the inside

ledge. Inside, but the window had not been opened. Archer stared
at the object for a moment, hesitating, searching for an explanation.
The window remained closed. The attempted intrusion hadn't been
successful, yet here was a small package that he swore had not
been there before.

Letting the curtain go, he raced to the front door, unlocked it and
flung it open, running into the small courtyard. A flash of motion
down the walk, somebody scrambling to get out of the confined
space and onto the street, and Archer sprinted after them.

He hit Bourbon Street, a bare-chested madman with a pistol in his
hand. In any other setting, in any other town, people would have run,
scattering every way possible. In the Quarter, it was entertainment.
The large crowd parted as he ran through it, but folded back in as he
passed. He dodged a toga-clad man with a snake around his neck,
and a guitar player sitting cross-legged in the middle of the street.

The detective looked both ways, the fleeting image of someone
running a good block away. He ran down the street, losing ground,
evading drunks and revelers. In thirty seconds he slowed down,
realizing there was no way he would find the person in the dense
crowd that still filled the boulevard.

'Hold on, hotshot.'

He felt a strong hand tighten on his shoulder. As he turned to
lash out, someone swung around in front of him and grabbed his
right wrist, wrestling the gun from his grasp. A second person
gripped his arm and pulled it behind his back, sending a sharp pain
through Archer's shoulder. He could have taken one, but two—

'Want to tell us what you're doing waving a gun on Bourbon
Street?'

Two uniforms.

Archer did his best to explain. The officer released his arm and
the detective pulled his ID from the wallet in his back pocket, and
both cops nodded. A homicide detective in New Orleans was gold.
They admonished him for possibly panicking the general populace,
although they admitted no one seemed that upset, and they let him
off with a warning.

He walked back home, a sheen of perspiration on his skin, gun
tucked into his trousers. What the hell had he been thinking? He
would have sworn it was his brother Jason, but there was no proof.
Another warning to leave the Detroit story alone. Because they knew

he never would. Archer walked into his tiny cottage and there it was on the windowsill. The mysterious package.

Then he remembered. He'd placed it there when he first walked in. Hours ago. *Gris gris*. The cloth covered gift from Solange Cordray. It was supposed to keep him safe.

His hands were shaking as he pushed aside the curtains and twisted the lock. Pulling open the window, he allowed the cacophony of music and the din of the crowds to pour in. Staring at the shadows in the dimly lit yard he reminded himself that someone, something had been attempting entry. Then out of the corner of his eye he noticed a glint of steel. An inch and a half long, it appeared to be the tip of a broken knife blade, resting on the outside sill, separated from the *gris gris* bag by the depth of the window frame. He studied it for a moment, wrapped a T-shirt around his hand and picked it up. The shiny steel came from a thick, heavy blade, and it appeared to have snapped at a weak place in the metal when the would-be intruder tried to pry the window open. Archer placed it on the end table.

He was certain there would be no fingerprints on the stainless-steel blade, but he'd try to run it anyway. Closing and locking the window, he considered the possibilities. The voodoo lady had told him his life was in danger. Thank God for the *gris gris*. Maybe her gift had saved his life.

22

She tied off the small cloth bags with twine, five of them, filled with different mixtures of herbs, seeds, pebbles and twigs. Picking up the first, which had seven silver-painted seeds inside, she rubbed lemon oil on the fabric and inhaled the fragrant aroma. This was a good *gris gris* and should be pleasing to Filomez. Tossing the bag from one palm to another she closed her eyes.

'Great Filomez, bring Roberto prosperity and new beginnings with a job. The job tears in this *gris gris* bag are my gift to you, a thank you for what you are about to grant him.'

Setting the bag down, she picked up the next, in a bright red fabric. She repeated the process, now praying to Erzulie Freda.

'Sandra wishes her marriage to find a firm foundation. Please, Erzulie Freda, accept the love seed, and accept her supplication. I ask that it be granted.' In the heat of the evening she felt a chill, and instantly knew that the marriage was doomed. Tears sprang to her eyes, and she closed them for a second, thinking through the process. There was nothing she could do.

Three more clients' wishes were prayed for. Three more *gris gris* bags set in a row, to be delivered tomorrow.

Picking up the final bag she gazed at it for a moment, then gently rubbed new oil on the cloth. Oil that smelled of cloves and cinnamon. For a moment she was transported back to her mother's kitchen, where the saintly woman would make roasted pears with honeyed cinnamon and cloves. The aroma was a clear path to the past. An oil for the *gris gris* bag, spices for the food. Tears once again sprang to her eyes as she remembered the vibrant woman who no longer made the potion, the mother who no longer roasted pears or baked brown bread. The lady who was taken at a young age by spirits that refused to respond to any spell Solange cast.

There were times like this that she felt she was too emotional for the job at hand. Then she realized: the entire job was one of emotion. Without it, she would be doomed to failure.

Tossing the bag back and forth she once again evoked the life forces.

'Baron, if you do not dig the grave, the body cannot die. I ask that you forgo the digging. There are evil spirits who are threatening Quentin Archer. I have prayed to you about this man before, and I have given the detective a *gris gris* bag, but if one prayer and one gift is good, aren't two better?'

She continued to toss the bag. There was a nagging message gnawing at her mind, that Detective Archer might be her most important client at the moment. Not important to the grand scheme of things, but important to her. And she wondered. Was it a romantic important? She surprised herself with the thought.

It was important to get back to her evening task.

'And, Baron, I am blessed that you did not dig another grave. Ma continues to survive, but I pray that her mind returns. If this is not possible, I am thankful for her life. I mean no disrespect.'

She placed the scented bag next to her bed, and felt a tremor surge through her body. Breaking out in a cold sweat, the woman watched the cloth covered seeds radiate a faint orange light. She'd seen it before. Once. And now, it was a miracle. Mystic, shimmering, lasting only for a moment. Less than a second. Still, an omen. A sign that something good was about to happen.

She passed a hand over her forehead, wiping away the perspiration. A prayer was answered. She felt it. She knew it. But it was impossible to know which one. Ma? Or had the detective been saved? Those were the two supplications most present in her mind.

Stripping off her clothes, she breathed deeply, then slipped a thin cotton T-shirt over her naked body and lay down on the bed. The heat and humidity prohibited her from crawling under the sheet where she wanted to be, taking cover from her responsibilities. The girl was alive, her mind conjuring dozens of scenarios and her lithe body on fire, every nerve alive and stimulating her core.

With the small package beside her, she closed her eyes, trying to settle down, praying for peace, praying for forgiveness, and praying that her prayers would be answered. It was an exhausting and complicated procedure. A true voodoo practitioner carried the weight of all of her clients. Their dreams, their desires, their ambitions. She interceded with the spirits. And if the spirits were cooperative, she could give the patron a path to achieve their goal. If the spirit was stubborn, and they sometimes were, she would try again. And again. And sometimes she would have to admit that as strong as her aura may be, there was nothing left to do. Possibly it was the clients themselves that were the obstacle. Their inability to believe.

Sometimes it wasn't her fault. But she always took the blame.

As the young lady finally drifted off, somewhere in the fog that filled her mind her mother was talking. Speaking clearly, succinctly, as she had in years past. And try as she might, Solange Cordray still couldn't understand a word the woman was saying.

23

n the phone the next morning Sue Waronker was able to give him three names, based on the initials. One was a judge, one a stockbroker and one an old friend. She didn't recognize the initials P.T. and had no recollection of any meeting that was to be decided.

'The three you recognize, those meetings all took place in his office?'

'To the best of my recollection, Detective. I'm not always here. I'm usually busy with running briefs or something to other offices and the courtrooms. I can't verify that they all showed up.'

A simple follow-up call to the three would answer the question, or he could just run the surveillance tapes. They had cameras in every corridor.

P.T. was another matter. P.T., the man without a name. Archer searched the Rolodex. There were fifteen last names beginning with T. None of those had a first name starting with a P. It could be the middle name. He'd call those names just to make sure.

P.T. had met Lerner at Cochon, a Cajun restaurant with an upscale menu. Archer called the restaurant, identifying himself.

'We do take reservations, Detective Archer, but looking at that day and covering eleven a.m. till we closed, I see no Lerner or anyone with the initials P.T. We weren't that busy for lunch so anyone could have walked in and they would have been seated.'

'How many people on your wait staff for lunch?'

'Oh, on a day like that, maybe five.'

'Can you ask if any of them knew the judge?'

'Sure. And I'll see if anybody recognizes the initials P.T. We get a pretty regular lunch crowd and our staff might recognize that combination.'

'You can talk to them today?'

'I don't have a chart in front of me, but I'll find out who was working that day and get with them.'

'Understand, this doesn't necessarily have anything to do with the murder. We're just trying to trace his steps.'

'Got it.'

'Can you get me this information by tomorrow?' Time was of the essence. He needed every bit of information today, it was critical, but that wasn't going to happen. End of the week. Sullivan had warned him. They were going to announce Antoine Duvay as the killer.

'I'll make every effort.'

'Check credit card receipts from that day. If Judge Lerner picked up the tab, it probably won't matter. But if someone with those initials on their credit card shows up, we may have our answer.'

'Anything we can do to cooperate with police, we're always happy to do, Detective.'

Most people in the town were happy to do whatever. Because they could call in a favor when something happened to them. And then there was the criminal element. They only gave out information when it benefited them.

'Call me.'

Archer crossed that task off his list, hoping the answer would come tomorrow.

He called the lab and was told they were still working on restoring the cell phone records.

'I've got a lot of pressure here.' Archer was matter-of-fact. He had to get across his point. 'As you know this is a high-profile case, and we need some answers fast. Can you speed it up? Make this a priority? I really need this before week's end.'

The voice on the other end told him that everyone insisted they had a priority case, but she would do her best.

Someone tapped him on the shoulder and he looked up. His errant partner Strand stood there, smiling, dressed in a deep blue shirt with a maroon tie smothered in gold fleur-de-lis. Go Saints.

'Hey, Strand. What's new with your suspect, Duvay?'

'Still working it, Q. He's got a lawyer, but we've got him in jail next door and I don't think a judge is going to set bail anytime soon. Judges tend to look out for other judges. I understand you've got a thing with some Krewe.'

'Sullivan told you?'

'Yeah, Sullivan.'

'I heard something.'

'Where?'

'I can't say, but apparently our judge was a member of . . .'

'Charbonerrie.'

'That's it.'

'Q, pray that we've got the right guy already in jail. Pray that he's our killer, because if you bring that group into the mix, there might be hell to pay.'

Archer nodded. 'Sullivan was a little concerned as well.'

Strand blew out a long breath, pulling a desk chair from the next desk and straddling it. Archer thought he detected the faint scent of alcohol.

'Honest to God, Q, this Charbonerrie is a nasty group. You know, it's mostly rumors, but they apparently go to great lengths to make things happen. According to local gossip, they've killed people who get in their way.'

'Killed people?'

He paused. 'Yeah. Killed people. People who go up against them, sometimes they just disappear. Not one or two people, but numbers, Archer.'

Strand lowered his voice and glanced around the room. Two detectives worked quietly at their desks and no one seemed to be paying Archer and Strand any attention.

'Literally. One detective who was investigating an embezzlement of funds never showed up for work one day, and he hasn't been seen in probably two years. A reporter for the *Times-Picayune* wrote a story about the Krewe and was found at a city construction site. He'd apparently fallen in and been impaled on a long steel rod. A city councilman who did some investigating several years ago fell off an excursion boat and drowned. Things like that. They happen to people who question this Krewe.'

Archer knew, only too well. Try to break up a drug business and they kill people. Kill your wife.

'They kill people? To what end?' Archer asked, already knowing the answer.

'To what end? What is the endgame for organized crime? Organized religion? Most governments? To dominate, to make sure the system works for them. It's a power thing, a financial thing, Q. King of the hill kind of shit.'

The two men were quiet for a moment.

'Katrina, man. It was – how can I tell you? It was a clusterfuck, where every poor sucker in this town got the shaft, but when the money started pouring in? When the Feds finally got their act together and sent money down here? Well, then the rich got richer. A lot richer. The scam artists also came out of the water like river rats. They swarmed in. Jesus, Q, if you were connected, you could have socked away millions. Seriously, millions. Contractors, guys who started up companies in twenty-four hours to get some of these grants. Engineers who had bogus ideas for the levies, I mean, there was, hell, there *is*, serious money to be made on the backs of the people who took it up the ass. Millions of dollars went to people in power who never did a damn thing for the recovery. They just sucked up government money. Even the mayor, Ray Nagin. Son of a bitch took bribes, free trips and handed out recovery contracts to his friends. I mean, it was like God opened up the heavens and just poured hundred-dollar bills from above.'

Archer nodded. He'd heard some of the stories. And where was all the stimulus money that had been poured into his home town of Detroit? In the pockets of corrupt business tycoons, organized-crime bosses, crooked politicians and a mayor who robbed the town blind. Dirty cops who ran drug rings in the inner city. Those were the ones who made the money, while the city went bust. And now, the State of Michigan ran the city, selling museums of artwork and whatever else the bankrupt city of Detroit owned to pay down its massive debt.

'And then, the BP spill?' Strand was just hitting his stride. 'Oh, man. The same cast of bad characters or those just like them siphoned off millions more.' Shaking his head, he continued, 'There was one guy alone who got a bunch of low-wage earners to give him three hundred dollars a piece so he would file a claim that they lost jobs because of the spill. It was bogus. Hell, Q, the guy then raked in fifteen million dollars from BP. Fifteen million fucking dollars. He's walking tall, man, with government money. I'm not sure he ever settled up with the workers.'

As Strand vented his frustration, Archer watched him, wondering whether the detective wasn't really upset about the fact that he hadn't been able to profit from these catastrophes himself. In the short time he'd known him, Strand seemed to be the guy who was looking for angles. Maybe small-time, but still someone who worked the edges.

'These opportunists, these rich motherfuckers who know how to manipulate the system, they are members of Krewe Charbonerrie. You want to know what power means to them? There you have it.' Strand took a deep breath. 'And they intend to keep that power. No doubt about it.'

'You never were presented with an opportunity?'

'What?'

'Come on, Strand, you've insinuated that there are opportunities.'

The detective was quiet. 'Not a fair question, Q.'

'No?'

'I can't compete with these rich motherfuckers. Couldn't begin to compare. We're homicide detectives, Q. Nothing like these other guys. Once in a while I get a bone thrown to me and I pick it up, but come on. I don't come close to these guys.'

'No fifteen million, but you do make some money on the side?'

'I'm not admitting anything, but try to live in this town, Archer, with a cop's wages.'

'Does the name Rayland Foster mean anything to you?' Archer asked, changing the subject.

'Everyone knows who Foster is.' Strand cocked his head. 'The guy is called the Chemical Czar of Nola.'

'Was there anyone who liked this guy?'

'No one. Believe me, nobody really likes this guy at all. He's ruthless. The guy owns at least six chemical plants between here and Baton Rouge. You know what that one-hundred-mile stretch is known as?'

Archer shook his head.

'Cancer Alley, Q. Man, the chemical plants, the landfills, the dumps – they are thick in that stretch. Why do you bring his name up?'

'Supposedly Foster was a one-time president of Krewe Charbonerrie.'

Strand had a tight-lipped smile. 'Wouldn't surprise me. He's a perfect example of a man making the system work for him.'

'I don't think that's working so well right now.'

'No?'

'Your chemical czar has advanced dementia. He's in a place called Water's Edge Care Center, down by the river.'

'Man. That's news. I hadn't heard that. And you think he was associated with the Krewe?'

Archer stood up, thrusting his hands into his pockets.

'It may mean nothing, but I've got a source who thinks we should look into a possible tie that links Charbonerrie and Lerner's murder.'

'Q, what the hell is this about?'

'What if Lerner was a member?'

Strand stood up.

'No way. Lerner may have been a judge, but give me a break – he was a juvie judge. He wasn't in that kind of stratosphere. And there's the financial issue. I think you've got to have some pretty big bucks to belong to an organization like that. Jesus, what can a juvie judge make? These guys in the Krewe are high stakes, Q.'

'This person, my anonymous source, they believe that Foster had intimate knowledge of the murder, months before it happened.'

'I'm telling you, Q, if you'd ever go public with that, your life wouldn't be worth squat.'

Archer sat down on the corner of the gray metal desk. 'It's not like that's anything new, Adam. I've been through some shit. Someday I'll tell you why my life isn't worth squat now.'

Strand ignored the comment. 'Seriously, I have never heard that Foster was the head of that Krewe. But you know, it sounds right. I can see it. He's the kind of guy they would want. Someone with a lot of power. And believe me, he has, or had, a lot of power.'

'So, if I can prove Foster has, or had, intimate knowledge of who is responsible for the murder of David Lerner, you'll back me with an investigation?'

Strand looked him in the eye, then motioned him into the hall.

'Look,' he said in a hushed tone, 'I don't know if that's strong enough. They want to charge Duvay week's end, and I don't think that's going to change their minds.'

'You won't back me?'

Strand closed his eyes for a moment.

'I'm not saying I do, but what if maybe I have certain relationships with certain people.' He looked down at his shoes.

'Certain relationships?' He'd been suspicious from the day he'd met his partner. This was not really a surprise.

'On the QT, OK?'

Archer nodded.

'There are certain people in this community. Certain people. People that make things happen. And yes, there are certain opportunities. Damn it, Q, to make a city like New Orleans work, you have to bend some rules. I'm not admitting anything, but come on, man, you worked a hard-core city. Rules aren't made for certain people. You know exactly what I'm talking about. Life isn't fair, so sometimes you take advantage of it.'

'All right.' Archer nodded his head. 'We all bend the rules a little, Strand. I've done it. But how far?'

'Don't be judgmental, my friend.'

'I simply want to know where we stand, Detective.' This was

exactly what he didn't need right now. Proof that he had a partner on the take. Archer just wanted to escape the entire system.

'I said I *may* have business dealings, Q,' Strand continued, his tone intense. 'There are a lot of cops who have side ventures. Don't play innocent with me, Archer. Look at what the fuck they're paying us. As I said, you can't live on that down here.' His palms open, asking for understanding, maybe forgiveness.

Archer had known it all along. The guy was too greasy not to be getting it on the side. He'd hoped he was wrong but—

'I don't know who is or isn't a member of this Krewe Charbonerrie. Really. But I've got reason to believe some of the people that I have business with . . .' he hesitated, finally making eye contact with Archer, 'people I may give some information to now and then, they would be very upset if they knew I was investigating that specific organization. So I stay away from them.'

'So that's the way it is?'

'Yeah. That and they kill people, Q.' The kid who had been bullied all of his life was cowering once again. 'That's exactly the way it is. And you need to chill. Come on, Q. I'll deny I ever said this if you try to narc me, but here's how it plays out. Listen carefully.'

Closing his eyes for a moment, shaking his head, Strand continued.

'I have information, they need information. I know something, they may pay me a little to clue them in. That's what it is, Archer. Sometimes I can help, you know? It doesn't go any further than that. Come on, Mr High and Mighty. Tell me there wasn't a lot of this going on in Detroit. Tell me you didn't play that game once in a while. I know better. Detroit has the same power struggles as any big city. Not that I'm painting myself into a corner, but there are a lot of crooked cops in your city. I'm talking about serious corruption.'

Strand had hit the nail on the head. There had been a lot of it going on. Corrupt cops, side deals, vice, bribery. It was everywhere. Archer's family was evidence. His blood family and his wife. Some were victims, and some of them were perpetrators. Archer nodded, breathing deeply, a cleansing breath, needed to settle himself in the current situation.

'What's the definition of crooked, Strand? Apparently it doesn't involve selling information. To you, that's not a crossed line.'

'I'm a survivor, Q, I'm not *that* crooked.'

Archer played the hand he was dealt. He'd tried to put a Detroit cop in jail for major drug crimes and it had all backfired. He'd had to implicate his brothers. But with Denise's death, he'd decided now was not the time to start another war. Later, not now.

'So . . .' Strand laced his fingers and rocked back on his heels. 'You don't have any proof about Foster or the Krewe. You have no motive. And some anonymous source is speaking about Rayland Foster, who can't speak for himself from what you've told me. Does that really make any sense?'

Archer shook his head. It was a long shot at best.

'A hunch,' he said.

Strand again gave him a grim smile.

'Well, listen, man, until it is much more than a hunch, don't bring me in on it, OK? There's a lot of things you don't know, rookie. Don't fuck it up for the rest of us. And if that's all it is, some lame hunch, I suggest you should go in a different direction, because we are about to get fucked by the press tomorrow. And it just gets worse from that point on.'

24

The Italian Pie was a hole in the wall restaurant, a block and a half from the courthouse. Green tablecloths, wooden chairs with vinyl seats, and on the wall a flat-screen television broadcasting *Fox News*.

Archer looked up to see the newscaster announcing breaking news. The sensational murder of a local judge had made national news and they were about to cover the New Orleans mayor's news conference. The mayor was first to speak about the dead judge, praising his work and calling for swift action. Then he introduced the Chief of Police. Archer couldn't wait to hear what his boss had to say, though he had been warned by Sullivan that the department would not come out looking good. Maybe the chief could stave off some of the criticism.

The conference didn't last long. All the chief announced was that they had a suspect in custody and expected to make an arrest by week's end. Archer tuned out when the questions started. He knew they were looking in the wrong direction and he had only until week's end to prove it.

The smell of fresh tomato, oregano, frying sausage and baking dough only stimulated his hunger and Archer approached the counter ordering a twelve-inch mushroom and pepperoni pizza. He wanted to see if it compared to Little Italy Pizzeria on 8 Mile Road in Detroit. Great food, and one of the places he and Denise had frequented, almost weekly. Closing his eyes for just a moment he saw her. Right beside him, a funny smile on her face.

When he turned around, the voodoo girl was sitting at a table by the door. The young lady seemed to appear and disappear at will.

'Mrs Cordray.'

She smiled and he felt that same uneasiness he'd felt the first time he'd seen her. Somewhat tongue-tied, not quite sure what to say.

'Detective Archer.'

Nodding, he said, 'Are you following me, or do you and I just have the same taste in restaurants?'

She glanced around at her surroundings.

'No,' she frowned, 'we do not have the same taste.'

And he thought about her ex-husband, a multimillionaire. Some guy who'd made a fortune from the misfortunes and misdeeds of others. Possibly she was more the Armand's, Commander's Palace, August kind of girl. Archer tended to go for the lower-class estab-lishments. The food was usually greasy, but there was more of it, and it was a whole lot cheaper.

'So then, you're following me.'

She nodded as he walked over and sat down across from her, facing the door.

'I needed to see you.'

He smiled. For whatever reason, she wanted to see him. This attrac-tive, mysterious girl *needed* to see him. This might be a good thing.

'Tell me something, Mrs Cordray. What are the worst things people ask you to do? If you are able to perform miracles, then . . .'

'I perform nothing. I ask for the intervention of the spirits.' A very stern tone to her voice.

'What do people ask? I don't get it.'

'Those who want serious help ask about their financial future, their romantic future, their own future. They ask about their health. However, there are those who ask to be fabulously wealthy. I don't think that's ever worked. And there are a surprising number of people who ask for a spell that will kill someone.'

'Really?' Archer actually wasn't that surprised.

'Really. If there is such a spell, I'm not aware of it. And if I were aware, I would refuse to use it.'

Archer nodded.

'And there are people who ask about the outcome of a project. They ask whether they should attempt a business deal, or take a certain trip. Will an investment pay off? They want approval before they make an important decision.'

'OK, you had to see me for what reason?'

'Two reasons. I have a question for you, and you may not have the answer. This may involve something that happened without your knowledge.'

Intrigued, Archer leaned in.

'Ask me.'

'Two questions, actually.'

'All right.'

'Did you keep your *gris gris* bag?'

Archer leaned back abruptly. How could she know about last night? He was somewhat afraid of the next question.

'I take that as a yes.'

Pushing her fingers through her thick hair, the girl smiled faintly, and Archer noticed the long eyelashes, the full lips and the dark, perfect complexion.

'Detective Archer, is there a chance that something happened last night that put you in danger? Something that possibly threatened you with bodily harm? Something that the *gris gris*, with its spiritual charm, helped avert?'

Archer was silent, staring intently into her eyes. Unless she had been the one trying to break into his cottage last night, there was no way she could have known what happened. Unless . . .

'Detective. As I said, you may not have been aware. It's an unfair question. I believe that the *gris gris* may have helped stop a crime upon your person. I needed to know if that were the case.'

Archer took a deep breath. If he told her she was right, he was admitting belief in her voodoo cult. A crime upon his person. Hell, that could be anything. It could be a drunk on Bourbon Street, almost colliding with him. It could be that he drank too much and was almost mugged going home. Actually, he'd been robbed in broad daylight by one Samuel Jackson, without his drinking a single drop of alcohol. It wasn't exactly uncommon in New Orleans. To answer, or not to answer. That was the question.

'There was an incident.'

That faint smile appeared on her face again. He'd pleased her.

'I was working last night, paperwork on the judge's murder, and I believe someone tried to break into my cottage. They tried to . . .' He hesitated, not wanting to tell her everything but compelled to bare his soul. 'They tried to pry a window open. It was locked and they weren't successful. Is that what you're looking for?'

Archer spread his hands on the green tablecloth, and Solange Cordray reached across the table, her palms on top of his hands. The detective shivered internally, the chill traveling down his spine.

'I felt it.' She shuddered and he felt the tremor. 'Was the *gris gris* bag nearby, Detective?'

It was the first time they'd had physical contact, and it was electric. The moment took his breath away and almost didn't return it. He'd never felt that from a touch. Almost like a sexual experience, but deeper. He felt it in his inner person, as ridiculous as it sounded, and he found himself wanting to tell her more. *Man up, Archer, man up.*

'The bag was one inch from where the person was prying. The window was locked. I'm not sure I can say that the *gris gris* bag had anything to do with it. It had to do with the fact that I had made sure the windows were locked.'

'Believe what you want.'

For that brief moment, Archer believed in *her.* But the feverish blush subsided and she removed her hand.

'And that's why you followed me here?' he asked.

'For another reason as well.'

'OK.'

'You are taking my presence lightly, and I understand that. I told you the last time we met that I've had a lot of experience with people, especially people in positions of authority, who do not understand what I – what Ma and I do.' Pausing, she closed her eyes. 'What Ma *did.*'

Archer nodded, remembering the conversation vividly. Her mother had been held for a crime she hadn't committed. It was a cop's nightmare to arrest someone and have them convicted for something when they were totally innocent. Unless the person was a lowlife who deserved to be incarcerated for a number of reasons. He never wanted that thought to get out.

'Detective, I know more than you think I do. I know about your wife and the trouble in Detroit, I know about—'

'Oh, you do?' At the mention of Denise, he stared at her, his defenses on high alert. 'Well, it's easy to find that information on a simple Google search.' He was surprised at the vehemence of his response. 'Don't try to dazzle me with your voodoo connections or your spiritual presence regarding my wife.' His voice was stern. 'I can tell you some rather shocking things about yourself, and it comes from nothing but working the Internet.'

She took her hands off the table, turned her head, gave him a sideways glance and remained quiet.

'You were married. To a Joseph Cordray. He is a finance guy who invested heavily in private prisons. One that's not too far from here. Made a ton of money with this investment, and moved on to a wife even younger than you. If I dug hard enough, I'd probably discover that he was able to low ball any settlement you received. Guys like that usually have some pretty high-powered attorneys who make mincemeat out of people like you and me.'

Archer was immediately sorry he'd said anything at all. The girl had pushed his buttons and now he'd stepped in it.

'I'm sorry,' he continued, his usual filter dropped, 'but to tell me about *my* problems, to bring up *my* deceased wife, it's an easy find. Anyone with a rudimentary understanding of their computer can—'

'Detective Archer, did your intruder use a knife?'

Archer froze. He knew it showed in his eyes, in his facial expression, and yet he was dumbfounded. How the hell could she know? Casting meaningless spells was one thing. Looking up information on the Internet, something else. Having proprietary information was out of the ball park. Especially information that could only be known to two people. The actual intruder and Archer. And she was so calm. So in command of the situation. He shivered again.

Finally able to speak, in a coarse, strained voice he said, 'Why would you ask that question? Is it a guess?'

'I had an epiphany.'

'A what?' He knew what the word meant, but he needed time to regroup.

'I had a dream, Detective Archer. A very vivid dream.'

'And you saw a knife?' He didn't want to believe.

'Detective, I needed to know if I was going in the right direction. I am now convinced of it. I have more information on Krewe Charbonerrie. Do you want it or not?'

Compared to her, Archer was not in control. He'd never felt more out of control in his life. His head was spinning.

'How do you know about the knife?'

'Do you want the information or not?'

'I do. I also want to know how you have intimate details regarding—'

'I have been informed of the new Krewe leader's name.'

He studied her. It wasn't often that someone one-upped him like she had. Archer leaned over the table.

'Rayland Foster? He told you?'

'Detective Archer, I can't explain how this information is transferred. The old man speaks to me, but he doesn't talk. I'm not sure I understand it myself.'

'Why does Foster want you to have this information?'

'He has yet to share that with me. Maybe he wants to right a wrong. I believe he has committed a lot of wrongs in his life.'

She remained calm, and he was taken with the softness of her eyes. Light brown, with a sadness he hadn't noticed before.

'So you believe you know the new head of Krewe Charbonerrie?'

'I do. If I'm correct, he is my client.'

'You really *know* the new leader of Krewe Charbonerrie? You do business with this man?'

'This gentleman has asked me to intercede in a business proposition he's involved with.'

'Jesus.'

'Damballa.'

'Damn what?'

'The supreme ruler. The voodoo snake god. Your ruler is Jesus. We worship Damballa.'

He was Catholic, not that it mattered much, but she seemed to know that. Archer tried to process the information. Never before had he dealt with emotions like this. She mystified him, humbled him, excited him more than anyone since Denise, and yet, in his white-bread culture, he couldn't help type her as bat-shit crazy.

There was no snake god. There was no voodoo culture. This sexy black girl had his mind spinning out of control. A snake-god-worshipping voodoo queen who had knowledge of the attempted break-in at his cottage. It was all too surreal.

'During our conversations,' she continued, 'I simply intercede for him. I make sacrifices, supplications to the spirits that affect his work. I had no knowledge he was involved in the Krewe. He seemed to be pleased with what I offered, and twice he has asked me for advice on projects and investments. Nothing specific, mind you. The man is very guarded in his talks with me.'

This young lady, a witch doctor sorceress, was giving out financial advice to billionaires. And they were paying for it.

'I did a Google search. I admit, Detective, that I don't see all the answers in my mind. OK? He's an entrepreneur. This gentleman, with whom I've consulted, for whom I have prayed, for whom I have gone to the spirits, is an oil tycoon. He owns over one hundred patents regarding new uses of oil.'

'He's obviously wealthy.'

'Wealth? I know of no one who approaches his value.'

'So, if he's the head of this Krewe, it may mean nothing,' Archer said. 'You are channeling the thoughts of someone who can't communicate with anyone.' He cleared his throat. 'Except you.'

'Do a web search for the head of Krewe Charbonerrie. Look for the name he gave me. Please, do it, Detective Archer. I know of no other way to prove to you that I have some important evidence in the murder of the judge. You won't find it anywhere.'

'I will.'

'I challenge you. Try to find that information on a Google search or anywhere on the Internet. I looked. It doesn't exist. And yet, I have intimate details.'

'So, if the name is unavailable on any search, who is he? And how does it effect the murder of the judge?'

'This man, if I understand the information that has been given to me, makes the final decisions for the Krewe. He was the person who gave the order to kill your judge.' She folded her arms across her chest in a defiant manner.

'Rayland Foster told you this?'

'I've explained that. Not in so many words. I sense things, Mr Archer. And my senses are usually very accurate.'

'And this man is your client?' The information was baseless. Yet Archer felt a burning need to find out everything this girl thought she knew.

'I don't know how to handle it,' she said. 'With no proof, there's obviously little I can do. If you could prove it—'

'You could be in a lot of danger, are you aware of that?'

She looked puzzled, her brow wrinkled as she stared at him.

'Danger?'

'This guy, your client, if you're accusing him, he may come after you. You do understand that you've put yourself in jeopardy?'

Cordray slowly shook her head.

'Don't worry about me. I'm concerned for you, Detective. My faith, my gods, they strengthen me. I think you are the one in danger.'

The knife under the window.

'Are you going to give me a name?' Archer asked.

'Detective, the information I give you is powerful. And I believe it is reliable. But without work on your part it is useless. I am simply trying to feed you enough fuel to start a fire.'

Archer sat back, shaking his head.

'I think you may be crazy.'

Smiling, she showed her near perfect teeth.

'I know that. I have been called much worse. So has my mother.'

'You've got a name to give me? The person who is your client? The person who may have put the hit on Judge Lerner?'

'Use it carefully, Mr Archer. Just the possession of this name may put you in serious jeopardy.'

'Stop stalling. Who is the new head of Krewe Charbonerrie?'

'Richard Garrett,' she said. 'I think you'll find him a very interesting character.'

'Garrett.'

'Richard Garrett. His father owned a successful oil business and my mother used to advise him.'

'Whoa. His father was your mother's client.'

'He told me. My mother never spoke of her dealings with him. And, Detective Archer, he wears something very interesting. Being a practitioner of my religion I noticed it immediately.'

'What?' He was tiring of the games and the back-and-forth subtleties.

'He wears the tattoo. A coiled snake on his wrist. Identical to the one Rayland Foster wears.'

25

Jonathon Gandal sat in the dining room of Broussard's, sampling the smoked salmon. He glanced at his watch and noticed his companion was fifteen minutes late. Not unusual for the man, but still inconsiderate. Gandal was an impatient man, who normally didn't tolerate inconsideration. In this case he made an exception.

His back to the wall, away from the window, he sipped his Sazerac. Whiskey, bitters, Pernod and simple syrup.

The gentleman walked in, casually glancing around the room. The man's head never moved, just his eyes taking everything in. Dressed in a pair of gray slacks, black tasseled loafers and a blue dress shirt with diamond-patterned tie, he looked like a New Orleans banker. Nothing to draw attention to himself.

'You're late,' Gandal announced guardedly as his guest slid out a chair and sat across from him.

'I was being careful.' The man's steel-gray eyes bore into Gandal's.

'If you were being careful, your back wouldn't be to the room.'

The man smiled, his perfect teeth a perfect shade of white. 'Look behind you, on the wall.'

Gandal turned his head. He was surprised to see the ornate mirror that reflected the entire room.

'I underestimated you.'

'Appearances can be very deceiving.'

'I won't make that mistake again.' Gandal sipped his drink. 'Can I order you something?'

'I'm hoping I won't be here long enough to enjoy it. Mr Gandal, you have a problem?'

'I do. It seems there is someone else who needs to be dealt with.'

'And you are looking for the same outcome?'

'A message was sent the last time,' Gandal said.

'That message received quite a bit of attention.'

'It did, and I'm certain it was received. But someone has been voicing concern about that message. In the company of friends. And we're concerned this person may eventually confide in someone else.'

The man looked up, studying the mirror.

'You have inside information?'

'We do. And that information tells us that we need to do some more quality control.'

'Same message?'

'We are concerned this person may have an accident.'

His eyes went back to Gandal.

'An accident?'

'We need to get rid of this person. An accident would mean there was no way to tie it to the other killing.'

'Harder to arrange.'

'Really? Faulty brakes, a fire?'

'You're reading crime fiction?' he asked in a very soft voice. 'I doubt that any fiction writer ever actually *staged* an accident.'

'Point well taken.'

'Is there a time frame?'

'Soon. Today wouldn't be soon enough.'

The man had both hands on the table, a simple Bell & Ross watch the only jewelry he was wearing. He tapped a manicured nail on his empty water glass, listening to the crystal ring.

'As always, I won't be involved, but I know someone who specializes in these types of things.'

Gandal nodded.

'Twenty thousand.'

Gandal sat back. 'What? That's ten more than—'

'This is an accident?'

'Yes. We don't think it should send a message. That didn't work out so well. We just need to remove a threat.'

He wore a thin smile. 'We can do that.'

'Half down?'

The man studied him.

'Normally.'

'What are you saying? This isn't normal?'

'No. This may require some expenses beyond normal. I'm anticipating other players.'

'No, no. We've been over this. You know damn well you can't involve more than two—'

'Mr Gandal, there were two players the last time. These other actors, they will be bit players who have no idea what the real mission is. It will not be apparent to anyone. They're contracted to do one job for an arranged price. The privacy factor has been,' he paused, 'factored in. Don't worry. We'll need the full price. Up front.'

Gandal took a deep breath.

'It's part of my job. To worry. You understand, the more participants the more chances of exposure. We don't need exposure. And full price up front? I don't know if I can—'

'How many people on *your* side are aware of the situation?'

Gandal looked beyond his tablemate. He wasn't sure how much information he wanted to share.

'Four. We have a board of directors, myself and . . .' He hesitated. 'Actually five, but that's not really your concern because—'

'Mr Gandal, I have exposure as well. Do you think that it's a risk-free business that I'm in? Five is a high number. I should refuse your request and walk away from here. Five people? Really?' The man pushed back his chair.

Gandal stared at the tablecloth, his smoked salmon and drink, and felt like a schoolboy who had been chastised by his teacher.

'Please, don't walk. We've done everything possible to keep your identity a secret. Hell, *I* don't even know who you are. You know that, don't you? I have no idea what your real name is. It was never shared. Just take care of the problem and everything will be fine.'

The gentleman nodded, pulling his chair back in, closer to the table. Checking the mirror on the far wall he seemed satisfied.

'You have an account?' Gandal asked.

The man pulled a small piece of paper from his shirt pocket.

'The number is here. It's the Iberia bank, and the company is Waterfront Seafood Distributors.'

Gandal nodded.

'This account,' the man continued, 'will only be open for two days. Then it will cease to exist. There's your window. Twenty thousand. And please burn the paper once the deposit has been made.'

He stood up, again studying the mirror with the brass frame.

'Mr Gandal, as usual, I wish you good fortune.'

The man wished him fortune only as long as Gandal had lucrative jobs for him. Gandal was certain of that.

He stood as well and reached in his pocket. Pulling out a similar paper he handed it across the table.

'Now, I have to tell you that our inside information has told us there are two people who need to be silenced.'

Studying the paper for a moment, the man finally looked into Gandal's face. His eyes were cold and he kept his voice quiet but serious.

'Two names?'

Gandal nodded.

'Are you holding me up, here? Two names is twice the price. Surely you do know that, right? You're not a stupid man. Are you?'

'We were hoping . . .'

'Hope all you want. Twice the price. Do you understand? There is a lot of work to be done here.'

'I understand.'

'This is going to raise eyebrows.'

'Are they going to look like accidents? These deaths?'

'These murders?' The man spoke softly.

'Yes.'

'Of course. But people will assume that—'

'Then please, do the job.'

'I hope you made the correct choice. You know what happened the last time. There is no reversing what I do.'

'It has to be done,' Gandal said.

'You know the old saying, Mr Gandal: *be careful what you wish for*. It may come true.'

26

L eaving his car by the restaurant, Archer walked the short distance to the courthouse. He hadn't settled on a gym yet, and the little exercise he did get was walking to the streetcars. Chasing the jailed suspect, Antoine Duvay, was the closest thing to a workout he'd had in weeks.

Greeted by the stark walls inside, beyond the metal detector he noticed an auction of foreclosed houses going on in the lobby; an auctioneer was pointing to pictures of properties tacked to a board that was mounted on an easel. At least fifty people crowded around, hoping to steal someone's home.

Further back to the right he saw hard plastic seats, green, brown and yellow, bolted to the floor. Black men and women occupied a handful of the chairs, some gazing at the wall, some staring at the tiled floor marred with black cigarette burns from another era, etched forever into the vinyl. They were waiting for their kids, their grand-kids, their nieces or nephews to be arraigned, tried or sentenced.

A mousy black receptionist with large breasts sat behind a battered metal desk, across from a colorful cartoon mural depicting a Dixieland band made up of kids.

Archer walked up to the desk and pulled his jacket aside, displaying the gold badge clipped to his belt.

'I need to see Judge Warren.'

He'd already spoken to Sue Waronker. No reason to revisit that at this point. But Warren was the one who had reported him as threatening. The man had called his office and told his sergeant that Archer was trouble. And, truth be told, that report hadn't bothered Archer. Judge Warren knew there was no threat. He simply wanted to distance himself from the detective. It was a front. But the fact that the judge had seemed to withhold information – that was something else. Of the six juvenile offender judges, Warren stood out as the remaining judge who passed very harsh, almost unreason-able sentences. Warren. A mirror image of Judge David Lerner. Archer wanted to know if there was a connection. He wanted just one more civil, unthreatening conversation.

The office was empty and he gazed into the next room. Judge Traci Hall was just walking out, dressed in her somber black robe, her blonde hair hanging low over her collar.

'Detective Archer, right?'

'Yeah. Good to see you, Judge.'

'I was going to call you,' she said.

'About what?' Radar tuned in.

'Something that came to my mind.'

It was always good when someone wanted to give him information.

'You wanted to know whether I thought Judge Lerner gave out harsh sentences. You asked me what my opinion was. Apparently you believe that his system of justice, the way he meted out sentences, was too severe.'

Shaking his head he said, 'No, you're wrong. It's not about what I believe.' Archer needed to be crystal clear on his ideas. 'I questioned the *why* of the severity of the sentences, and I wonder if other judges in this department give equally harsh sentences.' Pausing, he said, 'Like maybe you?'

She nodded. 'I think you'll see that every one of us has our own way of coping with sentencing. Personally,' she continued, 'I tend to be more lenient. If you've got a kid in trouble, try to get *me* to hear the case. I want the youthful offender to get help. The prison doesn't give them that.'

'That?'

'*Help*. Come on, Detective. Prison punishes. The fact that prisons are called correctional facilities is a joke. There is no correction. You know this as well as anyone. I want those kids to get help. That's what most of them need. There's the odd exception, where there's no hope, but . . .'

He nodded. 'So there is no uniformity?'

Pausing, she studied his face. 'Officer Archer, Detective, at one time I was in the public education system. I was a teacher before I got my law degree. I worked with troubled teens. Now I sentence them. You see, I'm trying to build a bridge to the other side. That's my way of doing things. And yes, you are correct. Judges like myself may let someone off while we try to find help for them, and another judge may give them a year in prison. It's the way the system works. I didn't design it and I won't apologize for it. Nothing is perfect.'

They were silent for a moment, as two uniformed police officers strode down the corridor, deep in conversation as they passed Archer and Hall.

'You were going to call me?'

Her eyes followed the two patrolmen as they continued their walk. Then she turned to Archer, her eyes narrowed as she addressed him.

'Apparently you had an exchange with Judge Richard Warren where he took offence as to your tone. You said something to him that didn't sit well.'

'I actually came by to see him again. Your Judge Warren took some comments I made the wrong way.'

'Did you tell him he may be next? The killer may be keying in on him? Was that the gist of your comments?'

Archer shook his head. 'No. I told him if one judge was hit, the others might be in danger. It's a truth. You are a target. Every judge in this building, in this system may be the next victim. I want to be sure you understand that.'

'Wow. That's not the way he spun it.'

Archer pursed his lips and thought back to the conversation.

'Judge Hall, I don't remember exactly how I phrased it. But the message was to watch your back. You never know.'

'Maybe I should hire a body guard.' She smiled.

'Look, Ms Hall, maybe you should. We're in the early stages of this investigation. We're going in a number of directions, and one of those directions is that someone has it out for the judicial system. I have no proof of that, but if that is the case, as I said, all of you may be targets. It's not a threat, just a fact.'

'Dick took it personally.'

'Well then, so be it. If he's vigilant it may save his life.'

That seemed to sober her up, the smile fleeing from her face.

'Detective Archer, I thought there were several things I should mention. You've probably already discovered this, but it hit me that when someone is in a relationship, their significant other may be a person of interest.'

'True.' He waited. Don't push. Let the information come out the way it's most comfortable for the informant to release it.

'As I said, possibly you know about Lerner's relationship. Or should I say relationships?'

'He was married. Has an estranged kid.'

'You do know.'

'What other relationships was he involved with?'

Judge Hall stepped from her doorway and motioned to him as she started walking down the hall.

'I have to be in court soon. Follow me.'

Their footsteps echoed down the corridor, sound bouncing from the walls of the empty hallway.

'Lerner was married. I never met his wife or child, but once in a while he mentioned them. His wife especially.'

Archer kept pace, not responding.

'So, his comments for the last several years were that she was a cold, callous woman who enjoyed the lifestyle and perks of a judge's wife but hated what she had to do to get them. He claimed that she took full advantage of all that was offered, but she detested Lerner himself.'

'He divorced her, right?'

'She divorced him. Took up with a State Supreme Court judge she met at a party in the Garden District, and she got rid of Lerner for good.'

'Would she have any reason to . . .'

'Detective. She got rid of him. She's now hanging with Louisiana State legal eagles. She's been invited to the governor's mansion, for God's sake. I believe she and the Supreme Court bigwig have visited the White House. Anyway, she's climbing that social ladder. No reason at all to look back. No reason that I can think of to come back and kill her ex.'

Archer nodded.

'Well, thanks for the information.'

She stopped mid-stride, reached up and put her hand on his shoulder.

'No, no, no. I haven't told you the whole story.'

Archer scratched his scalp, studying her for a moment. Blonde hair hanging straight down, full lips, a dimple in her chin. She looked nothing like he would picture a judge.

'Lerner, on the rebound, came up with a new partner.'

'And that would be—'

'A Rodger Claim.'

'What?'

'Rodger Claim.'

'So Lerner was—'

'Apparently. Always had been, had finally come or was temporarily out of the closet. I'm not sure.'

'I did not know that.' He'd already uncovered the wife story, but the gay lover was a surprise.

'I'm sure you would have found out. He tried to keep it a secret, but most of us knew. Judge Lerner was a strange duck. This relationship just added to his shaky reputation.'

'So who is this Rodger Claim?'

'Was. Lerner dropped him after a year or so.'

'Possibly this Claim didn't like being dumped?'

'I think that's very possible.'

'So you think that Claim could have—'

'Didn't know the man, and I don't want to go on record as suggesting anything of the sort.' She continued her walk, shaking her head back and forth.

He nodded. Hall believed there was a strong possibility this Claim person was a suspect but didn't want to verbalize it.

'Did you ever meet him?'

'No.'

'Know anything about him?'

'Sure.'

'What did he do?'

'With Lerner?' She turned to him with a coy smile.

Archer returned with a disapproving look.

'You mean for a living?'

'Yes.'

'He was supervisor of the guards.'

'Guards? What guards?'

'Here's where it gets interesting,' she said.

The lady judge enjoyed drawing out the story.

'So finish the story, Ms Hall. I've got an important appointment, and I don't want to be late.'

'OK, Detective, here's the punch line. Claim, Judge Lerner's lover, was supervisor of the guards at River Bend Prison, where Lerner sent most of his convicted offenders.'

'Oh?'

'I should stay out of this, but . . .'

'But what?'

'But I think there's something going on with some of our judges and that prison. Something very wrong.'

'You don't know this for a fact?'

'It's not gospel.'

'Then?'

'Just the fact that I even think it,' she unconsciously looked side to side, checking over her shoulders, 'makes me a marked woman.'

Archer found himself almost smiling. He swallowed the facial expression.

'You think someone is after you? Because you believe that some of the judges are involved in something to do with the prison?'

'Judge Warren has said a couple things to me that were rather strange.'

'Care to share them?'

'No. But I will tell you this, Detective. I was half serious about hiring a body guard.' She looked into his eyes. 'Do you by any chance freelance on the side?'

27

Sergeant Sullivan approached Archer's desk, peering over the detective's shoulder at the computer screen.

'Porter walked away today.'

'Porter? Walked away?'

'Turned in his badge and took a hike.'

'Private security gig?'

'He didn't say.'

'How many, Sergeant? This year?'

'Three.'

'Still . . .'

'It's high pressure. Pressure to make the case, solve the crime, and there doesn't ever seem to be a lull. Money isn't that good as you know, not to mention the horrible hours. You're going after someone who has killed . . . well,' he paused. 'Obviously I don't have to tell you.'

Everyone seemed to know Archer's situation. Or they thought they did. Surface stuff. There were actually only four people who knew the true story about his father, his brothers and the death of his wife.

'And of course now it's even dangerous for a cop to sit in his patrol car,' Sullivan said. 'Anyway, what new leads do you have regarding the Lerner murder? Anything at all, Archer, even if it's not in your report.'

'Do you know a Richard Garrett, Sergeant?'

'The oil guy? Sure. I know who he is. Met him a couple of times when he was a kid.'

'A kid?'

'His father, second generation, owned about thirty oil fields, maybe two hundred oil wells.'

'This Richard, he's a major player?'

'As far as I know Richard has grown the business quite a bit.'

'And Dad?'

'Earl Garrett. I played cards with him every Wednesday for years. He was very down to earth. Shrewd, and a really good poker player. Guy was very philanthropic. Helped a lot of non-profits in the city. Earl died about five years ago.'

'So Richard, he's a pretty powerful guy?'

'Why are you asking? Jesus, don't tell me that you're working on a Garrett angle as well as the Krewe Charbonerrie. Archer, I would suggest that you talk to your partner, Strand, and convict this line cook loser, Antoine Duvay. It's going to be a whole lot easier on us and the entire community. I hate to say this, but the kid is expendable. He goes down for the hit, the community gets a little crazy for a couple of days and then it all simmers down. You bring a Garrett or a Krewe into this and it gets more than a little crazy.'

'We keep dancing around this. Do you want the killer, or someone we manufacture? I really want to know, Sergeant. If you want the fast solution, I'm your next walk. Seriously, I'll pack my bags tomorrow. If you want a thorough investigation, then let me conduct that.'

Sullivan stepped back, one step, two steps.

'We're going public this Friday. You know that.'

'I'm not on board.'

'You get used to a certain vibe in this town, Archer. A certain way that things are done. OK? I want the outcome to be the truth. But damn, when it seems like a slam dunk, I want that too.'

Archer nodded.

'I want any information, Detective. You give it to me first. Because, at the end of the week . . .' He let it hang.

28

'Ma, some good news.' She studied the frail woman, too old too soon. 'There are doctors, scientists, who are experimenting with something that removes protein deposits in the brains of mice.'

The girl smiled in spite of herself. 'Crazy, isn't it. They use mice to find a cure. Mice. Anyway, this drug, it's called bexarotene. Doctor Kahn says it's much too early to tell if it will work on humans, but there are scientists out there, researchers who are exploring, Ma, looking for an answer. They're not going to give up, these doctors and scientists, and neither are we.'

Her mother's hands were in her lap, slightly shaking with a tremor that the girl had only recently noticed. Just another worry.

The lobby was awash in afternoon sunshine and Solange Cordray sat in an easy chair, her mother's wheelchair pulled up close. Potted palms cast shadows on the patterned marble floor and fresh flowers crowded vases in an array of bright colors on ornate tables scattered through the main area.

An aide walked by, nodding at them, smiling with a knowing look. Solange was the only volunteer with a relative in the center. Whether it was pity, or just bliss that their relatives weren't afflicted with dementia in any scenario, she didn't know. But she resented the condescending looks, the patronizing attitude from the staff. Her mother had been a proud woman, someone who made a difference in this community, and for them to humiliate her in any way left Solange with a bad taste in her mouth.

'It's a beautiful day, Ma. I picked up some fresh beignets at Cafe Du Monde, your favorite.'

She picked up a white sack beside the chair, opened it and presented the pastry with powdered sugar to her mother. No response.

'Extra napkins, Ma. You remember how messy these are? But they are so good. Remember? You used to take me there as a child.'

Sitting at outside tables in the warm morning air, the low-hanging ferns swaying gently in the breeze. Sweet fried dough and powdered sugar. And then, chicory coffee served *au lait*. Although, she remembered, her mother had served hers with more cream than coffee. Still, a delicious Saturday morning treat. And a cross section of New Orleans characters. The juggler who only wore a jockstrap, and the two black tumblers who fascinated the patrons with their cartwheels, somersaults and almost impossible acrobatics. There was a one-armed guitar player, and a host of other entertainers she'd since forgotten, all on the sidewalk, right outside her Saturday morning haunt. Ma allowed for the other patrons, but had told her the entertainers were there just for her. It was their special place, their special time. Ma and her special little girl. She sensed the tears in her eyes. It seemed she was crying a lot lately.

Setting the bag back down, she reached over and placed her hand on the trembling hands of her mother.

'Ma, I talked to the detective. I've done what I can do. I may have given him too much information. Or maybe too little.'

The old lady smiled at her, a sad smile, her eyes drooping and her wrinkled chin resting on her chest.

'I don't know enough. I wish that I could solve the case and present him with the murderer.'

Clotille Trouville's eyes closed for a moment and her daughter breathed deeply, wondering if her mother was asleep. She was always frightened the woman would simply expire and never open those loving eyes again.

'Baron,' she whispered, 'please let her live. Let her live so that a cure can be found. Give her life, new life that she can once again inspire and pray for the souls of those who need her.'

The matronly woman opened her eyes as if on command.

'Ma, it's a heavy burden we bear.'

Who was she to tell her mother about the burden? After all the old lady had been through. It was best if she left her alone and didn't bring up the witching. The voodoo spell that was cast from her moment of birth, from her mother's birth, her grandmother and before. And all the way back to the Voodoo Queen herself, Marie Laveau.

'The Krewe Charbonerrie, they're deep in this murder. I've felt it before, I feel it now and I'm certain that he will figure it out. With all the powers that I have, I'm not sure how much further I can go. Sooner or later, the detective has to follow my lead. It's just getting him to trust me.'

Drool dribbled down the chin of the old woman and Solange Cordray wiped it away with a tissue.

'Thank you for listening, Ma. These moments, these sharing times, are important to me. I feel you with me. Do you feel me with you?'

The lady lifted her head, a glint of recognition on her face. She nodded up and down, and Solange looked into her eyes, amazed at the acknowledgement. In an instant the once fiery orbs were clouded over as if the woman had never heard or acknowledged her daughter's presence.

29

To solve a murder you have to ask why, then follow the leads, the chain of evidence, until you've reached a conclusion, or, ask why starting with a suspect and go backwards, tying him into the crime.

Early in his career, he'd found an even easier way: someone simply comes forward and confesses or someone comes to you and gives up the perp. That hadn't happened in the death of his wife and now it hadn't happened in the death of the judge, and, since he didn't consider Antoine Duvay a suspect, Archer decided to follow a lead. River Bend Prison. End of the week, without a suspect, they were charging Duvay and that was not the way to go. He had to take some drastic measures.

The warden Russell Jakes seemed to have a personal relationship with Judge Lerner. They'd even had a photo taken in front of Lerner's piano, with the mug shots of convicted juvies sitting on the baby grand piano's lid. Definitely acquaintances, maybe friends, maybe more.

Then there was the former supervisor of guards, Rodger Claim. According to Judge Hall, Lerner and Claim definitely had a relationship. An intimate relationship that didn't last. Archer hadn't seen that one coming. Lerner, with an ex-wife and a child, seemed to be a straight guy. He should have explored a little further.

Finally, Solange Cordray's ex-husband had a vested interest in River Bend Prison. He had invested heavily in the company Secure Force, and apparently had done quite well as the company prospered. It could all be a coincidence, but seldom did Archer find that to be true. If two or more leads seemed to be headed in the same direction, there was something going on worth investigating.

Strand was off doing his own thing, probably still trying to tie Duvay up into knots so a strong conviction was inevitable. He secretly wished him luck but by now Archer knew full well that the killing went a lot deeper. This wasn't the work of a convicted petty thief who worked as a line cook at a waterfront New Orleans restaurant. The murder of Judge David Lerner went a lot deeper than a grudge shooting from a disgruntled criminal.

Archer's Chevy was in the lot, and even though the prison was an hour away, even though the temperature was eighty-seven in the shade, and even though his air conditioning was spotty at best, he decided to make the trip. Cold. No warning. He'd surprise everyone there and there would be no time to make up stories.

He didn't know if Rodger Claim was still employed at the prison, had no idea if Warden Russell Jakes would see him; he wasn't even sure if Joseph Cordray was still an investor in the prison group Secure Force. It didn't matter. Often, just showing up unannounced was enough to garner major information. If they knew you were coming, they'd conspire to stay silent. No, it was best to spring the surprise, and ask why.

River Bend Prison was northwest on Highway 10, about midway between LaPlace and South Baton Rouge, as advertised, on a bend in the Mississippi. It took him forty-five minutes to get there and it was four fifteen when he arrived. Not a lot of business time to see everything he wanted to see.

Pulling into a spacious parking lot he saw the familiar razor wire, reminding him of the jail right next to his office. But this was massive, rows and rows of the sharp thin shiny steel that would slice through your skin like a knife through warm butter. He'd read that in the last five years, two inmates had tried to traverse the deadly wire and both had died from loss of blood, their bodies sliced like beef *carpaccio*.

Four concrete towers anchored the perimeter of the site, cold and stark, and he imagined armed guards surveying the grounds below. These were the only weapons on the campus. Inside guards couldn't wear weapons for fear an inmate would take one and all hell would break loose.

Archer crossed the parking lot, the quietness almost unnerving. The prison atmosphere missed the sound of sawing cicadas, the croaking of crickets, the shrill call of the red-tailed hawk looking for romance. It was almost as if nature understood this was a place that sucked the life out of everything in and around it.

Approaching the reception desk where two guards were seated, a good two feet above the floor, he looked up and flashed his badge.

'I'm looking for a Rodger Claim, head of security.'

The small black girl in the blue uniform frowned.

'You find him, you come and tell us. We all been lookin' for him ourselves and if we find him we'll probably string the boy up.'

'He no longer works here?' It certainly didn't sound like it.

'Hell no. We run him out, that lyin' snitch. What you want with him?'

'I'm investigating a murder in New Orleans.'

She chuckled. 'Wouldn't surprise me if Claim was the victim. You think Claim is the killer? Well, he's a lot of things, but I doubt if R.C. has the' – she scanned the area with her dark eyes – 'the balls to do somethin' like that. You know what I mean?'

He didn't.

'Well, I can't help you, Mr New Orleans.'

'Where would I find Russell Jakes?'

Gritting her teeth the small woman gazed at him through squinted eyes.

'Warden Jakes lives on the property. He is not someone who sees you just because you choose to drop in. I *assume* you don't have an appointment.'

'No.'

'Then you're pretty much out of luck, Nola.'

He'd visited prisons before. It went with the territory. Sometimes he'd have to visit a suspect who was already serving time for another killing. Hardened criminals. And the power plays that employees pulled mirrored the men and women they kept under lock and key. Tough guys, tough girls, who threw their weight around. It was the culture of the system.

'You call him.'

'Can't be disturbed.'

'Look, Miss—?'

'Washington. And I can't bother the man. So why don't you just—'

'Miss Washington, this is about the murder of a judge. A good friend of Warden Jakes. He'll want to see me. And if you don't call him, I'll find his house, tell him what an uncooperative hard-ass you are, and suggest that even though I don't have any jurisdiction in this area, I'll bring so much weight down on this prison and you personally that you will end up in a job where the most important thing you'll say is "do you want fries with that?" Do you want to test me?'

Her eyes smoldered, her hands shaking.

'You got that? Miss Washington? Do you have an answer?'

She was breathing deeply, Archer recognized relaxation technique. Finally the lady picked up the phone. Archer reached up and handed her his business card.

'Mrs Jakes, this is Trystan at Central. Would you be so kind as to ask the warden to come to the phone?'

A moment later she leaned down and handed him the receiver. If looks could kill—

Ten minutes later a big burly red-faced Russell Jakes opened the door to his two-story antebellum-style home and, with a wary look, invited Quentin Archer into the house.

30

The man checked his watch, realizing he had a limited window to place the call. He had no idea who would answer on the other end, just that he needed to report.

'Hello.' That soft, deep huskiness, like a heavy smoker's gravelly voice or someone who was trying to disguise his voice. The caller assumed it might be a little of both.

'You wanted an update on the investigation? The judge? You suggested I may be paid if I offered some useful information?'

'Yeah.'

'Ex-con with the gun still looks good.'

'I thought you'd have something new.'

'Oh, I do,' he said. 'The other detective, he's without any hard evidence, but he's throwing around the name Richard Garrett and Krewe Charbonerrie.'

There was silence on the other end.

'Are you still there?'

'Really, those names came up?'

'He feels there is some sort of a tie-in. And, if it means anything, he is asking questions about River Bend Prison and Warden Russell Jakes.'

He could hear heavy breathing on the line.

'What else?'

'A Judge Warren has accused the detective of harassing him, and that detective has talked to another judge, named Hall. Apparently he finds those two interesting.'

'All right, visit the restaurant in twenty-four. I think you'll find our thank-you gift more than adequate. And give me another update as soon as something happens.'

'No chance you can tell me why you're interested in this case?'

'Don't ask again.'

'OK.'

'You do know that Krewe Charbonerrie has some high-powered members in its rank?'

He was afraid to admit to anything. 'Rumors.'

'I would simply suggest that you steer any thoughts of investigation away from that organization. I don't think Krewe Charbonerrie would appreciate anyone looking into them, and I can't imagine that they would be involved in the murder of a juvenile judge.'

The line went dead.

31

Some lady was talking on her cell phone, holding it close to her face, but not up to her ear. From his third-floor office window Judge Richard Warren pushed his thick glasses back on his nose and watched the woman across the torn-up street. Construction crews beat the pavement with jackhammers; front loaders dug into the broken concrete slabs, pulling the pieces out and dropping them into dump trucks lined up on the side of the road.

The woman was tall and shapely with straight dark hair that hung to her shoulders. She tilted the apparatus toward his office and studied the screen. Taking pictures of the building. It had to be.

And, Warren mused, our outside cameras are taking pictures of her. Did she know? Cameras were everywhere. Was this a tourist just documenting her trip? And who would take a photo of the juvenile justice building? With all of the tourist traps in this city, the hall of justice wasn't a place visitors wanted to remember. Was it?

'There seems to be an interest in our building,' he said to no one. Sitting back in his chair, hands splayed out on the desktop, the diminutive judge watched the lady, who seemed to have a singular purpose.

'Cell phone photographs.' He surprised himself as he uttered the line out loud.

The photographer studied her phone, then blatantly held the device away from her body and obviously clicked off several more pictures.

The judge thought about calling security. There was quite a bit of security in this building, but even then he sometimes wondered about his own safety. And now, with the Lerner thing . . .

Picking up his phone he started to call for an officer, but when he glanced out the window again the lady was gone. Disappeared. Warren dropped the phone onto its receiver and closed his eyes. He massaged his temples, wondering how lie upon lie happened. He'd certainly tried enough liars in his courtroom. Now, he was wading deep in lies himself.

At five fifteen he exited his office, almost bumping into Judge Traci Hall as she stepped into the corridor.

'Judge Hall.' Cold and officious.

'Judge Warren.' She mimicked his haughty tone.

'I understand you had a lengthy conversation with the detective who's handling Lerner's case. Quentin Archer.'

'I wouldn't call it lengthy.' She hesitated, not certain what he'd heard. 'The detective actually stopped by to see *you*, but we saw each other out here and had a brief conversation. There was nothing to it. Seriously. I guess he had some things to clear up and . . .'

'He wanted to see me again?' Warren's voice went up a tone. 'He wasn't satisfied with what I told him?'

'I believe he wanted to clarify his remarks to you. I think that was his purpose. But I don't want to put words in his mouth.' Hall put her hands up in mock-defense. 'I have no idea what the two of you discussed. Other than what you've shared with me. Not my concern, Dick.' It was time to get home. Leave this mess for another day, another conversation.

'What else did he say? Did he mention his concern about any sentencing I've been responsible for?'

Hall shook her head. 'Look, Judge Warren' – back to the formal response – 'I really don't know what his motive was.' Actually, that part was true. She hoped the entire mess would just go away. 'I shouldn't have mentioned it at all. Leave me out of this, OK?'

Warren looked at her over the top of his black-framed glasses.

'What? Because you've always been critical of my sentences, you told him you disapprove of my conviction record? Is that it? You told him that? I don't remember discussing your methods with anyone. Why do you feel compelled to discuss mine with other people?'

'No, Judge. I did not express any criticism.'

She should have just shut up. Never said a word. Now the diminutive man was almost hyperventilating, worried that he was in trouble with the police.

'Then what is it? Is he worried about me? Does he have some unfounded suspicion – do you, Traci?' The man was trembling.

She shook her head. 'No, Judge Warren. Nothing was said. He just wanted to clear things up with you. I won't talk to him again, and I won't mention you again, is that OK with you?'

'No, no. Please, if the man brings up my name again in any conversation with you, let me know. For some reason, I don't trust him. I don't think you should either. Please, Judge Hall, Traci, tell me.'

Outside, city crews were now breaking up the sidewalk and still tearing up the street. Throbbing jackhammers and angry bulldozers were ripping into cement and tearing out the rebar used for support. Getting to and from work was becoming more and more difficult. Becoming more and more of a hazard. Earth moving machines, dust, dirt; an army of construction workers had taken over the parameters and the judge had about had enough of it.

Richard Warren pulled out of the parking lot from his designated spot, driving through the thick dust, millions of fine particles of concrete clouding the area and clogging his nasal passages. Possibly he could sue the city for the damage to his black BMW 5 series and to his personal health. The construction mess had to physically harm every person and car that was parked at the courthouse. A class-action lawsuit might be appropriate.

He punched in his XM radio option and hit the number six setting, settling for Fox News as his entertainment on the ride home. *The Five* was on as he thought about dinner, the lamb chop he'd marinated, the endive salad. He should have invited someone to dinner. He'd open the 2000 Dunn Cabernet Sauvignon, a pretentious red that ran around seventy dollars a bottle. It should be just right.

Thinking of the word pretentious, he flashed back to the detective, Quentin Archer. Son of a bitch. Pushing him, pressing the issue. As if he knew what the hell he was talking about. And Traci Hall. The cute judge next door. Sexy, pretentious little bitch. She was critical of the way he handled his affairs, but never pushy. He just sensed that she was not his biggest fan. There was one way to handle that. He should have asked *her* to dinner. She'd walk in the door and he'd bang her once before and once after. In his dreams.

He looked up from the radio dial and gasped as the ink black Cadillac SUV swerved in front of him, the sun glinting off its shiny paint job, almost blinding him.

In a panic, Warren braked and spun the wheel hard, cranking it to the right as far as he could, to avoid a collision. The silver Toyota Corolla in the right lane failed to yield and Warren's car smashed into the driver's side, crushing the car's body and killing the Toyota driver instantly. Continuing its trajectory, his black five series muscled the Toyota off the road, and followed suit, spinning 180 degrees and slamming his driver's door into a concrete light pole. The last thought in Warren's mind before his spine snapped was his father's comment every time he left his parents' house as a teenager.

'Dick, be sure and buckle up.'

32

Traci Hall held her hand to her face, fighting the cloud of dust from construction in front of the courthouse. She coughed, spitting out phlegm on the coarse stone mix where a concrete sidewalk used to be. Where, God willing, it

would be again. She should have told Archer more about her
suspicions. Should have told him about her strong suspicions that
someone was paying off Lerner and possibly Warren. But there
was an allegiance between the men and women in the judicial
system. Lawyers looked out for lawyers, didn't they?

Walking to the parking lot at the rear of the building she frowned
at the panhandler shuffling on the grass beside her.

'Please, lady, a couple bucks for a sandwich.'

Judge Hall clutched her purse a little tighter.

'Lady?' The tone was a little firmer, more intimidating.

Hall glanced furtively, in front of her, in back of her. It was five
o'clock, for Christ's sake. Where were the other employees?

'I need the purse, bitch.'

She sidestepped his grab and started running toward her car, as
fast as she could.

Her heels were only about two inches, but they certainly weren't
track shoes. She struggled, pumping her legs but hobbled by the
high heels and straps.

She sensed the mugger close behind and knew he was gaining
on her. Either reach her car soon, or hope someone, another judge,
an office worker or a construction worker would see her dilemma
and save the day. She ran even faster.

Not fast enough.

Feeling the hand grab her shoulder, she jerked to break free. His
hand tightened on the muscle between neck and shoulder, bringing
her up short. Spinning around she screamed loudly, to no one who
could hear or care.

He chopped at her throat with his right hand, and as she crumpled
to the ground the man ripped the purse from her hand.

'No.' Her voice was more of a gurgle than a word.

He stepped on her throat, pressing his heel into her larynx until
she stopped breathing. Another murder, another purse snatching,
another violent crime in the Big Easy. A Nawlins crime that happened
on average at least once a day.

33

'**W**arden Jakes, thanks for seeing me.'

The big man examined him from heavily lidded eyes, his swarthy face creased with time, tobacco and alcohol abuse.

'I'm doing you a major favor, here. What do you want, Detective . . .?' He left the sentence open.

'Archer,' Q replied.

'OK, Archer,' he missed the r's saying *Acha* like a true Southerner, and his gravelly, weathered voice came from deep in his chest. 'You threatened Trystan, our Miss Washington. And you're inside my house and I don't ever invite strangers in. Make this relevant or get the hell off this property. I've got enough manpower to make that happen, as I'm sure you are aware.'

'Warden, I'm simply here on a fact-finding mission. Your Trystan Washington played hardball with me, and I only returned the favor.' Archer wanted to get under his skin, irritate him a little. The idea was to catch someone off guard so they would say things they wouldn't in a civil conversation.

'Play hardball? She can do that, that one,' Jakes said.

The two men were quiet. Finally, 'Warden Jakes, we are trying to get to the bottom of Judge Lerner's death. We're all on the same page, right?'

'Lerner was shot, right?'

'He was.'

They were still standing, Archer and Jakes, face to face, and Archer could smell the stale odor of cigar on the man's breath.

'I don't know who killed him, I don't know why. I was not a close friend of the judge and I have nothin' else to add. Good day, Detective.'

'Warden Jakes, I have a photo taken of you and Judge Lerner, in front of his baby grand piano. Inside the judge's home. You look pretty friendly in that picture. In the background there's dozens of framed portraits of inmates from your prison.' He paused for effect.

'I'm not sure that constitutes a camaraderie, but it's a bit peculiar. Wouldn't you agree?'

Jakes scowled at him, his eyebrows tightly knit.

'Look, Warden Jakes, I'm just trying to get a handle on what kind of man Lerner was. If you would just—'

'I have nothin' further to add to this.'

'Lerner was dating Rodger Claim, am I correct?'

Jakes froze, his eyes wide open, his forehead creased like an accordion.

'Who told you that preposterous story?'

'Claim was head of the guard unit. He and Lerner were having an affair, and you obviously were friendly with the judge.' Staring at the warden, Archer added, 'And you employed Claim. So if you were not aware of a relationship, pardon my comment, you must have been a damned fool. Am I right?'

Jakes squinted, his eyes adding to a nasty frown.

'Detective, I resent that remark and I was not that damned friendly with your dead judge.'

'Hey,' Archer shrugged, 'I'm not suggesting anything, but the prison personnel seemed to be a big part of Lerner's life. I was hoping you could tell me more. Like where Claim is now.'

'Look, Archer, I have a big responsibility here.' He tugged on the collar of his white shirt, pulling it away from his massive neck. 'There are a number of people I deal with on a daily, weekly, monthly basis. Not to mention stockholders who are depending on – no, demanding a satisfactory report. One little pissant judge doesn't mean a hill of beans in the scope of things. As for Rodger Claim, he was running his own little shakedown here with the guards and inmates. I do not, sir, know his whereabouts, but I hope he's in hell.'

Jakes took a deep breath, studied Archer for a moment and nodded.

'I've been to the judge's house, I even went out with him for a drink one time when I was in town, but I don't really know the man, I don't really care about him, and I'm not broken up about the fact that someone shot him.'

'What do you care about?'

'Truthfully?'

'I'm always looking for the truth, Warden.'

Jakes gave him a subtle nod.

'Detective Archer, I care about justice. I care about these kids in this prison understanding that if they fuck up again on the outside, there will be hell to pay the rest of their lives.'

Jakes looked down on him. Probably six three or four, the warden towered over Archer's five ten frame.

'Warden Jakes, this may seem like an off the wall question, but do you remember a prisoner named Antoine Duvay?'

'Of course. He was on my personal detail. Kept the grounds, the vehicles. Good kid. Sure I remember him. Why? Is he involved?'

'That's debatable at this time,' Archer said. 'One more question, sir. What kind of car do you drive?'

'Car? What kind of a question is that?'

'Warden? I can walk out of here, and probably see your vehicle in the drive or garage. What kind of a car?'

'The cars are a perk.' He was obviously put off by the question. 'Part of my compensation, OK?'

'What kind of car do you drive?'

'Believe me, Detective, it's not relevant to anything you are involved in. I actually have three vehicles.'

'What am I going to see when I walk outside, Warden? You're right, it means nothing, but it's just something that intrigues me.'

Jakes shook his head in disgust.

'You walked up here. Did you see one of my vehicles? You are a piece of shit. With someone as inept as you, how the hell will they ever figure out who killed Lerner?'

'What kind of car do *you* primarily drive, Warden?'

'Give it up, Archer.'

The big man walked toward him, crowding Archer out of the door.

'Warden, this doesn't have to end on a sour note.' He turned, sensing the edge of the porch about two steps away.

'It does, Detective. You may be some hotshot in Nawlins, but here you are nothing more than a fucking gnat on my eyelash. Got it?'

'I got it.'

Archer stepped back onto the brick pavers that led up to the stately home. Jakes slammed the door and Quentin Archer turned and surveyed the driveway and three-car garage. Pretty fancy for a prison warden.

A young black man in prison garb stepped out from the garage, smiling ear to ear.

'Sir, can I help you with something?'

'You are?'

'Nathan, sir. Nathan Peterson.'

About sixteen years old, probably in for theft, or assault.

'What are you doing here, Nathan?'

'Sir?'

'You're obviously cleared for some kind of freedom and . . .'

'I'm on probation here, sir. I've been given the chance to reha-
bilitate myself. The warden and his staff have given some of us a
chance to work within the system and prove that we can survive in
the world outside. I take care of the grounds, the vehicles and other
things. What can I do for you, sir?'

'Are you familiar with Antoine Duvay?'

He thought for a moment. 'I may have heard his name mentioned.
Worked here, like me.'

Archer nodded.

'Can you tell me what cars are in the garage?'

'Sir?'

'Nathan. What cars does the warden own. It's a very simple
question.'

'Warden Jakes has a Ford F-150 pickup, a Chevy Malibu, and
his most requested car.'

'What is that, Nathan?'

'A Jaguar XK-E.'

Archer glanced toward the garage, not surprised at the answer.

'It's a looker, suh.'

'Yeah?'

'A beauty. Cream colored and all. You want to see?'

34

Solange Cordray was in a hurry. Washing her face in the
employees' locker facility, she glanced at her watch. Today
she was off at three, with a three thirty appointment and a
throwing of the bones. The client wanted information, not just a
spell, and the young practitioner had some rather uncanny ability
to find information, details about people's lives and what the future

held in store when she tossed the bones. She wasn't happy at all about the job. This man was evil. She felt it, believed it. This was the man she'd gone to Quentin Archer about.

The problem always was that she had a hard time saying no. It wasn't the money although the cash always came in handy. It was the fact that she felt everyone deserved a chance. But this guy . . . He was bad news.

She concentrated on the bones, the only things that last in this physical world. Even when cremated, bone fragments remained. Every living soul, man or animal, leaves a trace of itself through its skeletal remains. Every one. And throwing bones went back to the ancient faith of the Yoruba. All that was needed was the four bones and the casting map, with three sections representing earth, plant and animal. With just those items, the voodoo lady could tell her clients things that would change their lives. But only if those clients knew how to interpret. The trouble with bones, they often told of unpleasantness that the client had no control over. It was a mixed blessing to have this information, possibly information that you wish you had never received.

She once threw the bones for a young white woman who was the picture of perfect health. The small bone, the *imbay*, pointed to the same plant segment on the casting mat as the *scita*, the broken bone. Solange had turned to the woman and told her she would be dead in three days and there was nothing she could do about it. The lady had laughed at her.

Three days later the woman suffered a stroke and died hours later. Ghende, the gatekeeper spirit, ushered her into the cemetery two days later.

The voodoo practitioner vowed never again to be so harsh with her predictions. There were some forecasts better left untold.

Picking up her small clutch purse she exited the locker room and stepped into the long hallway that led to the lobby and exit. She dreaded the meeting. She should tell the man her suspicions and suggest that he change his ways. This from a lowly practitioner to a wealthy business executive.

'Hey, pretty baby.' Clarence the orderly blocked her way.

'Please, I'm in a hurry.'

'You avoid me like I'm the plague or somethin'.'

'Clarence, I have an appointment.'

'I'm thinkin' we need to hook up, sometime after hours. You catch my drift?'

Reaching out with his large hand he touched her arm and she recoiled.

'You think you're better than me, is that it? You're too good for Clarence? I treat your momma special, little lady. You do good by me, you understand, and I watch out for momma.' He reached for her again.

Deep down, somewhere in the bottom of her soul she felt it roiling, an intense heat rising through her loins, her intestines, her heart and into her feverish head. White-flecked spittle formed on her lips, and her breath became hot and heavy. There was a fire in her eyes, and her nostrils flared like an angry mare.

The voice was a low, animal growl, like that from a mother bear protecting her cub. 'Go away.'

He pulled his arm back.

'Go away and don't ever come back.' A voice from the bowels of hell. 'Leave this place and promise yourself that you will never again enter the doors of this establishment.'

The man's eyes were wide open in fear and amazement. He took one step back, then another and another.

As she stared at him, the heat of her eyes burning into his, the big man slowly sank to his knees, whimpering.

'Understand that if you come back, the wrath of Damballa will be on you like the stink of the undead.'

He nodded, staring at the floor as tears streamed down his cheeks. He never looked up.

As if it never happened, the voodoo lady took a deep breath, gathered her composure, turned and walked in measured strides down the hallway and out the door into the afternoon sunshine. The river, the Mighty Miss, rolled by and she smiled at it, feeling some kinship to its awesome power.

35

Archer stopped at the office and saw the note on his desk. Other than Detective Davis's signature, it simply said, 'See me. Immediately.' He'd been in charge of Judge Lerner's cell phone. Davis was working late, so it must be important.

'You seen Davis?' Dan Sullivan walked up to him.

'Just got in. I was down talking to the warden at—'

'Go see Davis. Now.'

'Let me clear a couple messages here and—'

'Archer, come with me.' He tapped his watch. 'When I say now, I mean now.'

The sergeant grabbed him by his elbow and propelled him down the hall to his small office where they found the black detective sitting on the edge of Sullivan's desk.

'Didn't know if you were coming back today or not. Tried your cell a number of times, but—'

'Turned it off at the prison.'

He'd turned it off and left it in the car, then forgotten to turn it on when he returned.

'What have you got? Phone numbers?'

'Oh, hell. We can beat phone numbers straight out of the gate.'

'Then what?'

'The lab dried it out. The man—'

Sergeant Sullivan interrupted. 'Lerner recorded his own abduction and murder.'

'He what?'

Davis held up a playback device. 'It's all on here, Q. Guys are named Skeeter and James, and they picked the judge up at his house. They beat him up, stuffed him in a car, drove to a warehouse and they shot him. Some of the conversation is a little muffled and the guys are still trying to un-garble parts, but we got most of it.'

'The judge. He recorded it?'

'On his phone.'

'Why didn't he just call 911?'

'I don't think he knew they were going to kill him until it was too late. By the time they would have responded, he'd have been toast anyway. This all happened in about twenty minutes. We figured out who Skeeter is,' Davis said, holding up a photograph. 'Guy named John Lewis, nicknamed Skeeter, a low-level punk who does contract work for some of the mob guys in town.'

'What mob?'

'Actually, any mob. But we figure that's the guy who actually killed him.'

'My God, that's unbelievable. Did Lerner convict this guy? Was it a grudge thing?'

'So far we can't tie them together.'

'Sergeant Sullivan, I think it goes a lot deeper than a simple murder. There are a lot of threads.'

'We get this Skeeter Lewis, we should get some answers.'

'Priority,' Archer said.

'One more thing,' Sullivan said. 'We haven't reached Adam Strand yet. You know your partner isn't going to be happy. He still thinks he's got this thing wrapped up. Hoping and praying.'

You *were hoping and praying*, Archer thought.

'Strand had Antoine Duvay locked up for the long haul,' Davis said.

'Not after this,' Sullivan shook his head. 'Now Strand might actually have to do some work on this case. He thought it was going to be an easy conviction.'

'So you could actually hear the gunshot?' Archer asked. 'On the recording? I mean, how often do you get that lucky?'

'You can hear it,' Davis smiled. 'Muffled but loud.'

'What else?'

'Well,' Sullivan picked up the player, 'we'll play it for you, but at the end, at the very end of the recording, about fifteen minutes after the gunshot, you can hear this Skeeter character. It sounds like they're opening the door of a vehicle and struggling to pull something out.'

'Lerner's body,' Archer said.

'Probably. Here, I'll just play the last couple seconds for you.'

He pushed a button and there was a whoosh of noise, the phone inside the dead man's pocket loudly rustling over the fabric of the judge's pants.

'It's coming up,' Davis said.

More rustling, and some muffled grunts as if the man or men who were carrying the body were struggling with the dead weight.

'Here it is,' Sullivan was grinning, like a kid at Christmas.

Archer strained to hear some words, but they were more like groaning sounds. Then someone said, 'Ready?'

Another voice mumbled something, and the last words Archer heard came out in almost a shout.

'*Adios*, motherfucker.'

A count of three and there was a loud splash. A moment later everything went dead.

'Jesus, there it is. They just threw the body into the river.'

Archer couldn't say he was shocked. He'd been certain that Antoine Duvay had been innocent of the killing. But, the kid had run. He'd been scared of something. And since Archer had learned that Duvay had been in charge of the warden's grounds and vehicles, he wondered. Wondered if the newly innocent Duvay was really that innocent.

Exactly half an hour from the time Solange left the center, her client entered the small shop on Dumaine Street. Her Ma's shop, she reminded herself. The place where Clotille Trouville had practiced her brand of voodoo, a place where the matronly figure felt she could heal the world. It was her dream, one person, one problem at a time. It was the same place her Ma had advised Earl Garrett, Solange's client's father.

In the small cluttered store, with the shelves of ragged dolls and *gris gris* bags for sale, in this tiny room with a bare-wood floor and faded posters advertising lotions and potions hanging from the plaster walls, she was entertaining a killer. She was sure of it. Ma would not approve. Absolutely no way.

An aging hand-painted wooden sign nailed to the counter read *All Payments Must Be Made Before Services Are Rendered*. It had been there as long as she could remember. Ma was strict about it. Pay before you play.

'What are we searching for today,' she asked, carefully studying his reaction. She was certain who he was, and there was that very strong vibe that he was up to no good. She'd convinced herself. No good at all.

The casting map was laid out on the rough wooden floor in the back room and her four bones lay on top of a worn leather pouch.

Picking them up, she warmed them in her hand, studying the man who took a seat in the old cane-woven chair next to her.

'There's a project, a plan in place that may have gotten out of control.'

'Can you be more specific?' She wanted details.

'No.'

'Very well.' She would try a different tactic. 'What information do you want from the bones?'

'A *gris gris* bag you gave me several months ago, a spell that you gave me, surprisingly they had the desired effect.'

'Surprisingly?' she asked, raising her eyebrows. She herself was never surprised. It was part of who she was and what she did. 'Your father always trusted in my mother's abilities. Why would you doubt me?'

'I meant no disrespect. I am not a firm believer, but it was powerful medicine.'

She nodded, rubbing the bones like a shooter at the casino rubs his dice. Tools of the trade. *Roll a lucky seven and your dreams come true. Roll a thirteen and . . .*

'Miss Cordray, I believe you have some amazing powers. And I do believe that you can peer beyond the normal. As you said, my father relied on your mother from time to time. I think you know what information I want from the bones. Am I right?'

She studied him, the lines in his face, the furrows in his brow. He carried a lot of worries. If the bones blessed him, he would consider it a license to go ahead with his plans. And if they cursed him, he would probably do the deed in spite of them.

'There is this project, and I am hoping that it will have a satisfactory ending. I am hoping that the results will be in my favor. Am I being too vague?'

She considered his words.

'You want to know if your project will be successful. For you?'

'Yes.'

She studied him, then examined the bones in her hand.

'And this project, it involves my ex-husband?'

Studying her, he clasped his hands together.

'Does that matter?'

'Does the project involve profit or financial gain?' *Lead him. Make him tell you the nature of this project.*

'Again, does it matter?'

'Of course. I wouldn't ask if it didn't.'

'Yes.'

'Is this project you speak of moral?'

'Define morality.'

'Does your project revolve around good and evil?'

The man took a deep breath. 'It has nothing to do with morality. It is a simple project and I want to know if it will be successful. If the bones tell me it will be successful, I will proceed. If they say no, then I will decide whether I need to pull the plug and—'

'Mr Garrett, I must know if this is a principled project.' Damn it. He was being coy, avoiding the question.

The man shook his head. 'I was under the impression that you could forecast the ongoing success or failure of my plan.'

'I can't forecast anything. If the spirits are listening, if they are watching and weighing in on the event, then they may show their favor or disapproval. It's all about the spirits. It has very little to do with me. I am but their vessel.'

'So? Ask them for me.'

'I must know where the plan or project as you called it sits on a moral compass. Is that so hard to tell me? Yes or no. That's all, Mr Garrett.'

Watching her hand as she slowly caressed the smooth small bones, he shook his head again.

'I think maybe we have come to a parting of the ways.'

'Because you can't answer my question?' she asked. She didn't want to lose him; she still needed answers.

'Because I want a simple answer and you' – he pointed his index finger in her direction – 'you won't give me a simple answer. You know about this project, don't you? You see it, and you cast judgment.'

Solange smiled at his choice of words. 'Mr Garrett, there are no simple answers. We would all like simple answers, but they don't exist. They never have. And, sir, it is not *my* answer to give. You haven't listened to me. The answers come from far greater powers.'

'Oh?'

'The *gris gris* bag that you felt helped your cause, the spell that was given to you, they had little to do with me.'

'And I thought they had everything to do with you.'

She shook her bowed head.

'The spirits that deal with grief, loneliness, riches and wealth, the spirits of good fortune and health and everything else that humans have need of, these spirits are the ones who determine your fate. Please, don't look to me for an answer. Again, I must emphasize, I am simply the intermediary.'

Garrett studied the map at his feet. Earth, plant and animal. He glanced at the yellowed bones in the young girl's hand.

And the voodoo girl knew in an instant. He'd figured it out. There was no need for an answer. He didn't want definitive proof about whether he was successful or not. There was no sport in those answers.

The man stood, reached into his front pocket and pulled out two twenties and a ten. He handed the three bills to Solange and quietly walked out the store, the small bell tinkling as the door slammed shut. All payments must be paid before services are rendered.

Solange looked at the casting map, then closing her eyes she tossed the bones, hearing them rattle on the oilcloth.

Opening her eyes she saw the result. Four bones, four different possibilities. And every possibility was bad. There was no way, absolutely no way that his project could work. Every answer was a strong negative, every combination a formula for failure. In her normal business life, the man should be warned. In this case, she was exhilarated. He couldn't succeed.

Glancing at the door she knew what her next step should be. Garrett had made his own decision. He no longer asked for the intervention of the spirit world, and that was his decision to make. Solange was tempting fate if she forced her perceptions upon him. She needed to be quiet and let nature run its course, no matter how violent, no matter how bad the situation. The spirits were in charge and a mere human couldn't control the future.

The voodoo lady picked up the three bills he'd given her, placed them in a brown envelope and tossed the envelope in a large copper dish. Picking up a box of wooden matches, she struck one and ignited the envelope. As it burned, the black smoke rose and she smiled.

Folding up the map and putting her bones back in their pouch, she stored them and thought about the safety of her mother. If

Clarence didn't follow her direction and leave the employ of the center, she would kill him. She wasn't sure how, but realized that death could be the outcome. Maybe there *was* a spell for killing someone. She'd have to study that. And that possibility didn't bother her at all.

36

He woke up when a rooster crowed outside his window, the same window someone had tried to pry open with a knife. Had it been a drunk from the Quarter who thought no one was home? Not likely, although there were always strange characters out in the evening. Maybe a burglar who prayed on the area, knowing a lot of tourists who rented would be on the town? He didn't think so. He'd taken the broken knife blade to the lab. They had classified it as low priority, but he'd check with them in a couple of days. There was a chance they could match some prints.

He took a cup of instant coffee out to his miniscule front porch, listening to the early sound of the Quarter waking up, or for some, finally calling it a night.

Something told him the window incident involved Detroit. In the back of his mind he could hear and see Jason, his youngest brother. Jason, the one with the scraggly facial hair and the slight stutter, who just before he left had threatened Quentin's life.

He'd told him that until Brian Archer was free and Q was dead, he would haunt his oldest brother. Told him to his face. To be fair, Quentin Archer had tormented his younger siblings when they were children. Made them do his chores, even his homework. He'd just never figured that his kid brother, the young punk Jason, would go this far.

Jason and Brian Archer, his blood relations, but as distant as the ends of the earth. They'd become drug dealers who had hooked up with a very obliging Bobby Mercer, a Detroit cop who had creative ways of making money on the side. Bobby, still a respected cop, was a legend to the underworld. And the DPD refused to deal with it.

When Q had finally had enough, he'd gone to his father and

asked what *he* would do. The retired sergeant told him to relax. This was family and the boys would find their way eventually. Archer gave the old man token peace, but when the drug dealing escalated and a city councilman who was leading a probe into police involvement was found drowned in the Detroit River, he acted.

His department ignored him, siding with Bobby Mercer. His family shunned him, siding with Brian and Jason; and when Denise Archer, the love of his life, was the victim of that hit-and-run, Quentin Archer decided he'd suffered enough. Witnesses claimed they saw the driver chase the woman, coming up on the sidewalk with a Chevy sedan to make sure she was hit. The body was battered and broken when they finally cleared the scene. No one had seen the license plate number. Not until Tom Lyons and friends started a search for cameras. Archer would never get over that horrible afternoon. It had left him a broken man. The sorrow of losing his wife drove him from his home. But he hadn't forgotten. Her picture was by his bed, next to a cold, colorless framed photo of the street corner where she'd been killed. He needed to remember every day.

The rogue cop Bobby Mercer continued to prowl the streets of the Motor City, using his uniform and position as a license to earn a second income. Archer's brother Brian was convicted and was doing six months for a minor distribution charge. Jason, who had a larger sentence hanging over his head, had left town under cover and no one seemed to know his whereabouts. Quentin had a good idea of where his brother might be. But there were a lot of places to hide in New Orleans. And with the number of cases Archer was covering, he didn't have time to look. Not right now.

Finishing the coffee, he walked to Canal, grabbed the streetcar and followed the line to his stop, walking the rest of the way to work.

'Where the hell have you been, Detective? Everyone has been trying to reach you. What? You don't ever turn your phone on? There's no excuse for that.'

'Sergeant Sullivan, good to see you too. What's up?'

'Jesus, Archer, you're really clueless? Please, talk to your partner.'

As if on cue, Strand walked up to them, a sheaf of papers in his hand.

'A little news on the judge scene, Q. You seriously haven't heard? Are you shitting me?'

Archer shook his head. 'Everyone, settle down. We know that Duvay didn't kill Lerner. Is that what this is about? This guy named Skeeter?'

Strand gave him a long look.

'Really? That's the best you've got?'

Archer studied his partner for a moment.

'Strand, I'm sorry your suspect didn't pan out, but . . .'

'That's what you think this is about? That a suspect gets a free pass? Where the hell have you been?'

'Yeah. That's what I thought this was about.'

'Man, you're in for a long morning,' Strand said. 'We've got a shitload of problems, partner.'

They sat in Sullivan's office, Strand with his feet propped up on an extra chair. Archer was shell-shocked by the unfolding development. He couldn't believe it; he hadn't really thought they were in any danger.

'One automobile accident, one supposed robbery. Both judges that you'd interviewed, Archer. There's no way this was a coincidence, Detective. Not when the victims are all juvie judges and not when the crimes have been committed in this compressed time frame,' Sullivan said, almost accusatorially. 'They're dead, man. What the hell is going on, Archer? You're closer than anyone to this. What the fuck is going on?'

'The press also making the assumption that all three murders are related?' Archer said.

'They are,' Sullivan said. 'Channel Six led with it and the *Times-Picayune* has it online. It's early. Everyone will tee up on this, and we're still standing here with our thumbs up our asses. Plus, the *Advocate* is again saying we're totally incompetent. Especially after that news conference yesterday. We haven't looked this bad since Katrina.'

Strand sat across from him, a grim look on his face and his fists clenched tight.

'NBC news has called, Fox has a satellite truck outside, CNN is in the building, and the lieutenant is ready to come unglued. It's just the beginning, Q. We stand the chance of being the number one news story in the country tonight. The *country*, for God's sake. Forget the *Advocate*.'

Archer was still processing. Just when he thought things were possibly coming together . . .

'And we still can't tie it up,' Strand said. 'Lerner was a message. Judge Lerner's murder was a statement. Absolutely no question about that. Man, you blow a guy's eye out; it's a signal to someone. If this person or this group is so obvious with the first judge, why would they disguise the second and third murder? Try to make them look unconnected? Unless it's not the same killer. Doesn't have to be, does it? I mean, maybe the other two are totally unrelated, but what a coincidence. Of all the coincidences in the world . . .'

'Yeah, Lerner's death was meant to send a message,' Archer said, winging it. 'You're right about that. But whoever is orchestrating this plot decided the message didn't get through. They put a bullet through Lerner's brain but there was still some suspicion about these two judges, Hall and Warren. They were obviously afraid that Traci Hall and Richard Warren were liabilities, that those two knew something and they might talk.'

'You interviewed them. You didn't pick up any vibes?' Sullivan asked.

Archer took a deep breath.

'You don't want to hear this, but we are still in the beginning of this case. Warren was afraid of something. Very defensive of his harsh sentences. Hall? She was defending them as well, but from an entirely different perspective.'

'Any other observations, Q?'

'My observation was that Warren was a tough guy. He seemed to be of the same mindset as Lerner. And he seemed to be afraid of me. And he didn't like being questioned.'

'Traci Hall?' Sullivan asked.

'Knew more than she was telling me. Seemed to sense that Warren and Lerner were a little devious, but never said why. She told me someone was after her, but she wouldn't elaborate.'

'And that's it? We've got two more dead judges and that's all you've got?' He shook his head. 'Anyway,' Sullivan continued, 'this time they decided to just get rid of those two judges. Make it look like an auto accident. Make it look like a purse snatch. No message this time. I mean, if they blatantly killed them, bullet in the brain, we'd tie it all together immediately. So, rather than use drama, they decided to plant doubt about the way they died. It is entirely possible that an erratic driver accidentally cut Warren off, am I right? And a purse snatcher could have killed Traci Hall. Right now, we can't prove that they were premeditated murders. Right now, they aren't related, no matter how much pressure we get from the press.'

'And the lieutenant, the chief, the mayor and governor,' Strand said. 'Just a *little* pressure there.'

'By the way, we did cut Duvay loose.' Sergeant Sullivan changed the topic. 'I talked to Adam' – he nodded at Strand – 'and there is no longer any reason to hold the young man. We're pretty sure that this Skeeter Lewis character and his friend James killed Lerner. I don't think we'll have a hard time proving that. And there's an APB out on John "Skeeter" Lewis. We get him, we'll get his partner in crime. We can only hope that Lewis killed all three judges. Things would be a lot cleaner.'

'Or,' Archer said, 'at least he will connect us with who killed the other two judges. If they're related.'

'I'm going to tell you, Archer, I've been here eighteen years. I've seen the worst. Hell, I've been through Katrina. This is uncharted territory, even for New Orleans. And right now? When the Feds are meddling, trying to get some major reforms through here, I mean . . .' he tailed off.

'So we're still the priority?'

'Priority?' His eyes were budging. 'Are you kidding me? There is no other priority, Archer. Two more judges have been killed. We've got another detective who's walked off the force.' Throwing his arms up he said, 'This is beyond any situation I can remember. My understanding is the governor may make a statement tomorrow. Hell, this could go to the White House. The president. For God's sake, get to the bottom of this situation. Do you understand me? Three fucking juvie justices in less than a week.'

'Witnesses at these locations have been interviewed?'

'Hell yes, but interview 'em again,' Sullivan was crisp and to the point.

'Sites investigated?' Archer was crossing off a list he'd made.

'Yes, yes, but do it again. Find out who the hell is killing these juvenile court judges. I can't be more serious.'

'Security?' Archer kept asking.

'We're not idiots here, Archer. This isn't Detroit.'

It hurt, but he had a point.

'As of one hour ago, every existing juvenile judge has a patrolman assigned to them. Every one. Twenty-four/seven. They can't take a piss without an armed guard standing beside them. You want to talk about stretching the money in a budget that has no more elasticity? That is manpower that we can't afford.'

'I'm not sure he could have done much about it, but I did warn Warren about—'

'Don't remind me,' Sullivan said. 'Of course I remember. The guy accused you of harassment. Man, this thing has got be over soon, Q. We're in deep shit right now. We can't afford the black eye, we can't afford the community backlash and last but not least, we can't afford this period.'

Strand and Archer stood up, heading toward the door.

'You report directly to me on any new lead. Everything, understood?' Sullivan stood in the center of the room, arms folded. 'We have another judge killed and we're all going to lose our jobs.'

37

Counting down the seconds on his watch, he dialed exactly at 10 a.m.

'Hello.' The voice sounded tired.

'I've got more information on the murdered judge.'

'What now?'

'They're letting the ex-con go. There's a recording of the killing.'

'A what?'

'A recording. The judge recorded it on his phone. They've got a pretty good idea of exactly how it happened and who did it. Guys named John Lewis and James Gideon.'

A long slow exhale. 'Any tie-ins with these guys? To Krewe Charbonerrie or anything else in the mix?'

'No. It just changes the entire direction.'

'Nothing else?'

'I'll call the minute anything else breaks.'

'You do that. We'll make it worth your while.'

38

D etective Levy met him as he walked into the bullpen.

'Q, got a question.'

'Yeah?' He needed more input, more questions. Nothing at this point was coming together and it had to happen at warp speed. He felt the pressure in every heartbeat.

'We found a file box inside Lerner's Jag,' Levy said.

'OK.' Possibly more evidence. 'And?'

'Well,' Levy said, 'we found printouts, like spreadsheets. A whole pile of them. And they've got a series of numbers running next to each other. Two sets of numbers.'

'And what do these numbers represent?' Archer asked.

'I was hoping you could give us some ideas.'

'Let's see them.'

Walking down to Levy's desk, they passed Strand's station. The detective was not present. Probably off on a fact-finding mission of his own. Or working one of his side businesses. Archer was starting to wonder if the man was any help at all.

Reaching his desk, Levy pulled out a double-spaced sheet from the box and handed it to Archer. There were two columns of numbers displayed next to each other, probably forty to a page. No explanation. At the top of the left-hand column on the first page was the number 42981-201; next to it at the top of the right-hand column appeared the number 2000. Nothing more. Two spaces below, 38012-406 was printed in the left column; 2000 in the right. The pattern continued down the page, onto the next, and there appeared to be at least twenty-five pages in the file box.

'What do you think?'

'Have you run it up on a computer? See if there's any correlation between the two numbers?'

'Yeah. We ran it on Code Compare and a number of other programs. However, other than they're both whole numbers between one and one hundred thousand? Nothing. Because while the 2000 stays pretty constant in the right-hand column of each page, the numbers in the left-hand column are all different.'

Archer's brain was going in a thousand directions. Worst time in the world to do some concentrated thinking.

Levy put the sheet back in the file box.

Something about these numbers was familiar. Archer closed his eyes for a second.

'Levy, pull up the pictures on your phone. The one where Lerner is standing in front of his piano with the warden.'

Detective Levy grabbed his phone and with a few deft strokes turned the screen to Archer.

'This one?'

'Yeah. Look at the photos behind them. Numbers scrawled on every one.'

'Well, yeah. We guessed they are prisoner numbers. Their identification when they were in River Bend Prison. He'd scrawled them on the photos with a Sharpie.'

'Exactly. They're too small to see what they are. See if you can blow those numbers up and compare them to your spreadsheets. Left upper corner. I would bet that the numbers on those sheets correspond to juvie prisoners' numbers. The right-hand number, I don't know. Let's find out if I'm right. Left upper corner. Blow that photo up till you can read the numbers and run them.'

'Almost all of the right-hand-corner numbers are 2000. Some have the number 3000 and some 1000 and 4000. But you're telling me the left-hand numbers, the ones that are all different, you really think these are the prisoners' numbers?' Levy asked.

'I'd stake my reputation on it.'

Levy stood back and gave Archer a long look.

'You're reputation?'

'My reputation.'

'Detective Q, I know a little bit about you. Very little, but—'

'Yeah?'

'Yeah. No insult meant.'

'And?'

'Excuse me for saying this but your reputation isn't that great.'

Archer gave him a wry smile. The detective was right.

*   *   *

Twenty minutes later they had examined fifty of the numbers on the photos. Each matched numbers on the upper left-hand side of the spreadsheet. But not one number had any correlation to the number on the upper right-hand column.

Half right, thought Archer.

'Their prison number. I can't believe I didn't think of that. I'd forgotten about those numbers on the photos.' Levy whacked his head with the palm of his hand.

'But the other number, maybe it's a classification? The 2000 group, the 3000 group and so on. Maybe it's a code for the length of their sentence.'

The detectives stared at each other for several moments.

'What the hell does it all mean?' Levy asked. 'Why did Lerner keep these?'

'By God, we're going to find out,' Archer replied.

'Three judges now, Q.'

'You don't have to remind me.'

'Do you buy into the idea that all the deaths are related?'

'It has nothing to do with my "buying into it".'

'Yeah, it sort of does. You're the lead on this. Is there a vendetta on the juvie judges? What the hell did those three do? Apparently they either pissed someone off, or threatened to do so.'

Archer was silent for a moment. If he had the answer, he'd solve the case. What the hell *did* all of those three do? Better yet, what did those three know? Did they have information that determined their fate? Information that they took to the grave? Because all three were going to their grave. And the other common thread didn't escape him. Two of them had been interviewed by him.

Archer shrugged his shoulders and walked back to his desk. Strand was nowhere to be seen. He'd admitted that he did some side jobs for some important people in the city, possibly members of Krewe Charbonerrie. Strand had admitted to Archer that he may be involved in getting these power players information, and as much as Archer considered asking that Strand be removed from the case, he'd seen the effect of whistle-blowing on another officer. It destroyed his life in Detroit.

'Oh, Q, the lady is supposed to be here in about thirty minutes. You want to sit in on the interview?'

'Lady?'

'Lerner's neighbor. I interviewed her and she saw the black Escalade. Remember? You asked for a follow-up interview.'

'Yeah, yeah. Of course, include me. God, we need some new information.'

'I don't think she's going to remember much. Didn't when I talked to her, but . . .'

'Call me as soon as she shows. An eyewitness is golden, Levy. Even when they think they didn't see anything, they did.'

39

Nancy Olds showed up, her fiery red hair mimicking her personality. They moved her into a conference area and brought her bottled water.

'I watch everything that goes on down my street,' she stated emphatically. 'I mean, someone has to pay attention. We get a lot of wackos who visit our neighborhood, a lot of weirdos, and most of my neighbors either work or are not interested in who invades our space. I'm the watchdog, Detectives. Someone has to be.'

'Mrs Olds,' Levy nodded at her, 'on the afternoon in question, what did you observe happening on Judge Lerner's driveway?'

'Told you before, Detective, I happened to glance out of my kitchen window and saw a young man in a T-shirt and jeans confronting the judge.'

'Confronting?' Levy asked.

'Feet about three feet apart, arms folded over his chest. I would say he was confronting the judge. Yes. I would.'

'You could see this from your window? The man with arms folded? The confrontational attitude?'

'I'd be more than happy to bring you to my home and show you my window,' the lady said. 'I have a great view.'

'So what transpired?'

'Detective, I already told you. There was a conversation that obviously I was not privy to. They seemed to be arguing, back and forth. Then, a black Cadillac Escalade pulled into the drive. Usually these cars, they pull into his drive, back out and leave. This one didn't. The car sat there for four or five minutes. I remember watching the clock on my microwave.'

'Cadillac Escalade?' Archer asked.

'It was. Damned if it wasn't. Shut off my view entirely. I couldn't see anything that was happening. That car blocked all the activity.'

Archer glanced at Levy.

'You didn't happen to notice the license plate number?'

'No.' She seemed almost indignant. 'If I was sure of the license number, I would have told you.'

'Too bad. It would help our case,' Archer said. 'Are you sure you can't remember some of the numbers, letters?'

'Well, our house is not close enough to see details like that, although as the car passed my house I did notice *some* of the numbers. I did jot those numbers down. Nothing concrete, Detective. It all happened rather quickly, and I didn't know how important this information might be.'

Archer swallowed a smile.

'Yes, ma'am?'

'The first three were one-two-four, then an eight; I couldn't see if there was anything in between. The last letter was B, but there was mud obscuring the space between the eight and the B.'

'Was that it? Are you sure?'

'Of course I am, Detective. I have excellent eyesight.'

Levy excused himself and walked out of the room to check Mrs Olds's information against registrations. Time was of the essence.

'Well, thank you for coming in, Mrs Olds.' Archer reached out and shook her hand. 'It's observant citizens like you who help us solve crimes and bring criminals to justice. And we sincerely appreciate all of your cooperation. Keep looking out your window and let us know if you see anything else suspicious.'

'I try to do what's right,' the woman said as she rose from the chair. 'There's been so much activity at that house recently, I can't keep track of it.'

'I'll walk you out,' Archer said.

'Are they selling the property?'

'I have no idea, ma'am. Don't even know who is the next of kin.'

'My husband was interested. Said it would make a good investment property, once the story settles down.'

Archer nodded, reaching the exit.

'Detective, there's one more thing that I found a little strange.'

'What is that?'

'Well, not more than three minutes after the black Cadillac left the house, another car drove down the street and pulled into Judge Lerner's driveway. Then I saw that car drive up again when the police were at the house later.'

Archer nodded. 'You mentioned this happens frequently. Vehicles come down to the dead end assuming it's a through street.'

'Oh, it does,' she said. 'However, this was a little different, and very strange.'

'How's that?'

'The car was a cream-colored Jaguar XK-E. Same exact car as the judge owned. It was like he was pulling into his driveway. Only Judge Lerner's garage door was still up and his Jag was still in the garage.'

'Did you get the plates on that car as well?'

'I have them written down on my calendar,' she said.

40

Jonathon Gandal took a sip of his coffee, then a gulp.

'Will you be ordering breakfast, sir?' The black waiter stared accusingly at Gandal, his lip curled. The coffee crowd did not tip well and he didn't want to waste his time on this guy.

'Maybe,' he answered. 'Someone is meeting me and I guess we'll decide then. Thank you.'

The waiter walked away in disgust.

Gandal looked out the window, across the street. Just a block and a half away was the muddy Miss, and he almost wished he was on a riverboat, headed downstream. He turned and watched the door of the Mississippi River Bottom, where his boss had asked for the meeting.

Things were shaky at the moment. His situation was not as positive as it had been just a week ago. Looking out at the gray bank of rain clouds over the Mississippi River he shuddered, worried not only about the stormy weather front but his own stormy future. He'd simply followed orders, hadn't he? How those situations had transpired wasn't his fault.

'Jonathon.'

'Mr Garrett.'

Richard Garrett, impeccably attired in pearl-gray slacks, a soft, white silk shirt and royal blue silk necktie sat down across from him.

Garrett smiled as a second waiter in a bow tie brought him a cappuccino.

'How are things, John?'

As if nothing was wrong.

'Fine, sir. I mean, we've had some setbacks, but—'

'This is your definition of fine? This is what you consider "setbacks"?' He slapped his palm down on the table, rattling the coffee cup.

Garrett wore a sarcastic grin as he folded his hands in front of him. Speaking softly he said, 'We sent a warning, execution-style, telling people to shut up. We got rid of the judge who was going to go public with our business. We sent a message that if anyone talked, if they gave anything away, the same thing could happen to them. Isn't that what we did?'

'Yes, sir.'

'And what happened, Gandal?' Garrett's intensity increased but he kept his voice low, sinisterly quiet. 'All of a sudden these other judges are lined up to give their opinions. They can't wait to talk to the cops. Apparently that warning we sent didn't do a damned bit of good, did it?' He inhaled, seemingly getting more energy from the smell of the fresh-brewed cappuccino.

Garrett leaned forward, his elbows on the table and his chin resting in his folded hands. 'So the decision by you and the board was to get rid of the ones who might talk. The solution was to eliminate two more of the judges, one who was involved and one who knew what was happening and was possibly getting ready to talk to the cops. Ones who were likely to give information to this Quentin Archer. And now, since these two judges come to tragic endings within minutes of each other, there's no question that this is a plot. Did it not occur to you, Gandal, that killing two judges in a matter of minutes might raise suspicion from the police? Jesus.' He spread his hands on the table. 'The cops are all over this. This thing could, probably will, explode in our face, Gandal.'

'Mr Garrett, I . . .'

'You're shit, Jonathon Gandal. You're literally shit. There's going to be more law enforcement scrutiny on this case than any I can think of in modern times. And the sad thing is, this part of our establishment, this portion of our business that you are involved in isn't even that big of a deal. Do you understand? We make a lot of money, yes, maybe twenty million, but the money we make on this one project isn't worth the hassle, John. Lives have been taken, lives have been put at risk, and for a very small part of what we are about. I do not intend to gamble the Krewe's future on this incident. Do you understand?'

'Sir, I am sorry, but there were others involved in the—'

'You're sorry? You certainly are, Jonathon. You are fucking sorry. But that's another matter. Right now I need some solutions.' Garrett's hands were now pressed together, a stern look on his face.

'We made the deaths appear to be accidents. No one can prove that they weren't just accidents.' Gandal was sticking to his guns.

'Yes, you did. Both deaths appeared to be accidental. Someone cut off on the road and a purse snatching with an unfortunate ending. Accidents. I agree that you tried. But you also had someone kill those two at almost the exact same time. A little too convenient. And three juvenile judges in less than a week? Come on, man. You invited trouble.'

'Regardless of who's at fault, what are we going to do?'

'How many people are involved, John?' Garrett's voice was hushed, a low whisper. 'Besides you and your contact, how many were actually involved?'

Gandal glanced around the room, wondering how many people knew. He had to go with what his contact had told him.

'The man said that probably two people were responsible for each death. So, four people may have been involved.'

'OK, so there are five people, five including your contact, who were intimately involved in the killing of the two judges, am I right?'

'Yes.'

'And your contact, the fifth person, he doesn't know who you represent?'

Gandal shook his head, speaking in a hushed voice. 'God, no. He has no idea. I've never mentioned anyone to him. I cut the check from a place we own, the Blue Bayou Restaurant in Metairie.

Ownership is buried so it would take years to trace it to us. Our contact uses a seafood company front to cash it. The bank account only lasts for a few days.' Shaking his head, he continued. 'I don't know who he hires or how he pays them. There's no way Blue Bayou can be tied back to us. It's a dead end. I swear to you, Mr Garrett. There's no way this gets back to you or the Krewe.'

Garrett stared at the serpent tattoo on his wrist and considered the immediate chain for a moment.

'There's always a way, Gandal.'

'No. No. No. There are layers of privacy, secrecy. We covered every base.' The man was sweating.

'So those two involved in the death of Judge Lerner, they know nothing of the Krewe, myself or the board?' Garrett's voice was harsh, a whisper but a harsh whisper. 'You're sure about this?'

'They only know our contact person. They don't know who I am or what I represent. They have no knowledge of the Krewe. So you see, we're clean. We are in no danger of being discovered.'

Garrett stared at him for a moment. The number of people involved was almost unmanageable. Two people for every killing plus a director, and then there were those that Gandal didn't even know about. The board, along with Warden Russell Jakes and the investor Joseph Cordray. He shook his head. Jakes, Cordray, they were relatively safe confidants. As were the three members of the board. Again a safe bet, but what about that voodoo lady. The cute girl who threw the bones and cast spells, the ex-wife of Joseph Cordray. He'd almost handed her the entire situation. Somewhat naive of him. Did she have a clue? About her ex? About him? Garrett closed his eyes for a moment, trying to see the solution. Solange Cordray. She was dangerous. He'd trusted her advice, and even though he'd been secretive, this woman had the power to know more than anyone had told her. The girl could very easily know what his mission was. She was a witch. Not to be trusted. He'd been a fool to go to her for advice, and her ex-husband had subtly warned him time and time again. Joseph Cordray had warned Garrett to stop seeing her but he hadn't paid attention.

'No danger, Mr Garrett. No way this is traced back to the Krewe, to me.'

Jonathon Gandal wiped his brow with a napkin. Garrett watched, realizing it wasn't *that* warm in the room.

'Gandal, I think you are an idiot to believe that. What if I were to tell you that not only the Krewe was being mentioned at homicide, but my name as well?'

Gandal shook his head. 'Sir, let me say something. First of all, I am not thrilled with your depiction of me as an idiot, and in defense of my position, I did exactly what the board asked me to do. As far as I know, I did exactly what *you* asked me to do, lines of communication being what they are. Secondly, if the homicide department is mentioning you or the Krewe, it did not, I emphatically repeat: it did not come from this end.'

Garrett was quiet for a brief moment, as if collecting his thoughts. Was it the girl? Had she gone deep into his mind and seen that he and the Krewe were behind the killing? He believed and didn't believe. Maybe the voodoo lady was behind the information.

'You're quite certain that this contact you have, the one who sets up everything, has no idea of our organization?' It was redundant but he had to ask one more time.

Gandal took a gulp of his cold coffee. 'I can't emphasize this enough, Mr Garrett. What do you want me to say? None of the participants knows anything. They accepted a contract, did their job and were paid. I'm the only one who met with our primary contact and I feel certain he said nothing to the others. These people,' he paused, 'they are scum of the earth. They make money any way they can. There is no concern about where it comes from. They simply accept a job and see it through completion. Contract killers. That's all they are.'

'Who is the contact person?'

'But you wanted to keep a distance from the start—'

'Who is the contact person?' His voice was firm.

'I don't know his real name. He works out of Shreveport and we found him after inquiring with Sam Campari. Campari has done some jobs for us in the past. Nothing like,' he paused, looking around the small restaurant, 'killing someone, but Campari is connected and—'

'What's the contact's name?'

'They call him Loup-garou.'

Garrett gave him a puzzled look.

'My understanding is that it means *Werewolf* in French.'

'Campari knows where the man is?'

Gandal took a long, exasperated breath.

'When I contacted Campari, he just told me that this contact—'

'Loup-garou?'

'Yes, that he would contact me. He did and we set up the Lerner incident. I called Campari a second time when it was decided we needed two accidents. The Werewolf visited me again.'

Garrett shook his head. 'Jesus, another person to deal with. You don't think that this Campari character has figured out that every time he contacts this crazy wolf that a judge dies? Hell, this wolf guy sounds more dangerous than anyone.'

'Sir, I don't know what else I could have done. Do it myself? Bypass the middle man.'

Sipping the cappuccino, Garrett closed his eyes, as if in a deep trance. Finally he opened them, reaching up and tightening his necktie. *Do your own dirty work.* Sounded like a mantra.

'Yeah, do it yourself. Bypass the middle man. Maybe that's the way it should have been done.' He stared through Gandal. 'That's brilliant, Gandal. Brilliant. You should have done it yourself.'

Richard Garrett was silent for a moment. For a long moment.

'I've been seeing a . . .' he paused, weighing his words, 'a therapist. Not really a therapist. Well, someone who walks me through situations. I can't explain it exactly but I've relied on this person for personal advice. Do you understand?'

Gandal shrugged his shoulders.

'Anyway, I've had some good fortune with this person's advice. She, this lady, has given me some very good advice and made some things happen. I'm convinced of that. Pretty amazing. This last time I met with her I asked her for advice again. I asked her if I was on the right track.'

'And?'

'And I realized there are some decisions a person has to make on his own. There are times when you can't rely on others to solve your problems. So I left her, without ever hearing her advice. I didn't care anymore what other people thought. You have reinforced my feeling. At times it's better just to do it yourself.'

'And your point is?'

'I'm inclined to agree with you,' Garrett said.

'I did that, sir. It's exactly what I did. I hired the right people who did the right job.'

'So you take full responsibility for what happened?'

Gandal wrapped his hands around the coffee mug, squeezing tightly. He stared at the table then raised his head and gazed into Garrett's eyes.

'I did what I thought I was being asked to do. I did what I felt was right. These judges were a threat. You know it, everyone knew it.'

'The way you did the job, the consequences . . .'

'I will not apologize,' Gandal said. 'Won't do it, sir. It needed to happen, and it needed to happen now. There's no blueprint as to how these things work. You know what I mean? And I certainly wasn't going to do *that* by myself. That's asking a little too much, don't you think?'

Garrett nodded, pushing his chair back and standing up.

'Thank you for understanding,' Gandal said.

'You do understand,' Garrett said, 'that this Sam Campari and Loup-garou do know who you are?'

'I'm not certain that—'

'Oh, they know. You've talked with them, met with them. And chances are they know you work for me.'

'I'm not certain that—'

'They're not stupid people, Gandal.'

'And I am?'

'Maybe I'm the one who's stupid,' Garrett said. 'I turned this over to you and let this get way out of hand.'

Gandal glowered and said nothing.

'I am beginning to believe very strongly that you made a good point.' He took a deep breath and let it out. 'I'll walk you out.' Garrett put down a twenty on the table and walked out of the restaurant, Gandal by his side.

41

M ike wiped down the bar. Maybe a hundred times a day, five days a week for the past fifteen years. Three hundred ninety thousand times he'd cleaned the bar end to end. Damn. That was a lot of cleaning. But different people, different drinks, different dishes at each station, different personalities. That's what kept the job fresh.

'Hey, Mike.'

'Hey, beautiful lady. What brings you in today?' He'd never seen her before. He was sure of it.

'Mike, how fresh are the crawfish?'

Smiling at her, he kept wiping the bar. 'They were swimming this morning.'

'Mr Mike, you are involved in the unexpected death of the judge? The judges?'

He pulled up short. 'Involved? No. Interested, yes. Do you have information?'

The girl was about twenty-two and her brown hair fell below her eyebrows.

'Are you willing to pay?'

Mike smiled weakly. 'A free meal, a drink or two. I'm not a cash-for-info guy.'

She shrugged. Glancing to her right and left, she leaned forward and said, 'Krewe Charbonnerie. They had a hand in the killings. I was told to report this to you.'

Mike looked into her green eyes, her soul.

'Is there a name of a member of that Krewe?'

'Garrett. Richard. Now, I understand there is at least a drink and meal involved? Am I correct?'

The bartender swallowed his response. Richard Garrett was headline news. A capitalist among capitalists. An entrepreneur among entrepreneurs.

'There's a chance you could have gotten the name wrong?'

She smiled at him, blinking her eyes.

'No. There is no chance. Can I please have my drink and crawfish?'

42

G andal's car was half a block down the street and they walked quietly for a minute, Garrett keeping his head bowed low.

'Can you drop me off at an address on Canal?' Garrett asked.

'Certainly.' Gandal opened the driver's door. Garrett opened the rear door of the Lincoln Navigator and got in.

'I like the back seat,' he said to Gandal.

'Yes, sir.'

The maroon leather upholstery still smelled new and the heavily tinted windows kept the hot sun at bay.

As Gandal put the key in the ignition Garrett slipped off his tie and with a quick flip of his wrist looped the blue silk over Gandal's head. Pulling back as the tie reached the man's throat he jerked it, tightening and pulling with all his strength. The driver's head was flat against the headrest as Garrett kept pulling, harder and harder. As the tie collapsed the man's trachea, Garrett heard Gandal let out a strangled cry, reaching back with his hands, trying in vain to pull the tie from his neck to relieve the pressure. His weak effort gave Garrett more hope.

Richard Garrett pulled even harder, surprised at his own strength, his knuckles turning white. Gandal kicked his legs, almost as a reflex, furtively, then not as strong. His body convulsed, tremors running through his frame. Garrett could see Gandal's face in the rear-view mirror, swelling from the pressure, turning a shade of purple.

Finally, Gandal's clawing hands dropped to his sides and Garrett kept up the pressure for another thirty seconds. His victim needed to be dead. Only when Gandal's last breath was exhaled did Garrett release his grip.

When you want something done right, do it yourself. He'd heard it dozens of times and never really understood how true the statement was. *Do it yourself. Get rid of the middle man.* And it hadn't been that hard. Garrett was shaking, just slightly, the tremor mostly in his hands, but he'd learned something about himself today, and it felt good to know he could kill someone when the moment called for it. A man needed to know his potential and know his limitations. Another barrier had been breached and he was stronger because of it.

And as he sat there, gathering himself, collecting his thoughts, catching his breath, he wondered about the Voodoo Queen. The sexy, attractive young woman who cast spells for him and made his life easier. Did he believe in black magic? Of course he did, as did his father before him. And if he believed that she knew secrets, could implore spirits to give her mystical powers, then he believed it was possible she knew more than she admitted. She was aware of his every move. He felt it. At their last meeting, when she was ready to throw the bones, she'd asked him if his purpose was a moral purpose, practically accused him of committing a crime. She knew. And her ex-husband, Joseph, heavily invested in the project, he wondered again if she knew how far he was involved. She had her suspicions, he knew that much.

And then he was sure. She knew all right.

Maybe she was someone who needed to be dealt with. The situation needed to be addressed. And now that *he* knew he couldn't trust anyone else from the outside to take care of his business, it was down to him. How many people needed to be dealt with? Some serious thought had to be given to how many more lives were to be taken. No lackeys this time. He needed to re-evaluate the people who were involved.

Garrett unbuttoned his right shirtsleeve, using the cuff to wipe down the parts of the car that he'd touched, and he glanced out the dark windows. It would be almost impossible for anyone to have seen the murder, and even if they'd looked directly into the windows of the car the tint job was enough to block any long-range view. He was buoyed up with confidence, a new awareness of himself.

He smoothed out his wrinkled tie, then, looking in the Lincoln's rear-view mirror, he placed it back around his neck and tied it in a perfect Windsor, the entire time looking at Gandal's pale face, eyes wide open, staring at the roof.

The oil magnate opened the door, exited on the sidewalk side and quickly walked away, his head bowed and his shoulders slightly raised, shielding his face. You never knew when a camera might be in the neighborhood. In this city of high crime they were everywhere.

A short black man stood at the entrance to an ally. He studied the slightly crouched figure leaving the fancy black Lincoln. As the hunched-over man walked toward him, Samuel Jackson considered the effort, wondering whether he should ignore him or go for the wallet. Guy got out of a rich-bitch Lincoln Navigator. Probably carried a couple hundreds on him at all times. He prepared himself, taking a quick hit from the flask in his jacket pocket. If you smelled of alcohol, people dismissed you. Just another drunk, they'd say.

He stumbled out of the alley, colliding with the man, almost knocking him down.

'What the hell?' Garrett straightened up, glaring at Jackson.

'Sorry, governor. Just stumbled, that's all. Got a couple of dollars so a man might find a drink?'

'Go to hell,' Garrett said. He brushed at his shirt, shook his shoulders and walked quickly away.

Before he'd gone thirty feet Jackson had stripped a credit card and three hundred-dollar bills from the wallet. He tossed the fine leather billfold in the dumpster behind Joe Meany's Tavern, wondering what kind of rich white man would have a coiled snake tattooed on his wrist. Anyway, he'd had a good score and copped a credit card to boot. This had the makings of a pretty good day.

43

A musky, pungent odor hung in the air, morning fog still lingering on the bayou. Rotting vegetation, an earthy smell of mud and waterlife flourished in the swampy land that surrounded the water.

Solange Cordray stepped carefully, avoiding hollow areas where the earth gave way to a watery pool, endangering the walker who might break a limb or, worse, fall deep into the murky depth of the swamp and never be able to pull themselves to safety. Every year there were people who went for a walk on the wild side and never returned. Solange Cordray vowed not to be one of those statistics.

Smoke rose in a thin spiral a quarter of a mile away and she knew that Matebo was cooking breakfast, roasting a fresh kill on the fire and browning the homemade sourdough bread that he did so well.

A three-foot milk snake slithered on the watery surface to her right, its bright bands of red, black and white zigzagging as it headed home after a night of foraging.

Damballa, Papa, creator of all life.

Solange respectfully looked away, keeping her eyes on the ground so she didn't stumble. Deftly stepping in her worn hiking shoes, she kept moving, thinking of the reunion with her mother's old friend. The old man had been old even when she was just a kid and her mother would take her into the swampland. He seemed permanently ancient, his weathered lined face breaking into wide-smiling joy whenever he saw her. She dealt with ancient souls most of her waking hours, praying to them, asking them for intervention, so she identified very well with the old man in the bayou. She'd known him her entire life.

Now she could smell the campfire smoke and the simmering of maybe alligator meat and a piquant sauce, with tomatoes, chilies, garlic, rosemary, thyme and other savory herbs and spices. Breakfast Matebo-style was not for the weak. No. This was the main meal for the swamp man and it had to get him through the day. Breakfast on the bayou was unlike anything they served in the French Quarter.

Breaking into the clearing she saw the black cauldron hanging from a wooden stand, simmering over the open fire. Breathing in the rich aroma, she stood there for several seconds, waiting for his appearance. She guessed he had stepped behind one of two bald cypress trees that stood close by, and as she studied them he glided out from behind the second.

'Matebo.'

'Child.' He grinned.

'Matebo. Your breakfast smells wonderful.'

'How is Ma?'

'No change. As always there are new theories, new tests, new drugs, but not for her. Not at this time.'

'All the magic in the world, all the prayers and spells that ever existed and we are still at the mercy of the unspeaking forces.'

He motioned for her to sit on the brown blanket beside his fire. She eased down in a cross-legged position and nodded in agreement.

''Tis never our will but the will of the spirits, Solange. We are but vessels. Still, I pray for Ma. She means the world to me.'

Solange smiled. There was such a mystery between Ma and the swamp man. She remembered the quiet tension that used to accompany each visit, the unspoken language that seemed to float between them, just above her head.

'Sometimes I allow myself the luxury of thinking that I can control the spirits. Just a little bit, Matebo. But I am well aware of what you say. And all the prayers for my mother are appreciated. I firmly believe that one day she will be right, and our life will go back to—' she paused.

'Normal?'

'Life with Ma – and you – was never normal.'

'It's the spice that makes life nice,' the man said. 'Without that, life does become tired, old, normal.'

Solange laughed out loud.

'I never had to worry about that around Ma.'

'And how is Joseph? The man who told you to stay away from me. Who tried to take you from your Ma.'

'I don't see him often. I don't talk to him except through lawyers,' she said. 'He has his friends, his accountants, his lawyers, and his,' she spat on the ground, 'lovers. Putain.'

'Have some breakfast and tell me of your clients.'

The wrinkled, sunburned man wiped sweat from his brow with a red kerchief tied around his neck. His brown skin was in sharp contrast to the abundance of white hair that he shook from his face. With a carved wooden scoop he ladled the alligator dish into a bowl and handed it to the younger woman.

Pouring her a cup of amber tea, he repeated the procedure for himself.

'Please, eat up. I've been eagerly anticipating your arrival,' he said. 'It's been several weeks.'

The two of them ate, savoring the flavorful stew and when it was gone, they washed it down with the tea and a glass of fermented fruit juice that had more than just a slight kick to it.

'A little something for the walk back,' Matebo said. 'Citrus and herb left to steep for several months.'

'Someday you have to give me the recipe.'

'For the alligator?'

She laughed. 'No, for the juice.'

He joined in her amusement.

The subtle hum of cicadas and the shrill ringing call of a Louisiana waterthrush lent a Creole soundtrack to the swamp.

'Tell me what has happened.'

She told him about the judges' murders, about her messages from Rayland Foster the chemical czar and about Richard Garrett, her former client who she was certain was leader of Krewe Charbonerrie.

'Your head is very heavy with the knowledge of all this.'

She nodded. It was heavy.

'But, *ma petite*, you haven't mentioned the policeman. There's more to your story and you've left that out.'

She'd mentioned Archer the last time they spoke. Only in passing. Somehow the old man knew there was more to the relationship than she had shared.

'Is he a believer?'

'Is anyone a believer to our extent?' She smoothed her thick black hair with her hands, knowing the smoky fire would permeate her luxurious mane and knowing she would relish it when she returned home, a memory of her visit.

'I suppose not.'

'But, I've got his interest. He has taken some of my story to heart and I think since he is somewhat lost in regards to this case, he needs all the help he can get.'

'Does this go any further than his belief in the stories you tell? You say you have his interest. I think it may go further.'

'How much further can it go? I must convince him that Krewe Charbonerrie may be responsible for the murder of the judge.' A chill ran down her spine, and she momentarily lost her train of thought. Something had happened, something was not quite right. Something that upset the natural cycle of her life.

'What is it, child?'

'Nothing.'

But it was something. Serious. Had someone died? Suffered? A client? Possibly someone she was close to. She offered a silent prayer that Ma was alive. A prayer that Ma was immune to the incident.

'What did you see?'

'I don't know. The curse we have is that everything is not explained.'

'Damned if it isn't,' he said.

Solange shook her head, clearing it.

'Then tell me about Quentin Archer.'

'There is nothing to tell.' She stared at him.

'Is he an honorable man?'

'As honorable as a man could be. You know well I have no faith in men, present company excluded.'

Matebo smiled.

'Is he interested in you?'

'In the stories I tell him.' She swatted at a mosquito that buzzed by her ear.

'I think otherwise.'

'Oh?'

'Are you interested in him?'

'No. Not in that way. Well, if I wasn't involved in providing him information he might be someone who would be interesting, but—'

'I think otherwise.' Smoke from the wood embers filtered through the atmosphere, causing visions that were blurry and strangely exotic.

She reached over and punched his arm.

'What do you know, old man?'

'Not so old that I don't recognize the spark of love.'

'Where are my supplies,' she asked, quickly changing the subject.

'Wrapped in a bundle over there.' He pointed to the first bald cypress where on the ground a thin sheet of bark was wrapped around twigs, flowers and plants. The bundle was tied with green vines.

'Yellow root, indigo, Spanish moss to make your dolls, verbena, wild orchid petals and everything else you ordered.' Nodding at her, he struggled to his feet then walked to the package.

'Your ingredients, Matebo, they make the strongest potions, *gris gris* bags that are magical, and voodoo dolls that cast spells on all who see them. You are truly a rare spirit.'

'You just have to know where to look. I have special places that no one knows about. I cultivate, much like a farmer. All of my ingredients are fresh, handpicked and nurtured with love.'

'Still, your ingredients are magic.'

'The herbs, the roots, they are important, but you and me, we are but vessels. The spirits must agree to do the work. You understand that and because of your understanding, you are an effective healer.'

Nodding, she peeled off a stack of bills and gave them to him. Then she picked up the bundle, placed it under her arm and turned to him.

'You are the closest person to a father that I ever had. You know that, *mon protecteur.*'

There were tears in the old man's eyes when he turned from her.

'Go back to your motorbike. It's two miles and you must go now, before the sun is high and the heat and humidity tire you. Go.'

She turned and he called to her one last time.

'Solange, I feel there is danger in the city. I feel that you are a part of something that you may not fully comprehend, but I feel your spirit is in jeopardy. You said it moments ago. The curse we have is that everything is not explained, but I know it like I know my heart and soul. Promise me you will spend every waking moment being vigilant.'

She stared at him. Never before, not even during the Joseph ordeal, had she heard this degree of concern in his voice.

'I feel if you do not pay attention, I may not see you again, little one. Be careful for me.'

'I will, Matebo. If for no other reason than to come back and share a meal and drink with my favorite man. My life is not in danger, so dismiss your worries. I am more afraid for my clients. Many of them are in serious situations, and I pray for them and do my best to help them through their problems.'

'Your mother never worried about herself. She, too, only worried about the ones who trusted her, who relied on her advice. She worried about me, Solange. Always looking out for the other person. And now she has the worst set of circumstances. There is the lesson. You must look out for yourself.'

He smiled weakly, nodded and walked toward the trees. She thought she saw tears in the old houngan's eyes. In a moment he was lost from view.

44

A dam Strand was dressed down in his off-duty attire. Jeans, a black tee and canvas deck shoes. Keeping his head low he shuffled into the restaurant. Surrey's Cafe was nestled in the lower Garden District on Magazine Street and specialized as a fresh-juice early-riser establishment that served organic breakfasts, along with high-calorie offerings. After all, this was New Orleans. He studied the hand-painted sign on the wall, covered with lemons, ripe mangos, watermelon and grapes.

'A New Orleans coffee and bananas Foster on French toast,' he said to the comely blond waitress.

Studying him for a second, she said, 'Really? That's what you're having for breakfast?'

'Uh, yeah.'

'Ah, good choice.' She didn't mean it. She poured his coffee.

He knew the look, had been getting it all his life. It was that look that said *you stupid fuck, don't you know that this is a bad decision?*

He'd made a lot of bad decisions in his life. Hadn't his credibility just taken a hit due to his insistence that Antoine Duvay was the guilty party in the murder investigation? He'd pushed the envelope, lobbying to convince the important players in this case that Duvay was the one who killed Judge David Lerner. He'd even planted a weapon, for God's sake. Dropping a gun was a major transgression. And what did it get him? Absolutely nothing.

Strand reached into his pants pocket and pulled out a small bottle of Jack. Without checking his surroundings, he took a long sip of coffee then poured the bourbon into his cup. It helped him through the day. His girl chided him, even at age five. *Daddy, you act funny when you drink that stuff. Daddy, why do you drink that stuff? You smell funny.* His daughter, once a week. And she was scolding him already. He really needed to rein it in.

They'd found a recording of the incident. A phone recording, for Christ's sake, so all that work, all his jockeying to convict the kid had been for nothing. His attempt to make this case a slam-dunk deal had failed. There was no case left. The murder of Judge David Lerner had nothing to do with Antoine Duvay. He laid his head in his hands, closed his eyes and wondered what the hell he was doing.

Adam Strand had fucked it up most of his life and he knew it. Admitted it to himself. But he'd been able to pay the bills. Pay child support. A little payoff here, a paid favor over there. He'd look the other way and be rewarded for his effort. Somebody wanted information, he'd find a way to get it. Strand could make half his cop pay again on the side. Nothing other guys on the force didn't do. But he was going out on a limb on this one. This time he was pretty sure he was working for the Feds and if he got caught committing crimes, even for the government, it would be serious jail time. Something he couldn't afford. His part-time daughter couldn't survive without full-time child support. He loved her more than life itself.

Paul Trueblood was going to meet him, offer him a pretty good payday for his information, and give him a chance to walk away with no recriminations. If he could trust the guy. A lot of money, the crime would be covered up, and a chance to leave with some pay in his pocket. Tax free at that. Trueblood had actually told him that he'd be doing New Orleans a service. An undercover hero if you would. Someone who had worked for the good of the community. He had had a pretty good idea who Trueblood worked for. He'd tracked him down, and it seemed that the guy could very well be undercover FBI, but the important thing was, the man had told him that he could cover his tracks. This Trueblood had insinuated that the detective would actually be helping solve a crime, bring the perpetrators to justice if he cooperated. There was a nice monetary reward in this exchange, so Adam Strand was on board. The more money he could make the merrier he could be.

At least he thought he was working for the FBI. It was just that Paul Trueblood couldn't divulge who he was or how Strand was going to be a hero. He had to trust the man. Hell, he could be FBI and they could be trusted, couldn't they? And, if Strand produced the product, Trueblood could make sure he didn't get caught. At least that was what the promise held. No incrimination. This was a win-win situation. Wasn't it?

Trueblood was late.

Strand pulled his cell phone from his pocket and placed it on the table. Five minutes and he'd be out of there.

The second he made that decision, a man walked in, dressed in a flowery tourist shirt and cargo shorts, and he headed right for Strand's table. Pulling out a chair, he sat down.

'You've got access to the printouts, right?' Trueblood got right to the point.

'Yeah. They're in the evidence room. I'm a lead on the case so I've got access. Access doesn't mean it's going to be easy to get them out though. By the way, no one is quite sure what they mean. They've got some numeric code that we're not clear on. Apparently you understand it?'

'Doesn't really matter, does it? I pay you for the sheets and they disappear from the evidence room. My understanding is that stuff disappears from that room all the time, so it won't be that big a deal.'

'Drugs are high on that list of things that disappear. Drugs and cash.'

'Yeah,' the man said, 'but these spreadsheets aren't drugs. And they're not cash.' He cocked his head and looked into Strand's eyes. 'You guys keep cash in there? Like paper money?'

'We keep it there until it disappears.'

'Duh.'

Strand spread his hands on the table.

'Are there big investigations when that happens? When evidence other than cash and drugs come up missing?'

'Usually it's considered the cost of doing business,' Strand said. 'If someone wants something bad enough, somebody can smuggle it out. Money? Hell, since 2010 there's been hundreds of thousands of dollars that came up missing. Dozens of people have access, Trueblood. So in most cases, stuff just disappears and no one does anything about it.'

'So no big deal?'

'Usually. There's a Fed probe right now on cash that disappeared, but that's not the norm. Usually stuff disappears and no one makes a big case about it. Usually, you understand?'

'Usually? So you are telling me that this is not a usual case? I need to know what happens in this case.'

Strand sipped at his chicory coffee and Jack.

'In this case three juvie judges have been killed, Mr Trueblood.' He pursed his thin lips. 'Three judges. Oh my God. There's a ton of pressure to get results and everything about this case is being watched very closely.'

'Strand, can you get them or not?'

'Maybe.'

'You're holding me up for more money?'

'They're worth more now. Whoever removes those sheets is putting it all on the line. Like I said, the case is really putting a lot of pressure on a lot of people.'

'How much to make those things disappear?'

'What are you going to do with them?'

'Detective, it doesn't matter.'

Strand frowned. 'You said you could cover me. That there was no way I could be convicted if caught. Is that still a fact?'

'Things have changed, Strand. As you pointed out, there are now two more judges who have been killed. It sort of ups the ante. You know, nothing in this world is for certain, Detective.'

Strand's frown deepened. He'd finally stepped out on the long board. The big dive was imminent and he couldn't walk back. Either jump, or cower and wait for someone to come and take him back.

'So you can't protect me?'

'I'll try.'

So things had changed. His young daughter crossed his mind. God, he couldn't put her at risk. Could he?

'Not good enough.'

'How much, Strand? What do you want?'

He needed some time. To think it through. It didn't sound nearly as attractive as it had.

'What do they mean? The numbers? We figured out that the left side of the sheets reflects prisoner numbers. Identification. But what are the numbers on the right side? Do you know?' Pausing, stalling, trying to delay the inevitable.

'Can you get the sheets from that box?'

'Yes. Maybe. Are you going to tell me what the numbers mean?'

Trueblood ignored his question.

'How much?'

No amount was enough. How much? Hell, twenty million wasn't enough for the chance he was going to take. And his little girl would be left without a penny.

'Twenty thousand.'

'Are you out of your mind?'

'Really? If I get caught and you can't help me, it's the end of my career, it's jail time, it's obstruction of justice, theft and I don't know what else. For any amount of money I'm a fool to do this. I have a little girl. She needs to be protected. You said it, Trueblood. Things have changed. It ups the ante.' He held up two fingers. Then held them up again. 'Double that. Make it forty. Seriously. Forty thousand dollars. I'll get you what you want for forty.'

Paul Trueblood stood up just as the bananas Foster was served. Looking down at the platter with sliced bananas, thick brown sugar and a huge scoop of ice cream over French toast he shook his head.

'You trying to kill yourself?'

'Forty thousand.'

'When can you deliver?'

'I've got to do it by tomorrow. Maybe today. Tomorrow at the latest. They're going to scan and digitize them in two days' time. They'll be gone from the evidence room and I won't have access. Right now, the only record of them that we have is the actual sheets themselves. I'd rather get it done now.'

'Tomorrow, then.' Trueblood stared into Strand's eyes. 'Before they're digitized. I want every one of those sheets. You can do that, right?'

Strand closed his eyes for a second.

'Things have changed. You understand that.'

'Not so much changed, just that I need information right now.'

'I'll need half down.'

'You'll need shit. Deliver the information, we'll deliver the cash.'

'Half now.'

'Look, Strand, I can report your willingness right now. I can go to your superiors and tell them exactly what—'

'OK, OK. But have the cash when I deliver. I'm really going out on a limb here.'

'Yeah, yeah. The parking lot at the 7-Eleven.'

Strand nodded, wondering how the hell he was going to pull this one off. Forty thousand was a lot of money, almost his entire salary without overtime, but those sheets were going to be hard to produce.

45

'The car was stolen.' Detective Levy handed Archer the report. 'Black Cadillac Escalade, one-two-four-space-eight-space-B, was reported stolen five hours before the abduction of Judge Lerner.'

Archer nodded.

'Doesn't do us much good.'

'We found it.'

'Fingerprints?'

'All over the place, Q, belonging to that Skeeter character and a guy named James Gideon. And there are some signs that someone was in the back seat. Hair samples, maybe a trace of blood. Could be Judge Lerner, could be the owner. Anyway, the two guys are bound to turn up. Hell, they've been turning up regularly for the past ten, twelve years. Small-time crooks, then suspects in a couple of armed robberies, then carjacking – they've graduated to the big time now.'

'What do you think the chances are that they killed all three judges?'

Levy gave him a weak smile.

'Wouldn't that be nice?'

'What would have been nice,' Archer stated, 'was if Strand had been right. That Antoine Duvay, the cook, had committed the murder and if no other judge had been involved. We're now in a clusterfuck, Levy, and all bets are off. Find this Lewis character. It will be a start.'

'We're on it. Checking his mother's home, places where he hangs out, staking out his ex-girlfriend's house.'

'These guys always work as a team?'

'More often than not.'

'You've got Gideon's places staked out as well?'

'We do. Guys like that, they don't get up enough courage to leave town. They hang around, more comfortable in their own environment. We'll get 'em, Q.'

Some guys like that *did* leave. They did have the courage to blow town and hide out. Guys like Jason Archer, his brother. He'd left Detroit and so far had succeeded in eluding the authorities. Maybe he was hanging with some new friends, possibly carrying on his drug trade in a different city, but he was out there. And it was one of the reasons that Quentin Archer slept with a gun by his side.

Levy's phone went off and he grabbed it from his pocket.

'Levy . . . Hang on.' He punched the speaker mode.

'We've made John Lewis,' said the voice on the phone.

'Where?' asked Levy.

'House we staked out on Dauphine Street.'

'Girlfriend,' Levy said to Archer. 'Mila Jefferson.'

'He's in the house and we think she's in there with her daughter,' said the voice on the other end.

'How old's the girl?'

'Six.'

'Shit.'

'Potential hostage situation. How do you want to proceed?'

'Quietly,' Archer said. 'This guy doesn't know that we know. He certainly doesn't know we've got the entire murder with his voice recorded. There's a chance if we approach the house he won't put it all together.'

'There's a chance that he will, Q.'

'Mother and child? We can't go up with sirens wailing and lights flashing.'

'OK,' Archer spoke into Levy's phone, 'watch any exits. Have you ID'd any vehicle belonging to the suspect?'

'We have. White 2000 Pontiac on the street. A blue Chrysler minivan is parked in front of the house, registered to a Jason Jefferson. We figure it's the lady's car, or belongs to a relative.'

'If Lewis leaves by himself, stop him. If the woman leaves with the kid, somebody follow them, then stop them at a safe distance. If three of them leave, follow but don't follow too close. That's the worst-case scenario.'

'Got it.'

'We'll be there in ten minutes.'

Archer grabbed a jacket, pulling it on over his shoulder holster. Levy patted the gun and holster clipped to his belt. Archer briefly wondered where the hell Strand was, then let it go.

'Let's pray we don't have to use these babies today,' Levy said.
'Or any day,' Archer said.

Traffic parted as they raced through the city, red light on top. About three blocks away from their destination they took it off.

Cruising by the house, they saw the two vehicles parked on the street. Three patrol cars were strategically parked on side streets, the officers still in the units. The other detective's car was parked across the street under a chestnut tree.

'How do you want to handle this?'

'Give me the clipboard.'

Levy handed him a clipboard with a roster sheet on it.

'And what are you going to do? Share the duty roster with Mr Lewis? See if he approves?'

'I'm going up to the house, knock on the door and tell Miss Jefferson that I'm from Children's Services. We have a number of checks made out to her that have been returned unopened, and if she will go with me to our offices, I'll be able to clear it all up and give her about three thousand dollars. Three grand should do it. Of course, I want the six-year-old girl to go along too.'

'You think that will work? Really?'

Archer nodded.

'Worked all the time in Detroit. Levy, if I offered you three grand, come on, man, you tell me . . .'

'Yeah, yeah,' Levy said. 'It sounds good, and you know she needs the money. I get it.'

'A guy with a clipboard can go anywhere, Levy. Nobody questions a guy with a clipboard.'

'We'll cover. You get those two out of the house and we'll get Skeeter. Don't worry about it.'

It actually didn't work every time, and it was a scary scenario. Walking up to the house of a known killer and just knocking on the door. He'd been shot at twice in his life, a bullet actually grazing him on his arm for doing the same thing. You never got over that. But, it often did work, especially when the killer wasn't expecting any kind of confrontation.

Glancing at the patrol vehicles he saw officers standing by the cars, guns drawn. Hopefully there were no trigger-happy types who could be spooked if things didn't go just right. Hopefully there *were* some top-notch marksmen that could take out Skeeter if he tried to kill Archer. They should have sent in the SWAT team, but he had a short window of opportunity and he had to take it. Plus, Lewis had the little kid.

The detective slowly walked down the sidewalk, studying the clipboard while checking out the house in his peripheral vision.

A pink-and-blue plastic Big Wheel was parked by the door, and a tired patch of grass tried unsuccessfully to cover the brown bare earth. Archer turned and walked up the narrow cement walkway, a cracked and uneven trail. He stepped up gingerly on the rotted wooden stoop. Archer was surprised it supported his weight. No doorbell, so he opened the screen door with no screen and knocked.

Everything was silent. A quick glance to the street showed him that everyone was out of sight. In a moment's notice they could provide backup but right now they were keeping a low profile.

He knocked again, holding the clipboard in front of him.

Once again there was no noise.

He hadn't anticipated being shut out. Possibly Skeeter Lewis had looked out the window and told everyone inside to ignore the visitor.

Then he heard the door handle start to turn. Slowly. He prepared himself, ready to drop the clipboard at a moment's notice and pull the Glock.

The door creaked before he saw it move, as it inched open. Archer took one step back, anticipating the worst. The door opened to a four-inch crack before he heard the voice, and glanced down.

'My mommy is busy right now.'

The little girl had her face pressed into the slight opening. Her bright brown eyes were staring up at him as she waited for a reply. Hell, they'd sent the kid out to do surveillance. It wasn't right.

'Honey,' he spoke loudly, knowing that Mom and probably Lewis were close by, 'I'm from Children's Services. We've been trying to give your mommy some checks but every time we send them, they come back to our office. We've got a little over three thousand dollars to give your mommy and you, but she's got to come down to our office to get that money. Can you tell her that?'

'My mommy is busy.'

'I understand. But you should go tell her that I have three thousand dollars that belongs to her.'

She stood there a moment longer, then leaving the door cracked open she walked away. Archer could hear her talking to someone.

Thirty seconds can seem like an eternity when your life is on the line. He kept the board up near his chest, half tempted to push the door open the rest of the way. Whoever was inside had heard him. The next step was theirs.

Without a warning the door swung open, and a young man with disheveled hair and a white T-shirt and jeans stood in the entrance.

'You're with Children's Services?'

It was him. No question. The photograph Archer had seen matched the man he was facing.

'Yes sir. We have some checks for Miss Jefferson and her daughter, and I'm just trying—'

'You can give 'em to me. I'll get 'em to her.'

'They're made out to her, in her name.'

The man put his arms behind his back and Archer transferred the board to his left hand, his right hand poised to reach inside the jacket.

'You got them checks with you?' His voice was a little singsong, somewhat effeminate.

'In my car. If you want to come with me, I'll just need you to sign for them. It's simply protocol.'

The man hesitated, his hands still behind his back.

If he's got a gun, Archer thought, *he's going to pull it now.*

The man pulled both his hands from behind his back and immediately dropped them to his sides.

Archer stifled a sigh of relief.

'The checks,' he nodded to the car across the street. Repeating himself, he said, 'They're in the vehicle so you'll have to come with me.'

On blind faith he turned his back on the murderer and stepped off the wooden porch, slowly walking toward the sidewalk.

'You bring the checks up here.'

Without turning, Archer said, 'Do you want the money or not?'

Pausing for a second, he heard the screen door bang shut and footsteps behind him. He casually glanced over his shoulder and stopped, letting Lewis slowly catch up with him.

He looked over at the killer and smiled, and as Skeeter Lewis reached him, Archer lashed out with his right foot, viciously kicking

Lewis in the left leg and yanking his feet out from under him. The young man collapsed on the concrete and Archer whipped out his Glock, pressing it forcefully against Lewis's temple.

'John Lewis, you are under arrest for the murder of Judge David Lerner.'

Two uniformed officers were jogging up to the scene and as Archer read the Miranda rights, they cuffed the suspect.

'You have the right to remain silent . . .'

Yanking him to his feet, they walked him down to the sidewalk, Archer following closely.

'Anything you say or do may be used against you in a court of law . . .'

Levy stepped up patting Archer on his back.

They all paused while Archer finished his obligation.

'Are you willing to answer my questions without an attorney present?'

Lewis stared back at him with hollow eyes. Then in a thin, whiny voice he said, 'Fuck you, whoever you are.'

Archer took that as a no.

The officers pulled him away, heading toward a squad car.

'Amazing, Detective Q,' Levy was truly impressed. 'It's too bad Strand wasn't here to watch you in action. You pulled that off like you'd practiced all of your life. Impressed? Hell yes. I guess a Detroit boy can teach us Crescent City cops a couple of new tricks.'

'We've got two more killers out there, Levy. Lewis is a low-level punk, but whoever is orchestrating this is a serious threat. I'm afraid this is just the tip of the iceberg.'

46

Paul Trueblood punched in the numbers on his cell phone, watching his rear-view mirror to be sure that Strand wasn't following. He didn't think he would. The punk cop was only interested in the money. Working with blue was not his favorite thing to do. It exposed the weakness of the police force, as far as he was concerned, the lowest level of law enforcement.

The voice on the other end answered.

'Trueblood?'

'He said he can get the sheets.'

'Yeah? We'll see. If I remember, you were going to get them from Lerner himself. That didn't work out so well, did it?'

'Damn, don't remind me. It took months to get that set up. I was skeptical, and then all of a sudden he decides to turn, and then—'

'They're making us look stupid, Paul. They knew Lerner was going to go public. Hell, they knew Warren was involved. And apparently they suspected Judge Hall. What do you think? Maybe there's a leak in our system.'

'Where?'

'We're working on that. Maybe they're just a little ahead of the ball. Anyway, we've got to move forward.'

'And now, who's left?' Trueblood asked. 'Hall and Warren are gone. Hell, we may have to start all over again.'

'Not enough time. If we go back to square one, they'll torch every piece of evidence they've got.'

'They've already killed three.'

'They have. So it's even more important that we have the hard data.'

'We can't include the cops.'

'They would so fuck it up.'

'But we can use a rogue cop. Strand says he can get the sheets.'

'We could just demand them.' The voice on the other end of the phone was almost insistent.

'I'll guarantee that wouldn't work,' Trueblood said. 'Jurisdiction, blue pride, the whole thing would take weeks to sort out. We need that information right now. This can't go on any longer. Christ, all we need is another judge or two to end up on the kill list.'

'Got it. By the way, how much is this supposed to cost?'

'Forty thousand.'

'Whew. Forty thousand? This guy actually asked for that? No shit?'

'That's what he asked for.'

'Well, we go with the first plan. Inspect the merchandise, take it, then threaten to turn him in. There's no way he can say a word. Don't let him have the cash first. Are we going to need him for anything else?'

'No. We can burn him.'

'He's not the kind of guy who would go for his gun, is he?'

'He's a punk,' Trueblood said. 'A pussy. He's scared of his shadow. His courage is alcohol. I just hope he has the guts to get the printouts.'

'Yeah, well, we get the sheets, we should be good to go. And besides, what can that piece of shit do for us after that? He doesn't know anything. He's definitely not worth forty thousand dollars. He's not worth one thousand.'

Trueblood thought for a moment.

'OK. I'll tell him we had a change of heart, but to be fair, I won't report him. He's not going to be happy. I mean, he's going to be very upset.'

'Other than coming after you, there's nothing he can do. Anyway, I'd have a hard time justifying any money until this whole thing plays out. If it plays out.'

'Got it,' Trueblood said.

'Paul, treat those things like gold.'

'I'm bringing them in the second the transfer is made.'

Trueblood checked his mirror one more time. He didn't recognize any vehicle behind him.

'Paul, one more thing.'

'Yeah?'

'When you drop them off . . .' there was a slight pause.

'When I drop them off, what?'

'Plan on taking a little vacation. The Caribbean, a week in Mexico. I think we'd like to see you disappear for a short while. Come back with a tan, maybe a moustache, shave your head . . . we've got another assignment for you in a month or so.'

Paul Trueblood smiled. As a freelancer, someone who was on the fringe, he had the same exact idea. But maybe a little longer than one week.

47

H is leg was chained to the table, a cold Styrofoam cup of coffee in front of him, and Levy and Archer were sitting in chairs across from the killer.

'It's not often, John, that we get a gift like we got on this case. Would you like us to play the recording again for you?'

'It's not my voice.'

'Yeah, it is. We can prove it. You'd be surprised at the technology we have. Christ, all kinds of detecting devices, speech patterns, lots of ways we can prove it's you.'

'Didn't happen.' The young man rubbed his knee where he'd been kicked.

'Yeah, it did happen. The sooner you admit that the sooner we can start dealing. John, two other judges have been killed. Murdered. Do you want us to look at you for all three killings?'

'Two more?'

'Yeah. We've got you, excuse the pun, dead to rights on one. It's not much of a leap to figure you did number two and three.'

There was a little fear in the cocky kid's attitude.

'Look,' Archer said, 'actually, we don't think you were involved. The two murders happened almost at the same time. However, somebody is going to make the case. You may have been the ring-leader. You may have orchestrated the other two killings. Is that what you want on the record before this goes to trial? One is bad enough, but three judges? Man, you'd have no chance. Period.'

'I didn't do it.'

'You did Lerner,' Levy said. 'You and James.'

'And if I admit that?'

'You have to convince us that you didn't do Warren and Hall. You have to prove that you didn't kill the other two judges. That's all there is. Show me you weren't involved in all three incidents.'

'Hell, I didn't even know about this Warren and Hall. Maybe James did. Maybe he was in on it, but nobody offered me squat. I mean, I didn't do anybody, Detective. Why don't you grill Gideon? You're blowing smoke, am I right?'

Archer stood up and walked behind Lewis.

'Skeeter, it didn't work out. They offered you some good money to kill judge one, but obviously we found you. I'm telling you, if you don't cooperate, that we will work to get you on two and three. If you know who else was involved, I can even make it sweeter.'

'Doesn't sound that sweet as it is.' Tears formed in the man's eyes and started running down his cheeks. 'I want to help. I wish I could. I could use the information to cut myself a break. But I don't know. This was a one-time thing.'

Levy jumped in.

'What was a one-time thing? Explain.'

'Nothing, man. You've got the wrong guy.'

And they started over.

Half an hour later they were still at it. John 'Skeeter' Lewis wasn't giving them any more. It was obvious his employers had kept most of the details from him so he couldn't incriminate them.

'Who contacted you?'

'Nobody.'

'You're going to get at least life, and possibly the death penalty, John.'

'I don't have a clue what you're talking about.'

'Really?'

'Really.'

And so it went. For another hour.

48

The evidence and property division in Central City was a nondescript, concrete-and-brick structure that resembled a warehouse, which in fact was what it was. And there was a good chance very few residents in the neighborhood knew that the building housed hundreds of thousands of items critical to criminal cases. Probably no one knew that thousands of dollars – in the form of cash, drugs or whatever – walked out of the building on a weekly, if not daily basis. All that the neighbors knew was that cops frequented the building. Straight cops, crooked cops, but cops were there on a regular basis. The neighborhood actually felt quite safe with all the law enforcement personnel hanging around.

Detective Adam Strand was a frequent visitor. Any cop on homicide duty was. Only now, it was a personal matter, so this time was a little different.

'ID.'

Strand handed the bored lady his detective ID card.

She ran it through a scanner, asked him to empty his pockets, and put his folder and tablet on the table. It was a procedure he'd been through dozens of times. The real test was when he left the building. Usually there was no check. None. He was hoping that was the case this time. Strand was depending on it. Although, with all the missing evidence, things might have changed.

'OK, Detective, you can go in.'

Adam Strand walked through the detectors, picking up his tablet, folder, and personal items on the other side. He walked down the aisles; he had a good idea where the lock box was that held the printouts. Glancing to the right and to the left, when he finally reached 812 G4, he pulled out the key. He inserted the metal piece into the lock, turned it and the locker opened smoothly. Strand pulled the box out, set it on a long metal table that ran the length of the aisle and took out the spreadsheets, shoving them into the folder. The process took less than one minute. As he pushed the box back into the rack he saw the motion from the corner of his eye.

'Detective Strand?' A rather stern voice.

She was dressed in blue, a little chubby for his tastes and he couldn't quite place her. Didn't want to place her. Strand wondered how much she'd seen.

Strand nodded cautiously.

'And you are?'

'Patrolman Harris,' she said. 'You and I met maybe three years ago when a bank robber killed a guard in the Garden District.'

He did remember.

Nodding, keeping a close watch on her eyes, he reached out for her hand, shaking it with a firm grasp.

'Good to see you again.'

She smiled, moving in even closer.

'I always hoped I'd run into you again.'

'Well, thank you.' *What the hell do you say?*

The lady smiled again, almost waiting for a more positive response, but he couldn't think of one.

'So, you're working on the juvenile judge thing? Quite a buzz.'

'No, not this trip.' He was Peter after the crucifixion. Deny, deny, deny. 'Another case, can't keep track of all of them.'

'Two shootings just this morning over in Bayou Saint John,' she said. 'Gangbangers.'

'Hadn't heard that one.' Shaking his head, he took a couple of steps, moving away from the woman toward his exit.

'It was good to see you, Detective Strand. I hope we can work together again.'

He gave her a weak smile, and finally, she moved on. Strand let out a sigh of relief. Another time he might be flattered but not today. Not with the possibility of a forty-thousand-dollar payday or a couple of years in prison playing around in his head. *Not today, lady. Sorry.*

Smiling to himself, he glanced up at the ceiling, then the lockers and the walls of the large building. For whatever reason, there were no cameras anywhere. Like cops could be trusted, but the rest of the world . . . not so sure. He'd heard rumors that things were about to change. There was a move to put cameras in the room, but money was tight. Hell, if they just took the money that was locked up in the evidence room they could afford cameras. And considering what he was trying to accomplish right now, it was probably a good idea. Strand closed the box and inserted it back into the locker. Empty.

As he turned he saw a hulking black man, glaring at him from five inches away. The big guy reached out and grabbed Strand's shoulder.

'Detective.'

Gripping the folder and tablet tight, he said, 'I'm sorry, do I know you?'

The man was dressed in a blue blazer, gray slacks and a maroon solid tie. A square jaw and shaved head gave the impression he was a no-nonsense cop.

Strand's heart skipped a beat and his stomach rumbled.

'I saw that.'

Strand took a deep breath. So far he hadn't transferred the sheets to Paul Trueblood. He hadn't actually left the building, so there was no real crime committed. Wilting under the man's gaze he asked the question, hesitantly at best.

'What do you think you saw?'

The man paused, nodding his head at the departing woman.

Strand turned and watched the woman who was walking away.

'The lady?'

'Yeah, the lady.' He smiled, his pearl-white teeth shone against his dark skin.

'I had the impression,' the man released his grip on Strand's shoulder, 'that she was interested in you. Maybe hitting on you. But maybe I was wrong.'

What is this? High school? Thank God, apparently no one had seen the transfer of the printouts to his black folder.

'I don't know, but she was cozying up to you pretty good.'

'We worked together on a case a couple of years ago. That's all.' *And what the hell business is it of yours?*

Strand nodded as the other detective chuckled broadly at the missed opportunity, and walked back up the aisle until he arrived at the exit.

'Quick trip, Detective.'

'It was, Gwen. Had to double check on some information.'

She smiled.

'You're working on the judge's murder, right?'

Strand's smile froze. Did he have a sign on his forehead? *Ask Me About Judge Lerner's Murder.* Shit, the last thing he needed was the lady reporting that he'd been in just before the evidence had come up missing.

'I'm co-lead. But this visit was about something entirely different,' he was babbling. 'Checking up on a suspect from a couple of years ago. A bank guard who was killed during a robbery. Different case altogether. No connection. Thanks, Gwen. Look forward to the next time we talk.'

The lady studied him for a second, finally nodding as if she understood what he was saying. She didn't.

Couldn't catch a break. Probably another bad decision.

Strand quickened the pace, wondering whether maybe they *had* installed some cameras. Possibly they had a way of tracking what he'd just done. He concentrated on the forty thousand dollars he was being paid for his theft. What would it buy? What security would forty grand give him?

It was a load of crap. He was putting his life, his career on the line for forty grand. The worst decision of his profession. He pushed open the door and, turning right, almost ran into a uniform.

'Sorry,' he bowed his head. It was going to be a whole lot easier the fewer number of people who recognized him.

'Aren't you Detective Strand?'

'Jesus.' He said a silent prayer.

'Hey, man, three judges. You guys getting anywhere with that case? Sounds complicated.'

The man in blue removed his cap, brushing his hand through his short hair.

'You know,' Strand said, 'Detective Quentin Archer is the top on that case. He's got the answers. You know how it is, man. I've got seven cases I'm working on. One of 'em I just researched. Carry-out clerk got killed back in February? Anyway, have a good day, Officer.' There was a carry-out clerk murder, wasn't there? There was always a carry-out clerk murder.

The man nodded. The patrolman got it. After all, he was a cop in New Orleans. Everyone in law enforcement was overworked, overstressed. Every cop on the force understood that.

Strand double-timed it to his car, his folder held tightly under his arm. Jesus, forty grand. That was all? What had he been thinking? Forty grand wouldn't post bail if he was caught. Wouldn't even pay that much to get out of the country and start over somewhere else. Wouldn't do much of anything. What the hell had he been thinking? And he wasn't even sure that Paul Trueblood was on the up and up. Something disingenuous about that man. What if he was gunning for Strand? Maybe his bad decisions had finally caught up with him.

The guy could be with the Independent Police Monitor group, someone who investigates the way the NOPD handles cases. Damn. If he was on that board, Strand was in for a world of hurt. And of course there was Internal Investigations and the mayor's Committee on Police Action. Hell, there were a whole lot of ways that he could be nailed. A number of organizations that wanted to monitor every action the department made. And every entity tried to justify its existence. They would all be vigilant, hoping to open a hole in the dam, hoping they could find some violation that they could take credit for. And then there were the Feds, sticking their nose into the NOPD. This guy, this Paul Trueblood, could be with anybody.

Strand opened his car door as another uniformed patrolman walked by. Perspiration dotted the detective's face, and he felt sweat running down his chest. Stripping his jacket off, he tossed it along with the folder into the back seat.

He had to get the hell out of this area. Everyone who saw him was a possible witness. A detective in a sport coat and tie stepped from his car and walked toward the building.

Strand buried his face, shaking and wondering who would turn him in. Forty grand? He felt like fucking Judas. It wasn't worth this torture, was it?

He raised his head, peered over the steering wheel and finally saw no one. Turning the key, he backed out as soon as the engine engaged. There were forty thousand dollars' worth of spreadsheets in the back seat, inside his black vinyl folder. Lord let him deliver those before he was caught.

Skeeter Lewis was tired. His eyes were puffy and he blinked incessantly at the bright light in the interrogation room. Archer sympathized. He'd had fresh coffee and a sandwich while Levy covered, but they hadn't gotten too far.

'I want an attorney, man. Get me a lawyer.'

'We'll do it, Lewis. But tell me who talked to you. Tell us who was your contact. My God, man. Right here, on this recording we've got a solid case. You are giving up any chance of a deal once you go lawyer. A name, Skeeter. Give us a name.'

'I'm not sayin' that I talked to anyone.'

'Who hired you?'

'I'm not sayin' anyone did.'

'What are you saying?'

'If there was a name, if there was someone who was trying to hire people to maybe kill or consider killing a judge . . .'

'If there was?' asked Levy.

'There's a guy who I heard of.'

'Please, Jesus. A name.'

'Loup-garou.'

'What the hell kind of name is that, Lewis?' Archer was ready to strangle the guy. Hours and hours and he comes up with some silly French word. There was no given name of Loup-garou. Archer knew better.

'He's the Werewolf. If there was someone who was trying to hire people, it would be the Wolf.'

Archer looked at Levy and shook his head. Too much coffee, too little sleep, too many hours in the company of this crazy lunatic.

'Look him up, Archer. I'm just sayin'. If there was a guy, it would be Loup-garou. But I never talked to him. I never worked for the man. He's a crazy motherfucker. I don't go near people like that. You understand?'

Archer nodded.

'We pick up your partner, Jim Gideon, he'll tell us the same story?'

'Shit,' Lewis said, 'he's a crazy motherfucker too. Gideon is liable to say anything. Anything to save his neck. He may say we talked to the Wolf, and that would be a lie, man. Or maybe he talked to the Wolf. I would never talk to Loup-garou. Not me. I'm clean.'

'We will hook up with Gideon. You know that.'

'So?'

'If he doesn't back your story, if he tells us something different . . .'

'You find this Werewolf.'

'And if we do?'

'You find the man behind the Lerner murder. Maybe those other two judges too. You find him, Detective.'

'Loup-garou.'

'Loup-garou.'

Levy smiled, then started chuckling. Starting to shake, he finally let loose with a loud throaty laugh.

'This is crazy, Q.'

Archer didn't crack a smile.

'You lie to me, Lewis, and I promise you we'll bury you in the judicial system and you will never have a prayer, my friend.'

'You find him, Detective Archer. Then you come and see me.'

'Oh, I will. And I know exactly where you'll be. In that hellhole next door that we call our jail.'

49

'Another murder, Archer. Guy named Jonathon Gandal. Strangled in his car down in the Quarter,' said Sergeant Sullivan as he passed Archer's desk on his way to the coffee machine.

'Sergeant, you're not thinking about loading this on top of—'

'No. But wondered if you had any thoughts about him.'

'Gandal? I don't know the name. Look, Sergeant, I'm a little busy right now and I don't need to worry about—'

'You brought up his employer's name the other day. Out of the blue.'

'All right' – Archer threw his hands up – 'enlighten me. Who did this Gandal work for?'

'Richard Garrett. My friend's son. The oil tycoon, remember?'

Garrett. According to Solange Cordray, the head of Krewe Charbonerrie. Archer shook his tired head. If something would just come together.

'I've got nothing, Sarge.'

'Guy was a supervisor for Garrett. Don't know for sure of what, but I was hoping this might make some sense to you. He's sitting in his black Lincoln Navigator and someone strangles him from the back seat. It probably took a minute and a half and he was dead. No fingerprints in the car. Looks like it was wiped clean.'

'We just spent four hours with Skeeter Lewis in interrogation, Sergeant. Nothing is making sense right now. I've got the French nickname of some guy who hires killers, a guy who calls himself the Werewolf. I've got Skeeter Lewis who has heard the recording of himself killing Judge Lerner and still tells me he had nothing to do with the murder. We've got a rumor that Krewe Charbonerrie may be involved in the murder, plus a prison warden and the head of prison security that might be involved.'

'That's what we do, Archer. We put all that shit into a mixer and . . .'

'Yeah. And sometimes it comes out exactly like that. Shit.'

'You OK?'

'I need to take a breather. Be back in a couple of hours.'

'Stay focused, Archer.'

The detective nodded. 'Before I go, any unusual tattoos on Gandal? Like a small coiled snake on his wrist?'

'Didn't hear of one. Is it important?' Sullivan asked.

'Everything at this stage is important, isn't it?'

'Why the question?'

'Why do some of the players have the same tattoo? That's the question, Sergeant Sullivan.'

Why? Archer thought about it as he walked to the restaurant. He knew the answer. They were members of Krewe Charbonerrie.

A detective walks into a bar. The bartender says, 'On the clock or not?' The detective looks up at the clock and says . . .

'Hey, Q. What brings you in?'

'Tough day, Mike. I've been working on the murdered judges and . . .'

'Judges, plural?'

'Yeah. Multiples. Doesn't seem to stop.'

The bartender from the French Market smiled.

'Man. We've got to catch the dude at the top.'

'*I* have to catch him, Mike. Bring me a Sazerac.'

'Strong medicine, *mon ami.*'

'It's more than the judges' murders. It's a lot more. It's this city, it's Detroit, it's about family and it's about my wife and innocent people who shouldn't have died, Mike. But none of it is your concern. Thanks for showing some support.'

The man with the wild hair nodded, a faint smile on his face.

'I've got some information, my friend: the murder involves Krewe Charbonerrie and a Richard Garrett.'

Archer's eyes widened, and he tilted his head, looking at the bartender in a whole new light.

'Why am I not surprised that you suspected that all along,' Mike said. 'You see, it is my concern. Q. Did you hear about a Quarter murder in the last couple of hours?'

Archer paused, watching the 'tender mixing his drink.

'What murder?'

'Jonathon Gandal?'

Archer closed his eyes. When he opened them, Mike was staring at him, his gaze burning into his brain. 'What about it?'

'Worked for the aforementioned Richard Garrett. Big man in the oil business.'

'Yeah?' Where did this guy get his information? 'Why are you asking me about this murder?'

The bar manager took a step back, studying Archer with a cynical eye.

'Because if you are truly interested in solving the murder of Judge David Lerner, this murder, this Gandal murder, may be important to you.'

'You want to be a little more clear?'

'Think about this, man. There's a lot of killings in New Orleans. Blacks, minorities, hoodlums, gangsters, bangers and once in a while a cop gets shot in the line of duty, but high-profile white people? Three judges and a respectable businessman all in four or five days of each other? And Gandal worked for Garrett.'

'Mike, I appreciate anything you can bring to the table. And I suppose that the demographics of the victims skews a little higher than usual, but what you're suggesting is that Richard Garrett is involved in the murder of Judge David Lerner and Gandal.'

'Yes. It's a suggestion, Detective. I don't have all the answers, just good information. I can't solve the crime for you. If I did, you could turn your paycheck over to me.'

'You'd be very disappointed, my friend. Do you have any idea how much a detective makes? It's not that much money, trust me.'

'My point is,' Mike said, 'I can show you the evidence. I can introduce the stories, but it's up to you to make the case. It's up to you to tie everything together. Am I right? You are the one who has to find the answer.'

He was right.

'And, Q, I'm not the only one who is suggesting leads, offering theories. There are others who are coming to you with information. Am I right? Come on, man. Put it together.'

'Do you know who set Lerner up?' Archer was beside himself, wondering if everyone around him knew the answer except him.

'No one knows for sure except the guilty parties. Other than that, you are the only one who has all the information. No one else knows. No one but the persons who contracted the hit. No, Q. No one else has all the evidence except you. I believe that somewhere in your soul, you know who killed the judges and why. You have compiled all the information. Now, just sort it out.'

Archer took a sip of the strong cocktail. Then another. At one time the drink had been outlawed across the country. The devil's brew it was called. Now, for those in the Quarter who could make it, it was the bestselling drink in town. Absinthe, bitters and rye whiskey. A little bit of licorice with a hammer attached. The detective felt a rush to his head.

'What do you know about Gandal?'

'Only that he was strangled in his car. As far as I've heard, no one has a clue as to what happened.'

'Mike . . .' Archer took another sip and let it slide down his throat. 'You once told me you know almost everything that happens in the French Quarter.'

'I do.'

'Then tell me exactly what happened.'

'I've got some people who feed me, Detective. They've already given me some very interesting information. But, I need twenty-four hours, my friend. At least. I'm not a fortune teller, not a Solange Cordray.'

'What the hell do you know about Solange Cordray?'

'Everyone knows about the Voodoo Queen, Q. Listen, I visited her mother many years ago. Madam Clotille Trouville. Very savvy woman before the dementia. And I know Solange Cordray has taken her mother's place. She's a bright girl, despite marrying her ex-husband. Big mistake. But, she's talked to you. I'm right, aren't I?'

'She doesn't make any sense.'

'I read a lot of mysteries, Q,' the bartender said, 'and they're always different, but always the same.'

'What's that, a riddle? What's always different but always the same?'

'There's always a puzzle in mysteries. At least the good ones. The ones I like to read.'

'You're going to give me some pithy philosophy about solving a crime based on crime fiction you've read?'

'No. I give you a very simple truth.'

'That is?'

'The answer is always in front of you.' Mike's big eyes focused on Archer and he gave him a slight smile. 'It's in front of you, it's in front of the protagonist, it's in front of the reader.'

'I'm afraid not in this case. I've studied every piece of evidence, Mike. It's not there right now, trust me.'

'Come on, Detective, you've been through this before. There's never any magic. Even the locked-room mysteries don't have magic. There's no such thing. Once you explore the room, the characters, the circumstances, there's always a solution. You may not see it right away, but it's always there. Has to be. Because in a real world, there is no magic. It's a very controlled environment. You've solved a lot of crimes and you know what I'm talking about.'

Archer nodded.

The bartender picked up empty glasses from his bar and plunged them into a soapy mixture behind the bar, running them up and down on a soft brush, readying the vessels for the next round of drinks and customers.

'I remember one story where a man is killed in a hotel room. His wife finds the body and she is not in the room when he dies. The room is locked and we know the victim did not let the killer in. Locked room mystery, right? Well, I'm struggling to find the answer. How the hell does someone get into the room? Then it occurs to me. At check in, the couple is issued just one electronic entrance card for the room. They are issued one, not two. The writer tells us that the victim has nothing on him. No money, credit cards, no room card. So we assume the killer stole the room card and along with everything else.'

'The reader assumes that everything was stolen, but forgets that the killer would have to have been in possession of the key to gain entrance to the room,' Archer said.

'Exactly,' Mike said. 'So, the wife must have given the killer the card so they could gain entrance. And I'm reading this thinking the killer stole the card.'

'Except,' Archer nodded, 'the victim could easily have known the killer and opened the door and let them in. Then the killer would have taken the card and locked the door on the way out.'

'It took hundreds of pages to tie it all back to that entrance card. The evidence was there from almost page one. But there were at least three scenarios.'

'And you feel stupid that you didn't catch it right away.'

'Exactly. The evidence was there. You just had to sift through it.'

'It was the wife, right?'

'You figure it out, Detective Q.'

'I don't have a husband or wife in this case. No locked room.'

'You'll get it, man. I feel it in my bones. You've already got the evidence, you just don't know it yet. You'll figure it out, OK. It will happen and I think deep down you know it too. I'll look into Gandal's murder. Someone in this small village of ours knows something. Trust me. And I'm next in line. I'll hear about it before anyone else and you will be the first person I'll contact, Detective. I promise.'

50

H e left after one drink. That was one more than he should have had. But this time he felt that he really needed it. Archer headed for his car, two blocks away.

He didn't need some bartender to point out how his business worked. As much as he liked the man, the detective was somewhat put out with Mike's spin on the science of solving crimes. Put out because the son of a bitch had pretty much nailed it. Archer may have had enough evidence about the case to solve it, but he had yet to put those puzzle pieces together, and that was the frustrating part. It was always the frustrating part. Like a damned Rubik's Cube.

Turning a corner, he stepped aside as the short man brushed up against him, stumbling and moving on in the other direction. Spinning around Archer ran his hand over his rear pocket. To his surprise, he found his wallet intact. He looked after the retreating figure.

'Jackson.'

There was no acknowledgement from the would-be pickpocket. Without hesitation Archer walked after him.

The man in the worn burgundy sport coat kept moving up the street.

'Jackson, stop. Get back here or I'll arrest your sorry ass.'

Abruptly the short man stopped, seemed to consider the consequences then slowly turned around, a questioning look on his face.

'Hey, Detective Archer.' He acted surprised. 'Didn't even know it was you, sir.' Opening his hands and holding them out he said,

'I never did nothing. You check, sir, and see for yourself because I saw the light the last time we met, sir. No more pickin' pockets, no sir. I'm a changed man.'

'No pockets picked?'

'No, sir.'

'So what are you doing for a living? Now?'

Jackson bit his lip. Slowly walking back to Archer, he folded his hands in front of himself.

'Sir, what if I confided in you. Told you something that would possibly help you in your line of work. You know what I mean, sir?'

Archer didn't have a clue.

'Have you been charged with something? Do you want something from me?'

'Lord, no,' Jackson said. 'If I needed something from you, I think I'd look elsewhere,' he said. 'After all, you and I have a history.'

Archer studied the man for a moment, there on the street, cars passing by and tourists and colorful locals crowding the space.

'So what are you confiding?'

'Please, sir, this doesn't go against me?'

'How bad is it?'

'It's only an observation, Detective.'

'Jackson,' Archer cleared his throat, 'an observation is not anything that can get you in trouble. At least legally.'

Nodding his head, the short man smiled.

'Well, an observation may be a thought, or it may be something I saw. If it was something I saw and didn't report directly, I am afraid it may get me in trouble. I'll let you decide.'

Archer nodded, intrigued.

'Sir, before I tell you, did you seriously donate my money to some charity? You told me you would. You do remember taking some of my hard-earned money, right?'

Archer found himself smiling. The first time in a long time.

'Yes, I did. I most certainly did. Your twenty went to help police families who are facing a rough future.'

'I'll need a receipt for tax purposes,' Jackson said with the straightest of faces. 'A receipt, Detective.'

'Understood. I'll get it to you.'

'Thank you, kind sir.'

'Now, Jackson, about what you saw?'

'Well then, I noticed that a man named Gandal was killed today here in the French Quarter. Don't misunderstand, I didn't see any murder, but it happened. It did happen, ain't that right, sir?'

What the hell? The last two people Archer had talked to had made that murder a focal point of the conversation. Now a street-smart criminal?

'I heard the same thing, Jackson.'

'Well, I may have stumbled on some information regarding that murder. Something that might interest you.'

'Really?'

'Yes, sir.'

'What kind of information?'

'I'm paying this forward, Detective. You know, so if I run into a spot of bad luck, you'll remember I helped you out.'

The man reached into his pocket and pulled out a black American Express card. Holding it back, he said, 'No questions asked, Detective? Got to have your word on this. Is that OK?'

'I won't ask any questions, Jackson.' He might not, but what his superiors would do was an entirely different story.

Samuel Jackson handed the card to Archer.

'Never used it or anything,' he said. 'Hell, a Black Card? You just don't mess with stuff like that, you know what I mean? Man has to spend two hundred fifty thousand dollars a year just to own one. Two hundred fifty thousand, sir. Now you know I don't have that kind of dollars on me. Twenty here, maybe, twenty there and that just don't add up.'

Archer looked at it, then looked at it again. It was the shiny black anodized titanium card used by high rollers only. He'd heard about it, but never dreamed he'd hold one in his hand. The Centurion Black American Express Card. Archer was lucky to have a MasterCard with a thousand dollars charged to it, and that was probably delinquent.

'Where did you get this?' He studied the name, his hand slightly trembling. The entire encounter was getting stranger by the second.

'You askin' questions already? You promised.'

'Sorry.' He looked at the raised name again, not sure whether to believe his eyes. The name scared him.

'OK, Detective. I will volunteer one piece of information.'

'That being?'

'That Lincoln Navigator where Gandal was killed?'

'Right.'

'Please, Detective, now this can't blow back on me, understood? You and me, we got a history. I donated to that police charity, sir, am I right?'

Archer nodded.

'The man who walked out of that vehicle before they found Gandal's body, he carried this credit card. Understood? I ain't sayin' he did nothin', but he walked out of the back seat of that Lincoln.'

'You know this because?'

'Shit, you askin' questions again? Give me back my card then.'

'No. No.' Archer studied the card again, shaking his head. He couldn't understand how this entire puzzle fit together. 'Do you recognize the name on this card? Do you know the man?'

Jackson's eyes drifted as the two men stood on the sidewalk. He shrugged his shoulders, uncomfortable with the question.

'I heard about a guy with that name.'

'You lifted this off of him?'

'What? Lifted it? Hell no. What you trying to imply? He dropped it. I simply picked it up.'

'Ah,' Archer nodded. 'You picked it up. I see. Well, what do you know about him? This guy who dropped his card?'

'Man owns some big oil company or somethin'. Kind of guy who is used to having his own way.'

Archer nodded again.

'I would guess you're right.' Again he read the raised white print on the shiny black object. *Richard Garrett.*

'And here I am, being a model citizen, Detective. Check it out. I find this card on the ground and first thing I do is turn it in to an officer of the law.'

'You're cream of the crop, Jackson.'

'Yes, sir. Well, I got to go. Got a job interview as janitor at a club over on Toulouse Street.'

'Garrett. He walked out of the Lincoln Navigator? After Gandal was dead? And you saw him?'

'I'm tellin' you, Detective.' He paused. 'But you can't be tellin' anyone else. My life would be worth shit.'

Archer nodded. 'You checked the Navigator?'

'May have glanced through the driver's window.'

'And you saw—'

'Detective.' Frustration in his voice. 'How much more you gonna ask?'

'Let's say you saw someone slumped over the steering wheel. Let's just say that might have happened.'

'Let's say I did.'

'Jackson, you're aware I'm going to have to know where to reach you. I may not be the one asking questions but I've got superiors who will want more information.'

The small black man nodded. 'I may not have any more information, sir. Probably don't. You know, shit, I should have kept my mouth shut.'

'OK, if I'm going to get you a receipt for your taxes, where would I deliver it? You want to get a tax form, just give me an address.'

Jackson shot him a grim look.

'In that case, I hang at CC's Coffee House on Royal. You want to reach me, you just leave whatever you have there. A receipt, maybe an envelope with cash for the information I just gave you. Or how about you want to give me a "get out of jail free" card, but whatever it is you want to give me, leave it at CC's. Those folks know me well.'

'How did you know so much about the Black Card?'

'I, uh—'

'You tried to use it, didn't you?'

Jackson stared up at him, a thin smile on his lips. 'Apparently,' he said, 'you don't use one of those Black Cards to buy a po-boy and a beer. They 'bout threw me out of that place.'

51

He missed Denise every day. Every hour. Every minute. They didn't get to spend a lot of time together, the couple's two jobs in Detroit ate at their chance to be together, but they'd been close. Married just three years, dating on-and-off for ten. They'd grab ten minutes here, twenty minutes there, a cup of coffee, a fast-food sandwich, different spots around the city when he was working.

Denise worked as hard and almost as long as he did. She'd meet him during the day at the El Taquito food truck in southwest Detroit, where they would share a *ceviche tostada* and a chorizo taco, the sound of souped-up car engines and loud Harley-Davidsons gunning down West Vernor and Military ringing in their ears.

At night, they'd sometimes grab a bite near the Henry Ford Hospital in the north end, where Denise tended to emergencies like knifings, shootings, poisonings and a steady parade of hapless Detroiters who had the misfortune to get mugged.

She'd take her break close by, maybe at Park's Old Style Bar-B-Q on Beaubien Street and they'd share a slab of ribs covered in Park's famous sauce. He could almost taste it now. And if he closed his eyes for just a moment, he could taste Denise, her sweet kisses and soft, supple lips.

It seemed that he and Denise only saw each other over a meal. And of course the times they connected in bed. There was more than one time when one of them had been late for their shift because the loving lasted a little too long and was a little too intense. But then, like she once told him, when it came to making love, it could never be too long or too steamy.

As Archer drove back to the office, his thoughts turned to Solange Cordray. Strange to think it, but there was a food connection with her as well. She showed up at the damnedest times. He'd sit down to eat, and there she'd be, piecing out tidbits of information. Cryptic, mystic, just like Mike the bartender, the girl was playing with his head.

And he wondered what Solange Cordray was like in her moments of passion. He hadn't fantasized much about women since Denise was killed. Tried to keep his mind off anything but surviving, getting out of the Motor City, and starting a new life down here in the Big Easy. And of course finding Denise's killer. But the Cordray woman piqued his interest. He'd only seen her a few times, but there was something sexy about her. Possibly the mysterious way she approached him, but certainly for the soft dark skin, the thick dark hair. She was a beautiful woman to look at, with slight curves in just the right places. For some reason, if he were asked to conjure up images of witches or voodoo practitioners, they would be evil-looking women with warts, hooked noses and bad teeth. Solange's skin was smooth, her nose turned up just slightly, and her teeth appeared to be perfect.

'Where the hell have you been?' Sergeant Dan Sullivan walked to his desk.

'I told you, I needed a little time.'

'Well, here's what you missed.' Pointing his finger at Archer, he numbered the things they had learned in the brief time Q was gone.

'Number one, we found Jim Gideon, Skeeter Lewis's accomplice. Dumb-ass was hanging out at a place his wife's brother owns, wine bar called the Met. Gideon is next door but we're bringing him in for questioning in half an hour. Number two,' he continued, 'Gandal, the guy who was strangled in his Lincoln Navigator today, was seen having coffee at MRB this morning with a prominent New Orleans businessman. We're tracking down the identity, but several of the help said the man was a regular. Number three—'

'Sergeant, here's what I have for *you*.'

He handed the stocky man the black titanium American Express card.

Sullivan reared back, surprised by the presentation. Then he took the card, studying it for a moment.

'What is this?'

'Check it out,' Archer said.

'Richard Garrett? How the hell did you get this?'

'Garrett may be involved in the murder of Gandal.'

'No. I told you that Gandal worked for Garrett. There's no way Richard Garrett was involved in his murder.'

'Yes. Prominent New Orleans businessman. It all fits.'

'No. Do you understand me?' Sullivan was livid. 'This is not possible, Detective. Please understand what I'm saying.'

'Sergeant, you can't tell me—'

'I just did.' Sullivan handed him back the card. 'Leave this alone, Archer. I want no can of worms opened on my watch, do you understand?'

'Well, then let me tell you something.' Archer palmed the card. 'This guy was the last person out of the Lincoln Navigator where they found the body of Jonathon Gandal. It may implicate him as Gandal's killer, Sergeant. I suggest it does implicate him. What do you propose we do? I've got an eyewitness that I think will testify.'

'Give me the card,' Sullivan said, reaching for it.

'No.' Archer backed away.

'Do you understand the implications here? You're trying to destroy the reputation of a pillar in this community. I'll call Garrett and I'm sure he'll have a perfectly good explanation.'

'You don't get the card.'

Sullivan studied him for a moment, cocking his head and squinting his eyes as if deciding whether to officially confront him for his insubordination.

'Archer, I don't like you.'

'That has been obvious.'

'And if it had been my decision, no one would have offered you this job, knowing what I know about your background.'

'I'm lucky to have found this job,' Archer said, staring right back into the man's eyes. 'I will admit that.'

'Damn straight.'

'But your point is?'

'You're mucking up the water. And apparently your job in life is to take everyone else in your circle down with you. I've made it clear. There are certain people in this town that you don't want to fuck with. I'd rather you look in a different direction. Can I be any more direct?'

'I'm going in the direction of the conviction, Sergeant.'

'I'll almost guarantee you that this will garner you no conviction. Jesus, Archer, you lost your job in Detroit trying to take down people.'

'I was trying to get to the truth.'

'You're about to become a one-man train wreck. Don't fuck this one up the minute you get here.'

He'd started his tenure by pissing off the hierarchy. There was no place to go but up. Or, if he was fired, a spiral death.

52

G arrett stopped for lunch. Galatoire's on Bourbon Street, with its French Creole dishes. No hurry. It was probably best to take his time, act as if he was just in the area for a leisurely meal. With a copy of the *Times-Picayune* in front of him he finished his meal, finishing it off with a cup of cappuccino.

The waiter brought his check, and that's when the man started to sweat. His wallet was missing. He thrust his hand into his other rear pocket, then his two front pockets. Stepping out of the booth he studied the area, then looked under the table. Nothing.

All he could think of was the Lincoln Navigator. During the struggle it had slipped from his pocket and right now, as the police combed that vehicle, they already knew that he'd been inside the car. In the rear seat.

Closing his eyes he said a short prayer, hypocritical he knew because he believed in no higher authority. But this situation called for extra measures.

Asking for the manager, he explained the situation.

'Mr Garrett, we want to accommodate you any way we can. Just sign here, sir, and we'll send you your bill.'

With shaky hands, Garrett signed and left a fifty percent tip. Assuming he'd get the chance to actually pay the bill.

He walked back to his booth one more time, scanning the entire area, but there was nothing. Walking outside, he looked both ways, half expecting a cop to approach him and take him into custody then and there.

What if they hadn't found the body yet? He could simply go back, open the rear door and retrieve it. Then he thought about the cameras. Passing five, or seven or eight businesses, he was sure to be on camera. The damned things were everywhere. And by now, he was certain, they'd have found Gandal's body. Sure he'd had coffee with the man, but there was no evidence that . . . where was his damned wallet?

Then his thoughts turned to the short man who gave him a strong bump on the sidewalk. How naive of him to think the wallet had slipped out of his pocket in the Navigator. The guy who stepped from the alley was most certainly a professional pickpocket. Son of a bitch, that had to be the answer. Didn't it? So how much did the man know? Was he aware that Garrett had gotten out of the vehicle where Gandal had been killed? Had he watched Garrett actually open the door? It wasn't a good scenario.

On the surface, Richard Garrett was a man who oozed confidence. He'd picked up his father's sense of business, adding a quick decisiveness that almost always led to new avenues of profit for the growing oil firm. On the surface, Garrett was a force to be reckoned with. Someone who's wrath could bring down titans, destroy years of building, and often did.

On the surface, Garrett's magnanimous generosity cemented his contribution to the community and even people who had never met him had heard about the amazing work he'd done with Habitat for Humanity, the Cure and Wounded Warriors.

Beneath the surface, Garrett ran scared. The bluff and bravado of other titans of industry, captains of commerce and business gurus might fool most people, but Richard Garrett was always looking over his shoulder, assuming that someone else was going to figure him out, take over, do a better job and kick him to the curb. His band of handlers worked their magic and he'd never been uncovered, but damn. This wasn't a good time to have that facade fall apart. And he needed to immediately stem the tide.

He sat down on a street bench and watched the traffic go by. Pedestrian and vehicle alike oblivious to the biggest dilemma he'd ever faced. Someone, either the law or a citizen, had evidence that he was involved in a murder. Involved, hell. They may know he was the killer.

Grabbing his cell phone he punched in two numbers, and the voice on the other end answered immediately.

'Hey, Mr Garrett. What can I do for you?'

'There's a guy, short, black, wears a sport coat, in the Quarter Pickpocket.'

'There are dozens of pickpockets in the Quarter, Mr Garrett. Pick pockets, apple pickers . . .'

'Apple pickers?'

'Guys who steal cell phones.'

At least he hadn't taken that.

'There's one short black guy who has my American Express card. I want my wallet, my driver's license and that card and I want *him*. Am I clear?'

'On it, Mr G.'

'You'd damned well better be.'

Garrett stared at his phone for a second then made a second call.

He could hear the phone ring, one, two, three and four times. Finally—

'Joseph, your ex-wife is a liability.'

Garrett could almost feel Joseph Cordray's gut clench.

'Garrett?'

'Are you going to deal with this?'

There was a hesitation on the other end. A long hesitation.

'She can be a bitch. But a liability?' Cordray asked.

'I've got somebody inside and they say the cops are thinking the Krewe may be involved. And,' he hesitated, 'me. You tell me who else would figure that out. It's your wife.'

'Hell, you've been seeing her. Maybe you let something slip.'

'Listen, Joseph, I may have made a mistake in using her services, but I never . . .'

'So, what do you want me to do? Have a talk with her?' Cordray asked.

Garrett was silent for a moment. He'd acted on impulse and probably should have thought the call through before making it.

'I know now I never should have used her as an intermediary.'

'You think? I only warned you about twenty times,' Cordray said. 'Sometimes you don't listen, Richard.'

'Don't lecture me, my friend. I'll admit it was a mistake. My father swore by her mother when he made buying and selling decisions. I'm sure you'll admit he did quite well.'

'Your father and Clotille Trouville were of a different time, Richard. And you and I have stepped over some boundaries. We're in uncharted waters here. You should have left the past be the past.'

'Probably.'

'She's psychic, Richard. Maybe more than even her mother. One of the reasons I left her.'

Garrett cracked a smile. Joseph Cordray couldn't deal with the fact that his wife, the Voodoo Queen Solange Cordray, was aware of his numerous affairs. He suspected that she'd put a hex on several of them. Some serious shit. One of the ladies had walked into traffic; another one had put a pistol to her head and pulled the trigger. Another reason that Garrett should have been leery of the woman. But she seemed to be so intuitive. Everything she did seemed to work some sort of magic.

'Well, Richard, there's one more thing I should tell you,' Cordray sounded cautious. 'I have someone who keeps an eye on her. Don't take that any further, OK?'

'Follows her? You're her ex-husband. Isn't that a little creepy?'

'I like to know what she's doing. Where she goes. Solange usually works at that place where her mom lives down by the river, and when she's not there she's in that shop where she does her business. You've been there. The place she casts her spells.'

Garrett had been there. Probably one too many times, and deep down he knew that was a big part of the problem.

'And?'

'Several times in the last week she's been seeing a certain cop.'

Garrett took a deep breath.

'Seeing? Like dating?'

'I don't think so. If they were dating, I'd know. Trust me. My guy is pretty thorough. They don't arrive together and they don't leave together. It's a meeting over coffee, beer and I guess a pizza one time. Anyway, this cop, Quentin Archer, he's the lead on Lerner's murder, but I didn't seriously think—'

'Jesus. You didn't tell me this? She's talking to a lead detective on the Lerner case and you decide to keep that quiet? What the fuck is wrong with you?'

'What the fuck is wrong with *me*? *You* had a relationship with her, for God's sake. And you were well aware she is my *ex*-wife. Ex.'

'I asked her for advice, damn it. My father asked her mother for advice. I'd hardly call that a relationship.'

'Listen, Garrett, Solange should have been left out of this entire process. You call me and say "are you going to deal with this"?'

There was a long silence from the other end of the phone line.

'You seriously don't know where she's coming from?'

'She could come from anywhere. Solange is a wild card. She's capable of anything. You take it from there.'

Garrett heard the connection go dead.

Where the hell was his wallet? Where the hell was Solange Cordray? And what did she know?

His well-connected world, his stature in the community as a player, his entire front was falling apart. His desire to exceed his current wealth, build his power base, to go beyond anything his old man had dreamed of, this was what drove him. And maybe he'd pushed this just a little too far.

And maybe this witch, this voodoo lady, this seer, this soothsayer, maybe she was gumming up the works. She'd given him insight, helped with several spells and yet since he'd been using her, things had gone to hell. Three judges had become liabilities. Three judges had been eliminated. So maybe what he'd perceived as psychic intervention had been psychic *interference.* Maybe she was causing the problems. Maybe it was intentional. Maybe it was seriously time to eliminate the spirit. The voodoo practitioner.

If you eliminated the intermediary, then there was no connection to the spiritual world, right? If you cut off the connection, there was no connection. Events could happen without interference. Events would end with a logical conclusion. There would be no prejudice from outside sources. No spirits, no voodoo, no magic. It seemed like the perfect answer.

53

Garrett's phone rang and he glanced at the number, hoping one of his questions had been answered.

'Pickpocket's name is Samuel Jackson.'

'You've got him? Got the wallet and my card?'

'One thing at a time, boss. We don't have him but we know who he is. Hangs out at a place called CC's Community Coffee House on Royal.'

'Can you get him?'

'Eventually.'

'There is no eventually. That's bullshit. Get him now and get my wallet back.'

'What do you want to do with him?'

'Do I have to spell it out? Finish the transaction.'

'We'll get it done, boss.'

'Get the card. Get the wallet. Get my ID. Understand?'

Garrett terminated the call, shaking his head. What was this 'boss' shit? It should be Mr Garrett. He distrusted anyone who called him 'boss'. Hell, he distrusted almost everyone. Those who worked for him, those who didn't. Those who threw themselves at him and those who hated him.

Let the team deal with Samuel Jackson. They could find this

street punk, get the wallet and deal with him. But he knew where to find Solange Cordray and he also knew the woman had no fear for herself. None. She feared for others, her clients, her mother, maybe even this lead cop, but she'd never exhibited any fear for herself. Which left her wide open. Vulnerable. In no way defensive. He could walk up to her, greet her, stick a knife in her and she would probably never see it coming. And that was his advantage. He was going to have to kill her. Immediately. If you want something done, do it yourself.

The Cordray lady could see dark clouds for her clients. She could forecast evil, see signs of failure for others, but in the times he'd interacted with her, she never watched out for herself. Her selflessness, her concern for her fellow man, it would be the death of her. Garrett had penetrated her shield. He knew exactly how to break her down. And she needed to be dealt with. Right now.

He reached the Bentley, opened the door and slid into the sleek interior. His own private cockpit, his cocoon, the soft buttery leather seats, the wood-grained dash panel and Sirius radio with its array of choices. For a very brief moment he wanted the old relationship with Solange Cordray back. He wanted to know that his problems had been solved. He wanted to be certain that the pressure would ease, that all evidence leading back to the Krewe, back to him, had been eliminated.

He wanted to go to his spiritual leader and have her confirm his salvation. But that ship had sailed.

He sat there for the better part of half an hour, in the quiet, wrapped in his own luxury. He never even turned on the radio. He'd always imagined that he could skate on anything they threw at him, but he knew that if they eventually caught up with him, he'd probably kill himself. He was too big to fail. And if failure was an eventuality, then he'd end it all.

Finally, Richard Garrett stepped back out of the luxurious sedan and gazed down the street. Cordray's store, shop, boutique, place of worship, was two blocks away. No reason to park the car in front of the business. He could walk it. And, with any luck, she would be there. If so, the deed could be done. And if she wasn't available, he'd drive down to Water's Edge Care Center and wait for her to get off.

Where there was a will, there was a way and the sooner he got

rid of the fortune teller, the soothsayer, the better off he was going
to be.

54

T he old man from the bayou parked his bike near a lamp post
and padlocked the chain. He'd had a bike stolen from the
Quarter before and he'd spent more money this time to get
an Xterra chain, one that no one with regular bolt clippers could
cut. No one. The chain was almost as tough as he was.

He'd been to Clotille Trouville's store once before. Possibly he'd
violated the spiritual sanctity in that place. Possibly he had caused
the gods and spirits to become angry. He'd introduced a very physical presence there. Maybe, just maybe, he'd had something to do
with Clotille's slow descent into chaos. Whatever it was, he swore
he would never go back. The memories were too strong. The memories of her and what had happened.

More often, she had come to him. The comfortable woman with
the wide smile and good news. Always good news. She'd speak of
the changing weather, or the positive economic forecast. She would
glow about results she'd had with his herbs, spices, and magical
ingredients. And it had gone from there. Friends. More than friends.
And then the night at her shop. A clandestine meeting that ended
with carnal knowledge. A night of passion that was filled with lust,
a crazed aura that neither of them ever dreamed they were capable
of. He dreamed about it for months after. Years. Nothing ever so
intense had ever been a part of his life.

Then she disappeared. Vanished. He made some inquiries but no
one knew where she'd gone. He became a hermit, seldom venturing
beyond his swamp.

It was months before he saw her again, and one day she walked
into his clearing, smiled at him and sat down for a meal. And
although she was friendly, there was a distance that he could not
breach or understand and the relationship was never the same. Within
a couple of years she started bringing the girl with her, the shy one
who hid behind her mother's long colorful skirts and peaked out at

him. She was a beauty even then. Dark hair, long eyelashes and a nose that turned at the tip. He could tell from first glance she was going to be trouble.

And that girl was *in* trouble. Right now. He sensed it, felt it, knew it. Matebo had thrown the bones, stirred the leaves and prayed to the highest authority. There was no doubt in his mind that Solange was a target.

It could be the cop, although there seemed to be an attraction there. It could be someone involved with the murder of the judges. The image wasn't clear, but he needed to be there. To protect her, and truth be told, he needed to see her mother. Matebo knew he had to visit with Clotille Trouville one last time. He needed to know if he was the father of her child.

In her incapacitated state, could she communicate with him? The lady of mystical wisdom who had been stripped of all her senses? Voodoo was a strange medicine. A mixture of faith and mysticism, and Clotille was a mambo, a priestess, who could read the elements. In her prime she had been among the best and Matebo hoped that inside the shell of this woman there still stirred the spirit that remembered the voodoo ways. Maybe she could communicate with him. Maybe she could converse or give him a sign that would affirm his suspicion.

Anywhere else the old man would have drawn attention, the long gray hair, braided and hanging down his back. His dark brown leather vest hung over a naked, shriveled chest; his thin legs were covered by white cotton slacks that fell loosely from his waist. Alligator skin sandals, footwear that he had fashioned himself from a fresh kill, and a bracelet of feathers made from a hawk that had tried to steal a small rabbit he had killed. In New Orleans, in the French Quarter, he was almost normal. Almost.

Walking down the sidewalk he shook his head, embarrassed by the cheap bars and tourist stops that populated the street. They reinforced his need to hide in the swamps, to live in the bayou and cease communication with the normal people of the Big Easy. If it was even reasonable to call them normal.

A throng of Mid-Western tourists crowded the sidewalk, and he had to walk into the street to avoid their celebrations. Hooting and crowing they laughed at him as he passed by.

Concentrating on his mission, he thought about his talk with

Solange. If she was stubborn like her mother and refused to listen to his advice, then the next step was to kidnap her. Hold her hostage in his home in the bayou.

When the danger had passed, when he felt that things were back to normal, whatever normal was, he would release her to continue with her life, but Matebo was certain he was put on this earth to protect this woman. And right now she was in danger. Extreme danger. There was absolutely no question about it.

Matebo approached the shop, hoping she'd listen to reason.

Glancing across the street, he saw the man in the gray slacks, white shirt and blue necktie loosely knotted around his neck. The stranger was observing him, never taking his eyes off him. Matebo was aware that he stuck out in public, but this guy's stare was a little too intense.

There was something sinister about the man, but the swamp man couldn't quite put his finger on it.

55

Archer's phone rang as he was driving and he answered.

'Detective Q, it's Mike.'

His favorite bartender.

'Another report. The man Gandal last saw before he was killed. It was the oil tycoon Mr Richard Garrett.'

Confirmed.

'A contact saw them together. There seemed to be an argument. My contact says that the two of them were going back and forth. But they left together. So, my contact says they were a duo until one of them was killed. And we both know who that was.'

'Thanks, Mike. We've got a similar story.' The black AmEx card was privileged information. He'd kept it, stashing it in his back pocket, waiting for a chance to use the piece of plastic as evidence.

'Not done yet, *ami*. This Jonathon Gandal, the victim, has recently been seen with a Sam Campari, a low-rent borderline mobster who does dirty jobs for some of the Big Easy's connected citizens.'

'People have strange friends, Mike.'

'Ah, but this guy has been meeting frequently with our Jonathon Gandal. As I said, recently. Right around the time that the judges were being murdered. Trust me Q, these meetings have some gravitas.'

Stepping from the wheezing Chevy, wiping sweat from his brow, Archer walked away without locking the car, half hoping someone would actually steal the clunker and maybe he could upgrade to some drug dealer's repo'd Lincoln or Cadillac.

'This Campari, he's not the kind of guy that Richard Garrett would personally want to meet with?' Archer asked the question.

'I wouldn't think so. Jesus, Garrett works on a reputation as a wholesome son of a bitch, but I'm sure some of his employees would say different. By my accounts, Garrett has used other people to do almost all of his dirty work. That's why I wouldn't think Garrett would want to get blood on his hands, but he's apparently done that,' Mike said. 'We're pretty sure he killed Jonathon Gandal.'

Archer heard the word 'we'. He wondered what Mike had. An entire team of investigators?

'Maybe Garrett had run out of people he could trust.' Archer was getting to that point, too, wondering who he could trust. Family, the Detroit cops, and now his sergeant and his partner. Neither of the latter wanted to pursue Garrett. But to be truthful, he didn't trust either of them. Sullivan and Strand hadn't shown any support for his ideas this entire case; hell, ever since he'd gotten there. Maybe Garrett had the same problem with his staff. Whatever he was involved with, he had to make it happen himself. There was no one left that he could trust. No one else to do the dirty work.

Archer could hear the clinking of glasses and china and pictured the wiry-haired man behind the bar, talking in hushed tones.

'Campari has been rumored to solicit a man who goes by the name of Loup-garou. The Werewolf.'

'Go on.' That corroborated the information from Skeeter Lewis.

'Guy works the edge and I haven't been able to get a handle on his real name, but he arranges end-of-life scenarios.'

End-of-life scenarios. Serious shit.

Archer thought for a moment. If Mike had told him yesterday that Richard Garrett was guilty of Gandal's murder, he would have questioned the entire account. Probably dismissed it altogether. But he had Samuel Jackson's story, and Archer had the black American

Express card. Maybe enough evidence to bring before a judge. The puzzle just might be coming together.

'Loup-garou has worked for the Gagliano family, Q,' Mike continues. 'Big time mob name in New Orleans. He stays busy in this area. This Werewolf, he's a bad guy, trust me. So if he's setting up the hits, maybe the mob is involved.'

It was a stretch. Like six degrees of Kevin Bacon. Anyone could piece together enough relationships and trace themselves back to someone. But, if Garrett employed Gandal, and Gandal had had meetings with Campari, and Campari had had meetings with this Loup-garou, then maybe, just maybe there really was a Garrett connection to the murdered judges.

'I'm going to meet with your friend, Solange Cordray, Mike. Hopefully in a few minutes. I'm thinking she can help fill in some of the blanks. The lady seems to have a pretty good handle on what's going on. And you, my friend, you've been a big help. If it weren't for people like you, we wouldn't solve these crimes.'

There was momentary silence on the other end. Archer could hear the bar sounds, and the breathing of the bartender.

'Q, I told you that I would tell you everything I knew once I knew. So far, I'm fulfilling my promise.'

'Yeah?'

'Now you've got to do what you said you'd do.'

'And that was?'

'Keep asking why. Your question should be *why*. I can give you everything I've learned, but you need to know why, am I right?'

'Exactly.'

'You've got the pieces, my man.'

'Why? Why would someone with the strength and power of Richard Garrett kill someone like Gandal? What was he thinking? The guy is an oil magnate. A rich son of a bitch. What was he doing? Protecting himself?'

'You're on the right track, Quentin. Put the pieces together. If I have any other information I've got your number, *inspecteur*. I'll call you. In the meantime, you need to concentrate on what you know. Figure this out, because the story is not good for our community.'

The connection went dead.

Archer holstered the phone, shaking his head. The events of the last days flew through his head. Three dead judges, a list of numbers, a partner who admitted to being on the take, the former lover of Judge David Lerner who had disappeared, Warden Jakes's Jaguar showing up at Lerner's house and a murder recorded on a smart phone. The Krewe, Richard Garrett and Solange Cordray. Somewhere in there was an answer.

He found a parking spot just a block from Solange's shop. As he walked briskly toward the building he heard a shrill scream. At almost the same time, a disheveled man in his mid-thirties stepped from the store hunched over, running his hands through his hair and straightening his clothes.

Quickly looking one way then the other, the man walked down the street as if in pain, his head bent down as if to avoid detection.

Archer crossed the street with a burst of speed. Pushing open the door of Solange's shop he immediately saw the old man, crumpled on the floor. His white hair was splayed across the aged gray wood and a trail of blood spread across his exposed cheek and ran onto the floor. Across the small room stood Solange Cordray, her ebony hair in disarray, white dress torn so that her right shoulder was bare. Her dark face was flushed and tears streamed down her cheeks. Her eyes were wide open, sharing her terror with whoever stared into them.

56

Strand took a long swig from the warm bottle of Jack, feeling the whiskey burn down his throat and into his stomach. The bottle was almost gone. Even with the windows rolled down, the heat was unbearable. He watched the two Hispanics saunter into the convenience store, and almost wished they would try to rob the place. He could step in, level his Glock and save the day. Still vital. Still a damned good cop, right? The Indian who owned the place would probably treat him to a spicy tamarind sambar dinner, and he'd be on all the news shows. Finally, his claim to fame.

Thinking about a curry meal made him even hotter. He was tempted to go in and buy a cold six pack, drink a bottle in the car and hold it to his perspiring face. Where the hell was Trueblood?

The waiting was killing him. He should be working on the murders. Instead he was selling the evidence. He took another swig from the dwindling pint. Should have brought another bottle.

He saw the car pull in by the reflection in his side mirror. As Trueblood pulled alongside, Strand patted the file folder next to him. He kept thinking about the forty thousand dollars. He could catch up on child support, actually buy a nice present for his little girl. Take a vacation. Buy some love. It wasn't so bad. It was a lot of money for very little work. Be positive. No one was going to find out that he was responsible. This was simply a list of prisoners who were already documented. Just a list of their prison numbers. Nothing that couldn't be found again with a little digging.'

Then why was he being offered forty thousand dollars for these printouts? What could possibly make them so valuable that this organization, whatever it may be, would offer him that kind of money?

The two Hispanics walked out, a paper bag in the taller man's hand. Some wine. No bag of cash. No chance to be a fucking hero.

He watched Trueblood's car and everything was still. No movement. The glare of the sun cut off any visual through the windows. Who should make the first move? He considered the options. Eying the remaining warm whiskey, he took a long swallow, finally realizing he'd now finished the bottle. A little dizzy, a little woozy, but ready for the next challenge.

After two minutes, Strand finally opened the door. The heat was even more oppressive in the sun. Feeling a little tipsy, he walked around the back of his car and tapped on the window of Trueblood's driver's side.

The window came down and the man looked up at Strand and gave him a thin-lipped smile.

'Adam, you brought the sheets?'

'That was the purpose of our visit.' Strand gave a backward glance to see if a cop car was going to appear and arrest him.

'You've been drinking?'

'A little. Does that matter?'

Trueblood smiled. 'No. Can I see them?'

'Can I see the cash?'

'After I see the sheets.'

Strand wiped the sweat from his brow, running his hand through his hair. There wasn't a part of him that wasn't damp. He wished he'd remained a little more sober. A little less lightheaded.

'I'd prefer to know you brought the money.' He repeated the word. 'Money.' He staggered, slightly. 'Come on, man, just show me some of the cash and . . .' He was slurring his words.

'The money isn't going to materialize until I see the spreadsheets, Detective.'

Strand nodded. 'It appears we're at an impasse.' Impasse. Good choice of words. He smiled. 'An impasse, sir.'

'I don't think you've got them. I don't think you could get the file out of the evidence room. Too much for someone like you. Am I right? You don't have them, do you?'

'I think you're full of shit, Trueblood. I don't think you brought the money.' And at that point, he seriously wasn't sure. He was scared.

'Well, I guess this is a draw, Adam.' Trueblood started his engine, putting the car in reverse.

'Wait. Wait.' He wasn't going to let the money go. Not after all he'd been through. 'All right, man, I guess I can show you the evidence. You can see the merchandise, but I need to see cash.'

'Bring them here.'

Strand staggered back to his car, reaching in and pulling out the folder. It just seemed so cheap. Forty thousand dollars' worth of digital printouts in a plain folder. It didn't seem right.

Walking back to Trueblood's car he opened the folder and showed the man what was inside.

'Give me the folder. I need to examine it to see if this is the information we're after.'

'I need to see—'

'Strand.'

Hesitantly Strand handed him the folder.

'OK, Adam. Your worst fears have been realized.'

'What?'

Trueblood set the folder on the passenger seat.

'I'm not giving you forty thousand dollars. I'm not giving you anything. It's over, man.'

'What the—'

'The good news is, I'm not going to tell your superiors that you stole these from the evidence room. Nobody is going to know. Do you understand? That's the price, Strand. I won't tell anyone where

I got these. You want to argue with me, I'll be happy to tell your superiors where I got them. I'll be happy to destroy you, put you in prison. I get the printouts, everything is quiet, you walk away. That's kind of the way it is, my friend. Sorry.'

Strand stood there with his mouth open. He could see the folder, out of reach, and he could say absolutely nothing. His world collapsed. The spreadsheets, out of reach, no money to be transferred. He stared at the folder as Trueblood reached behind himself and pulled out a pistol. He laid it on the seat, his hand covering it.

Finally Strand blurted out, 'You can't do that. No, it doesn't work like that. When this evidence comes up missing—'

'I *can* do that. Try to understand. I just did. Don't you get it? You're fucked. But I won't tell a soul where I got them. If you left yourself as a possible suspect, hey, it's not my problem, Adam.'

'You said . . . you said we had a deal. I mean, this was a done deal. How can you . . .? I put myself on the line, for God's sake. No, no, don't, please. Jesus, don't leave me hanging here. Please. This is a huge fucking deal and . . .' His little girl, a trip to the Bahamas. 'Something. Ten thousand . . .' Tears sprang to his eyes.

As the window started to rise, Strand reached in, his hands going for Trueblood's throat. He could think of nothing else but killing the liar. He'd been through this kind of hell for nothing. The window caught him, his arms pinched now in the space and he wrenched them out, staring in disbelief as the man's car backed out and pulled onto the street.

Watching the car turn and disappear at the intersection he stood frozen on the blacktop parking lot. A fog clouded his brain and he tried hard to comprehend how he'd just been shorted his windfall. It was impossible to absorb. Strand wiped his face with his shirtsleeve, wondering how he could be that stupid, that naive. There was a degree of trust that should have been honored. It was impossible to conceive. Seriously? The guy had just shrugged his shoulders and driven off? Strand had plans for that money. Forty grand. And now, absolutely nothing. And he didn't even know for sure who the man was and who he worked for.

His feet felt like lead as he trudged back to his car. The passenger seat that until minutes ago held forty thousand dollars' worth of merchandise was empty. All because he trusted someone to honor his commitment. All because he'd believed that things always ended up working out. Even though he knew they seldom did. The detective wished himself sober, but that wasn't going to happen any time soon. No booze, no money, no spreadsheets.

Strand sat behind the wheel, staring into space as sweat and tears ran down his face, dripping into his eyes. Five, ten, fifteen minutes he sat there, no air conditioning, the oppressive humidity soaking him in his clothes.

A million thoughts went through his mind, and then it would go blank. He could put out an all-points bulletin, claiming the man stole the printouts, but there was no record of Trueblood going into the evidence room. None. He could try to track the man and confront him. Chances are the file would have been transferred to whoever he worked for long before he even got to him.

How many people had seen him in that evidence room? He could count five or six. Probably more. And if those records carried more important information than he could understand, well, that was even worse.

And at that moment, as if on cue, a long-haired bearded man came barreling out of the 7-Eleven, a paper bag in hand, and a pistol in the other. He turned on the sidewalk, a bullet ricocheted off the building as he fired back at the store.

Strand took a deep breath, calmly reached into his glove compartment and pulled out his Glock. Pulling back the hammer, he aimed the gun at the retreating robber. He held the pistol steady, watching the man run, then turn the corner and disappear from sight. Strand put the barrel in his mouth and pulled the trigger.

57

There was no question it was Garrett.

'He was a crazy man, Detective. After he knocked Matebo to the floor, he grabbed my throat and said I needed to be silenced.' She sat in a hemp-woven chair, gaining her composure.

The old man, Matebo, had argued, but the paramedics took him to Tulane University Hospital for observation. They assured Solange that he seemed to be fine, but to be safe they needed to transport him to the medical facility.

Archer had invited her to Cafe Envie, a neutral spot, hoping the young woman would give him a more substantial statement. Hoping she would . . . he wasn't sure what. Maybe just solve the case.

Cordray and Archer sat across from each other in Cafe Envie, the high, lazy ceiling fans slowly stirring the stale air, the girl with her dark espresso and Archer with his green tea.

'Why?'

She stared into his eyes and he steeled himself against any emotion. She had an effect, manipulative or unintentional, but Archer needed a clear head.

'Why? Why did Garrett say you needed to be silenced? What do you know that you were going to tell?'

'Because of what I've told you. He is the leader of Krewe Charbonerrie. He's responsible for the death of—'

'Why? Why did he have the judges killed?'

'It has to do with the prison. It has to do with the young men who go there.'

'How do you know that?' he asked.

'He told me.'

'Told you?'

'He said I must be silenced. And as he wrapped his hands around my throat, he said that I knew about the sentencing, I knew about the boys in prison, and I had to be silenced.'

Archer looked away, sipping his tea.

'No voodoo spell? No reading minds?'

'No, it was what Richard Garrett told me.'

'He thought you knew. As he was strangling you. As he was trying to kill you.'

'Just as he did with Jonathon Gandal.'

The detective shook his head. 'Garrett is about six foot two, weighs around two ten. If he wanted to kill you, he would have killed you.'

'I don't think so,' she said.

'You put a curse on him? Chanted something?'

Cordray wrapped her small hands around her coffee mug.

'Are you mocking me, Detective?'

'No. Not at all. I want to know. How did you stop this man from ending your life? You have some abilities that I'm apparently not aware of.'

'There are certain things we learn from an early age, Mr Archer.'

'Your mother taught you?'

Smiling, she nodded. 'I'm sure my mother taught me, and others as I grew older.'

'Voodoo secrets that you can't divulge?'

'A knee in the groin, Detective. And when he let go I screamed like hell. So did he. It has nothing to do with voodoo. It has to do with survival.'

Archer arranged for a patrolman to watch Solange Cordray, and put out an all-points bulletin to pick up Richard Garrett. When reached at his corporate headquarters, Garrett's personal assistant claimed to have no knowledge of his whereabouts and strongly denied any suggestion that the oil magnate had anything to do with murder or attempted murder.

On his way home Archer called Strand's phone, but after five rings he got an automated answer so he decided to try back later. His shirt was wet with sweat and he walked the short distance to his home, planning on a quick shower and a change of clothes.

Put the pieces together. Antoine Duvay was the first piece. Duvay was their first suspect. He and Adam Strand had admitted to each other that if Duvay had confessed, this case would have been perfect. But that piece didn't seem to fit.

Richard Garrett had told Solange Cordray that it was all about the boys in prison. And Antoine Duvay had worked personally for the warden. Duvay had run at the first sign of trouble. Archer took a chance that Levy would still be at the precinct and called his extension. Levy answered on the second ring.

'Antoine Duvay worked personal detail for Warden Jakes at the prison.'

'Yeah. A real model prisoner, seriously.'

'Listen, Levy, the kid Duvay runs when he hears that Judge Lerner has been murdered, but it turns out Duvay had nothing to do with the murder.'

'Unless he knows why the judge was murdered and he's afraid you know more than you do.'

'Yeah. I may have to actually apologize to Strand. Maybe Duvay was involved.'

'You haven't heard?'

'What?'

'Strand committed suicide. Shot himself in his car.'

'Jesus.'

'Yeah.'

'Did he leave a . . .'

'Note? No. But there was a note beside him.'

'What?'

'He'd scrawled one line. *Meet P.T. at 7-Eleven.*'

'P.T.?'

'They're running it now but all that came up immediately is the P.T. you included in your report. The guy that Lerner was supposed to meet just before he was murdered.'

'Somebody pick up Antoine Duvay. Bring him in and we're going to question him one more time.'

Strand, dead? And a meeting with P.T. The case got stranger every minute.

Once home, Archer threw his keys on the small kitchen table and headed for the bathroom. Quickly stripping off his clothes, Archer stepped into the lukewarm shower and let the water wash over him. A little soap, a little scrubbing and in five minutes he felt much better. Stepping out, he wrapped the worn white towel around his waist and took a deep breath. Tobacco, cigarette smoke. He remembered it well. Often longed for it. Someone outside his cottage must be smoking. He opened the bathroom door and the man sitting on his bed smiled at him, cigarette burning in one hand, Archer's Glock in the other.

58

She prayed for Matebo. To the spirits, all of them. The old man didn't deserve to die at the hands of a thug like Garrett. And she cast a spell, one she seldom used, wishing that Richard Garrett would be punished. She was responsible. She'd accepted the degenerate as a client and even when she knew he was evil, she had strung him on, hoping that she could learn more about his immoral mission.

It went against her beliefs to wish someone harm. But she followed the ancient ritual. His name, written three times on rice paper. Then she torched the paper, ashes forming in a ceramic bowl. Praying to Erzulie Dantor, goddess of vengeance, she stepped outside, nodding at her uniformed nanny, and blew hard on the black ashes. They scattered in the gentle breeze and she could feel the intense gaze from the police officer. Garrett deserved to be convicted and sentenced to death. He'd been responsible for killing three judges, and he'd hurt Matebo. She hoped the spell was powerful enough. And Garrett was responsible for the patrolmen assigned to her. She was not going to be held prisoner by anyone. The voodoo lady had a healthy distrust of all law enforcement officers, even Quentin Archer, and now to be surrounded by them twenty-four hours a day was almost unbearable.

'Ma'am, is there any trouble?'

'No.' She forced a smile. 'Some ashes I needed to get rid of.'

He nodded as if he understood. But no one really understood.

She walked back into her shop, thinking about Ma. What if Garrett decided to use her mother? There was almost no security at the home, no real reason for it. Yet Garrett knew her mother was there, and he was aware of the bond between mother and daughter.

She needed to do something. The worst thing that could happen would be if Richard Garrett used her mother as a bargaining chip.

Pulling her cell phone from her purse, she called Archer's cell. No answer, just an automated voice.

Solange walked into the back room of the small shop, opened the waist-high window and climbed out. In a minute she was on the next street and headed toward the Water's Edge Care Center.

59

Archer stood there, with just a towel for protection.

'You're looking a little tired, bro.' The man with the Glock hesitated, taking a deep breath. 'And apparently you-you-you're getting a little sloppy. I thought you took your gun with you-you know, every-everywhere.'

The slight stutter was familiar. Archer had grown up listening to it every day.

'What do you want?'

'A piece of y-you, my man.' Jason Archer aimed the barrel at Q's chest. 'For what you did. You fucked up my life, Quentin. And my brother's li-life.'

'You two fucked up your own lives.'

'We don't see it like that. And I don't think D-Dad sees it like that either.'

'I've got a killer on the loose, I've got an interview with a suspect, and a partner who just committed suicide. I've got a young lady whose life is in jeopardy and as you probably know, my job is on the line. So why don't you either do what you came to do, or get the hell out of my house.'

'Always the strong man, Quentin. Always the guy who was p-put upon but kept his backbone straight, like iron. What was that song Dad used to s-sing? "One fist of iron, the other of steel." I grew up thinking that was prob-probably you.'

'Didn't work out so well in Detroit, did it?' Archer asked.

'Bobby M is still driving the streets, bro. You should have left well enough alone.'

'Who killed her, Jason?'

'I th-think it was an accident.' He aimed the barrel at Q's head, then moved it down to line up with his crotch. Pointing with his free hand to the papers on the end table, he nodded. 'You've been doing a little dig-digging. Somebody in D-Detroit feeding you information?'

'Private security company. Nobody you know.'

'You were warned, b-bro. Leave it alone. We'll st-stop you if we have to.'

'Who killed her, Jason? Tell me. Because if it was you, you'll never outrun me. And if it was Mercer or somebody else, I need to know.'

'Denise was a noose around your neck, Quentin. You got all high and mighty when you finally hooked up. L-let it lie.'

'That was my wife, Jason. My wife.'

'I know, dude.' He snubbed the cigarette out on the faux wooden end table and the embers sizzled as they burned into the surface.

'So what's it going to be?'

'Pretty tough talk from a man with no clothes.'

'Get it over with, Jason.'

Jason Archer smiled, and stroked his scraggly beard with his left hand.

'No heroics? No desperate grab for the gun?'

'You've got to live with what you did and what you're going to do. It's pretty much your call right now. I just want to know who killed Denise. Who ran a vehicle up on a sidewalk to get even with me?'

'You put our brother Brian in jail, Quentin. You set back an, you know, an operation that was doing pretty well for everyone. There are a hun-hundred side deals going on in Detroit. Everyone looking out for themselves and you come along and decide to play Serpico. One man is going to bring down everyone. You arrogant piece of sh-shit. You pompous asshole. You could have stayed out of it and none of this would have happened. Even dad told you to b-back off. Your wife would be alive, you'd have your old job back and Brian wouldn't be doing time.'

'And you'd still be pushing drugs on the street and getting people killed.'

'Fuck you.'

Jason raised the barrel, aiming it directly between Quentin Archer's eyes.

'You were sent here to kill me, weren't you? You going to shoot me?'

Jason nodded and pulled the trigger.

60

Solange walked quickly, not knowing how long it would take until the policeman realized she had left the shop. His job would be on the line, and she felt sorry about that, but her main concern was her mother. That was all that mattered.

Avoiding the main streets when she could, she dodged into alleys and courtyards that she knew well, taking a shortcut here, going the long way around over there. A mongrel dog growled menacingly as she worked her way through a back alley, and she gave it a stern look. The mangy-haired animal cowered and whimpered as she moved on by. She dodged garbage cans overflowing with rotting produce and putrid meat, the stench permeating the air, and several rusted charcoal grills that stood on cement block porches, along with vinyl folding chairs that were torn and faded from wear and the sun.

She wasn't sure what her next move would be, but she felt certain that staying with Ma would be the first step toward insuring her safety. The helplessness of the old woman brought tears to her eyes.

Stepping out of a small courtyard, she saw the long, two-story building one block away. Water's Edge Care Center. She sprinted across the street barely missing a man selling ice cream from a pushcart. A family of four stepped aside as she ran past them. In between two small cottages and—

'Where the hell do you think you're going?'

The thick arm came out of nowhere, wrapping itself around her neck and picking her up off the ground.

She gave a strangled cry and started kicking, her small frame helpless against the big man who reeked of alcohol.

'You think you can threaten me, cost me my job? You think you are too fucking good for me?'

'Clarence, you don't want to do anything else. Stop it now. Seriously, you are going to be in so much trouble.'

He tightened his grip and she felt lightheaded, choking and desperately gasping for any air.

'Tell me about trouble, missy. You don't want to fuck around with me.'

Solange Cordray felt a sharp pain shoot through her brain. She needed to save her mother; that was her primary goal. *Focus. Ma.* Her eyes watched exploding stars, until there was no more air to breath.

CC's Community Coffee House on Royal was one in a chain of thirty in Louisiana. A popular gathering spot in the Quarter with an extensive coffee menu and a variety of baked goods, it was a great place to hang out. And hanging out was exactly what Samuel Jackson was doing.

He sat at one of the tables, rotating fans in the ceiling keeping him cool. He tried again to program his new iPhone. The trick was erasing the previous owner's programming. He'd searched this phone for bank account numbers, phone numbers and any other personal information, but he'd pretty much come up empty. Now he was trying to erase the information already in memory and program his own information. He could then sell the phone and capture any private information the new owner would download. Jackson had a market for all of that information. It was a complicated procedure, but very lucrative. He could make a couple hundred bucks a day just Apple-picking. He pecked at the keyboard, intently watching the screen.

'Sam?'

Surprised, he looked up and didn't like what he saw. Two bruisers with gray sport coats and their hands in their pockets. Only three reasons why someone has their hand in a pocket. To keep the hand warm, to steal something from that pocket (and he had plenty of experience with that reason) and to pull out a gun. Immediately he settled on number three.

'Who wants to know?'

Quietly the bigger of the two whispered, 'Richard Garrett. It seems you have something of his.'

'Oh, shit.'

'We can make this easy, Sam. Give us the wallet, everything included. We'll even roll on the money, sonny, but we need everything else.'

'I can get it. I don't have the Black Card, but I know where it is and if you just—' He'd already sold everything else and pretty much spent the money.

The two men picked him out of the booth, one holding him under each arm.

'No need to keep looking, folks,' the smaller man said. 'Nothing to see here. Go back to your business, do you understand?'

Several of the senior citizens nodded, not wanting to rile the local ruffians.

Jackson started screaming, imploring the management to step in and stop his abduction.

Amid the confusion, the two men carried him to the street and threw him in the back of a black Porsche Cayenne.

The smaller man sat with him, pinning his arms behind his back. The bigger man drove, two hundred fifty pounds sitting daintily in the driver's seat, squealing the tires as he pulled out onto the street.

'Sam, we need all the cards and personal shit that was in the wallet. Surely you understand that?'

'Please, I don't have that stuff, but I can get it.'

The big man put more pressure on the arms until they almost cracked.

'How soon can you get it?'

'Oh, my God, in two days.'

More pressure, and then more and there was a cracking sound. Shoulders separating from the joints.

The scream, the shrieking was enough to deafen someone. Jackson was crying, tears flowing from his eyes.

'Hey, Sam,' the driver shouted back to him, 'you fucked with the wrong man. It happens. Don't get crazy over it.'

The screams came even louder and the driver just laughed. He needed a diversion because when the boss found out that he didn't have the goods, the man wasn't going to be happy. Not at all.

61

Levy and another detective walked into the restaurant, Levy flashing an official warrant. The patrons and workers parted as the law enforcement team walked into the kitchen. Duvay looked up from chopping an onion and rolled his eyes.

'Oh, shit. Don't you ever give up?'

'Antoine Duvay, you are wanted for questioning in the murder of Judge David Lerner.'

The detective walked up and put his hand on Duvay's shoulder. For just a moment the young man gripped his knife, his hand shaking. Levy squeezed hard, sending a message that any attempt at escape would be a mistake. This was serious business.

As they led him away, Levy dialed Archer's cell. Good news needed to be shared, plus he wanted Archer in on the questioning because Levy had no idea where Archer was going with this.

The phone rang and rang and rang. No answer. Levy hoped he'd get an answer by the time he had Duvay at the station.

'Call me, Archer,' he muttered under his breath. If this was so damned important, he could at least answer his goddamned phone.

62

A rcher closed his eyes and held his breath. When he heard the click of the trigger he opened them again, his heart racing.

'Come on, bro. I wan-want a piece of you. Not everything. Not yet. I'll tell 'em you dodged the bullet. No matter how much I want to, I can't kill my own br-brother.'

'What the hell was that all about?' Archer's bloodshot eyes stared daggers into his brother's brain.

'Stop your Mickey Mouse investigation. You'll hear from me again, Quentin. Bri-Brian sends his best.'

Jason Archer rose from the bed, the gun still leveled at Quentin and he backed away toward the door. Reaching it, he laid the gun on the floor.

'No bullets. I did-didn't trust you.' He laughed as he walked out. 'Hell, I-I didn't trust myself.'

Archer stood there, a sheen of warm sweat covering his body and the towel wrapped around his hips. He couldn't exactly run through the streets of the Quarter naked, chasing his criminal brother, and he had no weapon other than a cold piece of steel which without its ammunition meant absolutely nothing. It was about as useless as a paperweight.

His phone was ringing and he grabbed for it, but the limit had been reached. He checked it for the number. Levy.

Archer called back immediately.

'Archer, we've got Duvay. What the hell do we do with him?'

From one crisis to another. The good news was he was alive to handle them. One at a time.

'Hold him till I get there. Give me twenty minutes, Levy.'

A minute ago he'd thought it was all over. He'd closed his eyes and expected to be on the other side by now. Quite a start. Quite an emotional upheaval. Now he was back, expected to solve the murder of three judges. Nothing had changed, except he realized his own mortality was in jeopardy. His brother proved what he already knew. No matter how careful he was, at any time someone could take his life. And almost had. Jason Archer was on the loose, and as long as that was the case, Q wasn't safe. He wasn't safe at all.

Should he alert the cops that a wanted man from Detroit was in New Orleans? In another minute the city would swallow Jason up and he'd only be seen when he resurfaced. When he wanted to be seen. Yet, in a twisted way, his own brother had spared his life.

Archer walked to his closet, and started to get dressed.

It took half an hour to get there but now they sat in the interrogation room, the suspect chained once again to the metal table.

'You ran, Antoine. Something scared you. I think you knew more than you told us,' Archer said.

'Not often a white man accuses me of knowing something. Hell, knowing anything. Most often I'm just some dumb nigger to you all.'

'You know why Lerner was murdered, don't you?'

'Shit, man, why do you think I know anything? What makes you think I've got that kind of information?'

'Because you worked for the warden. You worked Jakes's personal detail and you figured out a lot, didn't you? Lerner's murder had to do with the warden and the prison, am I right?'

'You understand that I tell you anything and it's a death sentence?'

'How is that?' Levy asked.

'How it is, is that this goes to the top, man. Governor's office, maybe further. I'm not shitting you.'

'What goes to the top?'

'You can't stop 'em, Detectives. You're two five-ohs who couldn't get a jaywalker ticketed if *they* didn't want you to.'

'OK, let's paint a picture and you tell me where I'm wrong.' *Pieces. Put them together and see what fits.* 'Lerner had a thing with Rodger Claim, head of security, am I right?'

'Claim was the one who suggested me to work at the warden's house.'

'Claim was gay, so was Lerner.'

'I'm gonna walk if I cooperate?'

'Pretty sure that can be arranged.'

'And how am I gonna keep safe once you have this information?'

'We're trying to get evidence, Antoine. With evidence, we won't need your testimony.'

But they probably would.

'They used Rodger Claim to get to Lerner. And then Lerner got to somebody else,' Duvay said.

'Why?'

'I'm guessing.'

'You ran, Antoine. You had a pretty good suspicion.'

Duvay was quiet, just slightly shaking his head.

'OK, was it Judge Warren? Was that the "somebody else"?'

'I don't know, man. I just got lots of bits and pieces. Maybe I heard Warren's name. I was just some dumb kid, so they didn't seem to worry too much about what I heard or saw. And, man, I saw plenty.' He hung his head low and shook it several times.

'Like?'

'I walked into the garage one time and Claim and Lerner were in the Jag, buck naked and—'

'Keep it PG, Antoine,' Archer said.

'I agree. But remember, you asked.'

'What else?'

'Some pretty high-powered people, they visited on a regular basis. Couple people, I think, were city council, and it was pointed out to me some senators and state big shots.'

Duvay hesitated for a moment and Archer kept quiet.

'Once or twice, the lieutenant governor of Louisiana. Had the same tattoo as the warden, and—'

'Why were they visiting?'

'Once in a while I heard and saw stuff I probably shouldn't have seen. They talked about stuff and when I was serving drinks or cleaning tables on the patio, I may have picked up some information.'

'The serpent tattoo?'

'The same.'

'Jesus,' Archer said.

Levy pressed harder.

'You gonna tell us what it was you heard? Because this is getting rather boring. You want to go back into that holding cell, Antoine?'

'They talked about SF. Big company that owned the prisons.'

'Secure Force.' Archer looked at Levy. 'Private company that owns something like twenty-five prisons in four states.'

'Wow.'

'So,' Duvay continued, 'we don't have to go there. They don't have to put all of us in private prisons. There are state prisons. State's got more programs, better food.' He paused, looking back and forth at the two cops. 'But that's where most of us end up. SF. It's crap, man. Pure crap.'

Homicide didn't deal with the juvenile justice system. Because most of the murderers under eighteen were still tried and convicted as adults. Archer didn't really understand exactly how the system worked. He just knew that Louisiana had more prisoners per capita than anywhere else in the world. The world. And from what he'd read and heard, the reason was cash. Jobs. Income. Taxes. It was hard to give any of that up.

'So what are you saying?'

'Petty crimes don't have to have long sentences. Come on, man, you know damned well that I got more time than most. Most of the cons in there are way long on their time. State prison, I would have done a month or two. Private prison, they need to find a way to keep you. It's a business, Detective. Ain't nothin' to do with corrections. You already figured all this out.'

'I agree,' Archer said. The pieces fit.

'What I saw was long sentences, and a full house. We were squeezed for space, man. And the state pen? Not full at all. Now I ask you, is that fair? Who's strokin' who?'

'So Lerner was funneling prisoners to his lover's prison,' Levy said. 'The state of Louisiana still pays for those prisons. They just pay Secure Force.'

'Yeah,' Archer stood up. 'I'd lay money they pay per prisoner. How much do you want to bet they pay per prisoner? And when River Bend or any of the other twenty-four prisons is full, Secure Force is making big bucks.'

'So Lerner and company were loading up the private prison,' Levy said, 'and—'

'Getting kickbacks. That's what the other number on those spreadsheets represented. Dollars kicked back per prisoner,' Archer said.

'Holy shit. Krewe Charbonerrie was getting a kickback and paying Lerner, maybe Warren, a finder's fee.'

'I'd bet on it,' Archer said. 'And the big shots in the Krewe owned stock in Secure Force.'

'Damn. Making it coming and going.'

'That was it, wasn't it?' Archer stared at Duvay. 'Prisoner number 12345 was worth two thousand dollars. It's that simple. It was right in front of us all the time. Lerner kept a list.'

'Jesus, it makes sense,' Levy said. 'Twenty-five prisons, a cut on every prisoner. That adds up to a nice chunk of change.'

'Plus, it keeps their investment healthy. These guys had it figured,' Archer said.

'Q.' Levy had his cell phone out, working his calculator app. 'If this prison holds eighteen hundred kids, and let's say half of them come from judges who are repping some organization who is on the take, that's one million eight hundred thousand dollars. Per year. From just one prison.'

'There are twenty-five prisons in the Secure Force network. By your equation, that's forty-five million dollars per year in kickbacks. Enough to pay the judges, the wardens and still pocket a tidy profit for Krewe Charbonerrie.'

'Plus a healthy dividend and growth in Secure Force stock,' Archer said.

The three men sat there, mouths wide open.

'Forty-five million dollars a year.' Archer shook his head. 'Just for sentencing convicts to these prisons.'

'Shit, man. I was robbed of time for two thousand dollars?'

'Even if it's twenty-five percent of all the inmates, hell, that's still some twelve million,' Levy said.

'Garrett and Krewe Charbonerrie,' Archer said.

'So, why kill Lerner?'

'Why?' Archer asked. 'Because he had the spreadsheets, the proof that each incarcerated kid was worth a dollar amount. And my guess is that he was going to turn them over to somebody. Maybe the P.T. that was on his calendar. Chances are there are account numbers on those sheets as well, showing where the money is.'

'Who did this P.T. work for?'

'A person or an organization that could have destroyed Krewe Charbonerrie. Whoever was behind Lerner's murder couldn't afford to have him rat on the Krewe. They must have known that Lerner was going to spill the beans. They knew if he gave any organization the information this multimillion-dollar business was going to be destroyed. Not only would the income stop, but the big shots would be arrested and thrown in prison.'

'FBI?' Levy asked.

'It apparently wasn't NOPD. I think we would have been notified.'

'Forty million,' Levy said, 'even if it was just twenty million a year, that's a hell of a lot of money.'

'Plus the stock in Secure Force. Don't forget that. We're talking millions and millions of dollars. I can't even fathom it,' Archer said.

'Cop, you gonna let me go? You gonna keep this conversation private?'

'We're going to do everything possible to keep you out of this, Antoine,' Archer said. 'If we bring this group down, I don't think you're going to have any problems.'

'We need to re-examine the evidence, Q. Especially that folder with the spreadsheets.'

'Get somebody to pull it from the evidence room.'

'I'll get right on it.'

'I want those sheets locked up. And not in the evidence room. Things disappear from that building way too often.'

'Good point.'

'The warden knew they were going to kill Lerner. It's all starting to make sense. Russell Jakes drove out to see if Skeeter had done his job. He was in on it and didn't trust the two killers, Skeeter and Jim Gideon.'

'So that's why the Jaguar pulled down the dead end street.'

'What was he thinking? No one would notice?' Archer asked. 'Nancy Olds caught him right away.'

'Criminals are never as smart as they think they are,' Levy said.

They were quiet for a moment, the three of them contemplating the information. Then Archer spoke.

'Levy, I know where Garrett is.'

'Just like that?'

'He's now hands on. He's doing everything himself.'

'And?'

'He's in damage control, and he's going to start destroying records.'

'His office?'

'No. He wouldn't keep things there. Jakes is in on it, so my guess is records are stored at River Bend Prison.'

'But it appears there are twenty-five prisons involved. Would he have records at all twenty-five?'

'We've got to start somewhere.'

'Guys,' Duvay was whining like a dog. 'Can somebody please unlock this chain? Come on, man.'

Archer motioned to a guard through the two-way mirror.

'Let's take my Buick. The shocks are shot but at least the air conditioner works,' Levy said.

Archer nodded. Trade a fairly smooth ride for air. Sounded like the best of two bad options.

'Q? Forty million. Plus all this stock you keep talking about. Is that worth the life of three judges?'

'Levy, I'm new to New Orleans. I have no idea what a judge is worth. In Detroit, you could have bought three judges for a couple thousand bucks.'

63

'I done told you, the wallet is in a dumpster near the alley where your boss was walkin' when I met him.' He spit blood from his mouth on the floor of the German car.

His lips were swollen from several punches to the face, and there was a purple bruise under his right eye. The man sitting next to him hit him again, a hard right to his jaw. It was hard to defend with his aching shoulders separated from their sockets.

'You kept the Black Card?'

'Don't hit me anymore, man.' He was slobbering. 'Gave it to the cop like I told you. Turned myself in. Look, I figure this Archer he's a straight dude. He'll return it to this Mr Garrett. I can't give you what I don't have, so stop beatin' the shit out of me.'

He shuddered. Garrett was a killer and he figured these two thugs were equally as bad. But he had nothing else to offer them. He'd told them everything he could.

'I got money. You know, you let me go, I'll go home and get some money. I can lay my hands on five hundred dollars right now, you know what I mean?'

The driver was on his cell phone, stuttering and stammering.

'Yes, Mr Garrett . . . No, Mr Garrett. Boss . . .' He shook his head as he drove. 'Mr Garrett, it's not our fault. We're pretty much convinced the little shit doesn't have anything. Gave your American Express card to some cop named Archer. That's the best we could get out of him.'

The big man gripped the wheel with his left hand and squeezed the cell phone with his right, a determined look on his face.

'You sure? That's what you want us to do? For real?'

Braking, he turned around and glared at Jackson.

The little black man grimaced and closed his eyes.

'What you gonna do to me? What? No, don't tell me, just do it. Just do it, you hear?'

The driver turned on a side street and came to a screeching halt.

'That alley over there, there's a dumpster.'

The man in the back seat opened the door and Jackson ducked his head as if to get out. As his captor leaned over, the pickpocket jerked his head up with a hard thrust catching the man under his chin. The thug's head snapped back and he rolled off the seat onto the floor.

It had all happened in a second and as the driver turned, trying to comprehend, Jackson was on the street, screaming in pain and running as fast as he could.

64

He'd parked in the employee's lot. He took another pull from his flask. Technically he still worked there. Solange had told him not to come back, but she had no right to tell him anything. Propping her up and dragging her useless body with him, the big man opened the door of his Nissan and pushed her into the passenger seat. He stared at the girl, her petite frame, and thought of what he'd do to her when she gained consciousness. As he smiled, she moaned.

Clarence felt the tap on his shoulder and he jerked around.

'What the hell are you doing?'

Clarence's eyes grew big as he stared at the tall, muscular white man in the white shirt and gray tie.

'Not what it looks like, man. This girl, she works here and passed out. I'm givin' her a ride to the hospital is all so they can—'

The right cross caught him on his cheek and he reeled, banging into the car.

'Hey, dude,' Clarence crouched, coming up for a head-butt, aiming for the man's chin. The white man dodged and landed a solid blow in the center of Clarence's face, his nose splattering, blood spraying into his eyes.

He landed in a heap on the ground and didn't get up.

The man looked in the open door as Solange Cordray managed to sit up. She stared at the crumpled body lying on the blacktop driveway. Then her eyes slowly raised.

'Joseph? What are you doing here?'

Massaging his right hand, Joseph Cordray gave her a brief smile.

'I had a talk with one of your ex-clients who suggested that he might do you some bodily harm. I wanted to warn you, and possibly protect you if it came to that.'

'It did, didn't it? It came to that.'

'I still care, Solange. I wasn't sure I did, but I do. Regardless of what you think. Who is the guy?'

'Someone who threatened me and Ma.'

'Does he work for Garrett?'

She shook her head and gingerly stepped out of the car, walking around the body in front of her.

'No. Don't worry about him. I told him to stay away or there would be trouble. I think he'll believe me now.'

Approaching him, she threw her arms around his waist and as he bent over she kissed him on the cheek.

'This time only, you are my knight in shining armor.'

Cordray smiled. 'I think you've got an army of knights and spirits out there. I've seen evidence. You and Ma, you're going to be just fine.'

'Your Mr Garrett, he already came after me.'

His eyes widened. 'Oh?'

'I sent him on his way. Hopefully he's another one who I won't have to worry about. He's rethinking his strategy.'

'Solange—'

'I know, Joseph. I just pray that you are removed enough from whatever it is that you are involved with that you won't be arrested.'

'Maybe we can have a cup of coffee sometime?'

'I don't think so,' she said. 'And, Joseph, I don't think you need to have me followed anymore. I'd hate to have to do something about that.'

His eyes widened and he opened his mouth to protest, but no sound came out. Joseph Cordray finally nodded, turned and walked away.

Solange looked down one more time, then walked toward the center. She wanted to see Ma and alert the limited security to deny any visitors. Things had escalated and she sensed someone was in trouble.

65

'Step on it, Levy. I hope to hell I'm right.'

'So do I, Q. Because if you're wrong, we're fucked. I can deal with a mistake, but you, my friend . . .'

'Yeah.'

'You only get so many strikes.'

Archer didn't comment.

They continued northwest on Highway 10, Levy running along at eighty miles per hour. Long silent periods were only broken by brief snatches of conversation between the two men, still putting pieces of the puzzle together. Archer called a judge and explained they thought they were ready to wrap up Lerner, Warren and Hall's deaths. The judge told them that a search warrant would be issued in record time, even though the prison was out of their jurisdiction.

'When it comes to the killing of a judge, we can bend a lot of rules,' he said.

'What the hell is this about Adam Strand?' Levy asked.

'We had a strange conversation about how he provided outsiders some inside information. He told me that everyone did it,' said Archer. 'It was like his sideline business, selling police secrets.'

'Obviously not everyone does it. Jesus, I wonder how much he made in his little sideline?'

'And then they found that note in his car, about his meeting with P.T.'

'Same guy Lerner was going to meet.'

'Exactly. Was Lerner leaking information to this P.T. person?'

'And when Lerner died, did that P.T. person go to Strand to get the information? What could Lerner provide that Strand could provide as well? It wasn't as if Adam had a law degree,' Levy said.

They were quiet for several minutes. Archer's phone rang and he checked the number. Sullivan.

'Sergeant.'

'Where are you?'

There was no reason not to tell him.

'Levy and I are headed to River Bend Prison.'

'We're down a man because of a suicide, we've got an old man in the hospital and possibly an attempted murderer on the run and you're going to the prison?'

'I think it all ends there. We believe that Lerner and other judges were getting kickbacks from Secure Force prisons.'

'At this point, I'm willing to believe anything.'

'Sergeant, we need those spreadsheets from the evidence room.'

'Funny thing about those sheets, Archer.'

'By the tone of your voice, it doesn't sound like it's funny.'

'It's not. The sheets aren't there.'

'Was Adam Strand on the list of visitors in the last couple of days?'

There was silence on the other end.

'Hello?'

'Yeah, I'm here.'

'Did Strand visit the evidence building in the last several days?' Archer asked. 'Any chance he was there?'

'So you think he stole them?'

'That's what I think.'

'To what avail?'

'I think he was going to turn them into someone or sell them.'

'What are they worth?' Sullivan asked.

'By themselves, nothing,' Archer said. 'But I think those sheets link everything together.'

'Q, who wanted the information? Why?'

'FBI?'

'This is *our* murder. Not the Feds.'

'Sergeant, this could involve twenty-five prisons. Four states. I'd like to believe we can solve this crime, get the convictions and be the heroes, but this is bigger than NOPD. I'm not giving up on the investigation, but understand: we may get buried on this case.'

'So Strand was contracted to steal the sheets?'

'My thoughts?'

'You're the only one on the other end of the line.'

'Yes.'

'And that's why he killed himself?' Sullivan asked.

'Guilt, concerned that he'd be discovered, I don't know.'

More silence.

'Sullivan, was Strand in the evidence room? I need to know. Yes, he visited in the last two days. No, he was never there.'

'We checked the list. Yes.'

Archer looked at Levy, the detective keeping his eyes glued to the four-lane highway.

'Bingo, Levy. We now know what Lerner and Strand could both provide. The spreadsheets with prisoner numbers and dollar amounts.'

66

'I need the bank account numbers.' Paul Trueblood aimed the pistol in his gloved hand at the warden's chest. 'Trust me, it will be a lot easier if you just give them to me.'

'I don't know what you're talking about.'

Garrett and Jakes stood plastered against the Jaguar, the garage feeling like a small morgue.

'Your friend, Mr Garrett, he also is a culprit.' The man nodded toward Garrett. 'One of the main players. We're going to close you down, Mr Jakes, Mr Garrett. I have the digital printouts, and that's just for this prison. I want the account where these deposits are made. Just need the numbers. I'll find them one way or the other.'

Jakes and Garrett looked at each other.

'We give you the information and what do we get?' Jakes asked.

'We'll work out something.'

Garrett stared at the man. 'You're FBI? Seriously?'

Trueblood smiled. 'Let's just say I do some work for them. Freelance.'

'So we're screwed no matter what? No matter what I tell you, I'm going to do serious time, right? So why should I volunteer anything?' Jakes played with false bravado, but it was thin.

'You're not screwed. Not if you give me the account number. Garrett? Jakes? If we can capture the money, then . . .'

Warden Russell Jakes was shaking. He'd always known it could happen, someone would figure out the scheme, but the Feds? That meant real time, Federal time. Jakes braced himself.

'I want access to the account,' the man stated.

'For River Bend?' Garrett was cautious. How much did this guy know?

'For Secure Force,' he said. 'For every prison. Just tell me where the kickback money goes.'

The guy knew plenty.

'I'm not sure what you think you know,' Jakes said, his gruff voice sounding dubious. 'What account do you . . .'

'I know that you don't have half of the information that Mr Garrett has, Warden Jakes. And I know that Mr Garrett has pretty much everything I need. Lerner's printouts, they pretty much proved how extensive this operation is. Mr Garrett has the account numbers. Mr Garrett is responsible for the depth and breadth of this scam you all are running. So you're not that important to the business, are you, Warden? I mean, other people have this information, right? Sorry my friend. I know the records are stored here. Other than that, you don't seem to be that important to the entire case. Am I right? You protect this prison, but in the scope of things . . .'

'Look, I can provide you with all kinds of information that you don't have. I can't do time, Mr Trueblood. Let me—'

'I can get all I need from Mr Garrett. Probably from his cell phone. I would bet the account number, that this brilliant businessman has the information stored right in his cell phone. Mr Garrett is a bright man, but all bright people think no one will figure them out and they get careless. Now, one of you give me the account numbers and we can all relax.'

Jakes swallowed, a gulp of saliva. 'I can't do time. I'd never last a week inside a prison. The convicts, man. Whatever you need to know' – the big man was sweating, wiping his brow – 'I can give you whatever information you need, but you can't threaten me with prison. Oh, Jesus, please let me—'

Trueblood pulled the trigger. Once, twice, three times and each exploding shot went through Jakes's body and into the Jaguar. Puckered holes dimpled the sheet of cream-colored steel covering the sleek frame. Each one was stained with bright red blood.

67

M a was safe, she was sure of it. Matebo was recovering and would be fine. But Archer was in trouble. There were forces, multiple forces that were at play, all of them conspiring against the detective. River Bend Prison was the focal point, and it was clear to her that Richard Garrett was a primary player. She wasn't reading minds; she wasn't casting spells or throwing bones. She just knew.

Shivering even in the heat, focused on her purpose, she walked back to her shop, stopping half a block away to scope out the security. There was no cop out front. Probably had checked on her, found her missing, reported in and now possibly there was a citywide search going on. Or, maybe they realized she'd blown her detail off and they gave up on her. Whichever way it played, she had to get to that prison. She entered the shop, went to the back room and pulled the canvas tarp off of her seldom used Honda Forza. The sleek red body beckoned and she stroked the smooth surface. It was one small pleasure she'd allowed herself. A top speed of ninety, a cruising speed of sixty-five, and eighty-five miles to the gallon. She almost never brought it out, but it was perfect for running around town. The bike was also touted as a great little highway scooter. Solange Cordray put on her helmet, pulled black leather boots over her tight jeans and wheeled the bike out the front door, locking the store behind her, and turned the ignition. The scooter purred, ready for the road.

*   *   *

The cell phone rang and Trueblood stared hard at Garrett. The oil man's eyes moved between the bloody body of Warden Jakes, slumped on the ground, and the pistol in Paul Trueblood's hand.

'Your phone, Mr Garrett.'

It kept ringing.

'Answer it. Say nothing about our situation.'

Cautiously, Richard Garrett reached into his pocket and pulled out the iPhone.

'Yeah.' His voice was a little raspy, a little tenuous.

'I've got some new information on the Lerner murder case.'

Trueblood still pointed the barrel at Garrett's head.

'Garrett, put it on speaker. Now.'

'Hello.' The voice on the other end was clear and loud in the garage.

'Go ahead.'

'Detectives Archer and Levy have decided that River Bend Prison is a focal point in the murder. They're pretty sure they've figured out that Secure Force is kicking back money to judges in return for sentencing juveniles to their prisons. And they think that one of our detectives, who just committed suicide, gave the FBI files that contain proof. Then he put the gun in his mouth and pulled the trigger.'

Trueblood shook his head. Strand ate his gun. The poor dumb son of a bitch. And now the cops were on the prowl.

Richard Garrett looked at Trueblood with a question on his face.

Trueblood signaled to Garrett to wrap up the call.

'OK, we'll make contact, Sullivan. In the meantime, keep your ear to the ground.'

'One more thing, sir.'

'Yeah?'

'Archer and Detective Levy are on their way to River Bend now. I'm guessing half an hour away. Is that enough information for another payday?'

'I'll get back to you.' Garrett terminated the call.

'Well played, Mr Garrett. So you've got someone on the NOPD who feeds you information?'

Garrett kept staring at the gun. 'You're going to kill me, right?'

'Who's your contact?'

'Dan Sullivan. He's a sergeant in homicide. He doesn't have a clue who I am or why I want the information.'

'But he's selling it to you?'

'You're going to kill me. Look, what do I have to do here? You know I've got money. More money than you'll ever need in a lifetime. I can write you a check and we can forget about all of this.'

'You know we can't do that.' He nodded at Jakes's body lying on the cold concrete floor.

'There's got to be a way.'

'There is.'

Trueblood stepped behind Garrett, reached around and wrapped the man's right hand over his pistol. Before Garrett understood what was happening, Trueblood forced Garret to pull the trigger, the bullet punching Jakes's body with a bang.

'Jesus.'

Wrenching the gun back from Garrett he pointed it at the man's head.

'I work with the FBI, Richard. I've now got you, a man who just killed his business partner. The gunpowder residue from the gun is on your hand. Now, I can make this go away, claim that the warden appeared to be pulling a gun and I had to shoot him, or I can say that you shot him and you can be tried for murder plus your kickback scheme. I detect a life sentence, minimum.'

'You want the account numbers.'

'I want you to release those account numbers to me. Release them, Richard.'

'Jesus, man. You're crazy. Do you know how difficult that would be to—'

'You contact the bank, you release those numbers. Right now. In my name. And if you don't, I promise you, you will be tried for the murder of Russell Jakes and a scheme to defraud the State of Louisiana and every other state that Secure Force works in.'

'You won't get away with this.'

'Neither will you, Mr Garrett. The only chance you have is if you give me those numbers.'

'OK, I'll give them to you.'

'No, you make the necessary transaction right now, on your phone. Release them. I want to see proof that the money is transferred to my name.'

'I can't just—'

'You've got a security code?'

'Yes, but—'

'You've got passwords?'

'Of course, but it's more complicated than—'

'You've got a second party?'

'Mark McKinley, my accountant.'

'You've got a code that allows him to second the transfer.'

'You can't just take the damned money.'

'You're a stupid man, Richard Garrett. Of course I can.'

Trueblood lowered the barrel and pulled the trigger, shattering the man's right tibia.

The surprise on Garrett's face was priceless as it turned to agonizing pain. Grasping at his leg, he crumpled to the ground, ending up on top of the bloody corpse of Russell Jakes.

'Are you going to make that call and enter those codes and passwords, or am I going to continue to break bones? One at a time.' Trueblood smiled down on Garrett, aiming the gun at his arm.

'No, no, please, don't shoot.' Garrett was screaming. 'Not again. I'll do it.'

'Quick, get your phone and let's get it done.'

The warden's house was much less secure than the prison. A lone guard gate protected the civilian buildings in the compound where Russell Jakes lived. An iron bar crossed the gravel driveway and the guard inside the small gatehouse simply pushed a button to raise or lower the bar. When Archer pulled up to the gate, he simply gave his name and told him the warden was expecting them.

A moment later the guard told him that the warden did not answer his call, and Archer and his companion would have to come back another time. Levy pulled his badge, showing it to the uniformed man. The guard shrugged.

'Nothing I can do, man. No one gets through if the warden doesn't approve.'

'Look, this is official business. There is supposed to be a search warrant already issued and sent here. Why don't you check? This could be a matter of life and death.'

'I've got no search warrant, and as far as you getting in here, never gonna happen, Nola.'

'Well,' Levy smiled at him, 'I guess all I can say is, never say never.'

Detective Levy pushed the accelerator to the floor and the car leaped forward, snapping the crossbar as the vehicle cleared the line and entered the compound.

'What you just did . . .' Archer said.

'Yeah?' Levy was headed right for the house.

'It's going to get us in a lot of trouble, Detective.'

'And?' Levy braked and turned a hard right, heading toward the warden's residence.

'And it's exactly what I would have done.'

68

S he didn't travel the highway much. Her world was small, confined, and in many ways she liked it that way. Her comfort zone, for what it was, was familiar. And flying down a concrete slab at eighty miles per hour was a little frightening. The tinted face shield blocked the wind, the bugs and the burn as she leaned over the handlebars.

She went whizzing by cars, overtaking vehicles when she could, swerving and maneuvering her bike. She had no idea what she was going to do once she reached the prison. Pray, ask for intervention, give up her life. She knew it was dangerous and that her immediate priority was to alert Quentin Archer to the possibility that his life was in danger. Serious danger. Having her connections, having her powers, working with the skills her mother taught her was exhausting. She wondered what it was like to be a cook, a teacher, a nurse, a mother. Oftentimes those occupations seemed preferable.

The girl heard the horn blaring as a car cut her off. Frowning behind the shield, she muttered a phrase. The blue Mazda swerved as the right rear tire blew and the car skidded to a stop on the edge of the road.

Solange Cordray sped on by. There was work to be done.

Wincing in pain, faint from blood loss, Richard Garrett worked his phone, thumbs punching in codes and passwords. Trueblood never wavered, the gun pointed at Garrett's head.

'If this doesn't work, I'm really not out anything,' he said. 'You – you're out your life; but me – still got a job, still make a living. You know, Garrett, when this is wrapped up, they've even offered me a paid vacation. Pretty nice, eh? So if you don't get this money transferred, I'll have to kill you, but my life pretty much stays the same.'

'Give me your account number once more. Where do you want the money transferred?' Garrett's voice was weak.

Trueblood recited the numbers, watching the injured man punch them into his phone. He'd been right. Richard Garrett had all the information on his phone. After all, who would ever think to look on Garrett's phone. He was just like all the dumb-asses who sexted, sent private emails and took dirty pictures on their phone, assuming it was all private business. They were certain they were protected.

Didn't they get it? There was a security camera on every corner, an alarm in every home and business and someone on the outside who could monitor what was going on in the inside. There was GPS on your phone, in your car, in your camera. There were listening devices that could pick up conversations half a mile away. The government monitored every keystroke on your computer and every call from your cell. Not one second of your private life was private anymore and there was a growing need from all sorts of organizations, private and public, to harvest all of that information.

Finally, Garrett put the phone down and leaned back.

'Damn, it's done.'

'And how much did you transfer?'

'Twenty-five. And that's a little low, so . . .'

Trueblood smiled, and took the phone from Garrett's hand. He studied the screen. Shock was setting in for the oilman. His leg was probably starting to go numb and his brain was slowing down as well. But it appeared that he'd had the lucidity to transfer the money.

'All the money in the world can't bring you happiness, my friend, but it's a damned good start.'

'Who are you really,' Garrett stared up at him.

'An opportunist.'

'Yeah, well we're all that, aren't we?'

'Some of us,' Trueblood said, 'see more opportunity than others.'

It was at that moment they heard the car roar up to the garage and two doors slam.

69

She turned onto the long drive, the prison in the distance. A low, concrete-block building painted a drab gray, sucking the color from an overcast sky. Rolls of razor wire layered the upper level and four blockhouses rose in the corners, where armed guards with high-tech workstations watched the facility twenty-four/seven.

Archer wasn't going to be inside the prison. Probably at the residence somewhere on the property. Solange Cordray lifted the faceguard and saw the paved road that ran beyond the prison. She gunned the engine and headed back the winding path. Finally, she saw the small guard shack and slowed. No one appeared to be inside and the cross bar that should have kept her out was broken, bent and pushed back off its hinges.

She braked, looked around the area and then gunned the bike through the entrance, following the path till it took a sharp right. The house to the left appeared to be the warden's domain, a large antebellum-styled home, and the garage immediately to the right was designed to look like a carriage house, with lantern-shaped lights on the corners.

Two cars were carelessly parked in front. The woman braked again, the throb of her engine the only sound in the eerily silent atmosphere. No birds, no insects, just a pressing heat and humidity, and an overcast sky.

Saying a silent prayer, she asked for victory in whatever situation she found herself.

One detective to check the inside, one to guard outside.

Levy cracked the side door and cautiously stepped in. As his eyes adjusted to the dim light he saw three vehicles. Gun drawn, he walked to the front. Two bodies lay on the floor, the one on top still breathing, eyes cracked open. As he knelt he felt the hard kick in his tailbone and he went sprawling, the Glock flying from his hand.

'Detective Archer, I presume?' The man stood above him, his gun pointed at Levy's head.

Inside they heard the scooter. A cop, security guard, just a visitor?

Trueblood held the pistol firmly, realizing nobody in the garage except him could leave alive. Also realizing that outside, two people were potential threats. He couldn't just shoot these two inside and walk out the door.

Richard Garrett was passed out, slumped over Warden Russell Jakes's body. The homicide detective was sitting on the ground, hands behind his head as he glared up at Trueblood, watching his eyes, not the gun. Trueblood wasn't sure what he was going to do if those eyes changed, but he wanted to be ready.

'So you're Archer?'

Levy nodded. 'And you're P.T.'

'I am. Your partner is still outside.'

'He is. You're kind of trapped in here.'

'Well, trapped is not the word I would use. I do have two hostages.'

'You think you're going to walk away?'

'I've stayed one step ahead of NOPD, and until now—'

'We were going to figure out who you were. FBI, right?'

'Well . . .' Trueblood smiled. 'I'm a bit of a freelancer. Usually I fold right back in, but in this case, the money was a little too tempting.'

'So you've got Garrett's records?'

'Hell, Detective Archer, I've got his money.'

'And it's not going back to the Feds, am I right?'

'No, it's already on its way to Belize, or wherever it is I keep funds like this.'

'You don't think they're going to find you? For that kind of cash?'

'Detective, they wanted this kickback scam stopped and they wanted evidence. I've got the evidence and I've stopped the scam. Took care of the problem. My fee may be a little exorbitant this time, but—'

The side door rattled. Trueblood swung the gun up and toward the door as the front garage door started sliding up at the same time. As he spun around again, the side door opened and he heard a girl's voice.

'Drop the gun or I'll shoot you, right now.'

He turned and fired at nothing but an open door.

'Drop it.' A steely voice now came from the open garage door. 'I'm Detective Quentin Archer and you're under arrest.'

The long slow sigh came from the floor where Detective Levy crouched. ''Bout time, bro.'

Trueblood raised his hands and slowly turned.

'Drop it.'

'The real Detective Archer.'

'One more time, drop the gun.'

He shifted position, the gun now pointing directly at Levy.

'I'll pull the trigger even if you shoot me, Archer. I kill him, or you let me walk out of here. You've got Garrett, you've got the records that you need. It's a win-win.'

'I can't let you go.'

'I just made a little transaction with your friend Garrett. I can work with you on this. You've got what you want, now I can sweeten the pot. Money under the table, Detective. But I am going to walk out of here, with or without your blessing.'

Archer considered the situation. It used to be called a Mexican standoff although he wasn't sure why. He couldn't put Levy at risk but he couldn't let P.T. go.

'You're planning on leaving and that's not about to happen.'

'Detective, Garrett is probably bleeding to death,' Trueblood said. 'In another minute, I'll shoot your partner right through his heart. Let me go or you will be responsible for two deaths.'

'Judge Lerner was going to give you the printouts, right? The prisoner numbers and the dollars that were paid.'

'He was, but the Krewe found out. They had him killed.'

'Krewe Charbonerrie seems to have found out a lot. They were suspicious of Judge Richard Warren, Traci Hall and—'

'One of your own, Detective. A cop named Sullivan? He was calling Garrett, filling him in on where the investigation was headed.'

'Dan Sullivan?' He didn't like Sullivan, but would never have suspected him.

'That was it. He called Garrett a short time ago and told him you and Levy were coming.'

'Really?'

'Kind of threw you under the bus, Detective. We were expecting you.'

It wasn't the first time.

'Sullivan's on the take?'

'Not my take. I just heard about him for the first time. Another little bit of information that makes me more valuable. You see, I haven't really committed a crime. I've exposed Garrett and company, I've obtained the records that the FBI wanted, and I've shown how far a rogue cop will go.'

'And you're threatening a police officer, and taking off with funds that are evidence in a Federal crime.'

'Well, there is that.'

'Drop the gun, Trueblood.'

'No, Archer, I think I'll shoot your friend.'

The explosion was deafening in the confined space, and Archer felt the concussion from the firearm. Trueblood's eyes opened wide, then he pitched forward, his face hitting the concrete floor.

Q blinked, the gun still clutched tightly in his hand. He stared at the side door, seeing her silhouette standing just inside.

'You're a pretty good shot.' His gun hand was trembling.

'Matebo taught me how to hunt game.'

Levy stood up, turning to the woman.

'Young lady, you may have saved my life.'

She couldn't tell him. It had been Archer's life she was concerned with.

'Detective Levy, this is Solange Cordray. She's been giving me advice on the murder investigation. I guess she came up here to check on me and see if I was following that advice.'

They nodded to each other as sirens pierced the air. Three security cars screeched to a stop and armed prison officers stepped out of the vehicles, pistols drawn.

'It's all over guys,' Archer said. 'You're a little late to the dance.'

70

The Werewolf, Loup-garou, and the contact Sam Campari were still on the loose, but Archer was pretty sure they'd show up eventually. When they were arrested, the people who killed Warren and Hall would be uncovered. Garrett, in what he thought may be a death-bed confession, had given up the names of the Werewolf and Campari. But Garrett was very much alive and, although crippled for life, had negotiated a reduced sentence in exchange for his testimony. The lieutenant governor, Sergeant Dan Sullivan, a Senator Marvin Shoemaker and others were all going down with him. The list was long.

The man known as Paul Trueblood was given a one-million-dollar bond, and even though he could now afford it, the judge had somehow frozen any access to his assets. P.T.'s shoulder was damaged by the thirty-eight-caliber bullet, but he was expected to heal. The FBI refused to comment on the man or the subject.

'Joseph Cordray, he had to have been a part of it too,' Levy said.

'Obviously, and the Feds are looking into it. I'm sure the whole Krewe is in disarray.'

They sipped chicory coffee and watched the Quarter come alive from the front seat of Levy's car.

'They haven't come out in half an hour.' Levy pointed to the small cottage on Magazine Street. 'Any chance there's an exit we don't know about?'

'No,' Archer said. 'They're in there.'

The 'they' were two women who had beat up a homeless veteran for his pension check. He'd died during the night and now the women were wanted for murder.

'And what about Sullivan? Everything we learned, he was leaking to Garrett.'

'Don't trust anyone, man,' Archer said. 'Adam Strand, too. Who knows who else is on the take.'

'I'm not too sure about you, Q.' Levy smiled. 'And tell me more about this Solange Cordray.'

Archer was quiet, obviously thinking about his response.

'It's pretty simple. You read the report. Mom was a voodoo practitioner, the girl is following in her footsteps.'

'You believe in that shit, Q?'

'Maybe. A little bit. I mean, she nailed it with Krewe Charbonerrie. There were a couple of other times that she . . .'

'She what?'

Archer shrugged his shoulders. 'Let's just say she surprised me.'

'Yeah. But following you all the way to River Bend? What is she, your guardian angel?'

Archer wondered about that too.

'She's passionate about what she believes.'

'Yeah, so is she passionate about you? She's pretty hot.'

Archer shook his head. 'In different circumstances . . .'

'You'd consider a fling?'

Archer was quiet, and he sipped his beverage. Finally he spoke.

'I'm still nursing a real Detroit hangover, Levy. I've got a ways to go.'

Just then two women walked out of the front door, looking left and right.

'That's them. Let's roll.'

71

The call came at 3 a.m. He figured it was Detroit. Another warning call. Another harassment.

'Q, it's Tom Lyons. We identified the license plate.'

Shaking the cobwebs out of his head, Archer concentrated on the call.

'You there?' Lyons asked.

'Who was it?'

'Car was stolen from a supermarket about a mile from the scene.'

'Damn.'

'No, Quentin. We were able to get the video from two parking lot cameras.'

'Damn it, Lyons, finish this story or I'm coming back to Detroit and I'll rip your tongue out.'

'Bobby Mercer or a dead ringer looks right at camera number one. We don't think there's any doubt.'

'Jesus.'

'We're being careful, man. As I said, we've got families. But we've got a DA who has promised to look hard at the evidence and, if he's convinced, we've got a case.'

'Tom, thank you. Thank you. Thank you. You've made my day. My night. My year.'

'Got a ways to go, my friend. A ways to go.'

'I'll come back. If you need me.'

'No! We don't need you right now. Stay there and let us handle this. You come back and the whole thing explodes.'

Archer closed his eyes. His heart was racing and he was sweating. They'd identified the killer.

72

T he wire-haired bartender pushed the drink down to him.
'Vieux Carré, Detective. Rye whiskey, sweet vermouth, cognac and bitters. First served at the Monteleone, a New Orleans original.'

The bar was filling up, and Mike moved to the man sitting next to Archer.

'Tell me, Ed, the best crawfish in Nawlins, am I not right?'

The man looked up from the heaping pile of red-shelled crustaceans and grinned.

She sat next to him, lightly touching his shoulder.

'You do amaze me,' Archer said.

'It's not my intention.'

'Well, I'm glad you're here. I think I owe you my life.'

She smiled. 'I am so glad you are alive.'

'Seriously, Solange' – it was the first time he'd used her first name – 'if it hadn't been for you showing up—'

'I know.' She folded her hands in front of her, staring intently into his eyes. 'Quentin' – the first time she'd spoken his first name – 'I know you have a hard time believing in this thing that I do. I respect that. And it's not my intention to interfere in your private life.'

'But?'

'I feel I have to tell you this. A feeling I have, something I can't explain to you, all I can tell you is that she is well. Adjusted. You can yell at me, ask me to never see you again, but I am committed to telling you that. Nothing more. She is well. Adjusted.'

Archer took a deep breath. Slow, long breaths. He believed her.

Wanted to believe her. Decided in a moment to believe anything she told him.

Tears sprang from his eyes, and he wiped at them with his hand. 'I needed to know.'

'Quentin, I am certain we will see each other in the future. If you need to contact me, you know where I am. At Ma's and at the studio.'

He tried to smile, but could only muster a confused look.

'When you've absorbed this all, when you are more comfortable with the situation, I hope we will talk.'

She stood and walked away.

73

They sat on the levee, the old man in a webbed lawn chair and the old woman in her wheelchair, staring out at the brown swirling water. She'd given him a faint smile when she first saw him, but now her eyes were glassy, seeing everything in front of her, seeing nothing.

'Clotille, your daughter is beautiful. She's smart, got personality; she's going to amount to something.'

A log washed by, and there were two men fishing on the far side, hoping to catch whatever the river had to offer.

'Are you comfortable? Do you need a shawl?'

She didn't respond.

'Clotille, about Solange, is there any chance that she is my daughter? I'd like to know.'

No response.

'Well, I treat her well, old woman. She is a joy.'

The lady nodded. Very subtly but she nodded.

It meant the world to Matebo. He felt it was a definite sign.

74

The phone rang in the middle of the night. Archer answered and there was silence on the other end. Archer hung up. It wasn't going to stop any time soon. He thought about Denise, her soft voice and healing manner, and drifted back to sleep, knowing that the killer had been identified. It was only a matter of time that he would be arrested, charged and convicted. That in itself would not bring back his wife, but it would satisfy some of his concerns.

She knelt on the floor, naked, the cloth spread in front of her. Two flickering candles threw shadows on the wall as she studied the bones. A chill went through her slender body, and she felt the presence of a spirit.

Tossing the smooth, worn objects, she closed her eyes. When she opened them Solange studied the display. The elements were against her. And against the detective. It seemed like he was in for a long spell of evil. She'd have to stay close and try to ward off the wicked signs.